The

TEARS OF GALLIA

All the best!
Karl J Morgan
June 2017

KARL J. MORGAN

The Dave Brewster Series
Tears of Gallia

Tears of Gallia may be purchased or ordered through all booksellers, at www.sacredlife.com, or at www.karljmorgan.com.

ISBN: 978-0-9860270-4-8
ISBN: 0986027049
Library of Congress Control Number: 2013938153

Cover and text design: Ronald Calica
Website: www.ronaldcalica.blogspot.com
Linkedin account: www.linkedin.com/in/ohnoitsronald/

Sacred Life Publishers™
www.sacredlife.com
Printed in United States of America

CONTENTS

Chapter 1 1
Chapter 2 9
Chapter 3 17
Chapter 4 21
Chapter 5 27
Chapter 6 35
Chapter 7 45
Chapter 8 51
Chapter 9 57
Chapter 10 65
Chapter 11 71
Chapter 12 77
Chapter 13 83
Chapter 14 91
Chapter 15 97
Chapter 16 105
Chapter 17 111
Chapter 18 117
Chapter 19 127
Chapter 20 141

Chapter 21 147
Chapter 22 161
Chapter 23 169
Chapter 24 177
Chapter 25 191
Chapter 26 201
Chapter 27 207
Chapter 28 217
Chapter 29 223
Chapter 30 227
Chapter 31 233
Chapter 32 241
Chapter 33 247
Chapter 34 253
Chapter 35 259
Chapter 36 267
Chapter 37 273
Chapter 38 279
Chapter 39 285
Chapter 40 291
Chapter 41 299

Chapter 42 305

Chapter 43 311

Chapter 44 317

Chapter 45 323

Chapter 46 329

Chapter 47 337

Chapter 48 343

Chapter 49 349

Chapter 50 357

Chapter 51 363

Chapter 52 373

Chapter 53 381

Chapter 54 389

Chapter 55 397

Chapter 56 405

Chapter 57 413

Chapter 58 421

Chapter 59 429

Chapter 60 435

About the Author 441

Other Books by Karl J. Morgan 443

CHAPTER 1

Several months had passed since Admiral Dave Brewster returned from the Andromeda Galaxy after receiving approval to create a Free Society in the Milky Way. All the colony ships under his control were devoted to moving equipment from the Hive under construction on Atar Pa to Tak-Makla to expedite the repair on the tekkan Hive. Dave and his best friend, Commodore Charlie Watson, were on the star cruiser Nightsky, in orbit over Nanda, where the Nan had been working with the locals to integrate them into the Free Society. Dave still thought fondly of the day he walked into the control room of The Hive and discovered that humanity had not originated on Earth or even in this galaxy. He imagined how the Nanda felt when thousands of their brothers from Andromeda landed.

Dave watched the planet below from the port in his ready room. He took a sip of his cappuccino and in his mind he thanked Aria Watson yet again for upgrading the coffee system. Aria and her assistant, Lieutenant Alana Albright had been called back to Earth to investigate some eddies in time that had been causing problems with some of the smaller portals. Dave's wife, Darlene, had joined them so she could visit their children and review some of the treaties forming the basis of the Free Society. A tone sounded on Dave's control panel and he walked over and pressed a button. The door slid open and Charlie Watson walked in carrying a tray with two coffees and several chocolate croissants. "Good morning, Charlie, what's the occasion?"

"Hi, Dave," Charlie smiled. "I've asked Jon Lake to join us." He set the tray down on the conference table and sat down. Jon

Lake, captain of the Nightsky, entered and sat as well. "Thanks for joining us, Jon."

"My pleasure," Jon said as he took a coffee and pastry. "What's going on?"

"I was wondering the same thing," Dave replied. He took a croissant and sat at the head of the table. "It must be important to warrant croissants."

"It is. I had a call from Aria a few minutes ago. As you know, they are holding the first meeting of the leaders of the Free Society on Earth now. Today, by unanimous acclamation, Mencius was elected President," Charlie explained.

"That is big news," Dave replied. "He was definitely the perfect choice. His role on Earth and working with the Galliceans and maklans has been very successful. I can still hear him making his speech to the High Council on Earth Prime. He had them mesmerized."

"I thought you did a pretty good job with them too, Dave," Charlie laughed. "I think you personally brought down the Brotherhood and the High Council."

"Thanks for the vote of confidence, but I'm pretty sure the High Council is still there," Dave replied. "And as long as the Society holds together, the threat of the Brotherhood or others like them will be real." A tone sounded on his panel and he pressed a button and said, "Yes, Lia, what's up?"

"Admiral, I have President Mencius for you," she said. "I told him you were with Jon and Charlie and he wants to speak to all three of you. Shall I put him through?"

"Of course, and thanks Lia," Dave said. A dimly lit office filled the view screen. Mencius of Kalidus was sitting on an overstuffed chair holding a full glass of whisky in his hand. High Commissioner Darak Daniels was sitting on the chair next to him and appeared to be asleep. "Mr. President, it is an honor to take your call."

"Thank you, Dave. It's good to see you three again. It's been some time since we jumped back from Earth Prime," Mencius replied. "Pardon me if I'm a bit tipsy, but we have been celebrating for hours now. As you can see, Darak has enjoyed himself too much. Our dear friend, Fa-a-Di provided us with many bottles of Gallicean whisky and I agree with you it is too strong." He took a sip and grimaced. "Very good, but too strong."

"I wish I could be with you, Mr. President," Charlie said. "It is early morning here and we're only allowed coffee. I think you are having the better time."

Mencius laughed and spilled half of his whisky onto his lap. "Damn, I'm making a mess of myself today. Hopefully, later in your day, you can share a drink and think of me trying to sleep this off. But I called for other reasons. Perhaps I should have waited until I'm sober, but this is just too important."

"Please tell us, Mencius," Dave said.

"Dave, mine was not the only selection today," Mencius began. "As you can imagine, there is much infrastructure to be built to support our Free Society. Hopefully, we have learned the lessons of Earth Prime and will not allow ourselves to become too drunk with power. Ours will be a more difficult road than theirs though. They were able to include only human worlds. Even though they developed their own internal animosities, they did not have to overcome species differences like we will."

"I thought we would give more power to the regional governments, like Greater Gallia and the Kalidean Federation," Dave said. "That way the central government would remain small and non-intrusive."

"We discussed that as well," Mencius replied. "But I kept thinking about the Lagamar system and especially the Nan. They were kept down and ignored by the larger groups in the Society of Humanity. I know most civilizations have known the Kalideans to be fair and peaceful, but that may not always be the case. Most of the Beings in our Free Society are either Kalidean or Gallicean. When we thought about this, we realized our union could only work if the integration of our species was more complete. All of our societies have been through aggressive periods and we have many blood stains on all of our hands."

"I hope we're not over-thinking this, Mencius," Jon interrupted. "None of us can control what will happen generations from now. Wasn't the goal of our Free Society mutual protection against enemies like the Paxran and Donnaki?"

"You're right, Jon," Mencius smiled. "However, the example of the Society is burned into my mind. We need to follow a different path. We've already set a separate course by including the Galliceans, Palians, maklans and others. But even the recent conflict with the Predaxians tells us it may not be enough."

"What is your plan?" Dave asked. "What did the High Council come up with?"

"First, our constitution will require us to select a president from a different species at every election. While a president can hold office for two five-year terms, they cannot be consecutive," Mencius explained. "There will also be two chambers in the legislature. The representatives in one will be based on population. The other will be based on species, with equal participation for all. I know it's not perfect, but it gives us a chance at avoiding some of the mistakes of the Society."

"That seems fair to me," Charlie responded. "What about the humans of the Kalidean Federation versus the humans of Earth?"

"Great question, Charlie," Mencius responded. "To be equitable to Earth and her colonies, they will be treated as a separate race, as will the various maklan species. That may change over time as we learn to live and work together. But none of this is why I called you, Dave. I'm sorry I've been rambling around, but the drinks and late hours are taking their toll on an old man."

"Please don't worry about that, Mencius," Dave said. "I've spent many evenings with Fa-a-Di and his brother-in-law, drinking his whisky. If you'd prefer to call us later, that would be fine."

"No chance, Dave," Mencius laughed. "This is one of the perks of being President. I get to give others new titles as well." Darak opened his eyes and sat up, seeming confused and disoriented. "Ah, Darak, I'm glad you are awake now. I was just about to give Dave the good news."

"I'm sorry I dozed off, Mencius," he yawned. "It's been a long day. Hello, Dave, Charlie and Jon. It's good to see you all. Mencius, please continue."

"The threats Jon mentioned are very real. There are rumors a Maklakar battle station is approaching our space. The Hive on Atar Pa continues to see Paxran and Donnaki espionage activity in the frontiers. We need to find more civilizations to join us. We need to construct more Hives to improve our defenses. Unfortunately, Hive 1008 has been permanently stationed in the Andromeda Galaxy. We were very fortunate to have two Chief Engineers sent to help us. We all believe we need to step up our exploration of this side of the galaxy. Dave, we unanimously selected you to do that."

"Okay, thank you, I guess. But I don't understand how that is different from what I am already doing," Dave replied.

"Think big, my friend," Mencius smiled. "We are pooling all the resources of our Free Society to enlarge your fleet. We are adding two Gallicean colony ships and three cruisers to be led by Admiral De-o-Nu. Predax has offered five cruisers and is currently converting two transports into colony ships. Discussions have begun with the Palians as well, although they seem preoccupied with Nom-Kat-Un."

"Wow!" Dave said. "That's really amazing, but what about my destiny to found a thousand worlds? I thought that was my focus."

"It still is, Dave," Darak replied. "But the goal is bigger now. We still hope you start a thousand human colonies, but there potentially could be many more for the other species. It always seemed unlikely that a single explorer could accomplish so much. However, when we consider the new larger fleet and other species coming to your aid, it seems much more attainable. What do you think?"

"I'll do my best," Dave said. "I guess I'm overwhelmed. Where do I begin?"

"We asked Fa-a-Di to present you with your new title and fleet on Gallia," Mencius said. "He told us you have promised a number of times to fly with him on his home world. I think this is his way of insuring you meet that obligation. Your ship should head there immediately. You can jump from Golden Dawn to Gallia directly. That should only be a day away from your current location."

"We'll lay in a course and leave for Golden Dawn in an hour," Jon said. "The two Kalidean research ships here can support the ground activity." He stood and left the room to join his bridge crew.

"Dave and Charlie, there is something else," Mencius said. "There is something wrong with Fa-a-Di. Ever since we returned from Andromeda, he has been distant and moody. Perhaps you can talk to him. Field Marshall Je-e-Bo has seen the same thing, but Fa-a-Di says he is fine. Thanks. Earth out." The screen went blank.

CHAPTER 2

Gallia was an immense gas giant. As Nightsky exited the portal, the space over the planet was filled with moons and star ports. The swirling bands of gas moved much more slowly than on Jupiter. The industrialization of Gallia had calmed the atmosphere over the millennia, but it remained very beautiful. A small, red Dar-Fa spun deep in the southern hemisphere.

The face of a Gallicean filled half the view screen. "Nightsky, this is Gallia Central Command. I am Captain Wu-no-Ba and I have been assigned to be your main contact point during your stay. Welcome to Gallia."

"Thank you Captain," Jon said. "I am Jon Lake, captain of the Nightsky. It is my pleasure to bring Admiral Dave Brewster to your planet. We both send our kind regards for your hospitality."

"Thank you, Jon," Wu-no-Ba smiled. "Lord General Fa-a-Di has requested that you and Commodore Watson join Dave for a fly over of our planet. I will join the group and have the honor of carrying you, sir. That trip will end in the Grand Courtyard of Gallia where the ceremonies are to take place."

"Very good, Wu-no-Ba," Jon replied. "Just let us know when to be ready."

"It is late evening here in the capital. Local time in No-Ja is 1900 hours. Please get some rest and I will contact you tomorrow at 1100 hours local. Please synchronize to our time coordinates. Gallia out." The image of the Gallicean disappeared.

Dave was sitting on a couch in his quarters and talking to Darlene over the com-link. "So, how are Bill and Cybil?" he asked.

"They are doing great, honey," she replied. "They both passed their exams with flying colors and are ready for the next term. Cybil is on top of the world. She and Rob Watson spend most of their time together whether in class or studying or dating. I think that's hard on Billy though. He hasn't seen or heard from Loni Arrak since we jumped back."

"When I talked to Mencius yesterday, he said that two Chief Engineers had been sent from Andromeda. I hope she was one of them," Dave replied. "We always knew this would be a difficult relationship given the problems with interracial marriages in the Society."

"I know, sweetheart," Darlene said. "I guess we'll have to wait and see. If Loni isn't one of the engineers sent here, I guess we know the outcome."

"I'm pretty sure she is one of them," Dave replied. "Ever since I spent time in the stone temple on Nan, my sense of what's going on is very sharp. It's almost like I can sense she is on Tak-Makla right now. Isn't that weird?"

"I've felt the same thing, Dave," she said. "Now you're going to think I'm a crazy, jealous wife, but I keep seeing you and that young girl Bea in my mind. I can see her sitting with you on a couch with her hand on your knee. It's crazy, I know. It feels like you two are spiritually linked or something."

Dave started laughing. "Wow! That's almost exactly right!"

"This is no laughing matter, lover boy," Darlene frowned. "Are you telling me all of that happened?"

"It's not what it seems, sweetheart," Dave said. "I promised Bea I wouldn't tell anyone. It could be very dangerous to the flow of time, but I can't sit here and watch you struggle with those images in your mind."

"Is this some kind of confession, Dave?" she asked. "I don't think I like where this is headed."

"It's not what you think, Darlene," he replied. "And don't tell me you never noticed how much she looks like you. Even Charlie recognized that. I think her resemblance to you is what caught my eye in the first place."

"This doesn't seem to be getting any better, Dave," Darlene scowled.

He laughed again. "Okay, but you can never tell anyone what I'm telling you now. Bea's life and my sanity are at risk here. Please say you promise."

"I promise, Admiral Brewster, but spit it out," Darlene said.

"Darlene, Bea is our granddaughter," he said. He could see tears welling up in her eyes and rolling down her cheeks. "Don't cry sweetheart. This is good news. Bea is Rob and Cybil Watson's first child, to be born on May 31, 3195."

"Is this really true, Dave?" Darlene whispered. "Our little girl is going to have a baby."

"Three actually," Dave smiled. "When I traveled back to the twenty-first to help Charlie convince his kids to jump forward,

I found out that Bea was not from our time. She had been sent by a future High Commissioner to make certain that Rob and Matt made the jump. She was ordered to divulge her identity if necessary to make it happen. She came to my room in Charlie's house to tell me because she was afraid something bad would happen if her secret was revealed."

"That's horrible, Dave," Darlene replied as she wiped the tears from her cheeks. "Think of the pressure that would put on Cybil and Rob's relationship. You must get married or Bea is dead. That poor girl."

"Fortunately, we got the job done and Bea kept her secret, until now," Dave said. "Now we both have to keep this secret to ourselves. If anyone else found out, it would be disastrous for her. Rob and Matt are already here, so the DNA project is safe. The only risk now is whether Bea is born or not. That's why we both need to keep this safe."

"And that's why you have the spiritual connection too," Darlene surmised. "She's your granddaughter, so you're connected. That's so wonderful and I'm so sorry I doubted you."

"There's a bit more to that part," Dave smiled. "The night before the Grand Conclave on Earth Prime, my string of light flew out of my body into space without the help of a Hive. I was floating along in Universal Power when another string smashed into me and we fused for a moment. It was Bea. She told me she was happy and that Rob and Cybil's relationship looked promising. I told her I was hoping to hold baby Bea soon. Before I could say anymore, the Elders of Nan took me away."

"You are a lucky man, Dave Brewster," Darlene smiled. "I would love to see her and touch her like you have." A tone sounded at her door. "Dave, I'm expecting Mencius and Darak to discuss the treaties and I think they're at the door."

"Okay, I know that duty calls. But let me tell you one thing. Tonight, when you are lying in bed, close your eyes and think of Bea, Rob and Cybil with all the love in your heart," Dave said. "You have been on Nan as well. Perhaps she will come looking for you too. I love you, sweetheart. Nightsky out."

A tone sounded on the control panel and he pushed the flashing button. The face of Fa-a-Di stared back. "Brother Dave, welcome to my home world," he said.

"Brother, I am thrilled to fly over Gallia with you tomorrow," Dave replied.

"I'm sorry, Dave, but I have had to cancel that trip," Fa-a-Di said. "I have been very melancholy since my return from Andromeda and I don't think I would be good company."

"Whatever is wrong, brother?" Dave asked. "Are you still worried about the Boley and Zula?"

"Yes, but that isn't the problem, Dave. After seeing the possibilities of the Hive on Nan, I know the Society will stay far away from Lagamar 7," Fa-a-Di said. "Exposing the horrors of the Society reminded me of too many blemishes on the souls of Galliceans. We too have done horrid things in the past. Every day I feel we are only inches away from doing the same things again."

"All of our societies were born from the blood of innocents, Fa-a-Di," Dave replied. "The humans from Earth were especially violent through much of our history. We cannot carry the blame for those who lived generations ago. We have learned from those mistakes and must do what we can not to repeat them."

"I used to feel the same way, brother," the Gallicean said. "After seeing the Society, I am beginning to think repeating the past is inevitable. I have told you before that Galliceans are not like humans. Our people crave order and discipline. It is a difficult transition to being free and peaceful. Some say it is in our blood to be conquerors."

"None of us can know what the future holds," Dave replied. "All we can do is our best to maintain the peace and love and care for our friends and families. Future generations will do what they do. We can provide a strong culture and a rich history for them, but that is all. I wish you could join me in Universal Power, brother. A few moments there and all doubt would be erased."

"That would be wonderful, Dave," Fa-a-Di sighed. "I am beginning to wonder if Galliceans will ever experience that. It seems little progress is being made in that area. Perhaps we have no souls."

"You and I both know better than that, Fa-a-Di," Dave smiled. "You are one of the greatest men I have ever known. Your honesty and sincerity are only outweighed by your courage and compassion. That is a rare combination in this galaxy or any other."

"Thank you for the kind words, brother, but frankly, I don't feel any of those things right now," the general said. "No-o-Ka suggested I stop drinking to see if that improved my mood.

That's only made things worse. Unfortunately, my wife has hidden all of my whisky."

Dave laughed. "Brother, I am going to try something tonight I learned from Elder Odo Pak of Nan. Do you remember when Odo and Obu appeared before the High Council on Earth Prime?"

"How could I ever forget that?" Fa-a-Di smiled. "It was incredible. I still wonder how it was done."

"Think about me with love tonight before you go to sleep," Dave said. "Perhaps someone will wake you during the night. Nightsky out."

CHAPTER 3

Dave Brewster was laying quietly in his bed, concentrating on his friend, Fa-a-Di. His spiritual light had flown from his body many times, but tonight nothing was happening. He knew his friend was in trouble, but could not figure out what to do to help. He sat up and dangled his feet over the side of the bed. He scratched his head and sighed. “Perhaps I’ve lost the ability now,” he said. He felt electricity coursing through his body and his hair stood on end. Out of the corner of his eye, he saw something glimmer. He turned to see two amorphous blobs of light coalescing in his bedroom. After a few seconds, the blobs resolved into Elder Odo Pak and High Priest Obu Neela.

“Hello, Dave,” Odo said. “We have felt your struggles and thought we would come here to help you.”

“It is wonderful to see you both again,” Dave smiled. “I think about you often. How are things going in your galaxy?”

“As well as can be expected,” Obu replied. “The High Council has resigned following the revelations about the Zula and Boley. Antar and Wendo are doing their best to work with the regional governors, but tensions are rising quickly throughout the Society. As we envisioned, the future looks bleak.”

“But we are not here to discuss problems in the home galaxy, Dave,” Odo said. “You already know that is not your problem to solve. The elders of Nan have been trying to determine why you have the exceptional abilities you displayed in our galaxy.”

"I am beginning to think those powers have left me," Dave sighed. "I have been trying for hours to reach out to my friend, General Fa-a-Di, but my light string doesn't seem to be cooperating."

"Dave, why would we be here now if we didn't sense your concerns?" Odo asked. "When you were in the stone temple, did you try to leave your body to follow me?"

"No, my light just surged out of my body," he replied.

"And when you left your body while orbiting Earth Prime, what did you do?" Obu asked.

"Nothing. I think I just fell asleep and it happened," Dave replied. "I think you're trying to tell me that I'm trying too hard."

"Something like that, Dave," Odo laughed. "The problem is not that your spiritual light is stuck inside you at all. You believe that string is an elemental part of your physical being. You may believe your body, mind and the Source are partners in your life. But that belief is false."

"Okay, I'm confused again," Dave began. "I'm sitting here, plain as day. My brain tells me my string of light is hidden inside me and can't get out. That's not true?"

Obu smiled and sat next to Dave on the bed. He put his hand on Dave's shoulder. "No, it is not. However, we are not here to expose ultimate reality or anything of the sort. Each of us must come to our own understanding of the nature of existence. As High Priest of Lagamar Ulu, it is my job to listen to my people talk about their struggles and give them tidbits of what I know so they may progress themselves. Tonight we are here to tell you to be patient and relax. Everything is happening as it was meant to happen. You cannot beg or force your mental string of light to reach out to your friend. You must relax and be patient. If you mind decides to fly off to his home now, it will do so. Otherwise, it will not. You must have faith that you can help Fa-a-Di through his challenge. That is the key, Dave Brewster."

"Dave, we have felt the pain in Fa-a-Di's heart," Odo continued. "Although he will deny it, the lesson of the Boley was too much for him. It reminded him that his people have been savagely brutal through most of their existence. Even though those days ended hundreds of generations ago, he cannot forgive himself or his people for their past."

"But Fa-a-Di had nothing to do with the ancient past, any more than I bear responsibility for the brutality of ancient humans," Dave said.

"Of course you are right, Dave," Odo replied. "But that doesn't change his feelings. Also, you do not know much about the expansion of the Galliceans into space. As leader of his people, he bears responsibility for everything. As a warrior, he has seen many battles and lost many friends. You and Fa-a-Di will have to opportunity to spend a lot of time together soon, and you can use that time to reach out to him and help him overcome the feelings he has now."

"Fa-a-Di already canceled our flight over the planet tomorrow," Dave said. "I am supposed to see him only at the ceremony tomorrow night, and then I will take my new fleet out of orbit immediately."

"Sometimes you need to change the rules," Odo replied. "After the Grand Conclave on Earth Prime and the ceremony tomorrow, you will be a very important man in the Free Society here. You don't need to follow every order if higher priorities arise."

"Get some rest now," Obu said. "Don't even think about visiting the general tonight. You cannot force that. On the other hand, he might. If he sincerely wishes you to visit him, your mental string will fly out of your chest whether you want it to or not."

"Okay, I'll try to relax and be patient," Dave said as he lay back down on his bed. "Thank you both for helping me. I hope you both fare well with the events in the home galaxy." He closed his eyes.

"About that, Dave," Odo said. "I've decided to relocate to Nanda. The elders realized at least one of us should help with the integration of the Nanda into Nan culture. Since I'm the most senior, we agreed I could do the most good without requiring more than one elder to move. My family and I are jumping there in the morning. I hope we can see more of each other soon." Dave did not reply as he had already fallen asleep.

"Honestly, Odo, I didn't think your speech was boring," Obu laughed. The two forms faded into blackness.

CHAPTER 4

"Captain, I have Admiral De-o-Nu calling for you," Lia Lawson said.

"Put him on screen, Lia," Jon Lake replied. The smiling face of Fa-a-Di's brother-in-law appeared on the right half of the view screen. "Good day, Admiral, it is good to see you again. I have heard your fleet is joining with ours. Welcome."

"Thank you, Jon," De-o-Nu replied. "I never would have thought this would happen. A new adventure awaits us all." Dave Brewster walked onto the bridge and sat next to Jon Lake. "Is that my dear brother, Dave? It's so good to see you again."

"De-o-Nu, it is our pleasure to visit your home planet," Dave said. "I was looking forward to flying with the general today, but unfortunately he was unable to fit it in his schedule."

"Yes, I know," De-o-Nu frowned. "The planning for the ceremony has been very time consuming. Also, my brother-in-law must begin the Sojourn tomorrow. That is the other news I am calling about. After much cajoling, I have convinced Fa-a-Di to allow me to join him on the Sojourn. I know this trip is tearing him apart, and I cannot allow him to wallow in self-pity any longer. I have ordered several dozen cases of the best whisky to accompany us."

"I suppose that will delay our first mission then," Dave replied. "Or would you prefer to catch up to us later?"

"Dave, do you think we could continue this conversation in private?" De-o-Nu asked.

"Of course, brother," he replied. "Lia, please send the call to my ready room." Dave rose, left the bridge and walked into his ready room, where he sat at his desk. De-o-Nu was already on his view screen. "Okay, brother, I'm alone now."

"Good. Dave, I am quite worried about Fa-a-Di," he began. "The events in the Andromeda Galaxy have burned into him. The memories of those days are now intertwined with the solemnity of the Sojourn and my brother-in-law seems to be spiraling downward."

"What is the Sojourn, brother?" Dave asked. "You keep mentioning that and if it is affecting our brother so deeply, I'd like to understand it."

"Of course, Dave, I understand," De-o-Nu replied. "As you know, the Galliceans were not always peaceful. In our antiquity, many factions rose and fought bloody wars for dominance. Our hatred for each other only abated when we discovered how to travel to new planets. Suddenly, we were finding other Beings who also believed they were the only intelligent life in the universe. We began to see ourselves as one people, not a collection of different races."

"That makes perfect sense, and we humans have a similar past," Dave said. "We were fortunate the Kalideans stopped our self-destruction."

"We were not so lucky, Dave," De-o-Nu replied. He walked over to his credenza and withdrew a bottle of whisky and a glass. He sat and poured a full glass and took a large drink. "The first Galliceans to venture away from Gallia were shocked by the terrestrial life we found. We had no idea life could thrive on other types of planets. The creatures we found had advanced societies and large vibrant cultures. None of them dealt with the difficulties of life on gas giant planets. And they were horrified by our appearance. Our fear of each other led to war. Unfortunately for the others, our forces were far superior. There are not enough teras of data to list the names of those we killed. The ultimate irony was we could never inhabit their planets anyway. Many of their systems had gas giants and none of those cultures had any intention of occupying them. We fought and killed for glory and pride alone."

"De-o-Nu, that was long ago and those days are over," Dave replied. "Your civilization is great and peaceful today. It's time to let the dead rest in peace."

"If only it were that simple, brother," De-o-Nu said with a slight smile. "The souls of our people have not changed that much, I'm afraid. Our first response to trouble is to draw our daggers and fight. When the Predaxians controlled our High Command and several Commissioners, the rest of our planet seemed happy to go back to strict discipline and conquest. It is only the Sojourn that keeps us from slipping back into our ancient ways. It was the events on the Tears of Gallia that made us look at ourselves and see our warrior ways could never bring happiness or peace. The memory of those events forces us to reevaluate our lives and ambitions and to calm down."

"I still don't understand, brother," Dave said. "Can you tell me more about the Sojourn and the Tears of Gallia? Please believe me, I really want to understand and help."

"Of course I will, but you must know these things are very personal and sacred to our people. Please do not tell anyone, even my sister Darlene about this," De-o-Nu warned. "There is nothing illegal or immoral about talking about them, but they do bare our souls in an uncomfortable way."

"I promise I won't tell a soul," Dave replied.

"Well, I recommend that you get a glass of whisky for yourself, as this will be a long story," De-o-Nu laughed. "First, did you ever wonder why my people are called Galliceans when the planet name is Gallia?"

Dave sat down again after retrieving a glass of Scotch whisky. "Frankly, I never thought about it."

"Throughout all of our history until we left Gallia, we called ourselves galli," the Gallicean replied. "We found several systems nearby with no sentient life and settled them first. But the old animosities between the races continued. In the beginning, the High Council suggested each race be given its own planet, similar to the Society of Humanity. But with hundreds of races and a few planets, it could never be done. Then we began to encounter other civilizations. Many resisted our incursions which infuriated our people. We vastly increased our fleet of warships and attacked. Over the following generations, we conquered dozens of other civilizations and grew our society to two hundred planets. The last of those planets we settled was given the name Gallicea." De-o-Nu rose and filled his glass with ice and returned to his seat.

"So, your people named their race after that planet," Dave said. "Why is that?"

"We'll get to that, Dave," he replied. "There was one inhabited terrestrial planet in that system. The name and appearance of the Beings there has been lost in time. All we know now is they were gentle and peaceful Beings who welcomed us to their system. They were eager to forge peace and trade treaties with us. However, our High Commissioner at the time, Za-a-Za was still consumed with blood lust. He ordered the fleet to attack the terrestrial Beings and slaughter them." Dave could see a tear slip down De-o-Nu's cheek. "Our people were happy to do exactly that."

"That is appalling, but also long ago," Dave replied. "We can't raise the spirits of the dead now. None of you were there or had anything to do with that."

"Yes, but the story did not end there, brother," De-o-Nu continued. "Our colony on Gallicea stood up for the poor Beings on the planet and demanded our forces end their attack. That made Za-a-Za mad with rage. He did withdraw our forces but sent them directly to Gallicea to put down the colonists. Za-a-Za led the attack himself. You can imagine the sight of hundreds of thousands of warriors fighting in the gas above the large Ka-la-a. The colonists were outnumbered fifty to one. But somehow, the colonists won."

"That's amazing," Dave said. "How could so few defeat the massive army?"

"No one knows, Dave," the Gallicean replied. "Those answers were lost long ago. The remains of the dead have been recycled through the Dar-Fa a million times over. History tells us a young priest named Fa-u-Bay fought with the colonists and personally killed Za-a-Za in combat. His forces declared him High Priest of Gallia. After the defeat of the army on Gallicea, no one dared to deny him anything and he became our High Commissioner for the next two hundred years."

"Wow! Fa-u-Bay must have been an incredible soldier," Dave said. "What happened to Gallia during his terms in office?"

"That one event changed us forever," De-o-Nu said. "We never attacked another planet and began to forge peace treaties with new societies. Our educational system was overhauled and began to focus on science and the arts instead of military studies. But none of those were his greatest legacy. Fa-u-Bay ordered all of our people to leave the Gallicea system forever. Gallicea and the terrestrial world were to be maintained as the most sacred sites in Greater Gallia and were off limits to settlements. He named those two planets the Tears of Gallia since they symbolize our regret and sorrow for the evils of our past. As the final atonement for our past, we were all to be known as Galliceans from then forward, so we are constantly reminded of the senselessness of war. He also commanded that every one of us visit the planets at least once every ten years to atone for the violence in our past and the blood on our hands. That trip we must take is called the Sojourn."

"Incredible, brother," Dave said at last. "Can I ask you just two more questions though?"

De-o-Nu shrieked with laughter. "Dave, I know you too well. Yes, Fa-u-Bay is my brother-in-law's ancestor; and yes, you can come with us."

CHAPTER 5

Dave Brewster was busy putting on his dress uniform for the ceremony to be held in the Grand Courtyard in No-Ja in one hour. Special transparent pressure suits had been made for Dave and Charlie so they could be better seen by the audience. Their face shields were based on the technology of the Society so they could enjoy the drinks and dinner after the ceremony. The breather packs containing their air supplies also utilized Society technology, doubling their capacity while reducing the weight by more than half. They would have enough air for several days, even though they were planning to return to Nightsky in four or five hours.

A tone sounded and he crossed the room to answer the door. It opened to reveal Charlie in his Commodore's uniform inside his clear suit. "How do I look, Dave?" he asked.

"Uncomfortable, I'd say," Dave laughed. "Please come in. I've asked Jake and Mitch to jump us down to the Grand Courtyard in a few minutes. Perhaps we have time for a quick drink. To tell the truth, I'm pretty nervous about this." Dave returned to his bathroom to finish donning his pressure suit while Charlie put ice and whisky into two glasses.

Charlie sat carefully on a couch and said, "There's nothing to worry about, old friend. I think the odds of being laid-off here are close to zero."

Dave was laughing as he entered the room and sat across from Charlie. "Thanks for the drink, buddy. I'm not worried about being fired or anything. It's just standing in front of those people and receiving a promotion. I don't know what I'll do or say."

Now Charlie was laughing. "Let me get this straight. You're nervous about being recognized by your friends, but you had no problem staring down the entire High Council of the Society and putting all of our lives in extreme danger. You never have a problem talking, Dave. And I should know. I'm as full of it as you are." Both men were laughing when Jake Benomafolays and Mitch Nolobitamore popped out of thin air.

"Mitch, these guys started without us," Jake said. "They've got whisky and are laughing it up. What's going on you two?"

"Yikes! You two almost scared me to death," Dave replied. "I'm going to put a bell on you two so I can hear you coming."

"Jake and Mitch, please help yourselves to the Scotch," Charlie said. "Dave was telling me how afraid he is of talking in front of the crowd tonight. Can you believe that?"

"That is pretty funny, Dave," Mitch said. "I've never seen you at a loss for words."

"I think I'm just used to having Darlene around to make me feel safe and secure," he replied. "She's my anchor. When she is around, I know I have to do my best or I won't hear the end of it."

"She'll be jumping back in a couple of days, buddy," Charlie said. "But I hear you won't be here. There's some trip you're taking with Fa-a-Di. What's that about?"

"I can't really talk about it now, guys," Dave replied. "Jake, I was hoping you could join us. Most of the trip will be either on a gas giant planet or the Kong-Fa. De-o-Nu is making all the arrangements, but being able to jump out quickly if necessary would be good."

"Of course, Dave," Jake said. "It would be my pleasure. I know Darlene will be happy to know I've got your back. I've studied the Sojourn and am interested to learn more about it myself. Mitch can take over for me here. By the way, it is getting late and we should jump down to No-Ja soon. We don't want to be late for the Dave Brewster Show."

Jake and Mitch flew up to Dave and Charlie and checked the fittings and gages on their pressure suits. They also reviewed the face plates to make sure they were working. "Whenever you guys think we're okay, we are ready," Charlie said. Mitch landed on Charlie's chest and held on. Jake did the same for Dave. Without a sight or sound, the room was empty.

Cheering and applause filled the air as Dave and Charlie appeared in the Grand Courtyard on Gallia. They were surrounded by fifty thousand Galliceans who were universally thrilled to witness this great event. The landing platform was guarded by twenty Gallicean Marines in their blood red armor. One of the soldiers approached Dave and extended his hand, which Dave shook happily.

"Admiral Brewster, welcome to Gallia. I am Major Um-de-Bo. I don't think we have met, but I had the honor to accompany General Fa-a-Di on Lagamar 7," the Marine said. He withdrew his Baloo dagger and presented it to Dave. "The general used my Baloo on Lagamar 7 to release our friend, Bola Deka from the Brotherhood agents. It would honor my family and my soldiers here if you would accept it."

"Thank you, Major," Dave said. "You and the general bring great honor to all of the Free Society and I gratefully accept your gift." Dave held out his hand.

Um-de-Bo frowned slightly. "Admiral, we have a ritual way of passing the Baloo, which only Marines are able to carry. Please hold your right hand over your head and be ready. If you don't catch it, it's okay, but we are a ritualistic people." Dave followed the request and Um-de-Bo threw the Baloo high in the air in the opposite direction. The throng of guests began to shout and scream in delight.

The Baloo flew through the air above the crowd. After fifty yards it began to curve and made a circle around the crowd who continued to hoot and cheer madly. As the blade began to fly back to Dave, Um-de-Bo positioned his hand directly behind his. The handle slammed into Dave's palm, pushing his hand backward into the Gallicean's palm. Um-de-Bo closed his hand around Dave's to secure the Baloo. Dave looked up at Um-de-Bo who was grinning and shouting as he removed his hand to show the Baloo securely in Dave's hand.

The crowd shouted and hooted more. The Marines jumped into the air and began to fly around the group with their Baloos waving in the air around them. Um-de-Bo grabbed Dave around the waist and flew up with them, while Dave waved his new Baloo. Another Marine grabbed Charlie and flew him around the crowd as well. The group circled for several minutes while the crowd chanted Dave and Charlie's names. Finally, the Marines delivered Dave and Charlie to a raised dais where Fa-a-Di and the entire High Council were clapping and cheering. Dave set the Baloo down on the table and went to his friend and hugged him. Dave could see joy and sorrow on Fa-a-Di's face.

Fa-a-Di knelt next to Dave and whispered to him, "Today, you are galli, my brother. The major has made you an honorary Gallicean Marine and I will have red armor made for you as well as a more manageable Baloo. Thank you for the incomparable gift of your company for the next few days. Perhaps by the end of our Sojourn, we will both be worthy to be called Gallicean." Fa-a-Di rose to his feet and waved to the crowd to quiet them down.

Major Um-de-Bo flew over to a large gong and banged on it. The noise quieted down the crowd and they returned to their tables and seats. The Marine said, "Good evening, ladies and gentlemen. Please take your seats and give your undivided attention to my dear friend, my mentor, the greatest solider in a thousand generations and the High Commissioner of Greater Gallia, Fa-a-Di." The crowd applauded again as they sat.

"Thank you, Um-de-Bo," Fa-a-Di said. "Your actions on Lagamar 7 and tonight bring great honor to your family and your Marines." Fa-a-Di turned his attention to the crowd. "Um-de-Bo was instrumental in our rescue of the Boley on Lagamar 7. He also fought proudly during thc Second Predaxian War, where several of his soldiers were injured or killed. His soldiers accompanied me on the attack that killed Emperor Zendo and ended his reign of terror near our borders. As a first acknowledgment of the evening, the High Council has approved the promotion of the major to the rank of colonel. Um-de-Bo will lead a team of one thousand Marines in the fleet of Admiral De-o-Nu." The crowd cheered again and the other Marines hugged their leader. Um-de-Bo faced Fa-a-Di and bowed deeply to express his gratitude.

Thousands of waiters moved through the crowd, placing glasses of ice and bottles of whisky on all the tables. Each glass was filled to the brim. "Charlie, that was one heck of an entrance," Dave whispered. He passed the Baloo to his friend. "Check this thing out. It weighs twenty pounds at least. I thought my arm would come out of its socket for a minute."

"That's quite a weapon, Dave," Charlie said as he tried to wield the curved blade. "Good luck with the thing. If you dropped it, you might cut off your own foot."

Fa-a-Di spoke to the crowd again. "As you all know, the High Council has unanimously agreed to join the Free Society of the Milky Way Galaxy. We have already authorized a fleet of ships led by Admiral De-o-Nu to join a new effort to find new worlds and civilizations for our Free Society. This effort will be monumental in scale. Our enemies have great power. We all need to work together to prevent their aggression and to build our might to equal or exceed theirs. That is the only way to guarantee peace. To accomplish this mighty goal, the High Council of our Free Society, of which I am a member, has unanimously chosen my dear friend Dave Brewster as leader of the Grand Exploratory Fleet." The crowd cheered and applauded wildly. Fa-a-Di let the crowd express their joy and Dave could feel the positive feelings wash over him.

After the cheering quieted down, Fa-a-Di continued, "We Galliceans owe much to Admiral Brewster. His efforts were instrumental in our victory in the Second Predaxian War, which saved the peaceful maklan society on No-Makla and stopped the Predaxians from invading our sovereign territory. Through the planet sharing agreement negotiated by me and the admiral's wife, our society has already grown by four new worlds. We expect this new effort to add hundreds more. His team discovered the maklans of Tak-Makla who have become our friends and part of the Free Society. Through them, Dave found the Society of Humanity and took many of us to the Andromeda Galaxy. There, we were able to find our own roots on the planet Lagamar 7. I have been able to negotiate with the Hive on the planet Nan to jump Galliceans and Boley back and forth between our galaxies so we can maintain and grow our relationship. I remember not too long ago telling Dave that many of us thought we were alone in the universe since we had never found any other sentient life that developed on gas planets. Not only did my relationship with the admiral change that, he actually led us to find our cousins two million light-years away. Those accomplishments over the last couple of years are amazing enough for any person in their life. Yet Dave Brewster's voyage is just beginning. Please raise your glass above your heads," Fa-a-Di continued as he raised his own glass. "At the request of President Mencius, I am overjoyed to announce that Dave Brewster is hereby promoted to the position of Grand Explorer and Supreme Fleet Admiral of the Free Society. Here's to Dave!"

After toasting, the crowd broke out in cheers again. Thousands of the guests leaped into the air and began to fly around the Grand Courtyard. The shouting continued as the waiters rushed more bottles of whisky out to the tables. After ten minutes, Um-de-Bo banged the gong again to signal everyone to take their seats. Fa-a-Di motioned Dave to come to the podium and say a few words.

A second human sized podium was quickly set up next to the larger one where Fa-a-Di continued to stand. Dave looked up at his friend who was beaming with joy. He could see De-o-Nu at one of the tables near the dais and waved at him. When the crowd was quiet again, he said, "Wow! I'm shocked. This has been an overwhelming experience for me. I am grateful to the High Council for their support and will do my best to exceed their expectations. I have been very lucky. My family left our normal lives on twenty-first century Earth without knowing what would happen. Everything my brother Fa-a-Di says is true, but those events are not what have been etched into my spirit. Through all of this, I have enjoyed the support of incredible friends and a loving family. Anything I have done to help Fa-a-Di or his brother-in-law has been more than repaid by them. While we did join in the fight against the Predaxians, it was mainly you people who made us victorious. We were led on a voyage of discovery in the Andromeda Galaxy by our friends Wendo Balak and Antar Arrak. They sent Fa-a-Di to Lagamar 7 to discover the atrocities there. I am thrilled the Boley have reunited with their cousins, but most of the credit goes to the general. I wish all of you could have seen the Grand Conclave on Earth Prime. My brother's management of the situation led to the dissolution of the Brotherhood and now to the collapse of the High Council. What I'm trying to say is that we were successful because we all love each other and work to help one another. Thank you for your confidence in me and for bestowing this great honor on me tonight. I cannot succeed at this mission alone though. It will be the efforts of each of us that will win the day. God bless Greater Gallia and thank you again."

CHAPTER 6

"Dave, I'm not sure I like this side trip," Darlene said. She could see him frowning on the view screen. "I still remember being stuck in my pressure suit for days when Darak and I were negotiating the planet sharing treaty. How long will you be gone?"

"I'm not really sure, honey," Dave replied. "Your trip was different though. Back then the Galliceans didn't know anything about us. De-o-Nu has set up a cabin on Kong-Fa with a breathable atmosphere for me. He has also made similar arrangements on the gas giant. On the terrestrial planet it will be Fa-a-Di and De-o-Nu who need the breathers."

"I know, Dave," she said. "Mencius and Darak told me you're an important man now and can make your own decisions. I just wish I could go too."

"Ambassador, I need you to manage the fleet while I'm gone," he laughed. "While I'm there, you should visit Nanda. Elder Odo Pak has moved there to help with the integration of the Nan. See if he needs any help."

"Now you are the funny one, Supreme Fleet Admiral," Darlene said. "Imagine me helping Odo Pak, a man who can transport Billy two million light years in the flash of an eye. Okay, we will head there right after I jump back. By the way, Aria and Alana might be delayed a while. The mystery of the time eddies is confounding everyone. The impact on the portal system is growing by the day. High Consul Zee Gongaleg told me his Hive will be up and running in a few days. We're counting on their help to find out what's going on."

"When you see Odo, let him know about the time eddies. He might be able to use the Nan Hive to help out. How are Cybil and Bill doing?" Dave asked.

"Very good. They are working with the High Council to set up the new campus for the DNA project. Bill keeps asking me when Jake can come join the team. What is his status?" she asked.

"I'm taking Jake with me to Gallicea," he replied. "Just in case there is some problem with the atmosphere or my breathers, he can jump me to safety."

"Thank God," Darlene sighed. "It's about time you thought about your personal safety. I still have the image in my head of you being shot on Aranar Zu."

"Hey, I wasn't the one who was kidnapped," Dave laughed. "But I don't know if that's why I asked him to come. There was a strange creeping feeling in my gut that called out for him. Odo told me to rely on that gut instinct, so I'm not about to ignore it now."

"I'm thrilled he will be there," she replied. "I've got to get going, sweetheart. I'm meeting with Mencius in a half hour to review our first mission. We've also been hearing about a Maklakar battle station moving in this direction. Hopefully he has more information on that too. Dave, please take care of yourself. I want you to have a good time and I know how much Fa-a-Di's mood is affecting him. I hope this trip helps him out as well. I love you."

"I love you too, Darlene. Nightsky out," he replied as he closed the call. A tone sounded on his control panel and he pressed it. The image of De-o-Nu appeared on his screen. "Good morning brother."

"Good morning to you too, Dave," the Gallicean replied. "I hope you are ready for this trip. Your quarters on my ship are now ready. In fact, I'm in your room right now. That's why I'm wearing this damned breather. It seems comfortable, but the new furniture looks as though it came from my daughter's doll house."

"I'm ready now, brother," Dave replied. "I've got a bag packed and Jake should be here any moment. How is your brother-in-law this morning?"

"He is remarkably well, Dave. I think the ceremony and dinner last night did a great deal to lighten his mood. You have a great impact on Fa-a-Di, Dave. Just being with you yesterday was therapeutic for him. Thank you for that. Oh, I see Jake has joined you now," De-o-Nu said.

"Jake, you know it unnerves me when you pop in and out like that!" Dave shouted. "Can't you warn me or something?"

"Sorry, Dave," Jake laughed. "I'll try to send you a card or something next time. Are you ready to go?"

"I'm ready. De-o-Nu, I'll cut the connection now and we'll be there in a couple seconds," Dave said.

"See you then. Kong-Fa out," he replied.

Dave tapped a button on his control panel. "Yes Admiral," Lia Lawson said.

"Lia, please advise Captain Lake that Jake and I are jumping to the Kong-Fa now," Dave replied. "We'll see you all in a few days."

"Aye-aye, Dave," she smiled. "Have a good time and we'll take care of things here." The connection was cut off.

"Let's do this, Jake," Dave said. He grabbed his suitcase and Jake floated over and landed on his chest. Instantly, Dave was standing inside the massive cabin on the Kong-Fa. The ceilings were more than twenty feet tall to accommodate the tallest Galliceans, like De-o-Nu. The human-sized furniture barely filled a quarter of the space. "Here we are, brother."

"Welcome to my flagship, brother," De-o-Nu smiled. "As you can see, we've left some regular furnishings here for any guests. I presume we will share some whisky here from time to time."

"Of course, that's a great idea," Dave replied. "By the way, Darlene asked me this morning about how long the trip will take and frankly, I had no idea."

"Dave, you can contact my sister any time while on Kong-Fa. It is not permitted to use electronic communications in the Gallicea system, except in emergencies. There is no portal in that system either. It will take two days at top speed to reach it. We will spend two to three days on each planet. Then we will leave the system and catch up to your fleet wherever they are."

"Sounds great. I don't want to keep you from your bridge, De-o-Nu. If you have to go that's okay," Dave replied.

"Don't worry about that, brother. Now that I am an admiral under your command, I have a captain to run this ship," the

Gallicean said. "I don't know if you remember Commodore Ka-a-Fa, who led the fleet to attack No-Makla?"

"I don't think we ever met," Dave replied.

"After that event, he felt disgraced and retired from the fleet. He believed his reputation was ruined after he almost started an intergalactic war while abandoning the Predaxian frontier," De-o-Nu said. "Ka-a-Fa went to the academy with me and studied martial arts with me as well, under the tutelage of Fa-a-Di."

"But none of that was his fault," Dave replied. "He was being manipulated by the Predaxians too."

"That's what I told him, but he couldn't face my brother-in-law or me. When I learned of our new adventures, I reached out to him again and almost begged him to join my fleet. Finally, I had Fa-a-Di reach out to him and convince him to join us. Ka-a-Fa is now captain of the Kong-Fa," De-o-Nu said.

"That is great news brother, and I look forward to knowing him," Dave replied.

"I suppose you've heard the rumor of the Maklakar battle station nearing our borders?" De-o-Nu asked.

"Yes, but only unsubstantiated rumors," Dave answered. "We're hoping the Hives on Tak-Makla or Nan can find out what's happening."

"No need for that, Dave," Jake interjected. "We have sensed their presence approaching from No-Makla. Their ship is still too far out for us to jump to it. After the attack on Tak-Makla, we are very concerned that No-Makla may be the next target."

"Dave, that's why I'm sending the Kong-Fa to the Earth system after they drop us off," De-o-Nu said. "We will have a shuttle capable of returning to Gallia if necessary. If everything calms down, Ka-a-Fa will return for us. But if there is trouble in the Earth system again, we need to be ready."

"Jake, what do you think?" Dave asked. "Are you still okay with going on this journey, or do you want to go home?"

"Dave, we've sensed the Maklakar for some time," the maklan replied. "We aren't sensing anything sinister right now though. Also, one single maklan can't do much if war comes. I think I need to be here with you. I don't know why, but I've been feeling drawn to Gallicea for some time."

"It is a magical place, my friends," De-o-Nu said. "While all Galliceans are required to visit every ten years, I have gone there every two or three years. When I am there, I feel completely at peace and happy. Of course, I'm speaking of the gas planet. Being on the terrestrial world is very troubling for me. When I am there, I feel the spirits of the dead staring into my soul. It is an even more excruciating experience for Fa-a-Di. He tells me those same souls seem to be tearing him apart. That's why he has skipped the trip a few times. Being High Commissioner, he can always find matters of state that trump this ancient ritual."

"Well, I can't wait to get there," Dave said. "So far this adventure seems a lot like our journey to Andromeda. Something strange happens every minute. When do we leave?"

De-o-Nu laughed, "We left already, Dave. I told Ka-a-Fa to leave orbit as soon as you two appeared in this cabin. My breather is running out of air, so I'm heading back to the bridge now. Outside your door, there is a pressure chamber. When you want to leave the room, put on your breather in here. There is a short delay to open the door while the chamber atmosphere is changed to match yours. Once you are in the chamber and the door is closed behind you, the atmosphere will change again and the outer door will open. Please have Jake double-check your equipment though. We don't want any surprises. I'll see you later. We are dining in Fa-a-Di's cabin at 1800 hours. Feel free to wander the ship and talk to my crew or come to the bridge. As our Supreme Fleet Admiral and an honorary Gallicean Marine, everyone will be thrilled to meet you. Bye now." De-o-Nu pressed the button on the door. After a few seconds, it opened and he left the room.

"Here we are, old friend," Dave told Jake. "The good news is there will be plenty of Gallicean whisky for you here."

"Thank goodness for that," Jake laughed. "We maklans can't eat normal food with our tendrils. But can I talk to you about something, Dave?"

"Certainly Jake. What's on your mind?" he replied.

"All of this seems oddly familiar to me," Jake began. "The Galliceans get strong feelings from the two planets. Something external is definitely affecting Fa-a-Di. His reaction to the plight of the Boley is too strong. I know the Predaxians have given up their mind control and there is no evidence the Maklakar have that ability. But something is going on here."

"Have you heard about the time eddies now affecting some of the portals?" Dave asked. "That seems to be another anomaly that can't be explained."

"No, I hadn't heard that. But time eddies are a strong sign that tampering with space-time is occurring. Do you remember Fola Untor, the shopkeeper and Chief Engineer?" Jake asked.

"Of course. I'm still confused by his comment that Chief Engineers can mask events to Hive agents," Dave replied. "I think it was Rence Rialto who told me traveling in time and returning at the same moment can create time eddies. Do you think that's part of this?"

"Probably, Dave," Jake sighed. "Right now we have many more questions than answers. Hopefully we will learn more on Gallicea. Time travel and contact with time travelers can negatively affect mood and health. We maklans are very sensitive to those things, so my presence should be helpful."

"Jake, since Fa-a-Di is already impacted, do you think we should have Mitch jump over and keep an eye on him?" Dave asked.

"Great idea, Dave. We should still be in range of Nightsky. I'll communicate with him now," Jake said, who began to glow bright blue. After a moment, he said, "Here's Mitch now." The second maklan floated through the air and landed next to Jake.

"Perfect," Dave said. "Mitch, please go find Fa-a-Di and ask him to let you stay with him. Jake will give you all the details. In the meantime, I'm going to put on my breather and take a look around."

"Just let me know if you need us," Jake said.

"Of course, my friend," he replied as he slipped the breather over his face and checked the readings on the heads-up display. Then he walked to the door and went to explore the ship.

CHAPTER 7

The battle station Mondor continued its trek from Zia-Makla, some fifteen thousand light years behind them. Ambassador Ont Valoo sat quietly in his office deep in the center of the massive planetoid. It had been months since they had left home on their journey to find and make peace with their neighbors. In their desperate attempt to mask their point of origin, they had side-stepped two maklan planets which were deemed too close to Maklakar space to risk contact. The top priority Ont had received from Supreme General Ulon Porto was to keep the location of the Maklakar systems a secret. All Maklakar knew if the Paxran found them, the genocide would begin again. Ont was still confused how he would maintain secrecy while negotiating for peace with another civilization. But he was an old man who had been given the job he had always dreamed of. The Maklakar could not remain hidden on the edge of the galaxy forever. Other civilizations were bound to find them eventually. He was saddled with the responsibility for forging alliances with others who would fight the Paxran with them.

A tone sounded on his control panel and he pressed a button, causing the door to open. Vard Kalak, his trusted assistant and commander of the battle station entered the office with a bottle of whisky and two glasses. "Lord Valoo, I have brought a drink for a celebration," Vard said. "We are approaching a system that includes a valakar civilization. I have just received approval from Oti-Makla to make contact."

"That is great news, Vard," he replied. "I could use a drink. We've been traveling a long time without reaching out to anyone. I was beginning to think this trip was a waste of time.

Have we been hailing the planet or have they attempted to contact us?" Ont asked as Vard passed him a glass of whisky.

"We began hailing them a few minutes ago, Ont," Vard replied. "Our sensors indicate several star cruisers are headed this way to intercept us. That's a great sign! They have a sophisticated stellar fleet. They may have the capability to help defend us from the Paxran."

A second tone sounded on the ambassador's panel and he pressed another button. The image of Uli Habol, the communications officer appeared on his view screen. "Lord Valoo, we are receiving communication from the valakar planet. I've sent the signal to our computers to develop a translation protocol. We have sent a translation signal to them as well."

"Excellent, Uli," Ont replied. "What is the status of their approaching ships?"

"They will intercept us in one hour, sir," she said. "Their defensive arrays are fully active, but their weapons systems are offline. What are your orders, sir?"

"Steady as she goes, Uli," Ont replied. "Commander Kalak is here with me now. As their ships get closer, bring down our speed so we are at a full stop when they arrive. Hopefully, that will give us enough time to have a large translation database available. The commander and I will be on the bridge soon. Valoo out." He smiled broadly and turned to face the commander. "This is the beginning my friend." He raised his glass to touch the other and sipped the drink. "This is exceptional whisky, Vard. Thank you for sharing it with me."

"Lord Valoo, you have been my mentor since the academy. This is only a minor token of my appreciation for your support," Vard smiled. "But may I speak to you in private for a moment?"

"Of course, Vard. We are alone now," Ont said, somewhat surprised by the turn of the conversation.

Vard pulled a small device from his pocket, set it on the desk, and pressed the single button. The button began to glow red. "That's better," he said.

"You need a privacy shield?" Ont asked. "That seems very irregular, old friend."

"Lord Valoo," the commander began, "you have to know Supreme General Porto has filled this ship with his spies. I believe he has a different goal for this trip and has his agents here to make certain you and I don't get in his way."

Ont laughed heartily. "Of course I know all of that, dear friend. Remember that I trained Ulon and his protégés at the academy. But you and I know our current situation in the Maklakar region is untenable. Eventually, the Paxran will find us. That may happen many generations in the future, but our inaction will still be the cause of our ultimate destruction. If you recall, I fought strenuously against the attack on Tak-Makla and the Gallicean system. How stupid could Ulon be to attack civilizations that don't know or care about us? That's why I sent the fleet of old ships to the Nom-Kat-La system. If Ulon had investigated further, he would have found the ships were unmanned. Even if the Galliceans turned out to be timid and peaceful, I couldn't let us attack them. It would have been the same on Tak-Makla, but Ulon insisted that his grandson lead that attack. That stupid decision will make it virtually impossible to get the alliances we need."

"You don't think the spies on board will try to attack other planets and blame it on us?" Vard asked.

"No, not at all," Ont replied. "They are here to keep an eye on us and make certain we don't divulge the location of our systems. I'm no fool. I would never do that. They will likely try to glean any information from our new contacts about the Paxran or the Hive technology we destroyed on Tak-Makla. If they are caught by our new partners, our mission will likely fail utterly. You and I will be blamed for that here and on Oti-Makla. I don't mind that happening to me. I'm an old man and the opportunity to take this voyage has already made my life worthwhile. However, I want you to get to know the spies better. I want you to be their friend. If all of this falls to pieces, I hope the blame will be placed entirely on me. You should be able to go home and keep your honor."

"I don't like the sound of that, Lord Valoo," Vard said. "I don't think I can stand by while you are disgraced."

"Let's not think about any of that now. Please pour some more whisky for me, Vard." Both glasses were refilled. Ont leaned back in his chair and savored the whisky. "Let us concentrate on doing our job right. If we can find some new friends to be a buffer between us and the Paxran, we will be heroes to all the Maklakar worlds. We will deny and rebuff any actions of the spies that threaten our treaties. Even General Porto would expect us to do that. If we overcome those issues, we will find more worlds to partner with. And if we are extremely lucky, we will be able to befriend the maklans of Tak-Makla and the Galliceans, and overcome the events of the past." Both men sipped their whisky again. "Vard, you should go back to the bridge now. I will join you shortly." He tapped the button on the privacy device and the light went out.

CHAPTER 8

"Rainor, my old friend, I think you are being difficult on purpose," Passor Valka said. "You have to remember I was your predecessor as President of the Ela High Council. You wouldn't be sitting in that chair if not for me and my friends."

"Things have changed in the Society, Passor," Rainor smiled. "The High Council of the Society is in shambles. You have been disgraced and expelled from Earth Prime. Your precious Brotherhood has been outlawed. Now you not only want me to allow you to stay here on Narta Ela, but you also want us to give asylum to Brotherhood agents. I think you ask too much, old friend. I do appreciate your mentorship and support, but I don't think I can do what you ask."

"The asylum is temporary, Rainor," Passor replied. "I keep saying that but you do not hear. The Brotherhood has other plans, but we need time to make bring them to fruition. Now, planetary leaders around the Society are rounding up agents and throwing them in prisons without charges. This is a great miscarriage of justice that cannot be allowed to continue."

"I feel your pain, Passor, but these times are very difficult for everyone. None of us can count on defense from the Society. We have been acquiring new cruisers as quickly as the Ulu planets can produce them. There are thirty ships in orbit here now to protect the Ela Council," Rainor said. "We used to rely on Lagamar Ulu to sell us a cruiser every two months. Now, they are building ships for their own defense."

"Please don't mention the Lagamar system, Rainor," he replied. "Those planets and Nan are responsible for the current situation. That's why I need to protect the Brotherhood agents. They are the only ones who understand the situation and can get those planets to pay for what they have done."

"Now you are being foolish," Rainor laughed. "I have seen the video of the Grand Conclave. Admiral Dave Brewster and the Galliceans had hard evidence to prove the High Council was at fault all around. They made you and the Brotherhood look like fools. The Lagamar planets were the victims, not you."

Passor laughed. "Rainor, you are the foolish one. The Brotherhood will not go quietly. I have spoken with the Supreme Leader and he is already devising plans to extract our revenge from those who have harmed us. Which side do you want to be on when that day arrives?"

Rainor went to his credenza and withdrew a bottle of whisky and two glasses. He poured two glasses and offered one to his guest. "Please be reasonable, Passor. You know you are putting me and this planet in a terrible position. Being known as the only planet giving asylum to the Brotherhood will make us a pariah in the galaxy. We will lose all of our trading partners. The enemies of the Brotherhood will accelerate their purchases of cruisers and come here to attack them. Eventually, the other Ela planets will abandon us and another will be named the capital. Is that what you want?"

"You know I don't want that, old friend," Passor replied. "There is no need to advertise any asylum for the Brotherhood. The Supreme Leader and I will let the agents know. Perhaps there is an out of the way spot where we can settle temporarily. We will also need two Hives, but the Supreme Leader can manage that. Hopefully, we will all be off Narta Ela within six months. Then you can go back to your normal life, confident that the Brotherhood will always count you as their friend."

"Okay, Passor, I can support that plan," Rainor sighed. "Please keep this very quiet and make certain the agents do not try to mingle with the permanent residents, unless they are Ela, of course. There is no need to raise any suspicions. And six months is the limit. After that, you all need to be gone."

"Thank you, Rainor. That will be satisfactory. I told you we could negotiate to an acceptable solution for both of us," Passor said as he raised his glass to touch the other. "Let's drink to our success."

"Cheers," Rainor said as he tapped the other glass. "Passor, you know more about the situation throughout the Society than I. What do you think the future looks like? Frankly, I'm terrified that we will collapse into anarchy."

"It's not good," he replied. "Without the semblance of central command and control, the planets are lost and confused. The Councils for the different races are totally ineffective, since their planets are so widely disbursed. You are very lucky to have five Ela planets close the Narta Ela. The only strong spot is the Lagamar-Nan Alliance. Other regions are trying to do the same thing, but it's a slow process, as most of the races never have trusted one another."

"It is a real tragedy that the High Council did not embrace Wendo Balak's plan for the Free Society long ago. Perhaps this could have all been avoided," Rainor sighed.

"I know that now," Passor replied. "But Wendo's plan never had a chance when he was on the High Council. By that time, the Council was so entrenched with their personal power they could not see the end coming. When I was elected President, my predecessor told me to just try and hold things together and to use the Brotherhood to help. And that's what I did.

Unfortunately, my term coincided with the end. Fate has not been kind to me."

"I have heard relationships with the nearby valakar planets are also at risk," Rainor said. "Once again, I'm fortunate to be deep in Society space."

"Only the Bandabar are causing trouble," Passor replied. "They have been trying to develop Hive technology for a long time. Now they see the opportunity to steal it from us while we are weak. My last executive order was to remove all mobile Hives from their frontier; however, there is one planetary Hive in the region. That is a big problem."

"Well, taking over a Hive is not the same as understanding it," Rainor said. "Let's hope they fail in their efforts or at least can't understand what they have."

"Hope is a rare commodity in the Society these days," Passor replied. "That is why we have decided to flee the home galaxy. Without a miracle, it seems likely that military dictatorships will rise and fight among themselves for ultimate power. I have heard that High Priest Obu Neela of Lagamar Ulu has predicted ten thousand years of conflict. Although it pains me, I must agree with him. We need a strong defense to protect our frontiers from invaders now. Instead, those forces will be focused on infighting, leaving our borders exposed. We may lose hundreds if not thousands of planets before we wake up and fight the invaders."

"Leaving the galaxy seems extreme, Passor," Rainor replied, "Although I can't argue with the conclusion. Unfortunately, with trillions of Ela counting on me for leadership, I cannot run and hide."

Passor laughed. “We won’t be hiding, old friend. We will be planning and rebuilding in preparation for our return. If we stay here though, our enemies in the Society will not give us the luxury of time. Any delay in our plans will make the remnants of the Society weaker. Plus, we have other enemies who must pay for their crimes.”

“You’re going after Admiral Brewster and the Galliceans, right?” Rainor asked. “I think that’s a terrible error, Passor. I think they were more than a match for you the first time. Why risk a second embarrassment?”

“First of all, I cannot comment on where we are going,” Passor replied. “As you know, the Brotherhood has enemies in other galaxies besides Ulagong. The Supreme Leader knows best and I’ll leave it to him to make those decisions. I must caution you not to ask more questions in this regard. The less you know the better. Call it plausible deniability. But if you must know more, I can call the Supreme Leader to initiate you into the Brotherhood?”

“That won’t be necessary, old friend,” Rainor said. “Let’s end this meeting before I put my foot in my mouth again.” He stood and stuck his hand out. “I wish you luck, Passor. And I hope you fulfill your promise to leave within six months.”

CHAPTER 9

Kong-Fa was due to arrive in the Gallicean system in a few minutes. Due to the blackout of communications in that system, Dave was calling Darlene one last time. He pressed a button on his console and her image appeared on the screen. She was wrapped in a towel and her hair was wet. "Oops! I hope I didn't catch you in the shower, sweetheart," Dave laughed.

"I'm afraid so, honey," she smiled as she dried her hair with a second towel. "We are just arriving at Nanda and I'm scheduled to meet with Odo Pak in two hours. How are you, Dave?"

"We will arrive in the Gallicea system soon and there is a communications blackout there, so I thought I'd better call to tell you I love you before then," he replied.

"I spoke with De-o-Nu's wife last night and she told me about the blackout," Darlene said. "I was going to call you after I got dressed, but I'm glad you called first."

"No problem, sweetheart," he beamed. "By the way, I was talking with Jake and he said the time eddy problem could be caused by time travelers or Hive agents trying to change the past or mask events. You might let Aria know that too."

"Chief Engineer Lanz Lagerfeld said the same thing, Dave," she replied. "Unfortunately, evidence is hard to find. Once the past is changed, the new past becomes the reality. But changing the past is very dangerous. If an agent changed one minor event, he or she might never have lived to make the change. The possibilities are too frightening to imagine."

"I'm not sure someone is trying to change the past so much as mask events from Hive agents. You remember our talk with Fola Untor, don't you?" he asked.

"Yes, but I can't say I understood what he meant. He was very cryptic with his words. I get the creepy feeling he is hiding a lot more than he told us," she replied.

"No doubt about that, honey," he said. "By the way, Jake also confirmed that a Maklakar battle station is approaching our space. Have you heard anymore about that from Darak or Arrin?"

"Yes. It appears the ship is approaching a system about five thousand light-years away," Darlene said. "Apparently, the system includes at least one valakar planet. So far, everything seems to be peaceful. Perhaps they are not as aggressive as we thought although I'm certain the tekkans would disagree. I also did speak with Zee Gongaleg yesterday. The Hive will be going online in three days. He did have to bring in a lot of maklans from No-Makla to replace the injured and dead. He has invited us to join The Hive as soon as your Sojourn is over."

"That would be great, but I'm not sure our schedule has any room," Dave frowned. "We've got a big fleet to manage now, honey. The sooner we find locations for new Hives or a natural Hive, the better. The Maklakar are too big of a threat to ignore." A tone sounded throughout the ship. "Darlene, that tone means we are entering the Gallicean system in two minutes, so I'll have to let you go."

"Okay, honey. You take care and keep safe. I love you and can't wait to hold you in my arms again," Darlene said.

"I love you too, babe. Take care and I'll see you in a few days. Kong-Fa out," he finished as he closed the connection. He sat back in his chair and pondered the absence of communication. He had become so accustomed to the constant connection to his family and crew that the quiet in his earpiece would be very strange. A tone told him that guests were outside his door. He pressed a button and the inner door opened.

Fa-a-Di and De-o-Nu entered his cabin. De-o-Nu carried a case of whisky under his arm. Dave rose to hug both men and offered them seats on the large couches. De-o-Nu opened a bottle and poured three full glasses of whisky and handed them to his friends. "Dave, this is a monumental event for us," De-o-Nu said. "You are the first non-Gallicean to visit these planets. I'm still amazed you are here with us."

"Gentlemen, to our health!" Dave said as he raised his glass to touch the others. "It is a great honor for me to share this Sojourn with my two brothers. I must say I'm very excited, but I don't know what to expect."

Fa-a-Di laughed, "Don't worry, brother, we will be with you the whole time. But let me give you some of the details."

"Jake should be here," Dave said. "I'd call him but communications are prohibited."

"Nonsense," Fa-a-Di replied. "Communications to the outside are prohibited, but we must talk to each other. Imagine if your translator was prohibited. We wouldn't understand each other at all." They heard the sound of glass clinking and turned to see Jake and Mitch pulling a second bottle from the case and flying it over to the table.

"Are you psychic, Jake," Dave asked. "I was just thinking about you."

"Dave, don't get crazy," Jake laughed. "You asked Mitch and me to keep an eye on the general and when we saw him coming this way with whisky, we knew our lunch was on the way." He extended a thin tendril into the bottle and drank. "That's better."

"I'm glad you're here, Jake," Dave smiled. "Fa-a-Di was just going to go over the itinerary for the next few days. Please go ahead, brother."

"Well, frankly there is no agenda to follow," Fa-a-Di replied. "The tradition requires us to visit both planets at least once every ten years. The visit is supposed to be freeform to allow us to experience the planets in our own way. My brother-in-law comes more often than me. For some reason, I find the experience of these planets very upsetting. I dread the trip each time and am rewarded with weeks of misery and nightmares."

"I can't say my experience is anything like that," De-o-Nu said. "Each time I am on Gallicea, my heart soars and I feel filled with love and contentment. The other planet is the opposite. I feel much the same as Fa-a-Di there. Since our custom dictates that we visit both, I generally spend only one day on the terrestrial planet and a week or more on Gallicea."

"Jake, why are you glowing?" Fa-a-Di said.

"Yikes! I hadn't even noticed that," Jake said as he saw his body filled with a deep blue light. "I'm not sensing anything, but my body tells me differently."

"Isn't the blue light a good thing?" Dave asked. "You seem to be happy when you glow that color, as I recall."

"Yes, blue is a peaceful color, but I don't know why this is happening to me," Jake replied. "When we glow, it's usually a sign of strong emotion, and yet I feel nothing special right now."

"It's likely the effect of Gallicea, Jake," Fa-a-Di said. "You can expect things to become stranger as we approach the planets. I can already feel a sense of dread growing in the back of my head. How do you feel, Brother-in-law?"

"I've been feeling great since you agreed to allow me to join you, brother," De-o-Nu replied. "But I don't feel any different than before we entered the system. How about you, Dave?"

"I feel fine too," Dave said. "I'm a little anxious about this trip and what might happen, but nothing else. Fa-a-Di, what do you want to do when we arrive at Gallicea?"

"First, I will take a shuttle to Sa-la-Na, the temple city that manages the system. Even though your presence was already approved, I need to meet with the High Priest and get his personal blessing before you and Jake come down to the planet," Fa-a-Di said. "It is just a formality, I can assure you. Once that is done, De-o-Nu will bring you to the city where our quarters are set up for the evening. I will need to make a number of perfunctory visits to different parts of the planet. It's part of my role as High Commissioner. De-o-Nu will see you are entertained tonight."

"And tomorrow morning, we will venture out to my favorite Ka-la-a," De-o-Nu beamed. "I have a small lodge there where we will stay as long as my brother-in-law can stand it. I have also made arrangements for a suite of rooms to have an Earthlike atmosphere there. Tonight, you will probably have to sleep in your pressure suit. I'm sure Jake will keep an eye on you though." He turned to Jake, "If Dave is having any air supply issues, please jump him back here."

"When I've had all of Gallicea I can stand, we will travel by shuttle to the terrestrial planet, where God willing, we will spend one day and one night only," Fa-a-Di grimaced. "The worst part of staying there is knowing my ancestor made the edict forcing me to go there in the first place."

"I was thinking the similarities between this system and the first time you encountered the maklans are amazing," Dave said. "Galliceans sense strong negative feelings and then correlate those to aggression. Remember that No-Makla was attacked due to a misunderstanding of maklan intentions."

"Are you suggesting that maklans live in this system and we are mistaking their thoughts for antagonism towards Galliceans?" Fa-a-Di asked.

"No, not at all," Dave replied. "However, the feelings of dread and misery could be a reaction to thoughts from another culture."

De-o-Nu and Fa-a-Di were laughing. "Dave, the Beings that used to inhabit that planet have been extinct for too many generations to remember. It's ridiculous to believe they could still be alive. Why haven't they reached out to us?"

“Well, the last time they did, things did not go too well for them,” Jake replied. “I don’t think we should discount Dave’s theory so soon. My body is glowing for a reason. Both of you have conflicting feelings about the planets here. Fa-a-Di has been in a somber mood for a long time. These things may well be connected.”

“Perhaps you are right, Jake,” Fa-a-Di laughed. “None of us thought humans and Galliceans originated in the Andromeda Galaxy until Dave casually ran into Loni Arrak in the Tak-Makla Hive. Maybe that’s why you two are here. Every Gallicean has visited these planets over the last thousand generations and no one found any sentient life. But maybe this time you will. It seems we are in orbit and I need to change for my meeting with the High Priest. You three can keep drinking if you like.” Fa-a-Di left the room, still laughing.

CHAPTER 10

The Gallicean shuttle slipped out of the shuttle bay and dove toward Gallicea. Dave Brewster was wearing his clear pressure suit over his clothes and Jake was clinging to his chest to monitor the readings. De-o-Nu was piloting the craft down toward the swirling atmosphere of the planet. After the shuttle had traveled some distance, the Kong-Fa left orbit and headed out of the system and back to Earth. As the shuttle entered the top layers of the atmosphere, it began to be pushed around by the high speed winds. Gallicea was the same size as Jupiter with similar bands of gas moving rapidly in opposite directions. That made it difficult and bumpy for the craft to travel north and south.

A small speck of silver appeared on the horizon and the shuttle raced toward it. Gradually the speck resolved into a large city floating in the gas. The island city of Sa-la-Na was very large, with a footprint of one hundred square miles. It was suspended above the planet by electro-magnetic field generators powered by thc rapidly moving gas and the planetary magnetic fields. The permanent population was only a few million, most of whom were either in the priesthood or hospitality industry, serving the billions of annual visitors. Shuttle docks formed the outer edge of the city. From there, rings of hotels and restaurants reached to the city center, which was dominated by a large hill covered with temples.

Given the importance of the visitors, the shuttle was allowed to land at a small star port in the temple zone normally reserved for the priesthood. The visit to the holy planets by the High Commissioner and non-Galliceans was very highly anticipated on Gallicea. Throughout Greater Gallia, people were concerned and anxious to find out what would happen on this trip.

De-o-Nu piloted the shuttle over the city and into the temple zone. A number of priests were directing the ship to its landing spot where De-o-Nu touched the ship down on its marks, and powered down. He unbuckled his harness and turned to his passengers. “Whoa!” he shouted, “What’s going on with you, Jake?”

Jake was glowing brightly and changing colors rapidly. “I have no idea,” he said. “I don’t feel any different at all. There is definitely something strange going on here on Gallicea. Dave, what do you make of it?”

“You look like a disco ball, Jake,” Dave laughed. “But I have to agree with you. The entire planet seems to be energized. Ever since we entered the atmosphere, I’ve been seeing flashes of light out of the corners of my eyes. It’s very distracting.” He unbuckled his harness and stood up and promptly stumbled. “Whoa! I’m feeling very light-headed.”

“Let me check your air supply,” Jake said. “According to the system, everything is normal. I think it must be the energy in the atmosphere that’s affecting us both.”

“Jake, do you think you and Dave should jump back to the Kong-Fa?” De-o-Nu asked. “We’ll be in range for several more hours.”

“No, I don’t want to do that,” Dave said. “I’m sure this is like landing in a high altitude city in the twenty-first. It just takes some time to get used to it. Let’s go.”

Chapter 10

A line of priests in dark gray robes were waiting for them as they exited the shuttle. Most of them had met De-o-Nu many times and they were happy to see him again. He introduced Dave and Jake to the priests, who seemed pleased to welcome non-Galliceans to their most sacred planet. No-be-Ka was the leader of the group of priests and spoke first, saying, "Admiral Brewster, it is an honor to welcome a friend of De-o-Nu and Fa-a-Di to our world. I also want to thank you for helping me choose to be a priest."

"You're welcome," Dave said, "but I really don't know what you mean. I don't believe we have met before." The group began to walk toward a terminal building next to the landing area.

"No, we have not met before," No-be-Ka said. "However, I was the helmsman on one of the three cruisers that attacked No-Makla when the Predaxians were controlling our captains. We were all frightened and nervous when we were ordered to attack, especially knowing our comrades were going to Nom-Kat-La to fight the real battle. We were a young crew and none of us dared to question our captain. When the soldier jumped onto our bridge and uncovered the Predaxian agent, we were stunned again. That day, I realized that I was never meant to be a soldier. I did continue to serve during the Second Predaxian War, but after that, I resigned and joined the priesthood."

"Your words are very kind, but I don't know how I helped you," Dave said. "It was De-o-Nu and his loyal lieutenants who ended the battle."

"Of course, Dave, but it was you who stopped the carnage by finding a link to the maklans and helping our leaders to learn their true intentions. Without you, I fear the worst would have happened," No-be-Ka replied.

“Well, then you are most welcome,” Dave smiled. “But most of the credit should go to my maklan friend here. No-be-Ka, this is Jacomofledes Benomafolays.”

“Jake the maklan!” No-be-Ka exclaimed. “This is a wonderful day for all of us. Thank you Jake for helping us to defeat the Predaxian Alliance.”

“You’re welcome; however, it was primarily the Galliceans who fought the war. We were happy to do our part, and fortunately, we succeeded,” Jake said.

The group entered the terminal building where hundreds of priests were just arriving or preparing to leave Gallicea for the other planets. Many had come to bear witness to the first visit of aliens to the planet. As Dave and Jake moved through the crowd, most stopped and stared. Dave smiled and waved, but the priests were too stunned to react. While Greater Gallia had trading relationships with many alien societies, the average Gallicean had little contact with them. As they continued through the hall, a single Gallicean in ornate ivory-colored robes approached them. The priests around Dave stopped and bowed deeply. De-o-Nu smiled and hurried forward to greet the man. The two hugged and shook hands. They then came over to Dave.

“Dave, please let me introduce you to my brother, De-o-Pa,” De-o-Nu said.

“How do you do, Dave Brewster?” De-o-Pa asked. “My brother has told me everything about you. Welcome to Gallicea! I have just arrived as well along with a contingent of my priests from Jupiter.”

"It is my pleasure, De-o-Pa," Dave replied. "As my friend's brother, you are now my brother as well."

"Prelate, it is an honor to have you with us," No-be-Ka said with his head still bowed. "How may we serve you today, sir?"

"Please straighten up, priest," De-o-Pa said. "There is no need for formality here. We are all just traveling through. I am simply here to welcome my brother and his friends."

"Thank you, Prelate," No-be-Ka replied. "We were just escorting them to their quarters. Would you care to join us?"

"Thank you, but no," De-o-Pa said. "I have a meeting with Fa-a-Di and High Priest Um-e-Ka in one hour. Then I'm afraid I must return to Jupiter. We have more settlers arriving every day, and I want to meet each one personally. They must know they are still Galliceans even though they are far from the home worlds."

"Pa, I was hoping you could spend a day with us at our family lodge," De-o-Nu said disappointedly. "You and Fa-a-Di always get along so well. Also, I have told you about his mood change. I need you to help me with that."

"I'll see what I can do, brother," the Prelate said. "When were you planning to go there, Nu?"

"Tomorrow at sunrise, I hope," he answered. "Fa-a-Di is traveling around on official rounds today. If he is ready then, we will go."

"Perhaps I will travel with him after the meeting then," De-o-Pa said. "I will use my wits to expedite our return."

"Perfect," De-o-Nu replied. "Hopefully, Dave, Jake and I will see you both later this evening."

"That sounds great, brother," De-o-Pa smiled. "Dave and Jake, it was a pleasure to meet you both. I hope we will share food and whisky tonight and tomorrow." He shook their hands, hugged his brother and walked away.

"I guess I should have known he was your brother, De-o-Nu," Dave laughed. "He's the only other Gallicean I've seen as tall as you."

"True, but good things come in really big packages," De-o-Nu replied.

CHAPTER 11

The Maklakar battle station had slowed to a dead stop ten million miles from the valakar planet. The defensive arrays were online but the weapon systems remained cold. Five small star cruisers had slowed and now blocked the path forward. Commander Vard Kalak sat in his command chair watching the scene unfold. His communications team had spent several hours building a translation database from the data stream from both the ships and the planet which hung like a crescent moon in the distance.

"Commander, our translation database is now complete," Uli Habol said. "We should be able to interpret eighty percent or more of their signals. We are continuing to hail them and have sent a matching database on a carrier signal so they can upload it."

"Very good, Uli," Vard smiled. He turned to his weapons officer, Paka Nopak and said, "What is the status of their weapons systems?"

"Still cold, commander," she replied. "We've been listening to the chatter among their ships and they seem to be calm. They are probably waiting for orders from their planet. Our systems are also offline."

"Thanks, Paka. Uli, please let Lord Valoo know the situation and advise him to come to the bridge at his convenience. I think he needs to be here to make the first connection," Vard said.

"Aye-aye, commander," Uli replied.

The view screen image split and the face of a valakar filled the right half. The creature was bird-like, as expected, with a thin beak and large green eyes. Its brown feathers were neatly combed. “Greetings, war ship,” the valakar said. “Thank you for the translation database. It has saved us many hours of work. Who are you and what are your intentions in our space?”

“Captain, I am Commander Vard Kalak of the Maklakar battle station Mondor. I am bringing our senior ambassador, Lord Ont Valoo to engage with new cultures and civilizations. It is our goal to establish peace, trade and mutual defense treaties with other peaceful planets,” the commander replied.

“Thank you Commander Kalak. I am Captain Zi At-at of the star cruiser Eet-O. I will pass your request back to our planet. Please maintain your current position until we get further instructions,” the valakar said. The image of the creature disappeared.

Ont Valoo rushed onto the bridge, saying, “What did I miss, Vard?”

“Lord Valoo, we have made first contact with a valakar captain,” Vard began. “I told him of our intentions and he has sent a message back to their world to get further instructions.”

“Wow!” Ont exclaimed. “I hope it won’t take too long. I must admit the anticipation of our success is getting the best of me. If they tell us to go away, I’ll be depressed for a month.”

Vard laughed. “Lord Valoo, please just relax. None of us are really diplomats. It’s not in our xenophobic nature. We could be sitting here a long time.”

"Or not," Uli said. He was pointing to the screen where the image of Captain At-at had returned. A second valakar filled the left side of the screen.

"Commander, thank you for your patience," Zi said. "On your screen you should also be seeing our Premier It Ka-la. When we informed his office of your intentions, he requested to speak to you himself. Premier, at your leave."

"Thank you Zi," the Premier said. "Dear Maklakar guests, it is my pleasure to welcome you to Vilu-Zan, the home world of the Vilu people. I must admit we were quite relieved to learn of your peaceful intentions. Your ship is quite impressive. As you have no doubt learned, our star cruisers are minute in comparison."

"Premier, thank you for your kind words. I am Lord Ambassador Ont Valoo, representing the Maklakar Federation. I am quite surprised you have heard of us. We are a very simple people who love our isolation from others who might wish us harm. I can assure you that our weapons systems are for defensive purposes only. Our Supreme General Ulon Porto has asked me to visit planets in our vicinity in order to form new bonds of friendship. Our military is very strong, but we have no desire to expand. Those days are far in the past for our species. In fact, we are very willing to offer much of our technology to our new friends. Do you think we could meet Premier? I know a new relationship between our peoples will be mutually beneficial."

"I think that is possible," It replied. "However, I do not think your ship in orbit around our planet would be accepted by our people. Do you have any smaller ships that can transport you to our planet?"

"Of course, Premier," Ont said. "This battle station has five star cruisers and dozens of shuttle craft. We can launch a single cruiser which my diplomatic group and I can take to your planet. Is that satisfactory?"

"That would be perfect, Ambassador," It smiled. "Captain At-at will arrange everything with our Central Command. It is early afternoon here in the capital city, so perhaps we can meet late tomorrow morning. Our local time stamp is 1745. Perhaps your diplomats can take a shuttle to our capital at 1000 tomorrow morning. The Captain will also send you a chronological translator. I look forward to our meeting."

"Thank you so much," Ont replied. "That will be perfect. We have already measured your air pressure and atmosphere and will need no accommodations. We will see you tomorrow morning. Mondor out." The view screen again showed open space and the Vilu cruisers. "Vard, I must tell you I am overjoyed right now. I didn't think we'd find such an agreeable culture so easily."

"It is almost too good to be true, Lord Valoo," Vard replied. "In my experience, that raises many red flags. Perhaps the Vilu are not as evolved as they appear. My science team is checking as much data as they can right now. My first fear was they were an offshoot of the Donnaki."

"You think they want to eat us?" Ont scoffed. "That seems highly unlikely. With their weak military, they can see that could never happen."

"I know, sir, but we must check everything. Fortunately, our scans of their ships and home world show them to be roughly our size, so we won't look like a snack to them. Also, the technology is far behind ours, so I doubt they'll be able to help us with Hive technology. I recommend caution on the first visits, until we can really understand their motivation," Vard noted.

Ont stood and paced around the bridge. "As always you are right, old friend. We should take a contingent of guards with us, although most of the troops should stay on the cruiser, ready for rapid deployment in case of emergency." He sat again heavily. "Our past is catching up to us, Vard. I can't tell if I'm afraid because of a potential threat or just due to our xenophobia. I can't let that stop us from this great mission."

"Lord Valoo, you are correct," Vard replied. "Perhaps we will keep all the guards on our cruiser. But we will have locked onto each of your team so we can jump them back if something happens. If we're in a close enough orbit, we can track your every move."

"I suppose a level of risk comes with any enterprise," Ont said. "There's nothing to do now but go and see what happens. I doubt I'll get much sleep tonight."

"If you would like, I can join you later for a whisky to calm our nerves," Vard offered. "I will also accompany you on the mission if I may. The Vilu have to expect some kind of support team for our diplomats."

"Great. I agree with all of that," Ont replied. "Having you around will calm my nerves, and your level headedness can only help in our mission tomorrow. Thank you, Vard. You are a true friend."

CHAPTER 12

Dave Brewster was sleeping uneasily. As De-o-Nu had expected, there was no breathable atmosphere at the hotel in Sa-la-Na. Dave had never slept in his pressure suit. He could only sleep on his side due to the supply pack on his back. He could not roll over either. If he needed to change position, he had to rise and move to the opposite side of the bed. Jake was a problem too. Even as he slept, his body flashed different colors. Finally, Dave had to ask him to stay in the bathroom with the door closed. Still, he could see random flashes of light under the door. He sat up in bed frustrated that sleep was eluding him yet again. If the city was higher in the gas, he could have survived with just a breather. At this level, the atmosphere was too dense and the pressure would collapse his lungs. He desperately wanted to contact Darlene and tell her how he felt and ask her how she had survived in a pressure suit so long on her first visit to Gallia, but communications were strictly forbidden. So, he sat alone on the edge of the bed hoping sleep might find him again soon.

He had become accustomed to seeing lights flashing in the corners of his vision since he set foot in the city. With his eyes closed, they were still there, but much less bothersome. He sat quietly wondering how long this night might last. Suddenly, the flashes began again and were painfully strong. Something was wrong with him. This just wasn't right. He thought about summoning Jake to jump him away from this dreadful place. He slowly opened his eyes and saw several blobs of light floating in the room. After a few seconds, they condensed into the light Beings of High Priest Obu Neela and three Nan elders. He did not know their names but remembered them from his meeting in the Andromeda Galaxy six months ago. "Obu, this is a surprise!" he said.

"It is a joy to see you again, Dave," Obu smiled. "Let me introduce you to Elders Olo Und, Zia Fal and Inu Atta of Nan. I don't know if you remember them."

"I do, although I don't think we were ever introduced," he replied. "To what do I owe the pleasure of your visit?"

The light Being of Obu sat next to Dave and put his hand on his shoulder. "Dave, there is much to tell you tonight. We could sense your situation here, even from our galaxy. I was visiting Nan and the four of us were in the stone chamber near Odo's home when we felt you."

"You felt me from two million light-years away?" Dave asked. "How is that even possible?"

"At first, we had no idea either," Zia replied. "You have a very strong connection to the Source, Dave Brewster. However, there is something else involved here."

"I know," Dave said. "I have a feeling the two planets here might be natural Hives. I've felt very energized since I arrived here and have been seeing flashes of light in the corners of my eyes. It reminded me a lot of Nan."

"And we sensed your maklan friend as well," Zia said. "The Source is coursing through every Being here. We've never seen anything like this."

"But somehow the Galliceans are blissfully unaware of any of it," Dave replied. "They sense elation or dread, but believe it relates to the war that occurred here generations ago."

"Hmm, that seems familiar to me somehow, Dave," Obu said. "Where have you heard that kind of thing before?"

"When the Galliceans first encountered the maklan on Neptune," Dave replied. "So, you're saying that Beings on this planet or the terrestrial one are communicating and the Galliceans translate that into emotion?"

"I think you said that, not me," Obu laughed. "It's the same with the feeling you had when you looked in Ulook's face in the fish market, or when Jake saw the Boley in a cage for the first time. Misunderstanding opens the door to understanding."

"That is one reason we are here, Dave," Olo said. "When we felt you from Nan, we knew something crucial must be happening. If you have indeed found a natural Hive planet, that will be a godsend. We need natural Hives now more than ever."

"Why? What's going on?" Dave asked.

"First, Odo Pak is dying," Obu said. "Without the constant connection to Source he had on Nan, his body has begun to decay. We all knew it was a risk when he decided to move here to help the Nanda fulfill their destiny. He felt his life was the most reasonable one to lose since he was already nine thousand years old."

"But if one of these planets is a Hive, then he can come here and survive," Dave said, dumbfounded by the shocking news.

"Perhaps, Dave," Zia replied. "But he is a stubborn old man. He won't want to desert the Nanda. He came here knowing his remaining life would be short and won't do anything to help himself if the Nanda suffer for it."

"Dave, please don't worry about him," Obu said. "We must have faith everything happens for a reason. We cannot change the course of the universe. If Odo is destined to survive, he will. But we have bigger problems."

"Things are deteriorating quickly in our galaxy," Zia said. "Obu has predicted ten thousand years of war. That has already begun."

"But it gets worse than that," Obu interrupted. "The Society is gone forever. With the planets of each race widely disbursed, those governments are collapsing as well. Wendo and Antar are working feverishly to set up regional governments, but they cannot succeed. The interracial hatreds are too ingrained. Many races claim they are superior and must be given power, but few accept that. There is a mad dash to build up militaries and civil wars break out every day. Several other species are beginning to invade the outer regions. Many planets are at risk of being overrun by the valakars from the Bandabar Fold. It is rumored the remaining Brotherhood agents will attempt to flee the galaxy to avoid prosecution and to rebuild their strength. We have sensed the Supreme Leader of the Brotherhood in this galaxy already."

"A great many planets are placing the blame for all of this on Nan and the Lagamar planets, and especially on you and Fa-a-Di," Zia said. "If they can form some kind of alliance, I'm afraid we are all doomed in the home galaxy."

"Dave, it seems Odo and I lied to you," Obu sighed. "We said you are not responsible for what happens in our galaxy. It now seems you have been drawn back into our affairs. I am so sorry for that."

"I am not afraid of the Brotherhood," Dave said. "They are cowards and do not stand a chance against our Free Society. They may kill me, but their whole organization will be wiped out. But what about Lagamar and Nan?"

"I doubt there will be time to save us, Dave," Obu replied. "When we felt you, we realized perhaps you had found a natural Hive. That may be our only chance. Do you remember what Alda Nackly told you about Balthazar Opa?"

"The Society relocated the entire planet by using thirty Hives," Dave said. "But I can't find thirty natural Hives so quickly. I swear I'll try."

"God will decide what happens, Dave," Obu replied. "But I don't believe you need that many. When Balthazar was moved, they used constructed Hives. That relies on human mental energy to coerce the universe to change. A natural Hive is part of nature. Each is many times more powerful than a constructed Hive. But you will have to figure all of that out. Imagine though the terrestrial planet is a Hive and this gas giant is not. You were able to connect to that Hive from one hundred million miles away and send a signal that reached two million light-years to reach us. That's unbelievable to all of us."

"I'm not sure that can happen," Dave smiled. "The Galliceans are very protective of these planets. I don't know how they'd feel about others running a Hive here."

"Who is to say they cannot do it, Dave?" Obu said. "Also, who is to say the original inhabitants of the planet are not still there? Perhaps they might even been Nan or Zula." Obu stood up and walked over to the elders. "Dave, thank you so much for reaching out to us. You give us hope for the future. We are going to visit Odo now before we return to our stone temple. Please get some sleep and we hope to see you again soon." He smiled again as the four shapes began to blur and finally disappear.

Dave noticed Jake was sitting on the bed beside him. "How long have you been sitting here?"

"Just a few minutes, Dave," Jake said. "That was pretty amazing. I can't believe they came from Andromeda because you called to them. By the way, I'm probably in big trouble with our Gallicean hosts, but I received a communication from No-Makla. There's trouble in Predaxian space again."

"What's happening?" he asked.

"Altamar Zendo has disappeared along with most of his loyal agents. It's feared they may set up a new alliance using their mind control abilities in another part of the galaxy," Jake said. "That's more trouble."

"Geez, as if we didn't have enough to deal with right now," Dave said. "Let's get some more sleep and think about that tomorrow."

CHAPTER 13

The early morning sun shone through the window in Dave Brewster's room and onto his face. He opened his tired eyes and looked around. Every muscle and joint in his body was aching from being immobile all night. After a moment he noticed he wasn't seeing the flashes of light on the periphery of his sight anymore. Perhaps he had become accustomed to the surges of Universal Power that seemed to dominate this solar system. He clamored to his feet in the bubble pressure suit. Looking back, he could see Jake still sleeping on the bed next to where Dave had slept. He smiled at his old friend. They had been through so much since he found Jake on New Dawn in the supply dump used as a safe house by Horace Hildebrand. They had met so many new cultures and even traveled to the Andromeda Galaxy together. Dave knew that Jake would soon leave to join the DNA project on Earth, but wanted to really enjoy his company while they were still together.

There was a knock at the door and Dave rushed to open it. Fa-a-Di and De-o-Nu were standing outside along with De-o-Nu's brother. "Brothers, I hope you had a better night than me! This pressure suit is impossible to sleep in. Please come in."

"Not now, Dave," De-o-Nu said. "We're ready to head to the Ka-la-a as soon as you and Jake are prepared."

"Well, since I'm stuck in this suit, I'd say I'm ready," he replied. "Jake is still sleeping. Let me go wake him up."

"I'm ready!" Jake said as he flew over and landed on Dave's chest. "De-o-Nu, make sure the whisky is there too. I'm famished."

The Galliceans laughed. "Don't worry my little friend, everything is there," Fa-a-Di laughed. "I'm had some men take our things to the lodge on a shuttle already. I figure we can fly there now." He held out his harness, saying, "As usual, I've got you Dave."

The group left the hotel and walked down the busy street toward a small park. Fa-a-Di had a spring in his step this day and Dave had to hurry to keep up. "Fa-a-Di, you must be feeling better today," he panted. "Slow down please. Remember how short my legs are compared to yours!"

Fa-a-Di stopped and turned to wait for Dave. "Sorry Dave, I'm just in a hurry to get away from all the people here. I'm starting to feel like I'm on a government junket rather than my Sojourn." When Dave reached him, Fa-a-Di lifted him up and secured him in the harness on the Gallicean's chest. "There, now your little legs can get some rest." The group continued across a broad pedestrian boulevard and entered the small park. A group of priests were gathered in the park, as it was the custom to be blessed before heading out onto the planet. As Dave's group approached them, the priests noticed De-o-Pa among them and began to bow respectfully.

"Please stop that, brothers," De-o-Pa said as he approached them. "Today I am just another citizen on his Sojourn. I am honored by the gesture though." The priests gathered around the Prelate and introduced themselves while kissing his hand. "That's quite enough, brothers. People are backing up now for their blessings. Attend to your flock. No-be-Ka, please join us."

The young priest bowed to the Prelate and kissed his hand. "Yes, Prelate, how can I be of service to you this morning?"

"My friends and I are leaving to explore Gallicea now and would appreciate your blessing, my son," De-o-Pa replied.

"I will handle this blessing personally," said an approaching voice behind them. They turned to see High Priest Um-e-Ka moving quickly forward through the throng of Galliceans. Most of the people bowed or stared in disbelief as the High Priest rarely left the sacred Temple of Galli. All of the priests and De-o-Pa dropped to one knee and lowered their heads in respect. "Please get up, all of you." He shook hands with De-o-Pa and his brother and then approached Fa-a-Di. "High Commissioner, I wanted to see your friend, Admiral Brewster before you all left."

"It is an honor to meet you, your Eminence," Dave said, bowing his head, which was all he could do strapped in the harness. "Thank you for allowing me to join my brothers on this trip."

Um-e-Ka touched Dave's helmet with his hand, saying, "My son, it is an honor for me to meet you as well. Fa-a-Di has told me of the adventures you have shared. I hope one day you can talk to me more about the tekkans and their Hive technology. Finding a connection between our physical world and the spiritual one is a miracle all believers have prayed for."

"Eminence, it is amazing technology, but I don't think it's proven that Universal Power is related to spiritual reality," Dave answered.

"Perhaps," the High Priest frowned. "Fa-a-Di, do you think I could have a private word with the Admiral?"

"Of course, Eminence," Fa-a-Di said as he unbuckled the harness and lifted Dave out, setting him gently on the ground. "But please walk slowly as his legs are much shorter than ours."

"Not to mention the pressure suit brother," Dave laughed. "It's awkward to walk in this thing too."

"Of course, my son. Please follow me away from the crowd for a moment," the High Priest said as he turned and began to walk away. Dave hurried to keep up. After a minute or so, they came upon a bench on a small hill. Um-e-Ka helped Dave get up on the bench and then sat next to him. Dave remained standing so he could look at the other in the face. "Dave, thank you for this moment of time."

"It's my pleasure, Eminence," Dave replied.

"Let me cut to the chase, Admiral," Um-e-Ka began. "I understand there is no conclusive proof on whether Universal Power is related to our souls, but what do you think? You are the only Being I know who has experienced it."

"Frankly I'm not certain how I feel, Eminence," Dave pondered. "In my experience with Universal Power I have seen and done amazing things. I have met the soul of a dead friend and my unborn grandchild. I have traveled back from the Andromeda Galaxy and then took my own son back with me. In my mind, there is spiritual energy in the flow of Universal Power, but I don't know if that energy is a small part or all of it."

"That is the most troubling part of Universal Power to me," the High Priest said. "Science and religion have always fought for the hearts and minds of people. While science seeks to define the knowable, only religion has attempted to define the unknowable. If Universal Power bridges that gap, the separation between science and religion would blur. I'm not sure that is a good thing."

"Eminence, my good friends, Odo and Obu, would disagree. The clerics in their society use the term Source for Universal Power because they believe it is the fountain of all physical and spiritual reality," Dave replied.

Um-e-Ka looked stunned. "Dave, I have heard those names before and my mind cannot believe you mentioned them." His head dropped to his chest and then rose again. "I have met two men with those names in my dreams. Some of my priests call them visions, but I am not so certain. Most often, I am dreaming I am asleep in my bed and wake up suddenly, unable to fall asleep again. As I sit on the side of my bed, two globes of light appear and slowly resolve into two human shapes. They called themselves Odo and Obu."

"That is amazing, Eminence," Dave remarked. "They never mentioned visiting you to me."

"So, they are real men, not apparitions?" Um-e-Ka asked.

"Oh, they're real men, Eminence," Dave smiled. "Each is the spiritual leader of their worlds in the Andromeda Galaxy. What do they tell you, if I may ask?"

"It's not easy to remember everything," Um-e-Ka said as he closed his eyes to concentrate. "They are always happy and grateful to be with me. I think they have told me I am not responsible for all of Greater Gallia and I should be happy in my life. That is not an easy lesson for someone in my position," he replied.

"They have told me the same thing," Dave said as he put his hand on the High Priest's shoulder. "If I may confess, Obu visited me just last night."

"I still can't believe any of this is true," Um-e-Ka gasped. "I was so certain these were just the dreams of an old man. I was also certain they showed Heaven to me. On a few nights, I will awaken and find myself in a very quiet place full of stone temples. I wander around until I find those same men sitting in a small temple overlooking a long range of mountain tops piercing a sea of clouds that stretches to the horizon. I feel so at peace there. Odo and Obu do not speak to me then. They look at me, smile and then let me sit between them. It is the most beautiful place I've ever seen. Isn't that Heaven?"

"No, Eminence, it is not, although the Temple on Mount Alila is a magical and powerful place. It is the most important temple on Lagamar Ulu and Obu Neela is the High Priest there," Dave said. "I have felt the same way when I was there. Unfortunately, the reality of that planet is not as glorious as the temple. Most of the planet is indeed shrouded with clouds, but they are made of smog and not water vapor. The Ulu race serve as manufacturers for most of the goods in the Society of Humanity. Now that the Society is crumbling, I don't know their fate."

"But Dave, you are not responsible for the people in that galaxy," Um-e-Ka said.

Dave laughed and smiled. "Eminence, those are exactly the same words that Obu and Odo have said to me more than once."

"Our visit has been helpful for me, Dave," Um-e-Ka said. "I have kept you too long from your friends. I can see they are becoming restless. Please have a blessed Sojourn and come see me again to tell me of your experience." He extended his hand and Dave shook it.

"Thank you Eminence," Dave replied. "Hearing your story has helped me keep Odo and Obu in my heart. I will thank them for this when I see them again. Goodbye, Eminence." Dave climbed down from the bench and began to walk back to Fa-a-Di.

"Dave Brewster, I bless you in the name of all of Gallicea. Have a wonderful Sojourn!" the High Priest shouted.

Dave turned around and waved back. Then he hurried over to Fa-a-Di who lifted him into the harness again. Then the three Galliceans took to the air and flew off.

CHAPTER 14

The sky was clear and warm as the shuttle from Mondor descended through the atmosphere of Vilu-Zan. Ont Valoo looked out the window as the capital city of Pa-Ka appeared on the horizon. It was clear these valakar had left the trees long ago as the mass of skyscrapers grew in front of them. As the shuttle moved into the center city area, thousands of Vilu could be seen flying to work or running errands. Ont felt a sense of dread about this place, but quickly pushed it back. Perhaps there was an instinctive fear of bird-like Beings for the insect-like Maklakar. There were ancient folk fables about flying creatures attacking and feeding on maklans, but most knew them to be just stories intended to make children be careful and listen to their parents. He turned away from the window and looked at his team. For this first visit, he brought only his confidant Vard Kalak and a security team. Vard had made progress befriending the spies on the battle station, and today the entire team was recruited from the Supreme General's agents.

The shuttle set down on the designated spot and powered down. After a final atmospheric reading, the shuttle bay opened and Ont led the team onto the tarmac. It was very warm and humid in the capital today. The door on a nearby building opened and a small group of Vilu approached them. Vard and Ont immediately recognized Captain Zi At-at at the front of the group. "Captain, it is a pleasant surprise to find you here!" Ont said.

"Thank you Ambassador," Zi said smiling back and offering his hand to shake. "The Premier thought seeing someone you already met might make you more comfortable." Everyone in the group shook hands and then turned back toward the building. "We will travel from here to the Premier's office. It is a short trip. Please follow me to the shuttle vehicle." As the group walked through the terminal building, every Vilu in the crowd stopped and stared. Most had never seen a non-valakar before. Most of the Vilu were about three feet tall, close to the size of the Maklakar. Their feathers were in a rainbow of colors and most were neatly groomed. There were a large number of soldiers with blaster rifles on their backs. "This terminal is the only one in the center of Pa-Ka, so we take security very seriously. Most shuttles leave here for our star port, where our people and goods travel to other planets where we have trading partners."

"Captain, are there other Vilu planets?" Vard asked.

"No, and please call me Zi. May I call you Vard?" the valakar replied.

"Of course," Vard replied. "We captains need to know each other. If the negotiations go well, we may see a lot of one another."

They exited the terminal and climbed aboard a large shuttle that then lifted a few inches off the road and zipped away at rocket speed. "Please don't mind the speed. All our vehicles are remotely controlled and integrated. The risk of an accident is extremely remote." Within five minutes, the vehicle stopped in front of a two-story stone building sitting in the center of a small park ringed by a wide boulevard. Past the road, the site was surrounded by skyscrapers hundreds of stories tall. "Gentlemen, welcome to the Premier's office and residence," Zi began again. "As you can see, the residence is modest as the Premier is the servant of the people, not the other way around. Please follow me inside."

While the building was modest compared to the buildings surrounding it, it was still large with each floor covering five thousand square feet. A large porch lined with stone columns led to the ten foot tall glass doors which opened automatically as they approached. They felt the cool of the air-conditioned interior as they stepped through the doorway. The entry was a large room suitable for celebrations or large meetings. There were doors all around leading to different parts of the building. The group approached one door and Zi opened it and then stopped. "Ambassador, as you can see, the Premier's office is not large. Perhaps your security detail can remain with me while you and maybe one other enter. Is that acceptable?" Zi asked.

"Lord Valoo, this is very irregular," Poli Zua, the head of the detail complained. "We cannot guarantee your security if we are not with you."

Ont smiled and put his hand on the other's shoulder. "Major Zua, I appreciate your concern, but Vard and I will go alone." He winked at Zi and turned back to the guard. "If anything happens to cither of us, you have my permission to destroy the planet." He laughed and stepped into the room with his friend.

Zi closed the door, looked at the guards and said, "Let's get some coffee guys. They'll be just fine. By the way, he was kidding about destroying the planet, right?"

Ont and Vard were alone in the office. A large desk sat on the opposite side with four chairs in front of it. Behind the desk were two large windows looking out at a small flower garden lined by short trees. The other walls were lined with bookcases and cabinets filled with awards and pictures of many Vilu citizens or historic figures. A small side door opened and Premier It Ka-la and another Vilu entered. The premier walked up to the two Maklakar and shook hands. "Welcome to my home, gentlemen. I am glad you made it here today. This is my personal assistant, Ai Uli and she will bring us some coffee and perhaps some pastries, even lunch if we speak that long. Please be seated."

After sitting, Ont began, "Premier, as I have mentioned, the Maklakar are keen to form positive relationships with other societies. We have lived in isolation for too long." The assistant returned with a tray of coffee and pastries and set it on the Premier's desk. She smiled and left again.

It poured his coffee and added cream. He put a pastry on a small plate and set it in front of him. He sipped the coffee and looked at the two maklans. "Frankly, we are more afraid of the humans and tekkans than we are of the Paxran or Donnaki," he said calmly and smiled at the two. The maklans looked stunned and bewildered, so It knew he had hit the correct nerve. "Don't be afraid or shocked by my words, gentlemen. I know quite a bit about the Maklakar society. That's why we were so relieved when you said this was a peaceful mission. As you can probably tell, our defenses are no match for your weapons. Peaceful trade and mutual defense treaties are exactly what we are trying to forge in this area of the galaxy."

"Premier, I am very pleased you share our desires, but also shocked you know so much about us. Where did you learn this?" Ont asked. "We believed ourselves to be well hidden in our little corner of the galaxy."

"If we are to be friends, then we should forego formality. In my home, you may call me It and I shall address you as Ont and Vard, if that is satisfactory to you," the Premier said. The Maklakar nodded in agreement. "Good, now we can get down to business. First of all, we know you have fifty planets at the end of this arm of the galaxy. Clearly, you should realize we do not have the technology to know these things. We are a single planet of small valakars."

"How do you know so much about us, It?" Vard asked.

"As I said, we have a trading network that includes many other worlds," It continued. "For generations, one of our key trading partners has been Tak-Makla. I am told you are very aware of that planet. The story I heard was you attacked their Hive."

"That was a terrible mistake in my view, It," Ont replied. "I argued against it, but I am just one man."

"Lord Valoo, perhaps we should not discuss such things here," Vard suggested. He turned to the Premier and said, "It, perhaps we can forget this incident."

It laughed. "Please don't take me wrong on this. I think you did the galaxy a big favor by taking out their Hive. Those tekkans have too much power for their own good. Now they know the risk they take by attempting to usurp the power of the divine for their business interests."

"I don't understand, It," Ont replied holding his head in his hands. "You trade with them but want them harmed. Are they your friends or enemies?"

It rose and walked over to a cabinet and withdrew a glass bottle and three glasses. "It seems like we could all use a stronger drink. This is the best brandy on the planet." He poured the liquor and handed each a glass. He raised his and the others clinked their glasses together and drank a toast. "That's better," he smiled. "To me, the tekkans are like a small child who takes a grenade to school for show-and-tell. The child has tremendous power over the other students and teachers, but can he be trusted with it?" It refilled the glasses and sat behind his desk again. He leaned forward and whispered, "You don't know what a Hive is, do you? You destroyed it not knowing why. That's amazing."

"What is a Hive then?" Ont asked. "Why do you trade with the tekkans as allies but then applaud us for harming them?"

"I have a couple friends visiting Vilu-Zan. Let me ask them to explain," It said as he tapped a button on his desk. "Ai, please send in my other guests." He sat back and smiled at the Maklakar. The side door opened and Altamar and Valamar Zendo walked in.

Ont and Vard jumped to their feet. Ont shouted, "Predaxians! This is an outrage, It! These monsters are a scourge on the galaxy."

"Calm down, gentlemen and sit down," Altamar said. "I guess you didn't hear my brother lost the war and the Alliance is gone. By the way, this is my niece, Valamar."

"We have been telling the Premier here how the tekkans destroyed our empire with their damned Hive. We were so happy to hear you attacked them. Thank you for that," Valamar smiled. "Why don't you two sit again and let me tell you all about Hive technology?"

CHAPTER 15

The Ka-la-a where De-o-Nu has his family lodge was expansive, covering more than five square miles. The lodge was constructed of very light wood imported from terrestrial planets in Greater Gallia. The floor was designed to spread the weight of the structure over a large area so the ice would not break. Dave was relieved to find a special suite of rooms had been upgraded for his visit. The pressure at this low level of the atmosphere would normally crush him, but this room featured lower pressure and breathable air. It was a pleasure to get out of the bubble suit and take a hot shower. Jake had accompanied the Galliceans on a tour of the local area while Dave refreshed and relaxed.

After dressing, he sat on the bed and thought about Darlene and the kids. Bill and Cybil were back in classes by now and would be studying hard. Darlene should be arriving on Nanda soon on her mission to help Odo. He was very worried about Odo Pak. Dave was convinced Odo's actions really ended the mock trial before the Conclave on Earth Prime. Odo had also taught him so much about the Source. It would only be fair now if Dave could somehow protect Odo in his time of weakness. There was so much to do now and here he was taking a few days off on Gallicea. Perhaps he should have declined the visit. He turned on his side and drifted off to sleep.

"Dave?" a soft female voice whispered in his ear. "Dave, wake up!" As he started to awaken, it struck him that a woman was talking to him, but he was alone on Gallicea with a group of men. He jumped out of bed and looked around frantically, but saw nothing. Then he saw a flash of light in the periphery of his vision and then a blob of energy began to resolve itself into the shape of Nok, the tekkan engineer. “Hi Dave,” she said. “It’s wonderful to see you again.”

“Nok, what are you doing here?” he asked.

“I felt you reaching out for help, so I came,” she smiled. “You worry too much, Dave Brewster. You need to relax a little.”

“I thought I was,” he replied. “I was sleeping and you woke me up.”

“It was not a restful sleep, Dave,” she said. “Everything is happening as it is meant to. You just need to stay true to yourself and allow events to occur. You are thinking it was a mistake to be here, but this is all part of the plan. Odo’s condition is part of the plan too, as is the conflict brewing in the neighboring galaxy.”

Dave frowned and sat heavily back on the bed. “Well, it’s not a very good plan if you ask me. So I’m supposed to sit here while Odo dies and Nan and the Lagamar system are ravaged by war?”

She sat next to him and put her head on his shoulder. He could feel the energy of her life force moving through him. “I wouldn’t be so judgmental if I were you, Dave.” She turned her head and kissed his cheek. “It doesn’t matter whether we like the flow of the Source or not. It will not change for us. We must align ourselves to it. Your life will be better if you just go with it.”

“I think that’s easier to say than to do, Nok,” he laughed. “After all, you go around making stars and traversing the multiverse. I’m here with a galaxy of problems to deal with.”

Nok laughed out loud. "You sure like to carry the universe on your shoulders. That's not your job, or did you forget that as well?"

"My job is to be happy and to love my family and friends," he replied. "I haven't forgotten, but sometimes it seems I can't help anyone."

"Your goal is not to fix their problems, Dave," she sighed as she held his arm. "Your job is to love them." She kissed his cheek again and stood up. "Well, Dave, I've got to get going. By the way, I probably won't see you for a while."

"Why do you say that?" he asked.

"I'm joining you in the physical universe again!" she beamed. "I'm being born to a family on Tak-Makla in just a few minutes. I'm so excited."

"I'm very happy for you, Nok," he said as he stood and hugged her, "but won't you miss the star creation and freedom?"

"Not really. I mean it was fun for a while, but I really miss the closeness and intimacy of the physical world. We are all of one mind in the Source, but the excitement of living, learning and the challenges of everyday are missing for me now. But not for long," she smiled. "Perhaps you will meet me again on Tak-Makla, and I hope we will recognize one another again. My hope is to be a trader this time. Spending my life in the Hive was great, but I really want to travel the universe, buying and selling exotic goods. That would be really exciting. But we'll see what happens. I love you, Dave." She kissed his lips and he closed his eyes. After a second, he was alone in the room again.

A tone sounded on the door and Fa-a-Di's voice boomed over the intercom, "Dave, we're getting ready to go to the Shrine! Get ready and we'll meet you outside in fifteen minutes!"

A few minutes later, the three Galliceans were flying away from the Ka-la-a. Dave was back in Fa-a-Di's harness and Jake was flying ten feet below him. "Brother, what is this Shrine? You haven't mentioned that to me yet."

"Let me answer that one," De-o-Pa said. "Dave, the Shrine is near the site of the final battle where Fa-u-Bay defeated the army of Za-a-Za. The battle occurred in the air, so there was no Ka-la-a to catch the bodies of the vanquished, whose flesh has now been recycled through the Dar-Fa a million times over. Now a small powered island sits there with a temple to commemorate the event. It reminds us of our last civil war and that we must insure good always conquers evil. No other place in Greater Gallia is more revered. That temple signifies our rejection of war and desire for peace."

"It is not far from the small Dar-Fa on this planet, so it is also constantly showered with dust from deep in the planet," Fa-a-Di added. "To us, that dust comes from those dead heroes and it is another honor to have it fall on you."

"Thank you, Fa-a-Di," De-o-Pa said. "That is not a traditional belief though. I believe it is more aimed to our warriors. We should be arriving there shortly." They continued to fly southward through rapidly moving walls of gas.

The Shrine appeared just as a heavy rain began to pour on them. Through the driving droplets, Dave could see thousands of Galliceans flying around the Shrine. Every minute or so, a group of ten would land on the Shrine and be blessed by two priests waiting there. Then the group would walk up the few steps into the temple. After a minute they would emerge from the opposite side and fly away. Dave's group took their position at the end of the long line and continued to circle the Shrine and watch others fulfilling their duty to visit this place.

"Fa-a-Di, we can move to the front if you like," De-o-Pa said. "You are an important visitor after all."

"That's okay," he replied. "Today I am just another Gallicean doing my duty. Besides I have told Dave many times that I would fly with him on Gallia with a group of thousands of people. This is his first chance to see such a sight."

"It is amazing, brother," Dave said. "The difference is color and wing shape and design is unbelievable."

"That is what this place is about, brother," Fa-a-Di replied. "Before Fa-u-Bay, many chose to segregate themselves from others due to wing shape or any other minute difference. Seeing so many together is indeed wondrous."

It took almost two hours before they approached the front of the line. Thousands more flew behind them awaiting their turns. The rain had stopped and the Shrine was illuminated in bright sunshine. They flew down toward the platform and landed near the two priests along with seven other Galliceans. "High Commissioner, it is an honor to host you. I am Iba-ali-Na, a humble priest. Bless you for fulfilling this sacred obligation," the nearest priest said.

"Thank you, Deacon," Fa-a-Di replied. "Please meet my brothers, Dave Brewster of Earth and Jake Benomafolays of No-Makla."

"Welcome dear friends, Bless you for accompanying your friends," Iba-ali-Na said.

The group walked forward and ascended the steps to the temple. Dave looked around from the security of the harness and saw the hundreds of Galliceans circling them. In the temple, he could see the previous group exit and head down the steps to the exit platform. Jake was sitting on Fa-a-Di's shoulder as they entered and moved up to the ten small benches, where each Gallicean sat to contemplate. To Dave's left was a marble statue of Fa-u-Bay, looking resplendent in pure white. A glass window behind the statue made the statue appear clothed in light. To the right was a statue of Za-a-Za. The statue was made of a dark gray stone. Two small windows behind the statue cast a pale light which made him look even more sinister than if he had been alive and standing there. The hilts of two daggers were imbedded in his chest.

After half a minute, the group rose and strode out of the temple and down the few steps to the exit platform. The group of Galliceans smiled at each other and hugged to celebrate their experience. Then they took off and flew away. "How are you doing, brother?" Dave asked.

"Pretty well, all things considered," Fa-a-Di said. "Thank you for being here. You and Jake really lighten my mood. But now it's time for whisky and dinner, I think." He shouted to De-o-Nu, "Hey, last one back to the lodge has to cook dinner!" Fa-a-Di flapped his wings as hard as he could and quickly left the other two behind.

"That's not fair, brother," De-o-Nu shouted back. "You know my brother and I are much larger and can't fly as fast."

"I guess you cook then friend," Fa-a-Di laughed.

"I don't mind, brother," De-o-Nu laughed back. "You are a lousy cook anyway!"

CHAPTER 16

“Now what do we do, Lord Valoo?” Vard Kalak asked as he poured whisky into two glasses of ice. He took the glasses from the cabinet and sat across the desk from the ambassador. “The Supreme General would chop off our heads if we suggested normalizing relations with the Predaxians, and I wouldn’t blame him.”

Ont was sitting at the desk with his head in his hands. After a minute, he looked up and smiled at the glass of whisky. He picked it up and took a sip. “Ah, that is just what I needed, Vard.” He stood and began to pace around the office. “Somehow we need to confirm their story about the defeat of the Alliance, but frankly, I don’t have a clue how to do that. What did you tell the agents?”

“I told Major Zua the Vilu introduced us to two Predaxians. When we saw them, we stomped out of the office and came to get them,” Vard answered.

“Good, that story is almost true, and I’m glad you didn’t try to hide this from them,” Ont replied “although this turn of events might mean the end of our journey. The only good thing is they were Predaxians and not Paxran. Our heads would roll for certain then.”

Vard pulled the security shield device from his pocket and pressed the button. “None of this was our fault, old friend. We had no way of knowing the Predaxians would be here. But now, it’s very important our next moves be well planned. I’m counting on Zua reporting the incident quickly. You should report it as well. Then we'll let General Porto make the big decisions."

"I know," Ont sighed. "I have a scheduled call to the general in a few minutes. I'm not really certain what to say though. We can't keep running from every other maklan we find. If Valamar was telling the truth, then we need not fear the Alliance anyway."

"Thank goodness our telepathy screens have been activated. If not, one of them could be here now controlling us and we wouldn't even know it," Vard continued.

"Assuming the screens work," Ont interrupted. "We have never had the opportunity to test them before. I am still confused why those Predaxians are here, so far from home. Why this little planet out of the entire galaxy? There must be thousands of worlds between here and Predax, and they are here. It doesn't make sense." A tone sounded on the ambassador's control panel. "That must be General Porto. Please refill my glass before you leave, and remember to keep close to the agents. The more trust they have in you, the better for your future, dear Vard."

Commander Kalak poured into both glasses and left the room. Ont pressed the contact, and the faces of Generals Ulon Porto, Udu Bora and Ava Liko were staring back at him. "My dear friends, I was not expecting all three of you. What a pleasant surprise!"

"Save the pleasantries, Ont and get on with your report," Ulon said. "We have many more such meetings today."

"Of course, Supreme General," Ont replied. "We had our first meeting with the leader of this planet today. The Premier, It

Ka-la was very pleasant and interested in establishing diplomatic and trade agreements."

"Excellent work, Ont," Ulon smiled. "What are the next steps?"

"Well, there was a problem, sir. I was very surprised how much the Vilu knew about our society, including the location of our planets," Ont said. He could tell the look of distress and anger on the others. "When I pressed him how he knew so much, he invited two others to join the meeting. Those others were Predaxians." Ont was not surprised the three generals seemed unfazed by the news. Clearly the agents had done their jobs well.

"And what was your reaction?" Ulon asked.

"I threatened to leave the meeting immediately," Ont said. "But then the Predaxians offered some free information I was certain you would want to have."

Now the three generals were noticcably irate. The sound was muted but he could see them talking to one another for some time. When they looked back at him, Ulon said, "Okay, what was the information?"

"Of course, I can't validate its authenticity, but they told me how a Hive functions," Ont said calmly.

"Really," Ulon gasped. "Is this some kind of joke, Ont?"

"Of course not, Supreme General," Ont gushed. "I was as surprised then as you are now. I had Vard Kalak with me to take notes and he is putting together the full analysis which we will send later today. As I said, I don't know if it is true, but it is what we were told."

"And the Predaxians want nothing from us?" Udu asked. "There must be a catch or this has to be a red herring." He looked at the others in the room and they nodded their agreement.

"With Predaxians, there is always an ulterior motive, generals," Ont replied. "However, they offered this information freely. But there was more. Apparently, the Vilu and some Predaxians hate the tekkans. The Predaxians said the tekkan Hive was a critical weapon in defeating the Alliance in a recent war. According to them, the Alliance is gone. I was hoping to find out if that is true as well. It could change our view of this galaxy."

"How did you leave the negotiation, old friend?" Ava asked. "Are we still friendly?"

"Of course, dear Ava," Ont said. "I explained this was a lot of information to internalize right away and I would have to report to my Supreme General for the next steps."

"What should we do now, Ulon?" she asked the Supreme General.

"Honestly, I'm overwhelmed with information right now. I need to think about that. What do you think Ont?" Ulon answered.

"Clearly, we all need time to come to grips with this," Ont began. "We can stay here and begin working on diplomatic and trade agreements. That can take as long as you like. I do think it is a good idea to be friends with the Vilu. There is probably much more they can teach us. While I do that, Vard will finish his report and send it to you. Perhaps the Science Ministry can review it to see if it's even remotely realistic. If everything works out well, I will establish an embassy here with a few of my men. Then we will leave and attempt to verify the death of the Predaxian Alliance. Perhaps we will meet more friends along the way."

"That is a very reasonable plan, General Valoo," Ulon said. "Now I know why I selected you for this mission. Work on the agreements for a week or so. That will give us time to review the Hive report. But please keep an eye on the Predaxians. It seems too coincidental they would be on Vilu-Zan. There must be another subplot to this story, and you need to find out what it is, understood?"

"Of course, General Porto," Ont smiled. "I've already asked Vard to test the telepathy screens. This is our first chance to try out that technology. He has also put ten officers in a secure site on board where they will monitor for non-Maklakar life-forms constantly. Even if they control my mind, they can't hide their DNA."

"A very sound solution," Ulon replied. "We will call you in one week for an update."

"Just one other thing, Supreme General," Ont interjected. "You know I was not in favor of the attack on the Tak-Makla Hive."

"Yes, I remember the discussion well, Ont. What is your point?" Ulon frowned.

"As you will read in Vard's report, it was the Hive on Tak-Makla that gave them the power to defeat the Predaxians and find our location. Thanks to your grandson's actions there, we have gained time and are safer. After I gave the premier his name, he immediately called for a national celebration in honor of Captain Awl Porto. I thought you'd like to know that."

The general was visibly moved. He smiled and said, "Thank you old friend. You have honored me greatly and I will let Awl know. Take care. Oti-Makla out."

CHAPTER 17

Dave was very pleased that De-o-Nu's lodge had an excellent coffee system. He was back in his bubble pressure suit and grateful for the Society of Humanity faceplate that allowed him to sip the hot beverage without compromising the conditions inside the suit. There was a slight pressure in his head, no doubt due to the copious amount of Gallicean whisky the group had enjoyed the previous evening. Dave had tried to control his drinking as the local whisky was too strong for his human system. It had apparently paid off as he was the only one out of bed at this hour. He had slept very well, finally rid of that pressure suit. It had taken him a few minutes to get up onto the Gallicean size chair. Thankfully the Gallicean size coffee mug kept him from having to get down again for a refill. From his vantage point, he could see the sun rising over the horizon, peering through the walls of fast moving gas marking the next band only a few miles away. He heard the sound of a door opening and turned to see Fa-a-Di walking slowly out of his bedroom. "Good morning, brother," he said.

"I hate this damned planet," was all the Gallicean could say. He grabbed another mug and filled it with coffee and sat at the table. He took a drink of coffee and said, "Between my head and my nightmare, I'm ready to leave right now! I've done my duty here."

"You're the boss, Fa-a-Di," Dave replied. "You'll have to convince De-o-Nu and his brother though. They seem to love it here."

"Fortunately, as High Commissioner and a member of the High Council, I still outrank him," Fa-a-Di smiled. "Or you could just order him to leave. You are his new boss, Dave."

"That is an option, brother," Dave laughed. "Now I understand your headache because I have a small one myself, but what was your dream about? It had to be something else to upset you so much."

"It was pretty much the same dream I have every time I come here," he began. "It always starts so well and then makes a big turn for the worse. Each time I have the dream it gets longer and more violent."

Fa-a-Di told Dave about his dream. At the beginning, he is leading a large army of Galliceans, flying over a massive gas planet. They are all wearing battle armor and carrying their daggers, blasters and their Ziga, or war blade. Galliceans have not carried the Ziga for generations, except for certain military ceremonies and parades. It was carried in an ornately decorated scabbard on their back, lying between their wings. The armor was also different, like that of an earlier age. The breastplate and other metal parts were brilliantly polished and engraved with their family crests. Those pieces were held together with straps of leather. As they flew, they sang the old war songs to build their confidence for the battle to come. Fa-a-Di felt perfectly content as a soldier doing his duty.

After several minutes he spies the smaller enemy force who are also Galliceans. The others wear blood-red leather armor. Even from this distance, he can see they also carry the Baloo. In his mind, Fa-a-Di becomes frightened. It was been thousands of years since his people fought each other. Why would his men attack the Marine army? Something must be terribly wrong, but he keeps flying with his men. The battle cries fill the air with noise. He wants to ask why they are attacking the others, but instead begins shouting as well. As they dive toward the opposing forces, he withdraws his Ziga and exhorts his men to be brave for Greater Gallia today.

The armies engage with thousands of soldiers swinging their blades and twisting and turning in the gas. He swings his Ziga and slices the left wing off one of the Marines. The enemy has a look or horror on his face and then spins downward into the gas toward his death. He looks around and sees his larger army is barely keeping even and many of his own soldiers are being killed. Something is very wrong here. This is the time when he would usually wake up, but this night the dream continued. Deep in the flock of Marines is a small circle protecting their leader. He waves to some of his comrades and they fold in their wings and dive toward the group.

They attack and hack at each other. Fa-a-Di sees several of his trusted lieutenants gutted by the Baloo of the enemy. He is losing the battle and must act now to end the carnage. He swings his Ziga at one of the guards, hitting him on the side of the head with the flat of the blade. The soldier is knocked unconscious and tumbles downward out of sight. The enemy commander is flying away. Fa-a-Di knows he must kill the commander to end the fight, so he follows him, flying as fast as he can. He is wondering why this coward is running and allowing his brave men to die for him. After several minutes, the commander lands on a small Ka-la-a and stops to face Fa-a-Di. Fa-a-Di lands twenty feet from the other, holding the Ziga in his right hand and his Falon in the left. For some reason, the face of the commander seems blurred, but that does not change his mission. He can hear himself say, "This is the end of your little rebellion, priest." He steps closer and sees the commander has his Nak and Falon in his hands. As he approaches, he swings his Ziga and hits the other on the shoulder with the flat of the blade, knocking him to the ground, where he lies on his stomach. "Turn over and look at your own death, coward!" he shouts. He stands over the other and prepares to plunge the Ziga in his back. As he starts the downswing on his blade, the commander flips over and thrusts the two daggers through Fa-a-Di's stomach upward into his chest. Waves of searing pain shoot through his body, but he still doesn't wake up from the nightmare. He stumbles backward and falls down with the hilts of the two daggers still protruding from his flesh. Rivers of blood pour out and onto the ice, freezing almost immediately. As he feels the life force leaving his body, he looks at the commander who is kneeling next to him.

The commander says, "Za-a-Za, this was your battle not mine. All I ever asked for was peace, brother. I'm very sorry it ends this way for you. May God have mercy on your soul." As he feels himself lose consciousness, he looks one last time at Fa-u-Bay and sees his face clearly now, but it is not the face of the true Gallicean. The face was that of Dave Brewster.

"And that's when I woke up today, brother," Fa-a-Di finished. "Now can you see why I hate this place? That dream will haunt me for the next ten years until I have to come back again."

"Wow!" Dave said. "You were Za-a-Za and I was Fa-u-Bay? That's unbelievable! Sorry about killing you brother."

The Gallicean laughed heartily. "Pretty bizarre, right? That little ironic twist at the end didn't bother me. You are here and that probably pushed you into my nightmare. But the horrible part is Galliceans killing other Galliceans. I know that war was long ago, but the specter of it is never far away. Look at the Society of Humanity. They are more advanced than any of us and now they are at each other's throats. If it can happen to them, it can happen to any of us." He looked around and was startled to see De-o-Nu and De-o-Pa standing on the other side of the room. "When did you two get here?"

"About the time your men attacked Fa-u-Bay's army, Brother," De-o-Nu said as they came over to join them. "You know, I never thought you and Dave looked alike enough to be related." Everyone laughed. "If this place bothers you that much, we can go to the terrestrial planet later today."

"Thank you, brother," Fa-a-Di replied. "Of course you know this planet does not bother me as much as the other."

"Yes, but the Sojourn requires both," De-o-Pa said. "I don't mind the expedited trip either. We are expecting three colony ships on Jupiter in the next couple of weeks. There are lots of folks to meet." The De-o brothers each grabbed some coffee and sat at the table with Dave and Fa-a-Di. "Dave, I cannot thank you enough for being here. If the High Commissioner really has this dream every visit, it's great he was able to confidc in you about it."

"You are all quite welcome," Dave said. "But I can't help but think this is more than a dream."

"Not everything in this universe is magical, Dave," Fa-a-Di scoffed.

"I have to agree with Dave on this one," De-o-Pa said. "There were a lot of details in your dream most Galliceans do not know, such as the red leather armor of Fa-u-Bay's army and the use of the Baloo."

“I don’t understand,” Fa-a-Di replied. “My imagination put them there. I’ve worked with Marines many times, as Dave can attest.”

“Perhaps that is true, but it would be an almost miraculous coincidence,” the Prelate said. “While it is generally considered to be legend, certain of our ancient texts confirm the use of red armor and the Baloo by his army. Before that, our Marines wore the same armor as other troops and there was no such dagger. The priests on this world proposed the red color to honor the Beings on the terrestrial planet. It is also written that the Baloo was created on that world. After the battle here, Fa-u-Bay put his generals in charge of the Marine forces and taught them their secrets to defeating the larger army of Za-a-Za.”

“And I suppose the real Fa-u-Bay had Dave’s face too!” Fa-a-Di laughed and everyone joined in.

“That is highly unlikely,” De-o-Pa chuckled. “However, no one knows how he looked for certain. The statue in the temple is the oldest known sculpture of him, but it may not look like him at all.”

“Good!” Fa-a-Di said. “If he really is my ancestor and had Dave’s face, my beautiful mug would never have been so pretty!”

CHAPTER 18

De-o-Nu had loaded the luggage onto the shuttle craft and was preparing to start the engines, while the others locked up the lodge and walked toward the landing area. Dave had a strange feeling in his stomach, stopped and turned around to see High Consul Zee Gongaleg of Tak-Makla standing not three feet behind him. "Zee!" he shouted. "What are you doing here?" The Galliceans turned as well and came to join them.

"Well, Dave," he began, "I wanted you to be the first to know our Hive is operational again. As you can see, the agents sent me here to be with you in person."

"That's great news, brother," Fa-a-Di agreed. "Now you can assist Dave in his new mission. Your people know more about the planets in this galaxy than anyone else."

"Of course, it would be our pleasure to help," Zee smiled. "However, there are many things happening around the galaxy right now and I was hoping you all could come back to Tak-Makla with me now. It is very important."

"How do you do sir?" De-o-Pa asked. "I am De-o-Pa, the brother of your friend De-o-Nu and it is a pleasure to meet you. Unfortunately, we are on a religious retreat and it would be very unusual to break the Sojourn in the middle. I hope you understand."

"Of course I understand. However, there are many developments I must inform the others about as soon as possible," Zee replied. "I can assure that you can return here within one or two days to this same spot. I would love to talk more now, but it is quite an urgent request."

De-o-Nu had become concerned that the others had not boarded, and he shut down the shuttle and came to see what was happening. "Zee, welcome to Gallicea!" he said. "But can't this wait another day or two?"

Zee frowned and furrowed his brow, saying, "Perhaps, but I think it would not be in everyone's best interests to wait. Honestly, just one day or so and you can return. Fa-a-Di, you are the senior official here. What do you think?"

"Well, I'm not an expert in religious protocol, however, I would be grateful for a day away from this place," he replied. "De-o-Pa, certainly this is not too much to ask to help the people who stopped the Predaxian invasion?"

"I could see that tactic coming a mile away, High Commissioner," De-o-Pa laughed. "I shall stay here and await your return."

"De-o-Pa, it would be an honor if you would accompany us," Zee said. "The reconstructed Hive is much improved, which we will discuss on Tak-Makla. I can tell you we have constructed several hundred chambers which should allow Galliceans to join with Universal Power."

"You're kidding, right?" Fa-a-Di quizzed. "You are bribing the Prelate of Jupiter with the chance to enter the Hive?"

"I suppose that's one way to look at it, Fa-a-Di," Zee smiled back. "What do you think, Prelate?"

"Let's go!" De-o-Pa said. "From what I've been told of Hive technology, this is exactly the right experience for a man of faith." Before the last words came out of his mouth, the group was standing on the beach in front of Zee's residence on Tak-Makla. The Galliceans were human sized again and no one required any breathing apparatus. "Oh, my God!" he gasped. "Just like that we're here?"

"That's pretty much how it goes, Prelate," Zee replied. "I've asked my butler Ton to serve a light lunch on the beach. It's going to be a warm and sunny day. Follow me." He walked up the beach toward the wide patio where one large table was set with fine china and glassware. "Ton will show you to your seats, gentlemen. Some of my key staff will be arriving by tube in a few minutes. I'm sure you will remember my Minister of State, Fak Mondoka and Mak Andeles, Minister of Internal Affairs. The Chief Engineers of the Hive will also join us. One is my daughter, Pua Napale. Please congratulate her when she arrives. She gave birth to my granddaughter, Nika just yesterday."

"And she's back to work already?" De-o-Nu gasped. "She must be very dedicated to her job."

Zee laughed. "Well brother, that is true, but we are maklans and our bodies work somewhat differently. She is on maternity leave, but offered to attend this meeting. She is also bringing little Nika. Val and I were unable to be at the hospital for the birth due to some of the issues we are here to address."

While Zee spoke, Dave was remembering the conversation he had with Nok last night. He had no way of knowing, but everything inside him was shouting that Nika was Nok reborn again. He felt warm and happy, but not certain he should mention this feeling to Zee. "Congratulations, Zee. I am very happy for you."

"Thank you Dave," Zee replied, smiling broadly. "Ah, I see they are arriving now." The second Chief Engineer was indeed Loni Arrak, who hugged Dave warmly. Everyone else was introduced and sat down to have lunch, which consisted of fresh fish and sautéed vegetables. "I hope everyone is enjoying the food. Fortunately, there was little damage to our crop lands from the Maklakar attack. Now that our Hive is back on line, we can probably reduce the defensive fleet from the Free Society. What do you think Dave?"

"It might be wise to move cautiously on that, Zee," he began. "With the Hive available, I think we need to focus some agents on investigating the motivation of the Maklakar and those races they are now contacting. Does that make sense, Fa-a-Di?"

"Absolutely, Dave," the High Commissioner agreed. "From what we've seen of Maklakar weapons and tactics, we must be especially vigilant. This planet is in extreme danger once they learn your Hive is active again."

"I agree as well," Loni said. "Until we can determine why they attacked this peaceful world, none of us are safe. Now that the Hive is working, it seems only logical they would want to attack it again. If they use their plasma bomb technology, this entire planet could be obliterated."

"Loni is correct," Pua interjected. "We have a large contingent of agents on Vilu-Zan to monitor the discussions between the Maklakar and Vilu. We even witnessed a meeting between their leadership and Altamar and Valamar Zendo. I thought we were finished with Predaxian aggression after the war?"

"That is disturbing to me as well," Fa-a-Di said. "As part of the peace negotiations, they voluntarily gave up their mind control. From our planets on the frontier, we have seen no untoward actions as yet."

"I spoke with President Panoplez Zendo earlier today," Fak announced. "He claims this is the renegade action of a small group of agents who remain loyal to Altamar Zendo. While Altamar did play a critical role in the defeat of his brother, apparently he was not ready to go quietly into retirement. Those agents have remarkable mind control abilities and were causing tremendous problems with the new government. Pan said it was a relief to have them gone, although he fears they will return to take power if possible."

"You know, that sounds remarkably like the Brotherhood in the Society of Humanity," Dave said. "Even though they were disbanded by the High Council, I have no doubt they are planning a come-back."

"No doubt about that, Dave," Loni replied. "Agents in our Hive and the one on Atar Pa have been monitoring Brotherhood agents. They seem to have some temporary asylum on Narta Ela, if you can believe that. We have heard hushed conversations about them moving to this galaxy to gain support and power for revenge."

"This galaxy?" Fa-a-Di gasped. "Won't they need a Hive to get here? Do they have one already?"

"Oh yes," Zee replied. "While we cannot penetrate any of their Hives due to security measures, we have seen several planetoid Hives near Narta Ela over the last weeks. One has been seen approaching the Lagamar system very recently."

"I need to send ten battle cruisers to Lagamar immediately!" Fa-a-Di shouted. "I will not allow those bastards to attack Lagamar 7 again."

"Please calm down, brother," Zee said. "We will all work together to keep them safe. Sending ships there now could be seen as a very provocative act. We must remember that the Society is crumbling. We have been helping the Lagamar planets get the tools and technology to build their own defenses. Their army is one of the most potent forces in Andromeda now. And we must remember the Brotherhood is at its weakest point. If they attempted to attack any other planet, the others would likely unite to eradicate them. They seem content to bide their time and lick their wounds. But we must keep an eye on them."

"If we're not going to do anything, then why did you bring us here, Consul?" De-o-Pa asked. "Why is this visit so urgent?"

"There seems to be a shift in the current of Universal Power," Pua answered. "We are aware of the time eddy problem being scrutinized on Earth. But it is much more than that. While those of us who know it believe Hive technology serves the greater good of all life, there are those who are beginning to believe it is the opposite of that. And for much of the technology's history, that has been true."

"Pua is quite right," Loni continued. "When Hive technology was developed in the home galaxy, its original purpose was to spy on other civilizations for defensive purposes. As it was refined, we found it could be used offensively as well. For example, if agents found a great planet with a weak military, we could jump several warships and thousands of troops there instantly. Within hours or days, the native population would be subjugated or eliminated completely. This was millions of years ago, but it is our past. That is how the Society grew to be so large. While there are many uninhabited planets, life always seems to choose the best ones. Rather than terraforming thousands of barren, lifeless worlds, it became easier to just take over developed ones. I'm sure you've all heard the story of the fifty-one races of humanity by now. The original Non-Ti, the ones who resembled the humans of Earth 47 were conquerors. When they finally learned that aggression was not the way, that race began to split until the Non-Ti no longer existed."

"But what impact does that have on any of us?" De-o-Nu asked. "We have not used Hive technology for aggression?"

Zee laughed. "Brother, you are forgetting the prison world of Localus. We dismantled that planet to end the Predaxian war."

"I'll never forget that Zee," De-o-Nu replied. "But that was done to stop aggression. We did not attack the Predaxians. We defended ourselves from them."

Zee was still smiling as he turned to Ton and said, "Please bring us some whisky, Ton. I think we might need it." He turned back to the group and said, "What you say is completely true, brother, but it is not our personal recollections that will fill the history books of this galaxy. There are many places where the natives are petrified with fear that a Hive might dismantle their populated world. There is no way to protect yourself or your family if the planet you live on dissolves into rocks and dust. We will never use this Hive for that. However, others may. We know the Brotherhood has access to more than one Hive. We also know they hate Nan, the Lagamar system, and most of all, our dear brothers, Dave Brewster and Fa-a-Di. In fact, you two are the primary reason we are here right now."

"I don't understand, Zee," Dave said. "If the Brotherhood chooses to act against me, there is little we can do to stop them. I don't fear them and I won't hide from them either."

"I agree with Dave," Fa-a-Di replied. "Let those slime try to kill me. The streets will run red with their blood. I would happily give my life today fighting to protect the Boley on Lagamar 7."

"Your bravery is commendable, but that is not the point," Zee interjected. "The Chief Engineers and I agree that a coalition of the willing is coming together outside our Free Society and the Society of Humanity in the Andromeda Galaxy. Most of the constituents do not recognize it, but the Predaxians and Brotherhood are likely managing the process. We believe societies are being convinced to be fearful of Hive technology. As that happens, there is a strong chance they will join forces with the Predaxians and Brotherhood to stand against us. That is why the Brotherhood is coming here. The Society is crumbling on its own, so their work can wait there. Our Free Society will come to be seen as the overlord of this galaxy."

"The Brotherhood will provide Hive access to help their allies. If the allies are not so willing, the Predaxian agents will use mind control to convince them," Pua continued. "This will start an even larger arms race here, possibly resulting in a galactic war of incredible scope and devastation."

"Yikes!" Dave replied. "They would start a galactic war just to get rid of Fa-a-Di and me?"

"I feel honored in a strange and horrifying way," Fa-a-Di said.

Zee took as sip of the freshly poured whisky and swirled it about in his mouth before swallowing. "You two are just a small step along the road they are traveling. Dave humiliated the High Council, leading to its downfall. Fa-a-Di humiliated the Brotherhood and personally dispatched Emperor Zendo to Hell. Killing either of you would be an act of revenge only, and provide some sense of progress and closure to their leaders. The goal is galactic domination, with the Brotherhood as the ultimate winners in the game."

"But the Predaxians could use mind control over them too," De-o-Nu interjected. "Perhaps Altamar Zendo sees himself as ultimate ruler of the universe?"

"He probably does, De-o-Nu," Zee replied. "However, I can't imagine the Brotherhood providing any Hive technology to the Predaxians. Our agents listened to the conversation when Valamar Zendo told the Maklakar about Hive technology. While they did reveal some things, most of the critical information was omitted. If the Maklakar attempted to build a Hive with that knowledge only, they would have a giant planetoid that does nothing, and might even electrocute most of the agents."

"Zee is right," Dave jumped in. "The Society of Humanity never wanted to give the technology to anyone. They made one exception here, which they came to regret, because the tekkans surpassed their knowledge over time. Isn't that right?"

"And you haven't seen anything yet, Dave," Loni smiled. "The tekkan Hive has been completely redesigned. I can't believe how advanced it is now. Perhaps that's a good segway, Zee?"

"Yes, I agree," Zee replied. "I think we should go to the Hive now. Once you all see some of that is happening, I hope you'll agree this visit was worthwhile."

CHAPTER 19

It had been a while since Dave had traveled in a tube. He thought about little Zak Louk whom he met in the tube on Hive 1008. Talking to that boy had calmed him down from the roller coaster ride every tube journey was. Entering the tube station, he noticed the panel was gone. A pale green light illuminated the room for a second and then turned off. A soft voice said, "Greetings High Consul, Ministers and guests. May I have your authorization High Consul?" Zee tilted his head upward and the green light passed over his face. "Authorization received. Please state your destination, sir."

"Hive, level one, ring one," he said. A large transparent tube shuttle entered the room and the door opened. The group climbed aboard and buckled themselves in. When they were set, Zee said "Ready" and the shuttle shot out into the tube system. After traveling level for a few moments, the shuttle turned downward and zoomed toward the center of the planet. The Galliceans and Dave hung on for dear life while the tekkans and Loni seemed totally at ease. "Pua, please explain some of the system enhancements we have made."

"Of course," she replied. "The primary upgrade was to the computer systems and power distribution network. The hardware and software were completely replaced with the latest technology. This is where we gained the best improvement. We can now perform twice as much work with one-half the number of agents."

"Think about that," Zee interrupted. "Now our Hive only requires five billion agents. The others are now able to pursue other careers. We will be able to greatly expand our trading networks and scientific investment. It also gives us the option of relocating a group of agents to Nom-Kat-Un to help with the construction and operation of a new Hive there. We also have the ability to transfer our latest technology to other members of our Free Society. It's very exciting."

As he spoke, the shuttle made a ninety degree turn and was flying level again. Dave remembered this area included a massive underground hydroponic farm, but now nothing but rubble from the Maklakar attack covered the ground below them. "I guess the rebuilding process will be ongoing for some time, Zee," he said.

"Sadly, that is true," Zee confirmed. "We have been focusing on the Hive exclusively, but now need to redirect ourselves to completing the restoration of our planet." The shuttle turned downward again and accelerated toward the center of the planet. "But not everyone is pleased with the changes we have made to the Hive, Dave."

"I don't understand, Zee. Why would anyone argue with this level of progress?" he asked.

"You said it yourself, Dave," Loni replied. "The Society doesn't want other species to have Hive technology. Now that the tekkans have surpassed the humans, jealousy is growing in the home galaxy. If the Society was still functional, they would be a severe threat to Tak-Makla as well."

"Loni, how do you know what's happening in the other galaxy?" De-o-Nu asked. "I thought communications were pretty much cut off."

"The Society sent another Chief Engineer to help this Free Society protect itself with Hives. He has very close communications with most Chief Engineers," she replied. "I think you met him on Hive 1008."

"It's Fola Untor, isn't it?" Dave asked.

"Wow! It's amazing you remember him. He was just a shopkeeper on Hive 1008, but I'm told he used to be one of the top Chief Engineers in the Society. He's been helping me a lot," Loni smiled. "Right now he's on Atar Pa helping Serena Vanatee learn more about being a Chief Engineer."

Dave thought again about Fola Untor. He seemed to know much more than he would ever say. His words were often clouded with vagueness and misinformation, although his skills as a Chief Engineer were unparalleled. "Charlie and I spent quite of bit of time in his coffee shop. He was a gracious host and made a real impression on us both."

The shuttle slowed and entered the tube chamber and then stopped. "Well, I'm sure you'll be seeing him again soon," Loni finished as she climbed out of the shuttle. "Pua, do you need my help or should I go back to the control room?"

"Actually Loni, I'm a bit tired and need to feed Nika soon," the other replied. "Perhaps you can take our guests to the new chamber and join them in Universal Power."

"Of course, it would be my pleasure," Loni answered. "You take care of that sweet little baby." She turned to the group and said, "Let's go, gentlemen!"

"Dave and Fa-a-Di, I think I'll return home with Pua," Zee interjected. "I still haven't had the opportunity to hold my new granddaughter! I hope you enjoy your visit and hope you can join us for a celebratory dinner at my house this evening. You are all welcome to spend the night in Ambassador Brewster's residence or my own. If you prefer, I can return you to Gallicea this evening as well."

"Enjoy your new grandchild, Zee," Fa-a-Di said as the two reentered the shuttle and it shot back out into the tube network. The group left the room and began to walk along the curved corridor. The circular doors of the chambers had been replaced with glass doors. They could see agents in each room lying on flat beds. The claustrophobic chambers were gone. Each room seemed to hold five or six agents versus the old standard of one or two. Bright blue lights came from the ceiling and illuminated each agent's face.

"The blue lights connect the agents to Universal Power," Loni continued. "We have also found having a group of agents in the same room improves their morale. Even though their minds may be millions of light years apart, the physical closeness of others is reassuring to them." Loni put her hand on a glass door and it slid open. There were six beds in this room and the group was startled to see Jake sitting on one of them.

"Oh my God, we left you on Gallicea! I'm so sorry Jake," De-o-Nu said.

"Not really, De-o-Nu," Jake replied. "Zee came to see me while you were all asleep and asked me to come here with him. I've been traveling in Universal Power since I arrived. The situation is not good. Take a seat and let's go back."

"Okay, the experience of joining Universal Power can be a bit overwhelming at first, but I think you will enjoy it," Loni said. "It has changed since your last visit too, Dave. It's hard to explain, but somehow it feels more connected, if that makes any sense. To me, the feeling I left my body behind somewhere is now gone. Instead of searching through all of space and time like before, now I feel like I am one with all of it. I know that sounds weird, but I'll let you judge for yourself."

"Loni, for your information, I am a Prelate of the Gallicean Church," De-o-Pa stated. "I have been told that Universal Power may be seen as spiritual. What do you think?"

"I guess that's up to personal interpretation, Prelate," Loni smiled. "In the home galaxy, many of our agents refer to Universal Power as the Source. They claim everything in the universe is the product of Source and it runs through everything with a set direction. My job is to manage the equipment and direct agents to look for specific physical things. There are agents here who look for bigger picture realities in Universal Power, but they are a separate unit that doesn't report to me. I would be very interested in your thoughts after our journey."

"What journey will we be taking, Loni?" Fa-a-Di asked. "From our meeting, there are many things going on that might warrant a visit."

"Zee thought the same thing, Fa-a-Di, and Fola even provided an itinerary to do some of that, but since this is the first time a Gallicean has knowingly entered Universal Power, I think the experience should be free form," she replied. "Dave has been fortunate enough to join with a natural Hive. What do you think we should do?"

"I couldn't agree with you more, Loni," Dave smiled. "I will never forget my first visit with Engineer Nok. It was very disorienting though, so I suggest that each Gallicean be teamed with one of us for support and comfort."

"Absolutely, Dave," Jake replied. "I'll take De-o-Nu. I'd suggest that Loni goes with Fa-a-Di and you go with De-o-Pa."

"But Dave and I always travel together," Fa-a-Di interjected.

"We will all be together in this room the whole time, brother," Dave replied. "I hope we all stay together in the Source as well. However, since my experience has been somewhat more metaphysical than others, I think Jake's idea is a good one." Dave climbed off the bed and walked over to Fa-a-Di who was looking apprehensive. "Brother, you and I will travel together in Universal Power very soon. I guarantee it. If you and Loni choose to stay with De-o-Pa and me now, that's great too. Universal Power is the ultimate playground of the spirit. Just try to enjoy yourself, okay?"

"Okay, Dave. I suppose that makes perfect sense. De-o-Pa, you are a very lucky man to be partnered with my dear brother. Make the most of this opportunity!" Fa-a-Di said.

When everyone was lying down again, Loni said, "Now, everyone try to relax. Take a few deep breaths and let them out slowly. When you are ready, just close your eyes. It's really that simple. If any of you experience any pain or discomfort, just sit up or open your eyes and you will be out of danger. I think the chances of that are very remote, however."

Dave felt his string of light move out of his body and he looked back down at his physical form. He looked around the room to see how the others were. He could see Loni's and Jake's string hovering around the room as well. He moved over to Fa-a-Di and touched his face. A brilliant red string of light shot out of him and zoomed out into the center chamber. Loni's light zipped out to follow him. Another red string shot out of De-o-Nu and Jake rushed to catch up with him. Dave moved over to De-o-Pa and looked at his face. He couldn't see any light energy in him and became worried the Prelate has flown away before him. Then he felt a surge of warmth and turned to see the red light wavering just in front of him. "I thought I lost you, De-o-Pa," Dave thought.

"This is unreal, Dave," De-o-Pa said. "I see my own body lying there, yet I am here. It is quite unsettling. Is my body dead?"

"Of course not, De-o-Pa," Dave thought back. "Move over here with me." Dave's string moved toward the glass window separating them from the center column. "Can you see the reflection in the glass?"

"I see a string of blue light and another red one," De-o-Pa replied. "I am the red one, right?"

"That's correct," Dave thought. "But this is just the beginning, De-o-Pa. Just think about where or when you would like to go. If you cannot find me, just think about me and you will fly to me."

"I was just thinking about the colony ships headed to Jupiter while I play here." Before Dave could reply, De-o-Pa's string shot out of the room and up the center column. Dave concentrated on the other and his string shot out in pursuit. Star systems and open space flew by as they moved forward at incomprehensible speed. De-o-Pa did not know what was happening and became worried about losing Dave. Dave's string caught up with him and wrapped around him.

"Don't worry, De-o-Pa," Dave thought. "I'm right here with you."

"Where are we, Dave?" De-o-Pa asked. "It looks like open space."

"That's what it is. You mentioned thinking about the colony ships headed to Jupiter. I'm sure we were on our way there when you became apprehensive and stopped. Before we go again, take a look around and tell me what you see," Dave answered.

"It is open space, but I seem to see a network of faint lines crisscrossing space. They are widely spaced here, but were closely aligned near stars and planets. Is that Universal Power, Dave?"

"I don't think so, De-o-Pa," Dave thought. "I believe those lines are the background of the universe and form the highways for Universal Power to travel. As I was told, all energy and matter are created from Universal Power."

"Can I see Universal Power?" he asked.

"In a way, we are Universal Power," Dave replied. "The string of light representing us now is not electricity or a stream of photons. It is just our spiritual energy. I believe the rest of Universal Power is the same as us, although I can't say whether spirits make up a significant portion of it. The experience of the Hive allows us to join with Universal Power, where there are no limits to where or when we can go. Do you still want to visit the colony ships? Just think of them again and we're on our way."

"No, I was preoccupied with those people coming to live on my planet," De-o-Pa explained. "Honestly, I feel guilty I'm here and not on Jupiter to welcome them."

"A very wise man once told me it is not my responsibility to take care of the universe. My responsibility is to love and care for my family and friends," Dave replied.

"A wise man indeed, Dave Brewster. He sounds like a man of great faith. I would love to meet him." Before Dave could reply, both of them shot away. The speed was so rapid the stars blurred into a faint glow around them. The glow disappeared as they entered intergalactic space. After a moment, the Andromeda Galaxy began to grow in front of them. They shot through the stars at blinding speed.

Then they were standing on a high mountain. It was a sunny afternoon, and a sea of clouds could be seen covering the planet below the peaks. They stood for a moment watching the range of mountains stretching toward the horizon. A group of men in dark gray robes approached them and bowed deeply. Then they sat on the ground in a circle around Dave and De-o-Pa and began to chant. Dave looked over at De-o-Pa and saw his light string resolve first into a luminous blob and finally into a Being of light in Gallicean form. Dave looked down and saw that he too had his human form again. "Dave, where are we? Is this the home of the special person you mentioned?"

"Yes it is, Prelate," Dave replied. "This is the Mount Alila Temple on Lagamar Ulu. The person I spoke of is Obu Neela, the High Priest here." The group of priests rose to their feet and pointed toward the small temple near the edge of the Temple. "I believe Obu is waiting over there for us. Let's not keep him waiting."

As they approached the temple, Obu stood and walked over to greet them. "Dave, it is a pleasure to see you again! I see you brought a Gallicean friend. Welcome!"

"Obu, this is Prelate De-o-Pa," Dave said. "He is Admiral De-o-Nu's brother."

"A man of the cloth? What a wonderful surprise. Welcome De-o-Pa!" Obu said. "Please join me over here and let's chat."

"Obu, it is an honor to meet you," De-o-Pa said. "Dave has the highest regard for you."

"Dave is generous with his praise, Prelate," Obu smiled. "I see you are one of the first Galliceans to knowingly enter the Source. What have you thought of this experience so far?"

"It is overwhelming, I must say," De-o-Pa replied. "You are the second person to state we knowingly entered Universal Power. What does that mean?"

"We clergy call it the Source here," Obu said. "We believe it is the source of all things and is the carrier of our immortal souls. We all come from it and go home to it when our life is through. Most living Beings never realize this, so they can never knowingly enter the Source. They die and find the truth again. They are reborn and forget again. It is the circle of physical existence."

"But if I require a Hive filled with billions of others to enter the Source, how can I hope to come back again?" De-o-Pa asked.

"For most, a Hive is the only way to do so while living," Obu replied. "However, there are natural Hives where a single person can enter the Source. We have also learned from Dave that some people become so grounded in the Source they can enter at any time. Isn't that right Dave?"

"It did happen to me, more than once," Dave admitted. "However, that ability seems to have left me."

"Only your faith has left you, Dave," Obu chided him. "We are all constantly connected to the Source. It permeates our bodies and fills our hearts and souls. It links us inexorably to one another. If someone is in need, their desire can pull our strings from our bodies and fly us to them, if we believe it and allow it."

"So I have been told, Obu," Dave replied. "I still think my proximity to the Hive on Nan was the key factor."

"Nonsense, Dave," Obu laughed. "You've been much closer to a natural Hive recently than you were when orbiting Earth Prime."

"This is all so different to me," De-o-Pa exclaimed. "I could never imagine any of this being true. Is this a dream?"

"No, it is real, De-o-Pa," Obu said. "You will remember every detail when you open your eyes in the Hive." He put his hand on the Gallicean's shoulder. "Before you go, I need to ask you a favor, De-o-Pa. Dave and his friends and family are in extreme danger now. The Brotherhood and the Predaxians are stirring up trouble in your galaxy as we speak. They would love nothing more than to make an example of Dave and Fa-a-Di for what they have done." He handed a jewel on a string to the Gallicean. "This amulet will be with you in the Hive when you open your eyes. Wear it always and keep close to Fa-a-Di. I believe it will give you the power to see the unseen. It will help you discover who the spies are and who you can trust. Personally, I believe it will let you rejoin the Source at your choosing, although our friend Dave here may doubt that."

De-o-Pa put the amulet around his neck. “Thank you, Obu, although I am not certain I will be allowed to relinquish my role on Jupiter. Are you certain about this risk?”

“Oh yes, the risk is quite real,” Obu confirmed. “And I think our friend Dave can put a name on that risk.”

“Fola Untor,” Dave replied. “He is the Supreme Leader of the Brotherhood.”

Obu laughed. “You see things much clearer here in the Source, don’t you?”

“I had a bad feeling about him for a long time, but it just coalesced in my mind,” Dave said. “Thanks for helping me to see.”

Obu turned back to De-o-Pa and said, “Dear friend, if I may ask another favor, could you please open your eyes now? I need a few moments with Dave before I send him back to the Hive.” De-o-Pa was gone. He turned to Dave, saying, “Thank you for bringing such a great man of faith into the Source, Dave. You’ve done the Galliceans a world of good. And give my thanks to Zee Gongaleg for making this possible.”

“Of course, Obu,” Dave replied. “But what did you want to talk to me about?”

“Dave, I had hoped we had more time, but unfortunately, Odo is near death,” Obu began. “The elders of Nan have given him their strength and begged him to return to Nan, but he refuses each time. I have seen the future for our universe and it is very bleak. Ask Loni and Pua about their journeys into the future and what they saw. The great peace I foresaw not long ago is now lost. The only factor that seems to have changed is Odo’s move to your galaxy. The universe needs him now more than ever. Without him, I fear all hope may be lost."

"But what can I do?" Dave asked. "If he won't listen to you or the elders, why do you think he'll listen to me?"

"Wishful thinking, perhaps," Obu sighed. "Both Odo and I have told you that you are not responsible for the problems of the universe. However, you must love and care for your family and friends. Is Odo your friend, Dave?"

"Of course, Obu, I resent you even asking that," Dave scoffed.

"I didn't doubt your love, Dave," Obu replied. "I'm just trying to clarify things for you. I'm afraid things are going to move very quickly now. It might take millennia for the Brotherhood or Predaxians to gain control, but they can set that in motion in a few days or weeks. Each action you and your friends take is part of the puzzle. The cornerstone is finding a way to save Odo. With him, we can win. If he dies, all may be lost."

"No pressure, right?" Dave laughed. "I'll do my best. When I open my eyes, I'll go to Nanda immediately to start working on him."

"Don't go crazy either," Obu said. "You forgot what Nok told you just a day ago, didn't you?"

"Everything is happening according to some misguided plan, right?" Dave replied.

"I wouldn't call it misguided, Dave," Obu smiled. "You went on the Sojourn to help your friend, Fa-a-Di. You went to Tak-Makla because your friend Zee Gongaleg needed you. Just go with it. As events accelerate, you will be called on for more and quicker decisions. Your connection to the Source is incredible. I can see billions of lines coursing through your Being of Light at this moment. Have dinner on Tak-Makla and drink too much whisky with your friends tonight. Then, complete the Sojourn and help Fa-a-Di come to grips with his problem. Have faith in yourself like Odo and I have faith in you."

"You make it sound easy, old friend," Dave smiled. "But I think it's going to be very, very hard."

"You'll be fine and your family will be fine. I want you to know that I've spent time here with your future granddaughter Bea. She's a remarkable woman, and I have a feeling you will meet her soon in the flesh," Obu replied as he put his hand on Dave's shoulder. "Dave, relax, have fun, and by the way, save the universe along the way. Now open your eyes and get to the party. Everyone else is already waiting for you."

CHAPTER 20

"Elder, I think you are being obstinate on purpose," Darlene said. "You must return to Nan soon. Please for your own sake, do not choose to die here."

"My beautiful Ila tells me the same thing daily, Darlene," Odo replied, sitting upright on his narrow bed. Ila and his children Alo and Uli stood nearby with tears in their eyes. The entire family was wearing their gray tunics smudged with black soot as a sign of grief, but Odo was wearing his normal Elder robes. His skin was pale and his cheeks were sunken. Dark circles formed around his eyes which seemed to stare off into space. "Each of us makes choices in life, and coming to Nanda was my choice." He coughed deeply. "Every Elder of Nan volunteered for this job. We all knew that our disconnection from the natural Hive would affect us greatly, but the greater good must be served. If it is my time, then so be it."

Ila sat on the bed next to her husband and held his hands. "Odo, please listen to Ambassador Brewster! The Elders and your best friend, Obu Neela, have all come to tell you the same thing. There is too much at risk in the universe for you to leave us now."

"I'm not planning on dying, darling," he said as he kissed her cheek. "The river of fate is leading us all in a specific direction. That direction is not of our choosing, but was selected by the Source. I have faith my decision to come to Nanda put me fully into the current of that river. But it is not a death wish on my part."

"But Father, you can save yourself so easily," Uli begged with tears streaming down her face. "The Elders of Nan can take you home in seconds. When your strength has returned, you can come back here."

"Perhaps I am an old fool," Odo smiled. "But my nine thousand years of life have taught me a thing or two. There are things Obu and the Elders do not know, but I do. I trust God to let things happen as He chooses."

"Please tell us about those things, Father," Uli asked. "If you die, all of that knowledge will be lost and we will not be able to carry on after you."

Odo laughed heartily. "My darling Uli, thank you for your love and concern for me. But there is nothing I know that is not known by others. While this flesh is very old, my spirit is as young as a new baby. Each of us knows everything, if we could just allow ourselves to accept the truth and let it flow out of our mouths and hearts."

"Odo, you have saved my family more than once," Darlene interjected. "Now it is time for you to allow us to save you. Dave is distraught over your condition and asked me to beg you to return to Nan."

"Thanks to both of you," Odo sighed. "Let Dave know I am thrilled he has allowed himself to flow down the river by my side. If there is a future in this life for me, it will only be because he completes his current journey."

"I don't think that's fair to burden Dave with your future when you could easily choose life by returning to Nan," Ila argued. She turned to Darlene and said, "Please forgive Odo for that, Darlene. I'm afraid his mind is going too."

Odo laughed again. “Dearest Ila, I am not burdening Dave at all.” He took her hands in his. “I have foreseen many events, including a brazen attack on Nan in the next few hours. Events in both galaxies are degrading very quickly. Without an incredible effort from all of us, the universe could fall into a darkness that will take millennia to recover from.” He stood feebly and walked over to the window. It had just started raining on Nanda and the residents were scurrying for cover. He smiled as he saw parents holding their coats over their children’s heads to keep them dry. “There is a chance that Dave and his friends may stop that evil from taking over.”

“Didn’t you tell him that it wasn’t his responsibility to take care of the universe?” Ila asked. “I seem to recall those words quite clearly.”

Odo laughed and walked over to her and hugged her. “You always had a perfect memory, darling. That is true, however, he must love and care for his friends and family. While he doesn’t realize it yet, his family is a lot larger than he once thought.” He sat again on the bed and motioned for Darlene to sit next to him. After she did, he put his arm around her shoulders and continued, “The intergalactic conflict that has already begun will affect each of us. If the evil forces prevail, all of us will be killed as enemies of the new state. That puts us, Dave’s family and friends, in extreme danger. If he continues down his path, perhaps the evil will fail, saving all of us. He will have succeeded in caring for his family and friends. It is only an ancillary fact that the universe will be saved. Do you understand, Darlene?”

“No, Odo, frankly I do not,” Darlene smiled as she kissed his cheek. “You know, I have envied Dave for his ability to join the Source and connect to people like my future granddaughter. After listening to you, I don’t think I do anymore. If that ability comes with the mission to save the universe, it is much too big for a single person. Can't you see this is why you must return to Nan to rebuild your strength? Dave needs you, now more than ever. Please help him."

Odo smiled back and replied, "I am helping him, every moment of his life. My spirit is connected to him now, as he sits down for a wonderful dinner on Tak-Makla. I will continue to push him along with me down the river of fate to hopefully, save us all."

"But Dave isn't on Tak-Makla, Odo," Darlene said. "He is on the Sojourn with Fa-a-Di and his brother."

"Trust me, dear," Odo smiled. "He, Jake and the Galliceans are on Tak-Makla right now. Today was a great day there. For the first time in all of history, Galliceans have knowingly joined with the Source. The spirits of all Galliceans have been set free from the chains of the past. Living Galliceans have seen the truth of the universe. Now we will see if they understand and accept that truth."

A tone sounded on Darlene's earpiece and she tapped it to communicate with the Nightsky. "And so it has begun," Odo said. "The time of darkness has arrived my darling family."

"Whatever do you mean, Father?" Alo asked.

Darlene stood up and appeared very upset. "That was the Nightsky. Ten Donnaki battle cruisers have appeared in orbit here. The Kong-Fa and her fleet will arrive within ten minutes to assist Nightsky. Dozens of Donnaki shuttles are heading down to the planet with an invasion force. Jon wants us to transport up while there is time."

"That won't be necessary, Darlene," Odo said. "I foresaw this as well. The Galliceans will arrive soon to help us." As he spoke, a brigade of two hundred Gallicean Marines appeared outside Odo's home. Each had a maklan clinging to his chest.

Colonel Um-de-Bo rushed into the room with two others. "Ambassador Brewster, I am here to escort you to safety. My men are establishing a secure perimeter for you and your friends. I'll leave two men with you and return shortly." He smiled and rushed back into the street. They could hear explosions as the enemy cruisers shot randomly down on the planet.

"Everyone try to be calm!" one of the Marines shouted. As he finished talking, another explosion struck just outside the home, shattering the wooden building and burying everyone in rubble. "Medic!" the Marine shouted. A column of Donnaki soldiers flew over the area and shot at the Marines, who jumped into the air to fight back. The two forces fought hand to hand in the sky over the wrecked home. The superior training of the Gallicean Marines was evident as the Donnaki quickly fled the scene with dozens of dead soldiers littering the ground.

Darlene tried to move, but her legs were pinned down by rubble. She could hear shouting and voices calling her, but her translator had been blown out of her ear by the explosion and she couldn't understand anything. There were more sounds of explosions but they seemed very far away. She wondered if Odo and his family were okay and if the Gallicean fleet had arrived on time. It would be the worst case scenario of Odo had died in this attack right after saying he had foreseen this. She prayed she could be on Tak-Makla now drinking a glass of whisky with Dave. Darlene felt something crawling on her body and looked down to see a maklan crawling onto her chest. She could sense it trying to communicate, but did not understand. The maklan smiled at her and glowed bright blue.

CHAPTER 21

Emperor Lok Zul was feeling very relaxed. For the first time since ascending to the throne of the Donnaki Empire, they were at peace with the Paxran. It was an uneasy truce to be certain, but the need was crucial. The new Free Society of the Milky Way would be the downfall for his society, he was certain of that. He took a sip of the glass of Paxran brandy. It was a lovely elixir, so smooth, sweet and potent. If nothing else came from the peace, this drink might be enough. "Perhaps you are right, my friend," he said at last.

"Of course, I'm right," Fola Untor said. "There will be plenty of time in the future to settle things with the Paxran, but we must face facts. The Hive weapon technology is too powerful to be trusted to the filthy tekkans. Until our allies have it too, the balance of power has turned against us all."

Lok sat up and faced the other. "But you are human and you say the humans invented the technology. Why don't you just give it to me? Wouldn't that be much easier?"

Fola rose and retrieved the brandy bottle, refilling his and the Emperor's glasses. "Well, it's not quite that simple, my lord. We made the mistake to give it to the tekkans and now they refined their weapon. I am not sure any human Hives can compete with it now. We must first strike at them from many directions so their resources are pulled from Tak-Makla. Then we can steal their new designs and destroy that Hive for good!"

"But you will give me the technology then, right?" Lok quizzed. "Otherwise, once my soldiers die giving you your sense of revenge, won't you just turn it on us?"

"Of course not, my lord," Fola lied. "I have already provided drawings and mechanical designs and your teams have started construction on two Hives. The computer systems and software must still be designed to work with your physiology. Also, there is the issue of population. With our current technology, you will need two to three billion valakars to operate each Hive. Most of your planets cannot support that many agents plus their families and the infrastructure to support it. Honestly, my lord, we have discussed this already."

"Yes, but I am a trained diplomat, Fola," Lok smiled. "I may ask you the same questions over and again. Perhaps I am looking for your story to change."

"Has it, my lord?" Fola asked.

"Not yet, human," Lok laughed. "By the way, the attack on Nanda went as you suspected. We bombed large patches of their cities before the Galliceans intervened. I have to tell you we have never had contact with them before. They are very formidable warriors. I lost a lot of good men today. Was it worth it?"

"The loss of life is always regrettable, my lord," Fola said sadly. "But this was just the first step in the plan to diminish the ability of the Free Society to defend itself. It will take some time to draw down their resources and force them to pull away from Tak-Makla. When that happens, we hit that planet with everything we have."

"And you say that planet is a manufactured world?" the emperor quizzed. "You think our plasma bomb device might actually destroy that world completely?"

"That is our only hope, my lord," Fola said. "If the tekkans use that Hive to attack this planet, they could dissolve it below our feet right now. We would have no place to hide from such a weapon."

"But the tekkans have never been aggressive to us before. We have traded with them for centuries, until the ongoing battle with the Paxran made that untenable. Perhaps we should convince them to join us?" Lok asked.

"They are the cornerstone of the Free Society, my lord," Fola scoffed. "If you ask me, they are using their Hive device to force the loyalty of the other cultures."

"Won't that make them like the Predaxians whom you want us to befriend?" Lok asked. "That seems counter-intuitive to me."

"Call that a friendship of expedience, my lord," Fola replied. "We need as many friends as we can to defeat the Free Society. Once that group is in decline, we can select different friends if we choose to."

"What exactly is your goal, Fola Untor?" Lok asked. "Let us say that your plan works perfectly. Tak-Makla is rubble and the other pieces of the Free Society are crumbling under our armies. What do you want the end game to be?"

Fola drained his glass and refilled it. He pulled his chair close to the emperor's and whispered, "All of us have disrupted the true course of the universe. The only significant species to evolve in this galaxy are the valakars and maklans. The humans, Gallicean, and Kalideans originated in my home galaxy. Of course there are others, but they represent a tiny minority. To me, that means God wants the valakars and maklans to have dominion over this galaxy. After we work together to eliminate the invasive virus here, you and the different maklan species can decide for yourselves who will rule well." He smiled broadly. "Frankly, if you rule the entire galaxy, that would be wonderful. Those spider-like maklans freak me out."

Lok laughed out loud. "Thank you for the vote of confidence, friend. I hope your prediction comes to pass."

"There is another issue though," Fola continued. "The humans originated in my galaxy and I want us to rule there. There are a few minor species, like the Boley of Lagamar 7, but they amount to nothing. Some valakar have settled in my galaxy and that is not acceptable. It is my hope to send them back here if possible."

"Or destroy them if not?" Lok asked.

"Only as a last choice, my lord," Fola replied. "Without the scourge of the humans, Kalideans and Galliceans, there is plenty of room here for them. Over time, they will likely fall under the Donnaki sphere of influence. That would obviously be much more acceptable than being slaves to the maklans."

The emperor laughed again. "You are a man of great dreams, Fola Untor. We shall work together as long as it suits me." He stood and pulled on his royal robes. "I must take my leave of you now, dear friend. I have affairs of state to deal with, as you can imagine. But I did want to suggest you might stay here with us as an act of faith that you will not turn on us. I will treat you very well here."

"Sorry, my lord, but I won't be a hostage to our agreement," Fola frowned. "Each of us has our lives and futures tied intrinsically to this arrangement. You must accept that."

The emperor smiled, "I don't know about that. You are just one man on a planet of valakars. Are you sure you can refuse my offer?"

Fola smiled, "You forget, dear friend. I have a Hive." As he spoke, his body dissolved into thin air. The emperor was alone in his chamber again.

"God damned Hives!" he shouted as he marched out of the room.

Darlene woke up in the sick bay of the Nightsky. Jon Lake was sitting on the chair next to the bed. "Jon, what happened?"

"Thank goodness you're awake, Darlene," Jon sighed. "I think you just passed out due to the trauma of the blast. The doctor says you're as fit as a fiddle."

She tried to sit up, but her head was pounding. "What happened to the Pak family? Are they okay?"

"Pretty much," Jon began, "Odo and Ila were not harmed at all. Uli broke an arm and Alo has a lot of bruises and contusions. But they have all be released from sick bay and have been assigned quarters on board. The doc said you might have a headache for a while. One of the beams hit your head when it crashed down."

"I don't understand what happened there," she said. "How could warships suddenly appear out of thin air like that? Couldn't you see them coming?"

"We only have theories now, Darlene," Jon replied. "Either the Donnaki have been given Maklakar shielding technology or a Hive was involved. We don't know which."

"Have you told Dave yet?" she asked.

"He is out of communication on the terrestrial planet in the Gallicea system, Darlene," Jon answered. "We are trying to get a shuttle there to get him."

"Odo told me he was on Tak-Makla at the time of the explosion," she replied. "How long have I been out?"

"Only an hour or so, Darlene," Jon answered. "But you're saying Dave is on Tak-Makla? How did he get there?"

"That's irrelevant, Jon," Dave said as he appeared in the room with Jake on his chest. "I just got the word, darling. How are you?" he asked as he rushed over and hugged her tightly. "Thank goodness you're safe now."

"Admiral, we don't know how the Donnaki ships jumped to Nanda without our noticing anything," Jon started. "We were alone in orbit one second, and the next we were surrounded."

"Was anyone hurt on board? How's the ship?" Dave asked.

"Everyone is okay here, Dave. Thankfully, we were running our daily drills at the time and our defensive shields were up when the Donnaki appeared," Jon replied. "It's like a miracle that the Kong-Fa and her fleet were close by as well."

Dave thought a moment and then said, "Well, we can't count on luck anymore. I need you to take the ship to Tak-Makla as soon as possible. Now that their Hive is operational again, our enemies will be trying to take it out. Nanda was a diversion. They are trying to split our defenses into enough small pieces so that Tak-Makla becomes vulnerable again. I won't let that happen."

"But what about the Nanda, Dave?" Darlene asked. "They are helpless without us."

Dave kissed her cheek and replied, "We'll do what we can, sweetheart. But Tak-Makla is the linchpin in this. If the Hive is disabled again, we'll lose all insight into what our enemies are planning."

"We'll be on our way in fifteen minutes, Dave," Jon answered. "I'll also contact Kong-Fa and see if they can send some ships with us and leave a few here."

"That's perfect, Jon. Thank you," Dave replied. "By the way, is Darlene safe to travel?"

"Sure! The doctors gave her a clean bill of health," Jon answered.

"Great!" Dave said as he picked his wife up in his arms. "Jake, take us back to Tak-Makla." Jake glowed and the three disappeared, leaving Jon alone in sick bay.

As soon as Dave and Darlene appeared on the beach outside Zee's house, the crowd assembled for dinner erupted in applause. A few seconds later, Fa-a-Di appeared next to them, having just returned from Nanda. The applause turned to cheers. As Darlene stepped up onto the patio, De-o-Nu, Zee and Loni rushed over to hug her. Ton was right behind them with two glasses of whisky, which he handed to Dave and Darlene before he led them back to their seats.

The group of waiters began passing out platters of appetizers. The crowd was buzzing with conversation and people were laughing and enjoying the night air. Dave touched his glass to Darlene's and they each took a sip. Darlene leaned over to Dave and kissed his cheek, then whispered in his ear, "Honey, this is unbelievable. After the house was destroyed on Nanda, I was pinned under the rubble and was thinking it might be the end for me. Then I prayed I could be here with you, sipping whisky together. And now look, my prayer was answered."

Dave kissed her lips and smiled back. "I love you, Darlene. When I heard about the attack, I knew I should try to find Odo to make sure he was okay. But I couldn't think about him at all until I found you safe. Things are going to get worse for a time now, and I'm not going to be separated from you again."

She kissed him lightly. "Dave, thank you for loving me. But you have to complete the Sojourn first. I'll be okay. But please do this for Fa-a-Di."

Zee, who was sitting next to Darlene, broke into their private discussion. "My dear friends, I fear we are neglecting our other guests. No one is happier than me that Darlene is well, but this was a great day for us. Three Galliceans have entered a Hive for the first time in history!" He pointed across the table. "This gentlemen is De-o-Pa. He is De-o-Nu's brother and a senior official in the Gallicean faith. I don't think you've met."

"It is an honor to meet you Ambassador," De-o-Pa said. "It is a great blessing that you are safe and with us tonight."

"It is very nice to meet you, De-o-Pa," Darlene replied. "What did you think of the experience of the Hive?"

The Prelate's face lit up with joy. "By the Daughters of Lubna, I've never had such a miraculous experience!" The other Galliceans started to laugh. "What did I say?"

When he could stop laughing, De-o-Nu said, "You have to forgive my brother. He travels in different circles from most, being part of the clergy. That saying, "the Daughters of Lubna" is generations old. Our grandfather used to use it all the time."

"We are sorry, Prelate, we meant no disrespect," Fa-a-Di gasped between fits of laughter. "But most Galliceans gave up those old sayings in primary school."

"But the Daughters of Lubna are a sacred part of our past, brothers. We should not so easily forget such things. There are priests who spend their lives researching the ancient texts for hidden meaning," De-o-Pa replied.

"I love that story!" Fak shouted. "It is one of my favorites, and I have studied many cultures and religions."

"Oh dear, now that the whisky is flowing, so is Fak's tongue," Zee sighed. "Can this wait until after dinner, at least?"

"Of course, High Consul," Fak acquiesced.

"I can't wait to hear about it, Fak," Darlene replied.

"And I am intrigued how a non-Gallicean would know our ancient texts," De-o-Pa asserted.

The dinner continued for another two hours with courses of seafood and fresh vegetables, followed by the traditional coffee and sweet offering. Dave told the group about his plan to safeguard Tak-Makla at all costs, which met with much disagreement, as each species was terrified of potential attacks on their own planets. While Dave explained how the tekkan Hive was the real target, there was little agreement on how to keep everyone safe. Only Loni Arrak was firmly on Dave's side, as she had seen hundreds of reports from Hive agents about activity among the Donnaki, Paxran, Maklakar and the rogue Predaxian agents. According to tradition, after dinner the primary guests joined Zee and his ministers for a walk along the beach and more whisky. Within a few minutes, the talk of the pending war slipped away and everyone grouped around Fak for her story.

Her face was already slightly blushed from the whisky, but being a student of galactic history, she was not about to lose her moment. "De-o-Pa, since you know this story as well, please interrupt me if I miss anything," she began. "The Daughters of Lubna comes from the story of Fa-u-Di, the brother of Fa-u-Bay. After the battle of Gallicea, Fa-u-Di was given the job to expand Gallicean influence by finding new civilizations to partner and trade with. He wrote about his adventures in the book, *Ten Years to Gallia*."

The book tells how Fa-u-Di was given a brand new star cruiser and asked to document all life within a hundred light-years of Gallia. The ship, Pal-No-Fa, was equipped with a new power system that would allow it to fly much faster than any others in the fleet. Unfortunately, there was a flaw in the system. When the ship left Gallia, it began to accelerate uncontrollably. Within hours, it was out of communications range hurtling through empty space. The crew was panicking, but they knew any escape pods would be destroyed if they tried to leave. After ten days of travel, Fa-u-Di ordered a core shutdown, which had only a ten percent chance of success. If it failed, the ship would be obliterated in a massive explosion. Every other option had been tried without success. He asked the crew to pray to God for their salvation. At exactly 1000 hours, the core was taken offline. The ship twisted and shook horribly, and the crew members were thrown around inside like toys. After a minute or two, the shaking stopped and the ship began to decelerate. Ten hours later, the ship was at a dead stop in orbit over an immense gas planet. When the core was safely reenergized, a large celebration was held. The crew was euphoric to be alive, even though no one knew where they could be. There were very few stars nearby, and Fa-u-Di correctly presumed they were on the edge of the galaxy, thirty thousand light-years from home.

The following morning, Fa-u-Di met with his command officers. The news was not good. From what astronomical data they could gather, it would take eight years to get home at top speed. There was not enough food or atmosphere to sustain them more than a couple of years. They would have to find planets with a breathable atmosphere and edible food to survive. Also, being enclosed in the ship for that long would undoubtedly lead to mass hysteria. The only good news was that the planet they orbited had a breathable atmosphere; but since they had only been gone a few days, their supplies were almost full.

The system they were in was very odd indeed. There was only this one planet orbiting the sun. The planet had only two moons, which were both terrestrial. The science officer noted that life was visible on the gas giant even from this high orbit. He and his men had seen what looked like enormous snakes moving around in the gas. He estimated they were hundreds of miles long and probably very dangerous. The recommendation was to avoid the planet at all costs.

The weapons officer was laughing at the story and Fa-u-Di chastised him. The officer mentioned the ancient story of Lu-Be-Na, the legendary female warrior who rid Gallia of giant snake-like creatures that had been attacking towns all over the planet. When one of the snakes stole her two daughters, she killed it and rescued her children. Then she set out on a mission to destroy all of the snakes to keep galli children safe for all time. Fa-u-Di smiled when he remembered the same tale from his childhood, and in honor of Lu-Be-Na, he named the gas planet Lubna, and the moons were named Fistan and Solander, after the mythological gods who created life on Gallia.

"I can't believe you know so much about Gallia," De-o-Pa sighed. "I feel young again, sitting on my mother's knee as she told me that story."

"As you know, that's only the first chapter," Fak replied. "The book tells the stories of every world they visited until they returned home. I can tell by Zee's expression that I've told enough for one night though."

"Thank you for that, Fak," Zee said. "After walking so much and drinking too much, I'm sure we could all use some sleep."

"May I share one thing that is wrong in that story?" Fak asked.

"If it is brief," Zee replied.

"I'll do my best," Fak began. "The book is not really about Fa-u-Di. It was really written by Fa-u-Bay."

"That's very slanderous, Fak," Fa-a-Di said. "How can you back up such nonsense?"

"You all must remember the Hive. Our scientists and historians have traveled all over space and time learning about other civilizations. We believe we must understand a people's motivation before we can be true partners," Fak replied. "I have seen the two Fa-u brothers together in the past. Did you know they were identical twins? After the Battle of Gallicea, Fa-u-Bay was overcome with grief. He was a priest and he had killed Za-a-Za with the blades his generals forced him to wear. Even though the people demanded that he rule, he could not come to grips with his emotions and the failure of his faith. Finally, he convinced his brother to rule in his place. They were so identical no one ever knew. His brother offered to let him travel the stars until he could come to peace with his actions. He said he would then allow Fa-u-Bay to rule. Gallicean history says that Fa-u-Di followed his brother into rule, but really it was the other way around. This is how the first ten editions of *Ten Years to Gallia* were written."

"That is preposterous," De-o-Pa said. "Can you prove this?"

"Of course. I'd be happy to take you back in time to see for yourself. We also have a first edition of the book in our archives," Fak replied.

"You stole a first edition from Gallia?" De-o-Pa gasped.

"Not really, De-o-Pa," she smiled. "We borrowed one from the past, which was taken one hour before a fire destroyed the building and countless historical texts. That was very long ago. We also digitized it so we can make copies. Would you like one?"

"I think we've heard enough for one night, Fak," Zee said as he led the group back up the steps to the house.

CHAPTER 22

Dave could hear the arguments raging as he walked toward the dining room in the ambassador's residence on Tak-Makla. He entered the room to see Darlene, Fa-a-Di, De-o-Nu, Odo Pak and Jon Lake eating and discussing how to safeguard the Free Society from their emboldened enemies. The Galliceans were demanding to keep their ships in their own space, while Darlene was supporting Dave's demand for protection for Tak-Makla. Odo was looking much better and listening silently to the others. The group quieted as Dave joined them.

"Odo, it is wonderful to see you here," Dave said as he sat next to him and put his hand on the Elder's shoulder. "How are you feeling today, old friend?"

"I feel very good today, Dave," he replied. "Consul Gongaleg suggested my condition might be improved on this planet. There is some magic in the place for sure."

"It is amazing," Dave agreed. "You can tell that our Galliceans friends are our size now and not gasping for air in this atmosphere. Zee told us when we met they could somehow set those differences aside here."

"Yes, I have heard that as well," Odo said. "It must have something to do with their Hive and the proliferation of lines of Source in this location. But I must return to Nanda soon, Dave. My job is not complete there."

"I'm sorry, Odo, but I can't let you go back there now," Dave replied. "That planet is too vulnerable and the current situation is extremely dangerous."

"Yes, I know, Dave, but I have chosen to help those people and cannot let that go due to extraneous circumstances, no matter how severe," Odo smiled. "I'm sure you understand."

"I do understand, but I'm not going to change my mind on this one," Dave said as he began to eat his breakfast.

"So, I am to be your prisoner here?" Odo asked with a wry smile.

"Not at all, Odo. In fact, you are going with me to Gallicea to complete the Sojourn," Dave answered, grinning happily. "Then you will stay with me on Nightsky until the danger either kills us all or we defeat it." Odo only smiled and turned back to his meal.

"This is very unusual, Dave," Fa-a-Di said. "I had to get special permission so you could come to the Gallicea system and now you are unilaterally adding Odo to our group? Shouldn't we talk about this first? I need to confer with the High Priest as well."

"I have already done that, General," De-o-Pa said as he joined the group. "The only condition is that Odo visits the High Priest on Gallicea before departing the system. He is honored to have a great man like Odo Pak in his system." De-o-Pa walked over to Odo. "It is my great pleasure to meet you sir," he said extending his hand.

Odo rose and hugged the Prelate. "It is an honor to meet you as well, De-o-Pa. I look forward to our adventure together." De-o-Pa sat next to Odo and took a sip of coffee.

A look of horror crossed Odo's face and he grimaced in pain. "Odo, are you okay?" Dave asked.

After a moment, the tranquil look returned to Odo's face, but a few tears were running down his cheeks. "I will be fine soon, Dave. I mentioned to Darlene that I foresaw an attack on Nan. That attack has just begun."

"Who would do such a thing?" Darlene asked. "Nan is a peaceful planet."

"You know that, but many believe the power of the Hive there was behind the decline of the Society. That lie is actively being spread by the Brotherhood agents still there," Odo explained. "The next target will be the Lagamar system. Hopefully those planets are better defended."

"Will Nan survive the attack?" Dave asked. "That planet is a jewel that must be protected at all costs!"

"Don't worry too much about Nan, Dave," Odo smiled. "The Guardians will protect the planet and her people. Only limited damage will be allowed so the attackers will feel successful. For example, I was told that my residence would be completely destroyed. The attackers blamed me for the dissolution of the Brotherhood, and now they believe they have their blood revenge."

"That's why you didn't want to go back to Nan!" Darlene shouted. "You knew they believed you were there and that your house was a target. How could you know that?"

"Perhaps Dave will learn some of those answers when we complete the Sojourn," Odo replied. "That is, if he doesn't already know. What do you think, Dave?"

Dave pondered the situation and came up blank. "I'm not sure, but I'd bet good money the Source has a lot to do with it."

"That's no bet, Dave Brewster," Odo laughed. "Everything is the Source, so it is involved in every action. But you are getting warmer, I must say."

"Elder, you mentioned something about the Guardians. Who are they?" De-o-Pa asked.

"Well, I'm glad someone is paying attention to an old man," Odo laughed. "Being a natural Hive, Nan must have natural guardians to protect it. It was the Guardians who convinced the Society of Humanity to make Nan the home of the Nan people. The Guardians knew the Nan would never use the power of the Source as a weapon."

"I would have guessed the Nan people were the Guardians," Fa-a-Di replied.

"In a way, they are now," Odo said. "But the planet existed long before humans colonized it. The naturally occurring life on any natural Hive planet will evolve to protect and defend the Hive. While one species may dominate that, all will work together. For example, the Nan people grow many crops there to support the population. If another species tries to take over the Hive, those crops might adapt to be poisonous for the invaders while still being edible by the locals."

"Brother-in-law, I must request to be released from the Sojourn," De-o-Nu said to Fa-a-Di. "Clearly the current situation demands that I command the fleet against the invaders."

"I have to disagree again, brother," Dave said. "De-o-Nu, I need you with me. There is too much at stake for us to go off in our own directions."

"Admiral, with all due respect, I think the safety of Greater Gallia comes first," De-o-Nu argued. "If I must, I will resign my commission and join the Gallicean Army as a private."

"No, brother, Dave is right," De-o-Pa said. "We must stick together on this one. I have already been given approval to be permanently assigned to Fa-a-Di's flagship. Dave requested that I do so. There is nothing you can do with a fleet of ships or a rifle over your shoulder to stop an enemy who can appear out of thin air. You might have fifty ships protecting Gallia when one hundred enemy ships appear over Gallicea or Nom-Kat-La. You could never get there in time to stop the atrocity."

"But I feel useless," De-o-Nu argued. "I am a warrior. I must stop the enemy."

"And we will," Dave said. "Today, we don't have many tools to help us against an enemy hell bent on terrorist tactics. We must find a way to do so. The Hive here is our only tool today. We must protect it at all costs. Once the resources are in place here, then we can start looking for other tools and ways to counteract the enemy."

"But don't we have the Hive on Atar Pa as well, Dave?" Darlene asked. "Doesn't that double our capability?"

"I'm not sure about that, Darlene," Dave sighed. "I believe Fola Untor may be one of our most aggressive adversaries in this battle. I would bet he's trying to turn that Hive over to the Brotherhood."

"But Wendo Balak would never stand for that!" Fa-a-Di scoffed. "That planet has always been loyal to him. Isn't Serena Vanatee his granddaughter? We must talk to her."

"I agree, brother, but it is still possible the Predaxians are using their special talents there to twist the minds of the locals," Dave argued. "If the planetary president and Serena are under their control, the agents can be forced to do whatever their controllers want them to do."

"That's a pretty bleak scenario," Odo replied. "I hope it isn't that bad, Dave. Are you suggesting that we attack that Hive?"

"Of course not, Odo," Dave said. "That would give our enemies the proof they need to bring more human planets into their fold. We would be branded as the aggressors."

"Then what do we do now, Dave?" Fa-a-Di asked. "Our enemies have all the cards in their hands and we have no plan. We have to do something!"

"Let's finish the Sojourn, brother," Dave answered. "Perhaps the Source will reach out to us with answers. If not that, then perhaps it will give us time to think."

"I will ask Zee to have the Hive prepare to send you back to Gallicea," Darlene said. "Then you can take the shuttle to the other planet."

"Perhaps we can change that plan a bit," Odo countered. "Please have the Hive move the shuttle to the other planet and then send us directly there. It will save time and we won't have to worry about our pressure suits."

"Well, that doesn't help us," De-o-Nu said. "We have no breathers here and can't survive for even a moment on that planet without one."

"The Hive can fetch those breathers here before we go," Odo replied. "Although I'm not certain you really need them."

"What are you talking about, Elder? Of course, we need them. The atmosphere is toxic to us," Fa-a-Di argued.

"Brothers, the planet is a Hive, just like Nan and Tak-Makla," Dave replied. "The power of Source will protect you, although I agree we should take breathers with us, just in case."

CHAPTER 23

Panzak was a verdant terrestrial world near the frontier between the Paxran and Donnaki empires. Somehow it had been spared the violence of the ongoing sparring between the two neighbors who constantly sought an advantage over the other. Panzak was only a few light-years from the other Paxran planet Tak-u-Baka, which was the last line of defense between the superpowers. If that stronghold ever fell, Panzak would fall as well. These were different times though. The odd alliance between the Brotherhood agents and the Predaxian rebels was growing, and their stories of the evil, so-called Free Society were enough to warrant a conclave of powers on this side of the galaxy.

Many smaller societies had eagerly joined the new alliance as it meant greater security not only from the Free Society, but the Paxran and Donnaki as well. The conclave was now in its fifth day. Each culture was given time to talk about their civilizations and strengths, but those narratives dragged on and on as each tried to impress and overshadow those before them. Thankfully, Emperor Lok Zul of Donnaki and Lord General Kolu Inzaka of Paxran had declined the offer to talk, allowing their reputations to stand on their own. As the speeches droned on, the patience of the leadership was wearing very thin. After lunch had been served, Fola Untor stopped the session and moved to begin the real narrative for this meeting.

"Bless you, Mr. Untor for stopping this endless posturing," Lok Zul said. "While I have enjoyed each of your speeches, I'm afraid we may all grow old and die before we come to any meaningful conversation on the problems facing us." He stood and began to walk slowly around the massive ring of tables where the various delegations were seated. "As you all know, as leader of the Donnaki, my military is the strongest in the galaxy..."

"One of the strongest, dear emperor," Lord General Inzaka interjected.

"Of course, friend," Lok smiled. "One of the strongest in the galaxy. My forces have seen the Hive weapon in action. Fifty ships were crushed to dust by a single weapon. Thankfully, the crews were magically transported back to Donnaki. And that may just have been a taste of their power."

"Shortly after that attack, the Hive weapon disappeared from your space," Kolu replied. "That weapon was thousands of miles in diameter and it disappeared like a ghost in the night."

Lok spun around to stare at Kolu and sneered. "For the moment, I will disregard the implications of your statement, general. Obviously, you are engaged in spying in my sovereign space."

"Gentlemen, let us please be civil," Fola begged. "We all spy on one another. That is normal for each society. We must protect our people and sometimes that requires us to monitor the activities of our neighbors. We cannot be distracted from the real enemy here."

Field Marshall Fongula Nokka of Palus rose and said, "I must agree with the human, friends. Frankly, I am not certain I agree with the need for a new alliance, especially when the Predaxians are involved. They enslaved my people for generations, and it was the humans, Kalideans and Galliceans who freed us."

"Then why are you here, brother valakar?" Lok asked. "Perhaps you are a spy for the Free Society?"

"With all due respect, that is ridiculous," Fongula laughed. "We have all been briefed on the capabilities of the Hive weapon. There could be ten thousand tekkan agents in this room right now and we wouldn't know it. Besides, while all of you wail and gnash your teeth in fear of the Hive device, it is only the Donnaki and Palians who have faced it. While the emperor lost some warships, one of my planets was dissolved to dust before our eyes." The others in the room groaned and whispered among themselves at the thought.

"The Field Marshall is exactly right," Altamar Zendo agreed. "I was in that battle, foolishly serving the forces of the Free Society. My only excuse is that my brother the emperor had sentenced me to life in prison and I was thirsting for revenge."

"Fongula is also correct about the tekkan agents," Fola said. "I was a Hive Chief Engineer in the home galaxy before our enemies came and destroyed our Society. I have the ability to detect agents in a Hive, but only human ones. I know little about the tekkans. That is another reason we must destroy their Hive."

"Then let's stop talking about it and do it!" Lok shouted. "I have two plasma bomb fleets at your disposal. Let's send them to Tak-Makla and blow that planet to rubble right now!"

"Unfortunately, Your Majesty, there are fatal flaws in your fleets," Altamar said. "They would be destroyed before they could fire one shot."

"What in heaven are you talking about?" Lok asked incredulously.

"Let's put our cards on the table here," Fola interjected. "Of all the societies we invited here, only one declined. Who was that?" The others looked around, but no one had any idea, as the list of invitees was very secret. "The Maklakar declined the invitation."

Kolu laughed out loud. "Now you're the crazy one, Fola. We destroyed the Maklakar civilization generations ago. How can ghosts decline an invitation?"

"They are still around, Lord General," Premier It Ka-la of Vilu-Zan replied. "I have entertained them on my own planet, only a week or so ago."

"I don't believe you, bird," Kolu scoffed. "Dead is dead."

"Unfortunately, Kolu, the valakar is correct," Altamar said. "I was there myself. I spoke to them and gave them some flawed information on Hives. After your armies destroyed most of their planets, the survivors fled to the edge of the galaxy and began to rebuild. They became incredibly xenophobic and focused all of their resources on defensive capabilities. They created the plasma bomb technology, not the Donnaki. However, they only gave them the earliest iterations. The plasma ball is very unstable until it can be launched at the enemy. If the tekkans fired a single shot at the developing ball, it would explode and send the pulses back to the ships, destroying most of them."

"They gave us this technology?" Lok asked. "How can this be? I was told that we did it."

"Don't blame your scientists, emperor," Altamar replied. "They would go home from work each night. In the morning, they might find one or two elements in their analyses or experiments very slightly different than they remembered. They likely passed that off to a poor memory or too much whisky."

"But they gave us flawed technology," Lok continued. "Isn't that worse?"

"Not at all," Altamar laughed. "It was the same technology they invented. They simply discovered flaws later and fixed them. When your scientists discover the flaws, they will fix them as well."

"But why would they do that?" Lok asked. "Why would they give us such a weapon?"

"Don't be an idiot, Lok," Kolu laughed. "We destroyed their civilization, so they gave you the capability to destroy us. It is the ultimate revenge, served by the only other empire capable of delivering it." He turned to Fola and asked, "So, the Maklakar will join the Free Society then?"

"I doubt that," Fola answered. "We must remember and forever thank the Maklakar. They attacked and almost destroyed the tekkan Hive. Without their actions, our plans would be meaningless. They have given us the gift of time. Their fear and hatred of the Paxran is probably all the incentive they need to sit on the sidelines. As Altamar said, the Maklakar are content to stay safely in their corner of the galaxy and be left alone."

"Then what do we do now?" Kolu asked.

"It has already started with the Donnaki attack on Nanda," Fola replied. "We have killed the leader of the Nan people who was the greatest expert in the galaxy on Hives and Universal

Power. The various cultures in the Free Society are already beginning to pull away from their alliance. Each attack will target a planet that seems totally helpless and friendly. Over time, the cultures will withdraw further from the alliance in order to safeguard their own people. As the alliance fails, we can turn our attention back to Tak-Makla and kill that Hive once and for all. After that, we take out our most dreaded enemies, Fa-a-Di of Greater Gallia, Mencius of Kalidus and Dave Brewster of Earth. That will throw the entire Free Society into turmoil. Then we can invade and take over."

Lok Zul was laughing. He said, "Okay, I understand the incentive for me and most of the people in this room. But Fola, what's in this for you? Are you and your Brotherhood planning on taking over our galaxy too?"

Fola thought for a few moments before saying, "No. Honestly, once those three are dead, my work here is complete and I plan to return to my own galaxy. If the battle is still raging here, I will offer what help I can, but I came here for them."

Now Kolu Inzaka was laughing as well. "So you came two million light-years to get personal revenge, and are willing to destroy billions of lives to get it? That sounds pretty sick and twisted to me."

"That may be true, but the Brotherhood was a powerful force in the greatest civilization the universe has ever seen. It was those three who brought the Society down and caused my men to be seen as pariahs on their own planets," Fola began. "I suppose that makes me like the Maklakar. I am here to provide weapons and support to those who can help me destroy my enemies. You can reject me now, and I will try other ways to complete my task. In that case, you will learn nothing more about Hives and will be forever at the mercy of the Free

Society. Once I succeed, I will go home and try to rebuild my civilization. From that moment forward, you will be on your own."

"And you, General Zendo?" Kolu asked. "You represent a few hundred Predaxian rebels. Are you hoping to rebuild the Predaxian Alliance and rule like your brother?"

"I'm still trying to figure that out, Lord General," Altamar smiled. "I fear the days of the Alliance are gone forever. The Predaxians have lost their desire to rule. I think the Field Marshall can attest to that. But my agents are now outcasts as well. I have no desire to take the place of my nephew Panoplez as President or to rebuild the empire we once had. But I don't fit in as a normal citizen there either. To be honest, I am no friend of the three individuals Fola is hunting. While Dave Brewster did save me from the prison planet Thuk, I believe it was his actions and those of the Galliceans and tekkans that put me there in the first place. Whether they live or die is of no consequence to me. My agents and I are looking for a place to belong. We have some incredible talents that are now shunned on Predax. If we can find a place to help and be treated well, we will be happy."

"Honestly, I think you are both full of crap," Lok Zul laughed. "Your sentiments of altruism are heart-warming, but I am not a young schoolboy. It doesn't matter today whether I know your real intentions. It may be that you want to destroy those others so you have the only real power in the galaxy. Or you may think you will ultimately rule all of us with your Hives or mind control." He waved his arms at the others in the crowd. "Each of us will make our own determination. For now, I will support you, if you can help me overcome the flaws in our plasma bomb device."

"I have to agree with my most hated friend," Kolu Inzaka replied. "While he and I have been sworn enemies all of our lives, I will make two pledges today. If all goes well and we succeed with our plans, I will graciously welcome our fellow maklans, the Predaxians, into our society. My other pledge is that if and when either of you turn on one of us, I will immediately join with Lok Zul to destroy you utterly."

"And you, Fongula?" Fola asked the Palian. "Will you join us or will you make your report on this meeting to the Free Society?"

Fongula laughed. "We already had this discussion, Fola. As I said before, Hive agents might already be here, so it would be a waste of time for me to make any report. As for joining you, I will have to think about that. We Palians are caught between the Galliceans and the Predaxians, both of whom have been friends or enemies at different times. So, it is not easy to pick one or the other to ally with. I hope you understand."

"I must agree with the Field Marshall," Premier It Ka-la said. "My society is a single planet. We have little to offer this alliance. Each of us will make our decisions after consulting with our people. I want to thank you all for this meeting, and especially Altamar Zendo for visiting my planet. It has been very informative."

As the group filed out of the room, no one noticed the four crystal maklans clinging to the ceiling. After the last people left, they glowed blue and disappeared.

CHAPTER 24

Dave, Odo, Fa-a-Di, De-o-Nu and De-o-Pa were standing near the water's edge near Zee's residence. Darlene rushed over and kissed her husband one last time before they headed back to the Sojourn. Then she stepped back and joined Zee and Loni. The Galliceans had donned their breathers and checked the settings. They would have enough air for two days, even though the shuttle could refill them for months if necessary. "Let's get this over with," Fa-a-Di barked. Loni touched a contact on her earpiece and spoke to the other Chief Engineer. In an instant, the others were gone. A shallow wave rolled onto the beach and erased the footprints where they had been standing. Darlene, Zee and Loni walked back toward the house.

Dave and the others were standing in a small clearing surrounded by very tall pine trees. The air on the planet was warm and full of the scent of trees and flowers. The Galliceans were back to their normal size and towered over the two men. "This is quite a beautiful place," Odo said. "It reminds me of Nan in many ways." He turned to Dave and said, "Do you remember the forest near my home, Dave? This looks very similar to me."

"You are right, Odo," he replied. "It's almost like we're standing on Nan, except I think the trees are much taller here." A gravel path cut the clearing in half, and led out into the forest on both sides. The sound of falling water almost covered the chirping of small birds in the trees.

"Okay, brother, where do we go now?" Fa-a-Di asked De-o-Nu. "You love this place. Show me the way."

De-o-Nu was laughing. “Brother, I never said I love this place. I love Gallicea, but this planet is frightening to me too.” He looked both ways to find recognizable landmarks. “The uphill path leads to the campsite, as I recall. The other will lead us to the temple and sacred river. What do you think, Pa?”

“That’s right, Nu. I recommend we go to the camp and check on the shuttle and our accommodations,” his brother replied. “Follow me.” He started following the uphill path and the others fell in line behind him.

The incline of the path was gradual, with the dense forest backed up against it. After a few minutes, the trees began to thin and the slope became steeper. After twenty minutes, De-o-Pa stopped to catch his breath. The clearing where they arrived could be seen below them as the trees were quite sparse at this level and they had climbed about two hundred feet in altitude. The forest stretched out to the horizon around them. A wide river could be seen cutting through the trees heading quickly toward lower climes. The group sat down to relax. Odo sat next to Fa-a-Di, saying, “General, are you going to try to breathe the air here without the mask as Zee suggested?”

“I’m not certain I’m ready to die just yet, Odo,” Fa-a-Di chuckled.

“I hardly think one breath would kill us,” De-o-Nu answered. “But I’ll have to get my nerves in check before I try it.” Before he could act, De-o-Pa pulled off his mask and took a deep breath. “Pa, what the heck are you doing?”

De-o-Pa took a second deep breath and then a third. “Apparently, I’m still living, brother.” He continued breathing normally. “The air here is sweet and full of energy. It reminds me of flying through a thunderstorm in a Dar-Fa.” As they gained confidence in their eyes, first De-o-Nu and then Fa-a-Di removed their breathers and were astounded to be breathing a nitrogen-oxygen atmosphere.

"Well, I'll be damned!" Fa-a-Di laughed. "Our people have been coming here for thousands of years with pressure suits or breathers. If anyone had ever tried this, no one would have believed them." He clapped Dave on the back and said, "You have to teach me a lot more about Hives, my brother."

At that moment, Jake and two other maklans popped in sight and landed on the three Galliceans. "What's going on here?" Jake shouted. "We've been monitoring your breathers and the signals went crazy. Are you okay?"

"It would appear so, little brother," Fa-a-Di laughed, "although I wouldn't have believed it if someone else said they did this." He stood up and breathed deeply. "This is great. I hate breather air. It's always so stale. Let's get to the camp. I'm sure we are going to be the hit of the century when they see us walk in like this." As the group continued, Jake told them about the report from the team that witnessed the conclave on Panzak. No one was surprised by the circumstances; however, Fa-a-Di was shocked that the Palian premier would consider such an act. After ten minutes, the path leveled again and they approached the massive encampment. A line of twenty shuttles clung to the edge of the camp, and hundreds of small cabins filled the center.

Fa-a-Di was right about the commotion caused by their appearance. It was very rare for such celebrities to come to this place, but even more so since they were not using breathers. The initial shock turned to curiosity after De-o-Nu brought out twenty cases of whisky from the shuttle and began to pass bottles around. Soon all the Galliceans had tossed their breathers aside and were singing and drinking as the sun began to dip toward the horizon. Platters of food were passed around and the crowd was having a wonderful, drunken time, which was a rare pleasure on this planet. Usually, the Galliceans were very reserved here and made their penance as quickly as possible and left, grateful for another ten years away from this place.

De-o-Pa was feeling the burn in his face when he asked the crowd to open a large circle in the center. A bonfire was started there and the Prelate began to lead the crowd in traditional folk dancing around the fire. Even the High Commissioner was drawn into the celebration and seemed to be enjoying himself immensely. The three maklans swooped through the air, dancing in their own way.

The party continued well into the night. As the temperature began to fall, the dancing became more frenetic and singing filled the air. Dave grabbed a couple of blankets and offered one to Odo Pak, and then sat next to him at the edge of the crowd, well out of range of the dancing Galliceans. Each held a glass of whisky in their hands and sipped it gingerly. "Dave, I must say that your friends do not seem so reserved for a religious retreat."

Dave laughed. "I know. Fa-a-Di has been dreading this visit for so long. Now it looks like he's having the time of his life. This is wonderful, although I'm not so sure they'll be feeling well tomorrow."

"Yes, I must say this Gallicean whisky is too strong. I must limit myself to only two or three more glasses," Odo smiled wryly. "And how do you feel, Dave?"

"I feel great," he replied. "But I can't explain that. Half of the galaxy wants to kill me. And it's not that they want to kill humans or defeat the Free Society. They want to kill me personally. But right now, I don't care."

"Perhaps your death may serve the greater good," Odo said. "Much the same way as my apparent death is."

"Are you suggesting that we fake my death too?" Dave asked.

"No, not at all," Odo replied. "And I am definitely not suggesting you actually die. That would be terrible for the entire galaxy. I'm just reminding you to focus on what's important to you. Even if your death would benefit the Free Society, it must still be avoided at all costs. There is nothing greater in the universe than life. You best serve the Free Society by serving your family and friends. But I think I'm rambling now. I'm sure I've told you that a hundred times."

"It always helps to hear it again, Odo," Dave said as he put his arm on Odo's shoulders. "I am so happy you are here with us now. I must confess I've been miserable since I heard your health was failing on Nanda."

"Thank you for that," Odo smiled. "But you shouldn't worry. As you now know, my relocation was part of a larger plan. But it was not my plan. I am just a servant of the Source. It led me to Nanda. And now it has led me to two Hives, which have reinvigorated me. I am feeling like a young boy again. I owe that to you."

De-o-Nu rushed up to them and sat heavily on the ground. His eyes were almost closed and his voice was slurred. "You two aren't having any fun! Come dance with us," he commanded.

He grabbed the whisky bottle Dave and Odo had been drinking from and took a long drink.

“Not a chance of that, brother,” Dave laughed. “Here we are the size of little children. That drunken mob would step on us and crush us like bugs.”

De-o-Nu frowned at them. “You know, you guys are just boring.” He scowled and tried to get up to leave. Instead, he rolled over and passed out next to them. Dave grabbed another blanket and covered his friend as best as he could, and then sat with Odo again.

“Yes, Dave, I love your friends too,” Odo said looking at the snoring Gallicean. Looking around the camp, it was clear that most of the crowd had gone back to their cabins or passed out on the ground. A single Gallicean woman turned off the music and stumbled toward her cabin. “Quite a party, don’t you think?”

“Yes it was,” Dave smiled. “I was just thinking we don’t know which cabin is for us. I guess we all sleep out here tonight.”

“Not just yet, Dave,” Odo said. “I think our night is just beginning.”

“What do you mean?” he replied.

“You didn’t notice the others watching us?” Odo asked. “I suppose not. You certainly remember the Nan are called the invisible people in the home galaxy? Apparently, Nan settled this planet as well.”

“There are Nan here?” Dave asked. “I haven’t noticed anything. What do we do now?”

"Just lay back and close your eyes, Dave," Odo said as he lay down. "Pretend you are trying to sleep and let's see what happens. And don't be frightened. I sense no danger from them."

"How many do you see, Odo?" Dave asked.

"Hundreds. But please be quiet," Odo demanded.

Dave lay quietly with his eyes closed for several minutes. His heart was pounding wildly in his chest and he feared a mob could come and kill him before he could act. He tried to push those thoughts out of his mind, but Odo's comment about his death was still vivid in his thoughts. Perhaps these Hive guardians sensed the threat to their safety he posed and were here to eliminate it. He squeezed his eyes tightly and tried not to think at all.

Suddenly a gag was pushed into his mouth and several hands were holding him down. He felt ropes being wrapped around him. After a few seconds, he was lifted off the ground and carried away. His eyes were open and he could see several others ahead of him carrying Odo. He couldn't move his arms or legs. He saw Fa-a-Di's sleeping body as they rushed across the opening and into the forest again. Looking around he could see dozens of others running along with them. Every few minutes a different group would take over for the three carrying him and then they would continue. He could see the forest was denser here and surmised they were headed downhill. After another ten minutes, he was lifted into a boat of some kind which set off across the broad river they had seen earlier in the day. It took another ten minutes to cross the river and then the group moved back into the forest. It was just a couple minutes later when he found himself in some kind of rig that was being pulled upward. When it stopped, he was pulled out and carried through a door and set into a chair. His limbs were freed momentarily and then he was tied to the arms of the chair.

A number of lights were turned on and he clenched his eyes from the brightness. When he was able to look, he saw Odo tied to the next chair and at least fifty humans in the large room. Most of them were women and all were around four feet tall. One of the women approached them and smiled. She was young and very shapely. Her face was clean and quite beautiful with bright green eyes, framed by flaming red hair. She came to Dave and kissed his hands, speaking a language he could not understand. Then she went to Odo and did the same thing. Odo began to talk back to her, which clearly shocked her deeply. The others moved back in fear.

"What is she saying, Odo?" Dave asked. "And how do you know her language?"

Odo smiled at Dave, saying, "She is speaking the ancient Nan dialect. I have had that language added to our database. Let me talk some more to her. If I can get my hands free, I can upload it to your communicator." He turned to the woman and spoke some more. Her expression softened into a smile. After a couple minutes of conversation, she untied Odo. He explained carefully what he wanted to do. The woman came over to Dave and gingerly pulled the communicator from his ear and gave it to Odo, who tapped it against his own. Then he asked the woman to reinsert the device in his ear. After she did so, she kissed Dave on the cheek and said, "I'm sorry, I hope I didn't hurt you."

"No, not at all," Dave replied. "Thank you." She looked blankly at him.

"You can understand her, but she has no communicator," Odo said. "I'll do the talking."

Odo talked to her some more and she replied giggling, "No, Elder Pak, we are not the guardians, although we serve them. They told us of the visit by you and Admiral Dave and asked us to welcome you and take you to meet them. I must apologize for the use of force, but the other creatures are very bizarre and we fear them."

Odo spoke some more and the group of Nan were hanging on his every word. After several minutes, the bindings were released and each of the Nan hugged both Odo and Dave and begged their forgiveness for the rough handling. The woman came to Dave and said, "Admiral Dave, I have been asked to take you to meet one of the guardians tonight. She asked for you personally. My only concern is I cannot understand your language. If you have a problem, I won't know what to do."

Odo laughed and joined them. He pulled the communicator from his ear and slipped it into hers. He spoke to them in the ancient tongue, "There, you should be able to understand each other."

Dave said, "Can you understand me? I don't even know your name."

She blushed and replied, "I am Dar Lini, and yes I can understand you now. Thank you Elder Pak."

Odo was laughing. "Did you hear that Dave? Her name is Dar Lini. It sounds like Darlene, doesn't it?"

"Let's not go there right now, Odo," Dave answered. "Okay Dar Lini, take me where you want me to go."

"Just call me Lini, Dave," she replied. "Dar is my family name." She took his hand and led him back out of the room and into the rig that lowered them back to the forest floor. Other homes were built into all the surrounding trees. All were dark at this late hour. There must have been hundreds of tree houses in this part of the forest. Dave wondered how the Galliceans had never noticed this before. Lini was very sure footed on the dark path and Dave struggled to remain standing and not fall too far behind.

After several minutes, she stopped and came back to him, taking his hand again. "I'm sorry Admiral Dave. I forgot you are not one of us." She led him down a narrow trail that ended at the edge of the river which moved slowly around a wide bend. The two moons of the planet illuminated them and the water like a full moon on Earth. She motioned him to stop and wait. She pulled off her clothes and set them in a neat pile. She pulled Odo's communicator from her ear, set it on her clothes, and then walked over to Dave. She took his hands and he tried not to look at her naked body. "You wait here, and I'll be right back." She kissed his hands and waded out into the river. When the water was waist deep, she dived in. Dave sat on the river bank watching the water and the thin clouds drifting by above them. Here he was on a strange planet with a beautiful young woman, wishing he was somewhere else. He thought about running away, but in the night, he had no idea where he was or how to get back to the camp. Why wasn't Odo here to keep him from himself. He heard a splash and saw Lini coming out of the water, with rivulets of waters pouring off her hair and down her chest and thighs. He wanted to look away but could not force his eyes to move. She smiled at him as he stood to greet her.

As she approached, she pulled him downward and threw her arms around his neck, pressing her lips against his. He tried to resist, but soon found himself kissing her back. When she released him, his shirt was wet and he was panting for air. She stroked his cheek and said, "I'm glad you find me pretty, Admiral Dave."

He stammered for words, but could only say, "You are very beautiful, Lini, and please just call me Dave." Thankfully, she did not have the communicator in her ear so he was certain she could not understand him.

She smiled again and giggled. "Okay Dave. I think you are very handsome as well."

"You can understand me now?" he asked. "How is that?"

"The guardians have enabled it Dave," she said. "They do many such things here. One of them is coming here to see you. She should be here soon. That's why I was in the river. I was calling her."

As she spoke, two blue eyes peered out of the water. Dave saw them and was shocked. They were exactly like the eyes of the Zula on Nan. He walked past Lini who was beginning to put her clothes back on. At the water's edge, he lay on the pebbly bank and crawled forward until he was inches from the Zula. He smiled and said, "I should have known Zula would be here."

"Not just the Zula, Dave. Don't you remember me?" the creature thought.

"Ulook, is that you?" he gasped. "How is that possible? You are from another galaxy. You can't be here."

"It's good to see you too, Dave Brewster," Ulook replied. "I have missed you. But I think it's pretty clear that I am here."

"I don't understand," he sighed. "How did you get here?"

"You're not even trying, are you?" Ulook laughed. "You used to be so grounded. What happened?"

"The Zula are guardians of all natural Hives. You can move freely among them to make certain they are all safe," he answered. "Is that close?"

"That is pretty close, my friend," she said. "But I can't say any more tonight. Your friends will be stirring in the Gallicean camp soon and will notice that you and Odo are missing. We don't want a bunch of crazed Galliceans flying all over Zulanan trying to find you."

"What do you want me to do, Ulook?" he asked.

"Tomorrow, you and your friends will make the pilgrimage to the sacred temple. The others will be in a hurry to leave after that. I want you to convince them to stay another night. I have programmed a course into your shuttle that will lead you all over the ocean. They can set the shuttle on hover there. All of you should don pressure suits and jump in the ocean. We will be there to meet you. There is so much you all need to know," Ulook said.

"It may be difficult to convince Fa-a-Di," Dave replied. "He had a great time tonight, but will likely be feeling bad tomorrow."

"You have to convince them Dave. Odo will help you. If you must, demand to be left behind here. The others and I will take care of you and Odo and make sure you get home if they do go, but I sincerely doubt that. Obu Neela told you things were going to go quickly now. The success of your mission depends on being in the ocean with us tomorrow," Ulook urged.

"I'll do my best," Dave replied. "If worse comes to worst, Odo and I will be here."

"Just one more thing, Dave," Ulook said. "Please bring Dar Lini with you. Find another pressure suit for her. She has been a great friend of ours, and we owe it to her to join this sacred mission. I love you, Dave. After I leave, kiss her lips again. When you do, you'll be back at the Gallicean camp with Odo."

"Why kissing? You know I'm married," Dave argued.

"Just do what you're told," Ulook laughed and disappeared into the water.

Dave stood up and brushed the dust from his uniform. When he turned, he saw Lini standing on a boulder to make her as tall as him. "You heard all of that, didn't you?"

Lini laughed. "One cannot argue with guardians Dave." He walked over to her and she threw her arms around his neck and kissed him. He opened his eyes and was standing in the clearing with the sleeping Galliceans. Odo and Lini were sleeping under a blanket next to his feet. He lay down and pulled another blanket over his body and tried to relax. Soon, he was asleep.

CHAPTER 25

Major Ulan Makwee was more nervous than ever as the Kalidus lifted off from Lagamar Opa and made another slag run toward the Lagamar sun. The controls were sluggish due to the massive load the ship carried today. Rising tensions around the Society kept most people tied to their planets where the fleets of star cruisers could provide some level of protection. This was to be the last disposal mission for the time being, so the hold was packed to the brim with the most dangerous byproducts of the mining process. The remaining slag would have to stay on Lagamar Opa until the threat level subsided. Two star cruisers would normally accompany the Kalidus, but today urgent shipments of metal needed to get to Lagamar Ulu to support the completion of four new cruisers there. News of the attack on Nan shot through the system, including the presumed death of Elder Odo Pak and his family when their residence was blasted from space. All efforts had to be focused on defending the Lagamar planets. Allowing one small disposal ship to run alone was a risk that had to be taken. If the materials in the hold had been blasted from an orbiting ship, clouds of radioactive vapor would circle the planet causing catastrophic lost of life.

Helmsman Balik Namm turned to Ulan and said, “All sensors read negative, Major. We should arrive at optimal distance in five minutes.”

“Is there unusual sunspot activity today, Balik?” Ulan asked. “I’m getting a lot of static and distortion on my headset.”

“I’m getting it too, sir, but Central Command did not mention anything about solar flares,” the helmsman responded.

"Forget about it. We have urgent business and I want to get back to Lagamar Opa as quickly as we can," the major said. "I'll ask the hangar crew to perform a systems check when we get back." Drops of sweat began to appear on their faces as the sun loomed larger and larger in front of them. The temperature on board was rising just as it should.

"Thirty seconds to yaw distance, Major!" Balik shouted. As he spoke, forty star cruisers appeared on their sensors, having just raced around the sun. "Shit! The enemy is on us Major!"

"Give me control, Balik!" Ulan shouted. The major performed a perfect yaw so the sun was now directly behind them, along with the enemy fleet. "Full thrust now!"

A voice crackled over their speakers, "Opa ship, surrender now or we will blow you into dust!"

"Major, we can't go any faster with this slag load sir!" Balik shouted. "One of the cruisers is gaining on us quickly. What are your orders?"

"Why haven't they destroyed us already?" Ulan asked. "They can certainly tell that we are unarmed. What are they waiting for?"

"Major, only one cruiser is following us now," Balik responded. "The others are headed toward the planets. I've sent a distress call to all planetary commands."

Ulan pressed a button on his console to open communications with the approaching ship. "Captain, this is not a warship, please power down your weapons. We are unarmed."

The voice over the speaker was laughing. "Do you think I care if you're armed or not, Opa? Your ship has new technology that we want. Prepare to be boarded. Power down now to save us all a lot of trouble."

"Major, what should we do?" Balik asked. "They'll just kill us or put us in a work camp anyway."

"Captain, I am powering down now," Ulan said to the other ship. The bridge crew turned and looked at him with disbelief on their faces.

"A wise decision, Opa. We will be in tractor beam distance in one minute. Don't do anything stupid or you will pay with your lives," the enemy captain said.

Ulan rose from his seat and walked over to Balik and whispered in his ear, then returned to the command chair. Balik was now visibly trembling as he held his hand inches above the power system panel. The enemy ship filled the view screen aimed behind the ship. "Nothing stupid Captain," he said to the other ship smiling.

"Major, the ship is only two hundred yards behind us now," Balik stuttered with fear.

"Now!" Ulan shouted as he pulled the lever that opens the bay doors and activates the ram. One thousand tons of radioactive slag was pushed out into space. Balik slammed his hand on the panel and the thrusters shot from zero to full thrust instantly. The crew was plastered into their seats as the ship accelerated wildly. The exhaust superheated the slag and pushed it toward the cruiser which had lowered her defensive array to activate the tractor beam.

The enemy captain saw the deception and ordered the array up and weapons brought on line. As the weapons officer reached for his panel, a fifty ton chunk of red-hot slag smashed through the hull and onto the bridge. The hull was breached in dozens of places and the ship drifted backward along with the searing slag. The thrusters exploded and the pieces of ship and her crew fell into the solar atmosphere and were vaporized.

"Shut off the thrusters, Balik!" Ulan shouted over the whine of the engines. Suddenly it became very quiet on the bridge. Ulan went to each member of the crew and asked if they were okay. Last, he came to Balik and kneeled next to him. "Are you okay, old friend?"

Sweat was pouring down the helmsman's face and he was breathing heavily. "Ulan, I thought we were all going to die back there, or at least spend our last days in a slave labor camp. What happened to the enemy ship?"

"It was destroyed by the hot slag, Balik," Ulan replied. "I sincerely doubt anyone on board survived. I hope you can live with that."

Balik laughed. "Live with it? That was awesome Major. You saved us all."

"Yeah, but for how long?" Ulan asked. "There are still forty star cruisers attacking our planets. And we can't even join the fight since we have no weapons. If we try to go home, their ships will finish the job the other failed to do." He stood and looked at the viewscreen. Only a field of stars could be seen, with one slightly brighter in the center. "We were only at maximum velocity for a few minutes, and I have no idea where we are now."

Balik was checking star charts and the ship's tracking computer. After a few moments, he said, "Well, that bright star is Lagamar, and it's now twenty light-years away. We're actually a lot closer to Nan now than home. What are your orders now, sir?"

"Tell the chef to prepare a gourmet dinner with wine for the crew," Ulan smiled. "I doubt anyone will interrupt us out here in open space. Tomorrow, we'll head for Nan. God knows how long the battle in Lagamar will continue. But we can't do anything about that right now. Perhaps the Elders of Nan can tell us more."

The remaining forty enemy star cruisers broke into groups of ten. One group each was sent to simultaneously attack the Vol, Opa, Ulu and Boley planets. Brother Luka Nance was commanding the entire mission and the smaller group to Lagamar 7, now renamed Lagamar Boley. It had taken the Supreme Leader months to forge an alliance large enough to gather this fleet. Tens of thousands of Brotherhood agents had been training on Narta Ela under the leadership of Marshall Passor Valka. Although he had done a good job with the soldiers, Luka despised Passor to his soul. While Passor was an adequate President for the High Council, he allowed Dave Brewster and Fa-a-Di to ridicule the Brotherhood and ultimately destroy the Society. Luka knew one day he would get his revenge against his former master, but that was not a thought for today.

Today was his opportunity to reestablish the Brotherhood as the preeminent power in the galaxy. After the Grand Conclave, the members of the Brotherhood were hated and rejected around the Society. After the battles today, they would be feared again and no human or Gallicean would stand in their way. Once their pride was restored, they could happily move to the Ulagong Galaxy and help the Supreme Leader rebuild their forces and weaponry. Ten Hives manned by Brotherhood agents would be an unbeatable force, even though it could take decades to come to pass. But time was on their side.

Luka was not a fool. He knew the real prize today was Lagamar Ulu. If his forces could damage or destroy their star cruiser factories, the rest of the planets would fall quickly. He sent the ten best ships there. There were five or six cruisers protecting each planet, but he was not there to fight ship to ship, but instead to target specific sites and instill the appropriate level of panic and terror in the hearts of the locals. To make that happen, one captain was given specific orders to target the Mount Alila Temple. The Ulu had great faith and confidence in their priests. Just as he had done on Nan, now he would take out the highest religious authority on that world.

The Opa and Vol planets were not significant targets, although he knew they too must be taught a lesson about respect. Those smaller ships were ordered to attack mines and large plantations at random, but keeping most of their fire power for the cities. Blasting an open pit mine might be fun but wouldn't have the same impact as targeting hospitals and schools. The key mission for those ships was to keep the local ships engaged so they could not assist on the other planets.

Even though it was not a real threat, Luka wanted to lead the attack on the Boley planet himself. He still remembered clearly how Fa-a-Di had held him over the open atmosphere and threatened to drop him to certain death. After today, the general would wish he had done that! The Galliceans had been building new cities for the Boley and many thousands had relocated there to staff new hospitals, schools and universities. The Galliceans had some crazy idea about making the Boley active participants in the Lagamar-Nan Free Society. How foolish they were? Soon enough, those migrants will be begging to come back home and forget the day they tried to get involved in the business of another galaxy.

“Brother Nance,” Captain Zinga Abalon said, interrupting Luka’s thoughts.

“What is it Captain?” Luka snapped.

“Our forward sensors do not indicate any ships in orbit over Lagamar 7, which is odd. There should be some defenders here, don’t you think?” Zinga asked.

“That is unusual,” Luka replied. “Perhaps that Opa ship notified them. If they’re smart, they relocated any ships here to Lagamar Ulu. We’ll find out soon enough when our ships arrive there. If that’s the case, we’ll head there and help them out. We can come back here anytime.” Luka smiled and took a sip of coffee. “When will we be in range?”

“Any moment now, sir,” Zinga replied. “I’ve ordered all ships to activate their defensive arrays and arm weapon systems.”

“Excellent! Have your sensor crew locate any new floating cities. We want to target them first. Keep shooting until your fingers bleed,” Luka laughed.

“Aye-aye, Brother,” Zinga replied as he turned his attention to his crew and barked orders. The ships dove into the upper layers of atmosphere. Zinga dispersed the fleet and told them where to attack. “We have a large floating city under construction ahead, Brother. I’m targeting it now.” A plasma bolt shot out and pounded the city, where buildings exploded and Boley could be seen flying away as quickly as possible.

"Captain, send some troop shuttles to land there," Luka ordered. "I'll go with them. I want to see those bastards pay face to face." Before the captain could speak, Luka bolted off the bridge.

"Stop firing!" Zinga ordered. "We don't want to hit our own troops." Ten shuttles flew ahead of the cruiser and headed to the city with the cruiser providing cover. Within a few minutes, hundreds of Brotherhood agents in pressure suits scrambled through the city, shooting anything in their path.

The Kong-Fa rose through the atmosphere at full speed, closing quickly on the aft of the Brotherhood ship as it yawed to face the attacker. Captain Ka-a-Fa ordered his ship to fire and a withering blast of plasma smashed the forward defensive array. Captain Zinga frantically ordered the ship to turn to show her shields to the enemy, but the second blast smashed into the bridge first, incinerating the crew and causing the ship to shudder and break up. A cloud of escape pods littered the sky as the cruiser fell downward, barely missing the edge of the city. It disappeared into the depths of the gas below. "Colonel Um-de-Bo, get your men down there now to defend the city!" Ka-a-Fa shouted.

The lower bay doors opened and hundreds of Gallicean Marines took to the sky, chanting the ancient battle cries and waving their Baloos over their heads. Luka and his men had witnessed the destruction of their ship and the approach of the enemy troops. They fired at them and were met with heavy return fire. Once the Marines had landed, the real battle began as they engaged the agents. Waves of blaster shots filled the air and the screams of death were all around them.

The Galliceans cornered the largest group of agents in a small city square. The buildings were heavily damaged from the battle and both sides tried to find cover where they could. Within minutes it became clear this would be a battle of attrition, with the larger surviving force winning. Luka was happy with that. He knew there were nine other star cruisers that would come to his aid. All he needed was time.

Um-de-Bo knew the facts as well. Two other Gallicean cruisers would be jumping here in the next few minutes, but for now, only Kong-Fa could protect them. He turned to his commanders and said, "Men, this battle will define us forever. We cannot win if we play a shoot and hide scenario. We couldn't call ourselves Gallicean Marines if we did that either. We must attack now and take the battle to them, regardless of the cost. Are you with me?" All of the officers shouted their approval. "Good. There is a group of agents near the far building. I think that is their command structure. We need to take them out. Give me fifty brave men, but no more than two of you can join me. Make sure their Baloos are sharp! Go now. You have two minutes."

Luka was communicating with the nearest ship when the assault began. The ship's captain said he could be there in five minutes at the most. He peered out and saw fifty Marines running and flying toward them and chanting. He ordered his men to fire. Just as they raised their weapons, the Marines threw their Baloos to their right sides and raised their blasters in one hand and war blades in the other.

Plasma blasts filled the open space and troops on both sides were blown to pieces or lay bleeding on the ground. The agents fired again and the lead Marines collapsed to the ground, including Um-de-Bo who died instantly from a blast to his chest. The remaining Marines took to the air and fired relentlessly on the enemy, who began to retreat. Luka ordered his troops to stand their ground. Suddenly, the Baloos flew back into Luka's group. He saw his best men eviscerated and maimed all around him. He shouted for medics just as Um-de-Bo's Baloo tore through his back, severing his spine and leaving a foot of its bloody blade protruding from his chest. He fell over dead. The second ship never arrived, having been intercepted by the next Gallicean cruiser to arrive.

With the leadership dead, the agents quickly surrendered and were chained together. Following the ancient rites, a group of doctors and priests joined the Marines and helped to remove the rank insignia, daggers, a DNA sample, and name tags from each fallen solder from both sides. Those articles were placed in black bags and sealed for their families. A prayer was said over each dead soldier and then two of their comrades committed their bodies to the Dar-Fa by dropping them over the edge.

CHAPTER 26

Dave Brewster slept very well after his adventure with Lini and Ulook. He dreamt of Lubna, the mysterious gas planet Fak Mondoka told him about. He was floating in space a few thousand miles over the swirling bands of gas. He could see the two terrestrial moons bathed the reflected light from the massive planet. He noticed he was wearing only his uniform yet was not surprised he was breathing normally in the vacuum of space. It could be said that traveling in Universal Power had changed his perspective. As he watched the colorful bands moving against one another, he saw one of the massive snakes breach the surface of the clouds and then dive back below. It was at least five hundred miles long and dark brown with mustard yellow spots. The site of the creature did not frighten Dave. Instead, he felt warm and safe in its presence.

Suddenly, Dave was riding on the back of the beast, plunging downward into the gas. He thought he might be thrown off, but the creature was very gentle and seemed to be reassuring him telepathically. Dave lay down on his stomach and stretched his arms out to hold on. The animal's skin was soft, elastic and quite warm. It seemed to be enjoying his company very much. It continued diving deeper and deeper into the atmosphere, and Dave knew he should have been crushed to death by the pressure by this point, but he still felt happy and safe. The creature dived through the last layers of cloud and into a clear level of air. The hard surface at the center of the gas giant stretched out below him. He imagined he was fifty or sixty thousand miles below the gas surface so far above him. The surface was flat as a table with no distinguishing features in this area. It was like a silver billiard ball, five or ten thousand miles in diameter.

He heard an odd singing sound and looked around. Dozens more of the giant snakes were flying through the air next to them. They seemed to be communicating with each other with their odd music, a harmonious combination of dolphin and whale song. The animals had heads and faces like whales, with large expressive eyes. Looking from side to side, he felt as thought they were smiling at him with their eyes glistening in the sunlight. The snakes began to spin and dive around one another, as if dancing or just playing together. Dave was filled with joy in their company.

The singing stopped suddenly. Far ahead, Dave could see countless tornadoes grinding away at the planet's surface. He realized he was seeing the base of a Dar-Fa. Even though their song stopped, the creatures seemed to be accelerating toward the funnels. Dave began to feel very apprehensive, knowing he would fall off the giant beast in the beating winds and heavy rain inside the swirling storm. He tried to hold on as tightly as he could, but his fingers were smarting and his hands let go. He felt his body float off the animal and became terrified at the thought of being alone on this alien world. He could see the snakes far ahead of them and tried to follow.

Then Dave was one of the snakes. He felt his body undulating to catch the wind. He was beginning to catch up to the others now. Where he had been a tiny speck on the back of the beast, he was now as large as them. He felt their minds reaching out to him, but could not understand their thoughts. A smaller snake moved toward him and touched his skin. His mind touched the other, who thought, "Welcome Dave. We are the Bolofaz, and this is our home world. My name is Ondeen and I have been chosen to be your guide here. I sense you have been on a world like this before."

“This is a wonderful dream, Ondeen,” Dave thought back. “And yes, I have been to several gas planets before, riding on the chest of my brother, Fa-a-Di.”

“You are a friend of the galli then,” Ondeen replied. “We have seen them, but they avoided our planet out of fear. That was a shame. Perhaps you can let them know that we are not dangerous to them.”

Dave laughed. “But this is only a dream. I will forget all of this when I awaken in the morning.”

“That will be up to you, Dave,” Ondeen replied. “We are approaching the helix. This is where we feed and play. I hope you enjoy it as much as we do.” As he finished speaking, the group flew into the sea of tornadoes. The Bolofaz opened their large mouths and breathed in the air laden with dust from the hard surface. Dave followed suit and could taste the sweet and savory flavors of the material around him. One by one, he could see the creatures diving into the funnels and shooting upward. He followed Ondeen into a very large vortex and felt himself rising up through the atmosphere. He was being pclted by the winds and debris, but felt warm and relaxed. The ride was exhilarating as he spun around in the tornado. He then followed Ondeen out of the funnel and into the open sky again. The Bolofaz were now thousands of miles up in the gas. Dave could feel the refreshingly cold rain washing his body. The liquid seemed to permeate his skin and his body relished the fluids. He was totally at peace flying with his friends and playing in the Dar-Fa. Now he knew why the Galliceans loved these storms so dearly. He hit the wall of the Dar-Fa and felt his body shaking violently.

Dave woke to find Fa-a-Di shaking him gently. “Dave, there’s been another attack,” his friend said.

"What?" Dave murmured, still half asleep. "What happened?"

"Last night, a fleet of ships attacked the Lagamar system," he replied. "I'm sorry to tell you that Colonel Um-de-Bo died in that battle along with two hundred other Marines."

"Oh my God!" Dave blurted. "But he was on the Kong-Fa and on his way to Tak-Makla. How did this happen?"

"Shortly after they dropped us off on Gallicea, Ka-a-Fa received orders to travel to Lagamar Boley. Our intelligence forces had heard rumors an attack on Lagamar was imminent. The ship arrived there just before the attack began," Fa-a-Di replied. "There are also reports of attacks on the Opa ship Kalidus as well as the other inhabited planets in that system. The reports are not good, brother. Information is sketchy, but we expect to hear more soon."

"What do we do now, brother?" Dave asked.

"There is nothing we can do now, Dave," the Gallicean answered. "The Kong-Fa will be returning to Gallia later today to make a full report. Since you met Um-de-Bo just a few days ago, I thought you should know." Fa-a-Di stood and walked away, then stopped and returned. "One last thing, Dave," he began, "who in the world is that woman with Odo?"

Dave climbed to his feet and said, "Her name is Dar Lini, and this is her home planet. I told you I sensed life here. Odo and I were taken to their camp last night after the party here ended. That's why we need to stay here one more night. There is something amazing here that we have to see."

De-o-Nu had heard the conversation and jumped in, "That's not possible, Dave. I need to contact the families of the injured and fallen soldiers. That sacred duty cannot be delayed. They deserve to know what happened."

"Fa-a-Di, please stay here one more day," Odo begged. "What Dave is saying is true. De-o-Nu and his brother can leave, but you have to stay here. They can handle the notifications, and you can contact the families personally tomorrow."

"I don't know Odo," Fa-a-Di winced. "Last night was fun, but I'm already feeling my skin crawl being here. I've completed my Sojourn and need to get back to work."

"Brother, please stay with Odo and me here," Dave replied. "Look at this young woman. Here is a person who has lived here all her life. I've seen their village in the tree tops not far from here. There are hundreds of homes there. All of you have cajoled me for claiming there is intelligent life on this planet. Well, here is the proof. Certainly this is significant enough to warrant one more day."

"That is pretty amazing," De-o-Nu said. He put his hand on Fa-a-Di's shoulder. "Brother, I will handle the notifications today and return early tomorrow to pick you up. I will tell everyone you mourn their losses and will contact them soon."

"Dave, why do you do this to me?" Fa-a-Di scowled. "Of all the places to be stuck, here I am on this rock. Do you have another good reason I should do this?"

Dave thought for a moment and replied, "Of course you remember the Grand Conclave, but do you remember the Zula we showed there?"

"Ulook!" De-o-Nu shouted. "Of course we remember her."

"She's here," Dave replied. "I spoke to her last night and we will see her later."

"That's not possible," Fa-a-Di laughed. He looked around the campsite and suddenly noticed dozens of humans at the edge, trying to conceal themselves in the brush. "Well, then again, it seems like anything is possible here. I'm breathing an oxygen atmosphere. It seems that Nan have been living here for generations. Why not Ulook? You have your day, Dave Brewster. I hope it's worth it."

"Just one more thing then," Dave smiled. "How many communicators can we get that will fit someone like Dar Lini? They only speak the ancient Nan language and I want you to talk to them."

De-o-Nu laughed. "A star cruiser will be coming here in a few hours to pick me up. I'll ask them to bring as many as they can. I assume you can upload the Nan language?"

"Of course! That's great news! And we'll all need pressure suits tonight. We're going for a swim in the ocean," Dave finished.

CHAPTER 27

The Kong-Fa was diverted from Gallia by Fa-a-Di. It headed instead to the Gallicea system so he could personally mourn with the crew for their losses and then celebrate their victory. When the ship arrived, De-o-Nu and his brother were jumped by maklans on board, where Ka-a-Fa provided a full briefing on what was known about the Battle of Lagamar. The Boley planet was heavily damaged before the additional Gallicean battle cruisers arrived. After the first two Brotherhood ships were destroyed, the rest of the fleet fled the solar system as quickly as they could. The only reported hand-to-hand combat occurred in the battle that killed Um-de-Bo and Luka Nance. The other ships targeted the few floating cities that were under construction. The floatation systems on two failed and the rubble disappeared into the lower atmosphere. Five more Gallicean warships were now on the way there to take care of casualties and provide more security.

The other planets fared somewhat better, as they each had a number of star cruisers for defense, although specific intelligence was hard to obtain or verify. Those planetary leaders were still sifting through reports and speaking to their military leaders to get a clearer picture of the situation on the ground. The attackers did not engage the defending ships, but instead targeted cities and major industrial facilities on those planets. Damage reports from the Opa and Vol planets showed minor damage as the attacking ships seemed to be quite weak. Once those ships were pursued by the defenders, they fled the area and returned to deep space. Each of the capital cities reported moderate damage to government buildings.

Lagamar Ulu suffered the most damage. The attackers focused their efforts on major defense industry sites. Two star cruiser assembly plants were completely leveled, along with twenty associated subcomponent plants nearby. Fortunately, the three other assembly plants were missed entirely, most likely due to poor intelligence. The attacking ships blasted away at unimproved lands miles from those locations. For once, the thick blanket of smog may have saved lives. Much of the capital city was also flattened. The President and his team were at the Mount Alila Temple at the time of the attack. There were spotty reports the temple was also a target, although no information on that location had been reported when the Kong-Fa was jumped back to the Milky Way. None of the leadership on the Boley, Opa or Vol planets had any contact with Lagamar Ulu.

De-o-Nu and his brother spent the rest of the day contacting the families of the dead and wounded. It was heartbreaking for De-o-Nu. Those men had been his crew and his friends. When he spoke to Um-de-Bo's wife, they both cried and tried to console each other. Later that day, De-o-Nu would ask his wife to travel to Gallia to be with her personally. Captain Ka-a-Fa made arrangements for the effects of the fallen Galliceans to be sent to their families by another star cruiser diverted to Gallicea for this somber mission. Before they had jumped back, an unmanned funeral probe was launched to Narta Ela with the effects from the Brotherhood agents who had died.

Looking out the window, De-o-Nu could see the terminator move over the site of the camp where Fa-a-Di was staying. Soon, they would be traveling to the ocean to be with Ulook. He remembered her dearly. He thought Dave Brewster was crazy for having him evacuate the Zula from Lagamar Vol and delivering them to Nan. When he was in the water with her and felt her touch him, he changed his mind. In those few minutes, she touched his heart and soul and he knew he would never be the same again. The only other extremely spiritual experience he had in life was his journey into the Hive days ago. He swirled the whisky in his glass and watched it. "I'm a fool!" he said to himself. "Dammit, I need a maklan!"

As if on cue, Mitch Nolobitamore appeared in his quarters. "De-o-Nu, Jake asked me to come here to help out. I heard about your journey into the Hive and wanted to hear the details," he said.

De-o-Nu laughed and clapped his hands together. "Mitch, this is an amazing coincidence! Can you tell where Jake is right now?"

"He's in the camp with Dave and Fa-a-Di," Mitch responded. "Why do you ask?"

"I need you to jump me down there with a pressure suit," he replied.

Dave Brewster had his bubble suit on again. He and Jake were climbing on board the Gallicean shuttle for their ride to the ocean, just as De-o-Nu suddenly appeared right behind them and followed them up the gangway. "De-o-Nu, this is a surprise. I didn't think you were going to make it here," Dave said.

"Brother, after the day I've had, I need something to distract me from my emotions," he replied as he strapped himself in. "The only good thing about today is that it's almost over," he laughed.

Fa-a-Di entered the cabin and smiled when he saw his dear friend. "De-o-Nu, this is a blessing. How did it go today?"

"Not well, as you can imagine. Everyone has been notified, and they all know you will call them soon," his brother-in-law replied. "Just so you are informed, Brother Luka Nance was also killed in the battle on Lagamar Boley. Um-de-Bo's Baloo killed him instantly."

Fa-a-Di sat next to the shuttle captain and strapped himself in. "That's a damned shame. I hated that idiot with all my heart, but death is the most extreme punishment. I will pray for his soul tonight as well."

After Odo and Lini joined them, the shuttle rose slowly off the ground. Lini provided directions, and in seconds, the ship hovered over her village in the trees. Hundreds of locals stood on their balconies and waved at the ship. "My God, I can't believe my eyes," Fa-a-Di sighed. "My people have been coming here for the Sojourn for countless generations, and no one ever saw this. That's almost impossible to believe."

"Don't worry, dear general," Odo said smiling. "There is much in the universe that can only be seen by one willing to look. Your people came here in fear and sorrow. The last thing you wanted to see was the truth. Your ancestors did attack this planet most viciously, but they did not destroy the life here. This is just one small village. Lini, what can you tell us about others on this world?"

She was almost too terrified to speak, never having been in a flying vehicle before, but Odo held her hand tightly and she finally replied, "I have been to several other villages with others like me. I am told that there are cities full of our people all over the planet, but we do not travel extensively, so I cannot verify that is true."

On her direction, the shuttle moved away from the village and followed the wide river toward the sea. As the vessel left the forest, it crossed wide plains where small farms could be seen dotting the landscape. Every few miles, another small village sat at the intersection of dirt or gravel roads. After another half-hour of travel, the ship moved over a cliff and out over the ocean. The sun was setting behind them and within minutes it was pitch black. The vessel continued for twenty more minutes until it reached the location Ulook had programmed and began to drop in altitude, until it hovered a few feet over the water. The sea was calm and reflected the light of the two full moons overhead. The pilot opened the bay doors and the team made sure their pressure suits were secure. Dave could not help but look at Dar Lini who looked so tiny in her bubble suit. It had only been last night when she stood nude in front of him smiling. Now she was clearly scared. The group sat on the edge of the opening with their feet dangling over the edge. Dave put his arm around Lini's shoulders and could feel her body trembling through her suit. "Lini, it's going to be okay," he said. "Ulook will take care of all of us. This is the greatest adventure of all of our lives. Don't be afraid."

She leaned against him and replied, "Thank you Dave, but I am a simple girl. Flying and diving in the ocean are totally alien to me. Your friends are like giants to me and I'm not sure they are friendly."

Fa-a-Di laughed. "Poor girl! Please don't be frightened by my people. We mean you no harm. We are just the product of our environment. Except of course for my brother-in-law. He is a giant and scares me too sometimes!"

"I don't think that's helping matters, brother," De-o-Nu scowled.

"Lini, these men are my best friends," Dave said. "I trust them with my life. Not so long ago, I was living on my home world in ancient times. I had never seen anything like them or like you. But life is an adventure. I'm sure that's what Ulook is trying to tell you. Just try to relax and enjoy the ride. Tomorrow, you'll be home with your family. I promise."

Jake flew over and landed on Lini's lap. "Imagine all of this from my perspective, Lini. Even you are a giant compared to me. But Dave is right about the Galliceans. They are our friends and mean you no harm. I promise I'll stay near you tonight. If you become too afraid, I'll jump you home in less than a second. Here, let me show you." Lini and Jake disappeared. Dave almost fell over as he had been leaning toward her. In a second, they reappeared. "See, you can be home in an instant, so don't be afraid."

She smiled at Jake and hugged him. "Thanks Jake. I do feel much better now. If I didn't have this helmet on, I'd kiss you." Everyone laughed.

Twenty eye-stalks appeared above the surface of the water. Dave recognized Ulook's eyes and waved. Then he jumped into the water and swam over to her. "Here we are, Ulook, all prepared for the adventure."

"Let's go!" she said. Dave waved for the others to jump in, and in a minute they were swimming and surrounded by dozens of Zula. "Each of you should stay in contact with one or more of us so we can stay in communication. Don't be afraid, we won't lose any of you. Now grab on and come with us."

The Zula dove downward, pulling the others with them. A group of three surrounded Lini, having sensed her fear. They held onto her tightly and Jake was clinging onto her chest. In the upper level of the ocean, thousands of fish could be seen all around them. Several schools spun around them and followed them downward. They all appeared to be gray or silver in the faint moonlight. Deeper and deeper they dove into the black water. After a few minutes, the moonlight had faded and they were in total darkness. Dave could see faint light coming from the eyes of the Zula, providing some view of what was ahead. At this depth, massive fish or whales swam near them, looking for plankton and other tiny organizations to ingest. Still they dove deeper. Dave looked at his heads-up display and noticed the crushing external pressure level. The internal readings were normal, so he ignored it and tried to enjoy the ride.

After twenty more minutes, they arrived at the sea floor and leveled off. Tiny crabs and other life were scurrying around on the ground looking for a quick meal. The ground was very flat with only a few rocks and boulders breaking the level surface. They continued along the surface for some time until a glimmer of light appeared ahead of them. The Zula quickened their pace and rushed forward. Soon an ocean bottom village appeared ahead of them. As they got closer, the apparent village became a massive city. The group moved into the city where towering buildings surrounded them, but they were unlike anything they had seen above the water. This was a Zula city. Tens of thousands of Zula were moving along the streets and going in and out of the buildings. The city was well lit and street signs marked each intersection. The writing was pictographic and in a language unlike any they had seen. Hundreds of Zula saw the strange creatures in pressure suits and began to follow them.

In the center of the city was a clear glass dome with several shorter buildings underneath. Ulook led them to a glass chamber that led into the dome. Once the group was inside, the door closed and the water drained quickly away. "Dave, check your external readings. You should be safe to remove your helmet," Ulook said.

The readings showed normal, but Dave was still concerned. "I don't understand, Ulook. What is this place and why is there a dome here?"

Ulook's eyes frowned at him. "Dave, can't you just trust me? This dome is for Beings like you. Don't you think we have contact with other civilizations?"

Dave began to depressurize his suit and the Galliceans tried to stop him. Jake jumped over to his chest and grabbed his hands. "Dave, I don't know if this is the right thing to do. There are thousands of feet of ocean over your head."

Dave pried his hands free and pulled off the helmet. He breathed deeply and laughed. "Ulook, I don't know how you did this, but the air is so fresh and clean down here." Reluctantly, the others removed their helmets and all were shocked by the normal pressure and atmosphere. The inner door of the chamber opened and the group walked into the dome. The door closed behind them. "Ulook, but don't you need water to breathe?"

Slowly the Zula began to twist and bulge. Their flippers morphed into feet and legs and they stood upright. Within a few seconds, they stood there, looking remarkably human, although nude. They walked over to a rack and pulled on robes and tied them together. "Is this better?" she said in a soft voice. "The transformation is not comfortable, but at least we can work together now." Ulook was now a beautiful woman with black hair, but the same startling eyes. "Follow me please."

Looking around, Dave could see thousands of Zula crowding around the glass dome watching the strange creatures walking inside. He wondered what they must think of the tiny maklans and the giant Galliceans in their city under the waves. Ulook led them into a small building and into a large conference room. Sitting at the table sipping a cup of coffee was Obu Neela, High Priest of the Mount Alila Temple. "It's about time you folks got here," he said as he rose to welcome the others. After everyone was introduced, they all sat together.

CHAPTER 28

Aria Watson and Alana Albright sat in Chief Engineer Lanz Lagerfeld's office. They were there to make their report on the time eddies detected recently. Lanz sat across from them with his hands over his face. The lack of progress was frustrating to all members of the Temporal Command. "You know this report doesn't tell us anything new," he sighed.

"We know Lanz," Aria responded. "We've never seen anything more contradictory than this before. It almost seems someone is trying to cover this up."

"We have contacted the Hive on Tak-Makla, Lanz," Alana interjected. "They've been sending agents into our past to find clues to help us, but without luck to date."

Lanz rose from his desk and carried his coffee mug over to the system outlet and set the cup down. A fresh stream of coffee, milk and honey filled it rapidly. He picked up the cup and walked over to the window and looked out on the early morning in Washington. He sipped the coffee and said, "Yeah, I know we've been doing what we can, but it's just not enough. I'm reluctant to send any more of our people back in time too. Any tiny change to the past could change the future forever. All sane people know that! What's to be gained by changing the past when the changes could destroy the future?"

"Before he went on the Sojourn with Fa-a-Di, Dave mentioned Fola Untor, the Hive engineer from the Society of Humanity," Aria said. "I don't think anyone on our side trusts him. He is also rumored to be in this galaxy now. Perhaps we should find him and question him on this?"

Lanz returned to his chair and sat heavily. Then he propped his feet up on the desk top and leaned back. "We are supposed to find one man in the galaxy who may or may not even be here and question him about time eddies happening on Earth? Even if we could find him, this whole thing might blow up before we got our hands on him."

"We could have the tekkans search for him too," Aria suggested.

"No way! They need to focus on the time eddy situation here. If we start parsing their agents to focus on different things, our little progress would probably grind to a halt," Lanz argued. "There has to be something in the data that we missed. Please check it all again and get back to me before the end of the day."

There was a knock at the door and Muncie Morgan walked into the room, shaking a handful of papers in the air. "Lanz, we think we've isolated something," he said.

"Thank God for that!" Lanz blurted out. "What have you got?"

Muncie stood next to Lanz and laid out the documents on the desk. Aria and Alana stood to better see the information. "You see here," Muncie began, "while we couldn't find any backward trails from the eddies, we were able to measure most of them. Rence and I have been studying the concept of time eddies and have a theory there is a correlation between the dimensions of an eddy and its endpoint in time. It's not much, but it may give us something."

"Interesting," Lanz said. "But it's only a theory, right?"

"I think we have to explore every possibility at this point, Lanz," Aria said. "We really don't have anything else."

"Okay, I know you're right," Lanz replied. "What does your theory tells us about these eddies, Muncie?"

"What was confusing at first is the sheer number and variety of distortions that have occurred. Rence started to see a series of patterns. Three separate patterns that is," Muncie began.

"Only three!" Lanz said excitedly. "That's a very good sign. From what I've seen so far, the whole mess looked random. Finally some progress. Please continue Muncie!"

"The earliest eddies were very narrow and weak. According to our theory, those only brushed the surface of time distortion," Muncie said. "That might imply they were more spatial distortions than temporal."

"Like someone moving from location to location at the same instant?" Alana asked.

"Exactly," Muncie acknowledged. "We can't tell, but it's as if someone came from another system to Earth instantaneously. There was a temporal distortion, but there was no forward or reverse time travel."

"So, we have a trail that some unknown Beings came to Earth," Lanz replied. "Can we tell where they came from?"

"No. Rence has been working nonstop to extend the theory to find a way to tell exactly that," Muncie replied. "Who knows how long that will take or if it is even possible."

"And the second pattern?" Aria asked.

“That was the biggest part of the mystery, Aria,” Muncie replied. “The first and third patterns were fairly clear. The second group was extremely diverse. After isolating those, the similarities within the second group began to appear. They were all quite weak, but a mixture of very broad to more narrow.”

“As if our culprit was searching in time for something, or someone?” Lanz surmised.

“Exactly!” Muncie confirmed. “It also seemed very clear that the searches were of the past only.”

“Shit! If someone went into the past, perhaps everything has already changed,” Lanz interjected. “If they did, we might never know. If they haven’t done it yet, we might all disappear from history at any time. What about the final pattern?”

“They were extremely narrow and quite strong,” Muncie said. “That could mean they were local to this planet but quite far in the past.”

Lanz rose and walked over to the window again. He could see hundreds of shuttles moving through the city around them. “It looks as though our culprit is searching for the ideal spot in time to change. Once he finds it, who knows what happens next?”

“How deep were the eddies, Muncie?” Aria asked. “Does that tell us anything? Can’t we compare previous legitimate jumps to estimate how far back this person is jumping?”

“It’s not precise, Aria,” Muncie sighed. “We don’t know what technology our friend is using. We did the comparison and the best we can come up with is around one thousand years.”

"Oh no!" Aria sighed as she sat down again. "This is starting to make sense."

"What is your theory, Aria?" Lanz demanded. "We don't have time to worry about the impact. We've got to do something!"

"I think our traveler is Fola Untor, the Hive Engineer," she said. "Dave has mentioned to Charlie that he thinks Fola is tied to the Brotherhood. As you know, Dave and Fa-a-Di pretty much brought the High Council and Brotherhood to their knees. Both Dave and Charlie come from that far back. If Fola can stop them from coming here, all of our history will change and the Brotherhood will have never lost power."

"Let's say you're exactly right, Aria," Lanz began. "The good news is we're still talking about Dave and Charlie, so Fola hasn't completed his task yet. I need you, Muncie and Rence to go back in time to the first time any of you met either of them. Somehow, you are going to have to make sure nothing in the stream of time changes. This is a major task and our chances for success aren't very good, but what else can we do?"

"I agree, Lanz," Muncie said. "I've have Rence configure the portal. We should probably go to different times so it's not so obvious. If we leave right away, perhaps there is time to save them."

"Lanz, you don't want me to go too?" Alana asked.

"No. I have another task for you," he replied. "After the others leave, I'll share it with you. It's better than no one knows except you and me."

CHAPTER 29

"Obu, I was so worried about you!" Dave said. "I heard that the Brotherhood attacked Lagamar Ulu and the Mount Alila temple specifically. What happened?"

Obu smiled and patted Dave's hand. "As you can see, I am quite well. The attack on my home world was quite vicious, with many factories and cities heavily damaged. The explosions and fires rapidly increased the smog level all over the planet. My priests and I sat praying in the temple as the clouds and smoke rose and completely enveloped the mountain range and our temple. I feel confident the Source was helping us that day. The directional systems on some Brotherhood ships were also affected and they blasted away at a nearby mountain, destroying only rock and snow, until our defending fleet could force them to flee."

"I am glad to hear that," Fa-a-Di said, "although I will pray tonight for the loss of life on your planet."

"Thank you general," Obu smiled. "You should know your own troops were very brave during the attack on Lagamar Boley. I have seen those who rejoined the Source and can report they are at peace."

"But none of this is why we are here," Ulook interrupted. "There is very little time, Obu."

"Yes, of course you are right," Obu apologized. "I do appreciate your help in this difficult time."

"What has happened will eventually ripple through time even here, regardless of our actions," Ulook frowned. She stood to address the group. "My friends, the past has been changed by a bandit moving through time. We Zula have some control over these things, but before long the change will move through here as well."

"What change?" Odo asked. "Why wasn't I informed?"

"There is nothing you or Obu could have done, blessed Odo," Ulook said. "I'm afraid this change will also affect you."

"What has happened?" Dave asked. "I don't understand."

"After this change reaches us, none of you will be here any longer. I fear some of you may already be dead," Ulook said. "An evil force has changed history by distorting the past in a heinous way. While we can delay its impact, we cannot control time forever. Shortly everything you know will change and this meeting will have never taken place. We have been praying for intervention from the Source, but unfortunately, that cannot succeed. The Source knows only its perfect self. When Beings die, they simple return to it, however, the physical universe can change terribly."

"But there are others," Odo replied. "Do you think there is a chance they might intercede?"

"Who can know that?" Ulook questioned. "Only time will tell."

"What change?" Dave shouted. "You are all being very cryptic. Just tell us."

"That's impossible to know, Dave," Ulook said as she stood behind him and put her hands on his shoulders. "We Zula can sense a temporal wave surging through the universe, but its full contents cannot be known. I can tell you that I will likely be dead after the wave arrives. I can feel it in my bones. I have no regrets and have faith that all will be well."

Dave stood and put his arms around her. She nestled her head into his shoulder, and he could feel her tears on his uniform. She kissed him on the cheek and walked over to De-o-Nu and put her arms around him. "Thank you for rescuing me from Lagamar Vol. I fear that now may never have occurred."

"This is insanity!" Fa-a-Di shouted. "There has to be something we can do."

"We are trying our best, general," Ulook sighed. "If we had seen the eddies in time, perhaps action could have been taken. Unfortunately, the culprit has masked his activity very well. I doubt there is time to do anything other than accept it."

"I wish we never had this meeting," Fa-a-Di said. "Now I am scared to death. If you never told us, then we would just be part of the new reality."

"There is one thing we can do, my friends," Ulook replied. "Everything that has happened from the moment of the change will be forever saved into your memories. While they may seem like only dreams, you will remember all of us and this moment forever. We can only hope one of you can find a way to restore the past."

"That's why we are here," Obu said. "It will be up to those of you who survive the change to fix the damage. If that happens, we may all return here and continue the lives we were meant to lead."

"How much time do we have?" De-o-Nu asked.

"Only a few minutes now," Ulook said. "The ripple in time is moving very fast now. Just remember each other and dream of the truth. God willing, all will turn out for the best."

"I'll remember everything," Dave promised. "I'll do everything I can to get us back here together."

"Me too!" Fa-a-Di shouted. "I will use all the resources of Greater Gallia to correct this disaster."

"I have a feeling the torch will fall to you again, Dave Brewster," Odo said. "My mind tells me you are the key to all of this. I hope you do remember and find a way to stop this plan."

"If he survives," Ulook interrupted. "If any of us do."

The room was empty. Tens of thousands of Zula swam around the dome traveling to work or home. None of them had ever seen any meeting, as it had never occurred.

CHAPTER 30

Dave Brewster lost his job six months ago, and looking for work during the horrendous recession of 2009 to 2012 had made him bitter and forlorn. He spent most days looking for job postings and trying to network with his friends and acquaintances. As the weeks slipped by, and his prospects did not improve, he let his feelings of inadequacy and helplessness take over. Darlene, his wife, tried to keep things normal, but Dave was sinking. Today, he just had to get away from home and at least interact with some other people, so he decided to visit his neighborhood Starbucks for a coffee and a Danish pastry.

He felt better as he pulled out of the driveway and drove the short four blocks to the closest Starbucks. Dave did not like people parking too close to his car, and he had plenty of experience dealing with dings and nicks in his car to justify his actions. He parked at the far end of the lot where most spaces were empty. He could feel a spring in his step as he felt separated from home and his laptop. The day was fairly cloudy, but he could see the cloud cover starting to break already, which was a great sign for a June day in San Diego. Typically, the cloud cover did not break until early afternoon. Things were looking up.

At the other end of the small parking lot sat a Ford sedan with a single man sitting behind the wheel, idling the engine. Fola Untor had been monitoring these few days of time for weeks now, waiting for a key moment in time when he could strike out at Dave Brewster, the stupid human from twenty-first century Earth 47. It had been difficult to mask his activity moving through time. He knew even the simple people of thirty-second century Earth 47 could time travel and therefore find signs in time of tampering and unapproved travel. But that could not be helped. It was this Brewster fellow who led humanity to find the Hive on Tak-Makla and eventually reconnect the Society of Humanity with their lost colonies in this galaxy. Fola had tried to dissuade him when they met on Hive 1008 and the Nightsky in orbit over Earth Prime, but failed. The events of the Grand Conclave led to the breakup of the Society and the persecution of his beloved Brotherhood. The most difficult jobs had already been accomplished when his fleets destroyed much of Lagamar Ulu and Nan, killing Odo Pak and Obu Neela. Those two held the keys to protecting Dave, but now they were dead and buried. It would be a simple thing to do. Fola had watched this day a dozen times already. Dave would park at the far end of the lot and walk slowly toward the coffee shop. He only had to wait for the moment when there were no other cars moving and Dave was exposed. He would run him down with this stolen car. If that failed, he had his blaster clipped to his belt. Then he could return to Narta Ela and begin the long task of rebuilding the Brotherhood.

Dave was walking through the parking lot. The fragrance of coffee was heavy in the air, pleasing him all the more. Good coffee was one of Dave's few remaining passions. As he crossed the pavement, he heard the sound of wheels screeching and turned to see a car racing toward him. Reality seemed to slow down. He could hear his heart beating and the pounding of his shoes on the pavement as he rushed for the curb. He even noticed the driver had light blonde hair and a look of intense anger in his silver-blue eyes. That sinister look made Dave wonder why this person was trying to kill him. Dave raised his foot to step on the curb as the bumper of the car struck him. He felt his body smash against the vehicle and become airborne. Before his body struck the ground, he passed out.

The driver slammed on his brakes and jumped out of the car. He held an odd pistol-like device in his hand. He looked around for Dave, having followed the arc of the flying body through the air. But he wasn't there. A crowd of people had heard the commotion and were beginning to gather around. The killer pointed his weapon at them and they began to scatter. He rushed over to the bushes where Dave should have landed, but could find no trace of his body or any impact site. Something was terribly wrong, he thought. He heard an odd click and spun around. Rence Rialto stood next to him with a revolver pressed up against his head. "Fola, you son of a bitch," Rence said as he pulled the trigger, spraying a nearby wall with blood. Fola fell to the ground dead. Rence grabbed the blaster from Fola's hand and ran around the corner of the building and into an open portal, which closed behind him in a flash of light.

A crowd began to form around the dead body as a squad car arrived and the officers pushed them back. They called for reinforcements and cordoned off the area. Within ten minutes other officers arrived and began to question the by-standers. Muncie, who had appeared through the portal with Rence and Aria moments before the attack, searched the area where Dave's body flew after being hit by the car. He could find no sign of him and gave up as the police pushed the crowd further back. "Muncie, where's Dave?" Aria asked.

"I don't know, Aria," he replied. "Fola's car struck him hard, but even he couldn't find where Dave's body went. It's a though he disappeared into thin air. That's good news isn't it?"

"The fact that any of us are here is very good news," Aria replied. "Somehow time must get changed back, but I have no idea how."

"All we know is that if Dave was dead, none of us would be here, unless Charlie is the key," Muncie replied.

"Kally and Taron have Charlie on lockdown now," she said. "I got a message seconds ago saying he was okay, so it looks like Dave was the target."

"But where the hell is he!" Muncie said.

"Someone else must have intervened," she replied. "We were obviously too late. We should get back and make a report. Lanz is not going to be happy we let Dave get hit by a car. Also, Rence is in a lot of trouble for killing Fola. We should have taken him back with us."

"I disagree," he replied. "If he survived, he might try to find another way to change the past. Now, that can never happen, although we cannot know if this is the only change Fola made to time. Perhaps other more subtle changes are yet to be found. But Rence should not have left the body. His fingerprints and identity don't exist here."

"It will be just another John Doe homicide," Aria continued. "How the police will explain it is anyone's guess. Lots of people saw Dave hit, but there's no body. They saw Rence kill Fola, but Rence is gone. But we do have another problem."

"Darlene and the kids," Muncie answered. "I know. She'll be out of her mind with Dave gone. We need to contact her. You and Charlie became her friends, but none of that has happened yet. That's going to be very hard."

"Let's go there now," Aria replied. "but I think we should wait for a while to let things happen the way they were meant to."

"Something better happen soon, Aria," Muncie said. "Since we're still here, Dave has to end up in our time somehow. But it doesn't make any sense to me at all."

"We also need to get Charlie over here right away," Aria replied. "Dave could reappear at any moment to resume the normal flow of time. If Charlie isn't behind him in line when he gets here, the time line will change again.

CHAPTER 31

Passor Valka and his top aides were sitting quietly in the conference room of their headquarters deep in the Valandes Desert of Narta Ela. More than five million Brotherhood agents had arrived over the last few weeks. Soon, they would have enough Hives to move all of them and their fleets to the Ulagong Galaxy. The Supreme Leader was overdue for the meeting. He had asked Passor to gather the men at 1000 hours local. It was now almost 1130. "Passor, how much longer do we have to wait?" asked Agent Armand Coos.

"Patience, my friend," Passor replied. "We are waiting for the Supreme Leader. All of us have sworn sacred vows to him and his tardiness is not our concern. We must wait until he chooses to arrive."

Agent Febo Loo asked, "Passor, where has the Supreme Leader been? None of us have had any communication from him in months. This is very unusual. Are we certain he is well?"

"It was only yesterday when he asked me to set up this meeting," Passor replied. "As you can imagine, he is a very busy man. He has been working with me to gain influence with enough Hives to transport us to Atar Pa in the Ulagong Galaxy. Also, you can see how many of your fellow agents are arriving here daily. None of that happens without a lot of work on his part. You men are being quite overzealous on this matter."

"We meant no disrespect to you or the Supreme Leader," Armand said softly. "We are just concerned about his health. Please forgive us if we gave you another impression."

"Don't worry about it. I feel the same way myself. It is difficult for us to keep moving forward without his help. However, we must wait for him to lay out the strategy for our next steps," Passor replied. He rose and began to walk around the table, patting each agent on the back as he passed by. "You know, I have worked with each of you for many years. Together we have seen the heights of joy and depths of despair. Now we are already climbing back from the abyss caused by Dave Brewster and Fa-a-Di. Our enemies are being punished and soon we will move to a place where they cannot reach us. In time, we will return to greatness. In the past, we were the enforcers for the Society. We will never be in that role again. Now we will become the rulers!"

"Passor, aren't there serious threats in the Ulagong Galaxy as well?" Armand asked. "I have heard stories of the Paxran, Donnaki and other empires. How will we fight them while we are still rebuilding?"

Passor chuckled softly. "Again, thanks to the brilliance of our Supreme Leader, we are already building a coalition in that galaxy to stand against their Free Society. We should have an ample period of peace and cooperation with those others to safeguard our planets. If the Paxran or others choose to attack us later, we will have Hives and weapons to easily defeat them. You have all read the Supreme Leader's manifesto. So you know this is all planned. All we have to do is carry out his orders. I know that I can count on each one of you to do your part."

There was a flash of light in the room and the agents averted their eyes. When they looked back, Alana Albright and ten tekkan soldiers were in the room, all pointing their laser rifles at the men. "Good morning, Brotherhood," Alana laughed. "I hope we're not interrupting anything important."

"What is the meaning of this?" Passor shouted.

Alana lowered her blaster and opened a pouch on her belt. She removed another blaster and set it on the table. "We brought you a gift from your Supreme Leader, Fola Untor," she replied.

"Who is Fola Untor?" Passor asked. "I have never heard that name before."

"The lies just roll off your tongue, don't they Passor," she chuckled. "We already know about him and have for some time. If you are all waiting here for him, you needn't bother. Fola Untor is dead. This was his blaster. You can see it is stained with blood. That is his blood of course. You can do a DNA check if you like."

"This is ridiculous," Armand scoffed. "Passor Valka is our Supreme Leader. Ask any of us."

"Fine, say whatever you want," she replied. "Whoever Fola Untor was, he is dead now, buried many centuries ago in an unmarked grave. He chose to change the course of time by altering the past. He succeeded, but the major change he achieved was his own death."

"How did this man die? What did you say his name was?" Passor lied.

"You mean Fola Untor? Unfortunately, those secrets are lost in time as well," she said confidently. "None of you will ever know. But this is not all I came to tell you."

"You must realize that our security forces will be here any minute," Febo sneered. "They have undoubtedly noticed your sudden arrival. Your own deaths will come soon."

Alana laughed out loud. "Poor little Febo Loo. Yes, your teams will come, but we will be gone before then. However, I am also here to give you a warning. The actions of your Supreme Leader have put all societies on high alert. We know your people will distort time without regard for the consequences on the present. Every free Hive is now monitoring time travel and sharing information. Any attempt to travel in time by Brotherhood agents will be met with the same quick justice that claimed Fola's life." She and one tekkan stepped up to Febo and touched him with their hands. "Let me show you what I mean." The three disappeared from the room. The other agents jumped up in surprise, but sat again quickly as the tekkans aimed at them.

Febo was standing in a hospital room with the tekkan. A young woman was sleeping on the single bed. She looked familiar. Alana whistled softly and he turned his head. She held a long knife menacingly at the throat of a newborn baby in a bassinette on the other side of the room. She waved him over to the baby and pointed to the chart at the foot of the tiny crib. He stared and a look of abject horror crossed his face when he read the name "Febo Xanther Loo" on the form.

Alana put the knife back into its scabbard and walked over to Febo, who could still feel the laser rifle poking into his back. She whispered, "You were such a cute baby, Febo. And your mother looks so happy and beautiful. Please know that I would never hurt this child, however, if we find that you have been traveling in time, this tekkan or any of a million others would gladly come here and slit you open in your crib. I hope I am being quite clear on this." Febo could only nod his head as he looked down on his earlier self. Alana reached over and kissed him on the cheek. "Now, go over there and kiss your mother and we'll go back."

He walked over to the bed and smiled down at his mother, dreaming so peacefully. He fought his tears and kissed her softly on the cheek. She smiled but remained asleep. Alana and the tekkan touched him and instantly they were back in the conference room. "Febo Loo now knows exactly what we are capable of," Alana said. "For God's sake, please don't make us do what I could have done. But it is up to you to decide." She and the tekkans disappeared from the room just as the security agents broke in the door.

"Is everyone okay?" the lead guard shouted.

"Yes, we're fine," Passor answered. "Now get out of here. But first take this blaster and have the blood stains compared to any current or past agents and let us know the results as soon as possible."

When they were alone again, Passor walked over to Febo and put his hands on his shoulders. Febo was sitting again with an odd combination of joy and horror on his face. "Are you okay, brother?" Passor asked. "What did that bitch do to you?"

He thought for a moment about resigning on the spot and returning home to Ednak Ela, his home planet. His parents were still living, but getting quite old now. His father had always wanted him to be an astrophysicist like himself, but Febo chose the Brotherhood instead. "We were in the hospital room," he started at last. "My mother was sleeping soundly. She looked so young and beautiful that I almost didn't recognize her. Then the woman made a sound. I turned to see her holding a long knife against the throat of a newborn baby. She motioned me over and I read the chart. The baby was me!"

"What did she do then?" Armand asked.

"Nothing. She put the knife away and kissed me on the cheek, saying how she would never hurt me, but others would if I traveled in time," Febo said staring into space. "Then she told me to kiss my mother. After I did, we were back here." He turned to look at Passor in the eyes. "What do you think our Supreme Leader did to them? What would make people think about doing something so diabolical?"

Passor sat heavily his chair and sighed. "God only knows, Febo. Fola always played his cards close to the chest. He said he had a plan to change the past so the Grand Conclave never took place and we would still have power. Since that woman and the tekkans were here, and we're not on Earth Prime right now, I have to assume that he failed. What do we do now?"

"Passor, we have to elect a new Supreme Leader," Armand said. "We're all here and I recommend we pick you. You were the closest to Fola and were the President of the High Council. Who else has your qualifications?"

"If I may say one more thing," Febo interrupted. "If the Brotherhood wants to use time travel as a weapon, I have to resign right now! You didn't see what I saw. If Fola did anything like that, he deserved to die. I won't be part of that anymore."

"Dear brother Febo," Passor said softly, "I can promise you if I am Supreme Leader, time travel will be strictly forbidden. The unknown consequences are just too great. Besides, we don't need that to get back at our enemies. We have Hives and battle cruisers!"

Febo stood up and shouted, "Passor Valka for Supreme Leader!" The other agents joined in the chorus. Several bottles of whisky and brandy were pulled from the cabinets and opened. The men cheered for their new leader and toasted to their future success. Even though he drank and cheered with the rest, Febo Loo could not get the image of the woman holding a knife over the baby who would become him. Perhaps he should go home soon, he thought. His parents would love to see him again.

CHAPTER 32

Dave Brewster knew he was dead. He had just been run over by a speeding car in the parking lot. He remembered the sound of his bones and joints cracking as he slammed into the front of the car. He snapped over at the waist on impact, causing his head and face to slam into the hood of the car. Then he was airborne, tumbling in the air toward a wall and some bushes. He was about to hit the wall when suddenly he was far away, speeding through space surrounded by millions of strings of light. The searing pain and agony he had felt at the crash was gone. He felt perfectly fine, but not quite conscious. Was he in shock, or was this the road to Heaven or a quick ride to Hell?

He noticed he was being carried by a giant angel. But it was made of light and not flesh and bone. As he watched it, he noticed it was more like a massive featherless bird. But this bird had two arms which were wrapped tightly around him. He had never imagined the afterlife being anything like this. Then the thought of Darlene filled his mind. If he was dead, how would she survive alone? He prayed for her health and safety. Then he thought she would have Bill or Cybil move back in or maybe sell the house and move in with them. He realized he could not control that anymore, making him desperately sad.

That thought dissolved into the image of the man driving the car at him. Why would someone want to kill him? He was out of work with little savings. He had no enemies that he knew about. It just did not make any sense. The intense look of hate in that man's odd eyes was locked into his mind. Perhaps he thought Dave was someone else? More likely, the poor soul was insane and delusional. But he was alive and Dave was dead. He realized he could not change that either and looked around himself more closely.

He seemed to be traveling in deep space with solar systems zipping by at an incredible rate. As he continued, he noticed fewer and fewer stars in front of him. He had no idea how long this ride would last, so he tried not to think about where he might be going. He looked at the strings of light all around him. They were in many colors and were spinning around him like a Fourth of July fireworks display. As he tried to look at individual strings, he saw them morphing into other shapes. Some seemed like people, but others were like spiders or even lobsters with hands instead of claws. What a magical place, he thought.

After what seemed like hours, he had the sensation he was slowing down. A single star was visible in front of him and the winged beast seemed to be taking him there. As they approached, he could see only one large gas giant planet circling the star. There were very few other stars visible, and he assumed the few he saw were actually distant galaxies. Approaching the planet, he noticed it had two moons. One seemed lush like Earth, while the other was red and sandy like Mars. He hoped he was going to the lush planet, but the creature instead chose the red one. As they entered the atmosphere, only the bird creature was still there, holding him tightly. They descended through the air which smelled sweet and clean to Dave. He thought it was very odd that a spirit could smell anything. He could feel himself inhaling and exhaling. Was he dead? He was not certain anymore. As the creature landed on the planet, Dave fell asleep.

Hours later, Dave woke to find himself in a small bed. He looked around and discovered he was in a small stone building. Several candles provided light. He was very surprised he could sit up after the crash had crushed his legs and pelvis. He was overjoyed when he stood with no pain. He looked down and noticed his clothes were stained with blood and ripped in many places. He also had no shoes. He quickly pulled off his clothes, but could find no evidence of cuts or breaks anywhere. "This is freaking weird," he said. He saw several robes on a hook and found one that fit. There were pairs of simple sandals by the door. After he put a pair on, he stepped outside.

The sun had been down for some time and it was very dark. The air was warm and the land smelled like desert. The fragrance of wild flowers permeated the air, but remained unseen in the darkness. There was a long bench on the porch, so he sat down to ponder his situation. "Where in hell am I?" he said out loud. "Hello!" he shouted, but there was no reply. He sat back and closed his eyes. Perhaps the crash had been a dream? But if so, why was he not in bed in San Diego with Darlene? He noticed a glimmer of light in his peripheral vision, opened his eyes and turned to see a light string on the bench next to him. Gradually, it began to swell and turn into a large blob of light. He kept watching it as it twisted and changed until the ten foot bird man was sitting beside him. Somehow it had transformed from a string of light into a massive flesh and bone creature towering over his head. "Well, that was impressive!" he said.

"Hello Dave Brewster," the creature said. "My name is Fa-u-Bay. I hope you're feeling okay now."

"Thank you for saving my life, Fa-u-Bay," Dave said reaching out his right hand.

Fa-u-Bay shook his hand and said, "You're welcome, but it wasn't really me. I did bring you here though."

"That I remember," Dave replied. "But where exactly is here?"

Fa-u-Bay laughed. "Long ago, I gave this moon the name Solander, after one of the gods who brought life to my home world."

"But why me?" Dave asked. "People die in crashes everyday. Why am I here and can I go home? My wife will be agonizing that I disappeared."

"She doesn't know you are gone yet," Fa-u-Bay said. "And she never will. I will make certain you get home in time to get that coffee at Starbucks."

"I'm not so sure I want to get hit by the car again, if you don't mind," Dave chuckled.

"That can never happen again. But I need you here for a while. There is so much to explain, even though I cannot tell you much of your future," Fa-u-Bay replied. "Time will play out as it was meant to. Hopefully the only change will be you arriving at the coffee shop ten or twenty minutes later."

"But I've been gone a lot longer than that!" Dave argued. "I feel like I've been sleeping for hours. And how long did it take to heal my injuries?"

"Dave, you believe that time moves along a straight line, but it does not," Fa-u-Bay said. "Your people have not yet discovered time travel. But the man in the car came from a different time. He knew the man you were going to become and he hated you for that. So he went back in time to kill you."

"So, you're telling me I can be back home just minutes after what I remember last and go on with my life?" Dave asked. "That's seems pretty hard to believe."

"But it's easy to believe you are talking to a Gallicean on a moon at the edge of the galaxy with no injuries following a major crash," Fa-u-Bay mocked.

"I keep thinking this is a dream and I'm going to wake up from a coma in some hospital," Dave replied. "Then if I can ever walk again, I'll need months or years of therapy. I mean, look around, this can't be real."

"Dave, get some sleep," Fa-u-Bay chuckled. "Lubna and the sun will be rising in a few hours. Then we can talk some more. I'll make certain there is food and water. I doubt there is any coffee here."

"That is a shame," Dave replied. "Right now, I need a cup to get my brain straight." Dave rose and walked over to the door. "Good night, Fa-u-Bay. And thank you again for your part in saving my life."

"Dave Brewster, it was my honor to help you," Fa-u-Bay smiled. "If you had any idea how much you were going to do for my people, you would understand why. I am the one who owes you more than I can ever repay."

"Tell me more about it in the morning," Dave yawned. "Maybe the nurse in the hospital looks a bit like you. That would make sense. If I'm still here in the morning, I'll listen to everything you want to tell me. Good night." He went inside and lay back on the bed. In seconds, he was sound asleep again.

CHAPTER 33

The intensely bright sunlight poured through the small window near the bed where Dave was sleeping. In his mind, the light seemed like the headlights of an onrushing car, coming back to finish him off this time. He struggled to run away, but the vehicle was gaining ground on him quickly. He could not imagine being hit by yet another car! Just as the car reached him, he woke up with a start. He was still on that small bed in the stone building. He could see the candles had all burned out. His bloody clothes were still in a heap on the floor next to him. After he climbed out of bed, he tied the robe around him and slipped on the sandals. The room was very simple, with just the bed, one small table and two side chairs. There were small windows on two walls and the single door. The floors seemed to be made from the same stone as the walls. It was rough as though hewn from a quarry with ancient axes.

He walked out the door and felt the heat of the sun on him. It cast an odd light that did not seem natural. Looking up, he saw the massive gas giant filling one quarter of the sky. A brilliant white star was rising above the opposite horizon. There were very few clouds in the sky to block the light. Looking around the building, he could see sparse fields of cacti and boulders baking in the heat. A few small birds circled overhead looking for breakfast. A single bird appeared to be heading his way. He watched it approach. As it came closer, it became larger and larger. The image of the bird man last night reappeared in his mind. Fa-u-Bay landed twenty feet in front of him. He hadn't noticed last night, but the Gallicean wore blood-red body armor and carried four daggers on his belt.

"Good morning, Dave," Fa-u-Bay said as he removed a bag that was slung over his back. "Is this still a dream to you or are you beginning to believe you are really here on Solander?"

"It's still a dream," Dave replied. "I want to believe it's real, but you have to imagine how strange all of this is to me."

Fa-u-Bay sat on the bench and opened the bag. "I'm not surprised. No one from your time has ever left your solar system. You were in a major accident and woke up with a giant Being from another world. It does seem far-fetched, even to me." He removed a set of clothes and set them next to him. Then he pulled out bags of food, two bottles of water, and what appeared to be a thermos of coffee. "Perhaps this coffee will make it more real to you." He opened the thermos and poured some of the coffee into a mug that he had also removed from the bag. He offered it to Dave.

The coffee smelled real to Dave, but he could not imagine where Fa-u-Bay could have found it on the edge of the galaxy. He sipped it and found it to be wonderful. "See, this proves my point. If we're on some isolated planet, where did you get all of this?"

Fa-u-Bay took a sip of the coffee from his own mug and laughed. "I see your point. Do you remember the other moon in this system from when we arrived last night?"

"I remember hoping we would go there rather than here," he replied. "It looked more hospitable than this rock. Is that where this came from?"

"That's correct. Fistan is a heavily populated world, full of people like you, although they are not quite as tall. I believe they are called Nan," the Gallicean replied.

"Nan? Gallicean? I don't know what any of that means," Dave said. "If that other moon is inhabited, why didn't you take me there?"

Fa-u-Bay frowned. "Dave, this is not a joy ride. I didn't bring you here to make new friends on Fistan. Drink your coffee and eat something. Then we can have our talk and you can get back to saving the universe."

A dazed expression crossed Dave's face as he took a biscuit out of a bag. "Save the universe! I think you have the wrong guy." He nibbled the biscuit. It was delicious and reminded him how hungry he was. He ate it quickly and took another.

"I was being a bit melodramatic, I know," Fa-u-Bay laughed as he took a biscuit. "Let's eat now and work out the details later."

Half an hour later, Fa-u-Bay was flying Dave high over the planet again. Dave was wearing the clothes the Gallicean pulled from the bag. They were identical to the clothes he had been wearing during the accident. Even at this altitude, the heat was becoming unbearable. Solander was not inhabited, so there were no air conditioned buildings to escape the heat. A range of tall mountains was approaching in the distance. Dave could see snowcaps at the peaks, so cooler weather was possible here. After another twenty minutes, the two landed halfway up the tallest mountain, where scrub brush broke the monotonous red clay and sand. The temperature here was much cooler. Looking back from where they came, he could see waves of heat rising off the desert. Fa-u-Bay led him over to some smaller boulders that could serve as seats. He handed Dave one of the water bottles and took the other himself. Sweat was rolling off both of them.

"Okay, I'm starting to believe this is real," Dave panted as he drank water. "I've never sweated like this in a dream before. And the heat is unreal here. Are you sure you don't want to go to Fistan instead?"

After drinking from the bottle, Fa-u-Bay poured the rest over his head. "I'm sweating pretty good for someone who has been dead for thousands of generations!"

"You're dead?" Dave gasped. "How is that possible? You look very real to me."

"I am real, Dave," he replied. "As I told you before, time, life, and existence are not as linear and simplistic as most Beings believe. When you return, you will learn more about that. In fact, you will remember all of this adventure as well. However, it will be like the memory of a dream."

"Why am I here, Fa-u-Bay?" Dave asked. "I still don't understand."

"The acts of the man who tried to kill you seriously affected the flow of time. If you had remained there, he would have made certain you were dead. The accident had a major impact, but your death would have been disastrous to the future," he replied.

"But I'm just an out-of-work accountant living in San Diego," Dave argued. "I'm nothing in the scheme of things. Of course, my death would devastate my family."

"You forgot what I already told you. That man, Fola Untor, was not from your time. He was from more than one thousand of your years in the future. You know who you are and who you have been. He knew who you would become, and the effect you would have on his future," Fa-u-Bay responded.

"Who will I become and what did I do to him to make him so homicidal?" Dave asked.

"I cannot tell you any specifics, as any memory of this visit might change the time line as well," Fa-u-Bay replied. "Reverse time travel is incredibly dangerous, as you know firsthand. That is why the Bolofaz guard it so well. When they sensed this impending change, they asked me to help you. They are the ones who saved you and had me bring you to their world."

"They brought you back from the dead to help me?" Dave asked. "Why didn't they take me themselves? And what the heck is a Bolofaz? Are they around here somewhere?"

"You ask a lot of questions, Dave Brewster," Fa-u-Bay replied. "Life and death are not what you believe either, but this is not the time or place to discuss that. I am here with you for two reasons. First, the Bolofaz asked me, and second, the things you will do for my people are so important even death couldn't keep me from helping you."

"I guess I'll have to take your word for that!" Dave exclaimed. "I have no idea what I can do, but I will do my best. Why am I still here?"

"Fola Untor, the man who attacked you had been traveling extensively to your time while planning his crime," Fa-u-Bay answered. "Such travel causes ripples and eddies in time. It takes a while for those to calm down. If you were there, other things could change and risk the future. Also, several of your friends from the future jumped back in time to help you and then jumped right back. That is upsetting the flow of time as well. So far, the only change the Bolofaz have detected is the car accident and the shooting death of Fola Untor. Those two changes appear to have no real impact so far. The Bolofaz asked me to keep you here to insure the distortions have stopped. When they are satisfied the normal flow of time can resume, you will be home."

"Wow!" Dave sighed. "I have friends from the future who tried to save me? That's really cool. Did one of them kill Fola?"

"Yes, thankfully," Fa-u-Bay said. "That man would stop at nothing to kill you and my descendant, Fa-a-Di, who would have been his next target."

"So how long do we wait?" Dave asked. "If I'll be back at the same time, I guess it doesn't matter. I'm just curious, although I'd love to get off this sizzling planet."

"I don't know. Only the Bolofaz can make that determination," the other replied. "I know they want to spend some time with you before you go back." Dave was gone. Fa-u-Bay smiled, saying, "I guess we know now." The Gallicean dissolved into a shimmering blob of light and shot out into the stars, leaving Solander to bake in the midday sun.

CHAPTER 34

Dave was flying through vast clouds over a mysterious planet. But something was very strange. He looked downward and could see no land, just bands of differently colored clouds rushing by at amazing speed. He moved upward toward a layer of clouds hundreds of feet above him. As he pushed to the top of the clouds, he was in space. The mammoth planet spun below him. He could see Fistan and Solander in their orbits nearby. He imagined Fa-u-Bay was still there wondering what had happened to him. Suddenly he realized he was on Lubna, the gas giant. But he was not a bird, so how was he flying?

A massive snake came out of the clouds underneath him. He thought this must be a Bolofaz. The creature came up under him and Dave landed on its back and held on for dear life. He could feel the creature speaking directly into his mind. "Hi Dave. My name is Ondeen." The two dived back downward into the gas clouds. The snake was impossibly large, and Dave was a tiny spot riding on its back.

"Ondeen, are you a Bolofaz?" Dave asked.

"Yes I am," Ondeen replied. "My friends and I wanted to meet you firsthand before we send you home. How are you feeling? I hope you have no remaining injuries from the attack."

"Frankly, I feel fantastic," Dave laughed. "The air here is so refreshing. It makes me feel alive! But I thought gas giants had mostly hydrogen and helium atmospheres. I can't breathe that!"

"That's very true, but we have compensated for that," Ondeen replied. "We wanted to meet you, not kill you. If that was our motive, we would have left you with the assassin."

Dave could see thousands of similar snakes flying with him now. They would turn their heads and smile at him, their eyes shimmering in the light. "Thank you all for saving my life. Right after the crash I thought about my wife and children. I didn't want them to suffer at my loss."

"It was our pleasure," Ondeen replied. "As Fa-u-Bay told you, we are the guardians of time. This planet and others throughout space are home to our species. We exist outside of your sense of time, because it is our duty to make certain the past does not change. Fortunately such disturbances have been rare so far. Life and reality flow along a defined course and changes to what has already happened cannot be allowed."

"What Ondeen says is correct," another Bolofaz interrupted. "Your life will end one day. That is the nature of physical existence. However, disturbing the past to change the present has terrible consequences. That is why we watch reverse time travel. We make certain changes do not occur that could affect the future."

"That's a relief!" Dave sighed. "For a minute there, Fa-u-Bay had me believing this was about me, Dave Brewster, the accountant. But it's more about safeguarding time. That makes more sense."

"Fa-u-Bay was partially correct," Ondeen said. "Each life has an impact on the future. Most impacts are modest on a cosmological scale. All are profoundly important on a personal level. If you had died at Fola Untor's hands, another future would have taken its place. Your family would be impacted the most. However, the things you might have done never would have happened, and no one would know the difference. The future would just be different. In your case, you had already done many things which your friends value greatly. Fola wanted to make it as though none of those things occurred."

The other Bolofaz continued, "Even we do not know the future, Dave. The rest of your life may be wonderful or horrible. But it will be the future that was meant for you, not the delusions of a madman bent on revenge."

"That's not very reassuring," Dave said coldly. "But I must have done something to get Fa-u-Bay to help me. So there's that at least."

Ondeen laughed. "The future up to the moment when Fola Untor left his own time to kill you has been written. That should give you some clue about your near term prospects. If you were an accountant in San Diego, why would the greatest leader of Greater Gallia come out of time to help you? However, you will have to experience those things yourself. While we cannot tell you about those events, we know you did some great things. Your future can be very bright!"

"Perhaps, but there is more," the other said. "While the timeline is now secure, there is great danger approaching you and your friends. You will all face incredible odds at great personal risk. That future awaits you. How it will end is up to God."

"If I can be with my family, I'll be fine," Dave said.

"We wish you the best of luck, Dave Brewster," Ondeen stated. "Believe it or not, your future will likely affect us as well. If and when that time comes, and you are drawn back here, you can count on us to help you in any way we can."

"Thank you, Ondeen," Dave smiled. "It would be a joy to be with you and your friends again. What happens now?"

"Just relax and close your eyes," Ondeen said. "Now stand on my back with your eyes still closed." Dave complied and could feel the strong winds lifting him off the creature's back. "When you're ready, just open your eyes."

Dave was floating in the atmosphere of Lubna. He could not sense the Bolofaz anymore but was enjoying the feeling of floating in the air. He thought of Darlene and their children and smiled. He hoped he would remember all of this so he could tell her when she came home from work. She probably would think he had been sleeping and dreamed the whole thing. After all, being hit by a car and then traveling to a distant planet was not believable. It was beginning to seem like a dream to him as well. The images of the Bolofaz, Fa-u-Bay and traveling in space were already slipping away. He tried to hold onto them, but was failing. He remembered Fa-u-Bay told him it would be like the memory of a dream. Too bad, he thought. It would make a great sci-fi book. He laughed out loud. He took another deep breath and opened his eyes.

Dave was standing next to his car in the Starbucks parking lot. He noticed a number of police cars near a section of the lot that was cordoned off with yellow tape. An ambulance was there and two paramedics were examining someone lying on the ground. Dave thought he could see blood on the sidewalk. He imagined some poor guy had been run over on his way to buy a coffee. He looked at his watch and thought if he had left home a few minutes earlier that could have been him lying there. He shuddered at the thought of being stricken by a car.

Deep in his mind, it all seemed too similar, as though he was the victim or knew him well. He felt bad for the person and hoped he would be okay. As he approached, he could tell the man on the ground was quite tall and had light blonde hair. At least he knew it was not his own body. It took longer for him to reach the coffee shop as he had to walk around the large crowd of bystanders.

As Dave opened to door to the store, he could smell the fragrance of coffee and scent of cinnamon in the air. Before he could step in, a woman in a business suit rushed toward the open door with a large coffee in one hand, and a cell phone in the other plastered to her ear, forcing him to step back and let her go by. He thought of a smart response but only managed a soft "Have a nice day," as she dashed to her car without even noticing him. As he stepped into the store, he could not decide if he was upset by her gruff actions, or just jealous that she had somewhere to go. *That used to be me*, he thought to himself.

Three others were in the line ahead of Dave, so he took his place at the end of the line and browsed the menu.

CHAPTER 35

"Obu, I was so worried about you!" Dave said. "I heard that the Brotherhood attacked Lagamar Ulu and the Mount Alila temple specifically. What happened?"

Obu smiled and patted Dave's hand. "As you can see, I am quite well. The attack on my home world was quite vicious, with many factories and cities heavily damaged. The explosions and fires rapidly increased the smog level all over the planet. My priests and I sat praying in the temple as the clouds and smoke rose and completely enveloped the mountain range and our temple. I feel confident the Source was helping us that day. The directional systems on some Brotherhood ships were also affected and they blasted away at a nearby mountain, destroying only rock and snow, until our defending fleet could force them to flee."

"I am glad to hear that," Fa-a-Di said, "although I will pray tonight for the loss of life on your planet."

"Thank you General," Obu smiled. "You should know your own troops were very brave during the attack on Lagamar Boley. I have seen those who rejoined the Source and can report they are at peace."

"But none of this is why we are here," Ulook interrupted.

"Of course you are correct, Ulook," Obu apologized. "Why don't you continue?"

"The leader of the Brotherhood has been very busy building an alliance in this galaxy," she began. "Fola Untor has been promising Hive technology to the Paxran, Donnaki and Maklakar among others in order to gain their support against your Free Society."

"Fola Untor is dead," Dave said.

"How can you know that?" Obu frowned. "He was monitored in Paxran space only a few days ago."

Dave shook his head as though his mind was full of cobwebs. "I don't know. I'm sorry I blurted that out. I just had this image in my mind of him lying on a sidewalk in a pool of his own blood. It must have been a dream."

"Hmm. This is very unusual," Ulook said. "That is a pretty specific memory. I will ask some of my people to look for him again. Regardless of his status, we need to worry about the possibility of a coordinated attack from those other races."

"That would be especially difficult if the Maklakar share their plasma bomb technology with the others," Fa-a-Di replied. "Several Maklakar battle stations could destroy any of our planets, even this one."

Ulook shuddered at the thought. "I think that is a low risk General. Even with their fear of Hives, they can never forgive the Paxran for destroying their civilization."

"I agree," Dave replied. "I think that may point to a solution. If we can somehow convince the Maklakar we are not their enemy, they may join us instead."

"You trust them after what they did on Tak-Makla?" De-o-Nu asked. "I don't think Zee will be pleased to hear that."

"It's not a matter of trust, brother," Dave replied. "Something made them strike out at Tak-Makla. It's probably a lack of understanding of the purpose of Hive technology. I have seen it used for combat and the power is much greater than their plasma bombs. Being xenophobic with a long history of defending themselves from aggressors, I can't imagine they want to build an empire."

"Dave is right," Fa-a-Di said. "And it's not like we have any other options. We only have two active Hives. With the disarray in the Andromeda Galaxy, it is very unlikely any more will come here anytime soon."

"Except for Hives for the Brotherhood," Odo said. "It is very likely the Hive on Atar Pa has already been compromised. Then it will be down to one for us and one for them." He patted Lini on the knee and asked, "What do you think, Dar Lini?"

"I'm just a local girl, but I think you are forgetting another Hive," she said meekly.

"Right here," Dave agreed. "This planet is a natural Hive. That's why Ulook and her people are here and why the original human setters are Nan."

"I'm so proud of you both," Odo laughed. "And as Dave knows, there are others yet to be found. Adding natural Hives to your defenses will overwhelm the attackers."

"Odo, Fistan is another natural Hive," Dave said.

"What?" Fa-a-Di questioned. "You are saying a mythical planet is a Hive? How can you say that? The planet is an old legend from thousands of generations ago."

"I don't know. It's just in my mind from somewhere," Dave sighed. "This is so strange. I keep getting these odd memories. I know I've never been there or seen Fola Untor dead, but the images keep popping into my mind."

"Like the memory of a dream," Obu said.

"Exactly! Maybe the pressure of the ocean above is getting to me," Dave replied. "I'll try to keep my mouth shut until I think it through."

"Don't do that Dave," Lini countered. "I think it's wonderful. The Source is speaking through you, right Odo?"

"I don't know for sure," the Elder replied. "I know Dave's connection to the Source is strong and here we are at the core of a natural Hive, but some of his comments are unbelievable."

Ulook shook her head. "This is impossible. The Zula have found no sign of Fola Untor. Millions entered the Hive and searched, but it's as though he disappeared from time and space. Perhaps Dave Brewster was right about him."

"You think that's strange," Dave began, "Here at the bottom of the ocean in a system with no communications, I'm getting a signal from Earth on my com-link."

"That's impossible," De-o-Nu said.

"Let's see what they want," Fa-a-Di disagreed. "Ulook, can we put the signal on a screen for all of us to see?"

A screen appeared on the wall. Dave tapped the com-link and the images of Lanz, Aria, Muncie and Rence appeared on screen. "Dave, thank God you're safe!" Lanz shouted.

"What are you talking about? Is there an attack imminent?" Dave replied.

The group on Earth recounted the story of the time eddies which had since ebbed. They told the group how Fola Untor traveled back to 2012 to kill Dave Brewster just minutes before he was to meet Charlie Watson for the first time. Rence admitted shooting Fola after he saw Dave struck by the car. Fola had gone searching for Dave with his blaster to make sure he was dead. No charges were filed against Rence. Aria and Muncie told him how they searched for Dave's body after the accident and were frantic when they could not find him. They waited in Charlie's automobile for ten minutes until they saw him reappear next to his own car. Then Charlie followed him into Starbucks. The others then jumped back and had arrived in Lanz's office only moments before this call.

"I remember seeing that accident," Dave remembered. "When I got out of my car, I saw the taped off area and all of the police. But it wasn't me on the ground. I wasn't even there. The man struck by the car had light blonde hair."

"That was Fola Untor," Rence said. "He wasn't hit by the car, you were. I shot him at point blank range, right in the temple. I couldn't risk allowing him to escape in time to try again."

"But if I was hit by a car, how come I have no recollection of it?" Dave asked.

"I have no idea," Lanz said. "What I really want to know is where did you disappear to? His car was going pretty fast when it struck you. You must have flown twenty feet in the air before you just were gone! Do you remember anything after that?"

"Lanz, I hear you asking me the question, but I really don't remember any of that," he replied. "Odo and Obu, what do you think?"

"Time is pretty resilient," Obu said. "Somehow the Source keeps contradictions from occurring. I don't know any more than that."

"The Source fills the universe and beyond," Odo replied. "Nothing is beyond its capabilities."

"We Zula believe there are others who guard time," Ulook answered. "Most cultures believe in some entity or entities who watch the worlds and the people there. Whether that is their interpretation of God, or demigods or angels, they are always there. Perhaps this was their intervention to prevent Fola Untor from changing the course of time. Whoever they are, I am most grateful. Without Dave's intervention, my people would still be hunted on Lagamar Vol."

"We are all grateful that Dave is still here with us today," Fa-a-Di said. "I can't imagine a galaxy without my dear brother. But we still have to decide how to cope with the threat posed to us today."

"You're quite right," Dave replied. He faced the screen and said, "Thank you to all for helping keep me alive. We need to disconnect, but I will fill you in later. Zulanan out." The screen went dark and disappeared. "I think we need to meet the Maklakar. We need their help to defend ourselves. And we need to move more Nan to this planet to train the locals to join its Hive."

Fa-a-Di laughed. "Two days ago, I would have slapped your face if you suggested allowing foreigners into this sacred system. Of course, two days ago I was dreading this Sojourn with all my heart. All of that fear is gone now. I see these planets for what they are. If this is a Nan Hive, then we will support it wholeheartedly. Now I realize this has always been a Nan and Zula planet."

Ulook stood and began to morph again. After a few seconds, she was a female Gallicean wearing Marine battle armor. "Dear General, this was never a Nan Hive. It is natural. It is as much a Gallicean Hive as anything else. Anyone who is here can join it. Perhaps that will add to its appeal in your worlds. No longer is Zulanan a place to be feared for one or two days every ten years. Now it can be a place of joy and contentment where humans, Galliceans and others can be together without issues like atmosphere or language. All can enter our Hive and experience the joy of the Source."

"Well, I think I can return home now," Obu said. "This has been a great day. I hope all of you can resolve your issues and continue to live in peace. Unfortunately, that is not the case in the home galaxy. Also, even without Fola, the Brotherhood will likely come here and occupy Atar Pa. With our disarray at home, there is little we will be able to do to help you." He patted Odo Pak on the shoulder and asked, "And what of you, my dearest friend. What will you do now?"

"With Fa-a-Di's approval, I would like to move my family here," he replied. "The Hive will protect us and I already feel reinvigorated by its power. The Nan on this world will need education and training. Also, any Galliceans coming here will need help and understanding of the power of this Hive."

"You have my blessing, Odo," Fa-a-Di said. "Dar Lini and Ulook, do we have your permission to keep this planet as a stop on our Sojourns?"

“Of course, Fa-a-Di,” Lini replied. “As Ulook said, we hope it can be much more than that!”

Odo put his hand on Lini’s. “You have lived your whole life in that small village, watching the Galliceans come and go. What do you want to do now?”

“All of this is amazing to me,” she replied looking at the faces around the table. “A part of me is so overwhelmed it wants to go back to my village and hide. But now that I am learning about all of you, I think I want to be part of the adventure. I don’t know if I’m qualified, but I would love to be part of Dave’s crew. I’m a quick learner and very well educated for this planet. I know I’d probably have to get more education and attend a military academy or something, but I’d like to try.”

Dave smiled at her. “When I first came to this time, I spent three months learning about the new technology and the chain of command. They wanted me here, but I was just an accountant. I don’t see why Lini can’t have the same thing. We’re not making her a soldier or anything of that sort.”

De-o-Nu laughed. “You might want to consult your wife first, brother! Bringing yet another beautiful girl into your life might upset her.”

CHAPTER 36

The Hive on Paranon Nar did not have sufficient time to react when the hundred Bandabar star cruisers crossed the frontier at incredible speed with their weapons and defensive arrays fully charged. For the last several months, the Hive had been undergoing deconstruction in order to move sensitive equipment and personnel away from the border area with the Bandabar Fold. Just yesterday, five cargo ships had left Paranon Nar for safer planets deep within the Society sphere of influence.

President Patak Gerfaz sat at his desk in a state of total disbelief. Against his wishes, ten battle cruisers had been ordered to protect the cargo ships, leaving only ten more to protect the planet. Ten to one odds meant almost certain defeat. In its weakened state, the Hive only had one billion agents; not nearly enough to push back the attackers or even to dismantle their ships. If this had happened two days before, the Hive could have easily crushed the invasion. Now Paranon Nar was defenseless. The defending fleet had left orbit and would be engaging the enemy within minutes in a hopeless suicide mission. Then the Bandabar would land on the planet and attack the cities and the Hive. His forces would outnumber them on the ground, but for how long? While he had begged Wendo and Antar to send reinforcements, he doubted that would happen. The whole Society was in turmoil, with factions growing quickly and attacking their neighbors. The remnants of the central government needed to focus on internal conflict before worrying about the frontier.

A tone sounded on his control panel and he pressed a flashing button. The image of Lord Wendo Balak appeared on the screen in front of him. "Lord Balak, any news for my planet? The battle is to begin any minute and I fear we are already lost."

"I am so sorry, Patak," Wendo replied. "I have spent hours begging your neighbors to help defend Paranon Nar, but each is more concerned about defending their own space. What are you going to do now?"

"I don't know," he answered. "If I stay the course, many brave soldiers will die very soon. However, if I surrender, God knows what the Bandabar have in mind for us. Either way, our Hive technology will be taken."

"Let us hope and pray the Bandabar do not know what to do with it," Wendo replied. "I am not in your shoes today, old friend, but I stand with your decision. Just do what's right for you and your people."

"Pray for us, Wendo. Paranon Nar out," Patak said as he closed the contact. He rose slowly and walked over to a credenza and removed a bottle of brandy and a glass. He poured a short drink and swallowed it. He looked around the office he had occupied for the last eight years. It had been an honor to lead this Nar planet. Paranon had been singled out many times in the Nar Society for their educational system and military prowess. Now that would all be lost. He walked back to his desk and sat heavily. He pressed a button and the face of Admiral Bonol Imbal appeared on the screen.

"Yes, Mr. President," Bonol said. "Please make it quick sir. We are closing in on the enemy now."

“Order the fleet to stand down, Bonol,” Patak said. “I would rather surrender to the Bandabar than watch you all die. The battle can never be won. I will contact their commander now.”

“Aye-aye, Mr. President,” the admiral replied with a confused look on his face. “But sir, are you certain this is the right course? We are soldiers and are prepared to do our best.”

“Bonol, the Society is dead. Let us live to fight another day. Out,” he said as he clicked off the screen.

A button flashed red and he touched it. The face of the Bandabar commander appeared before him. His head was much like a crow, with a long curved beak and jet black feathers combed neatly in place. “President Gerfaz, I am Admiral Veek Alar of the Bandabar Fold. Am I to understand that you are surrendering to me?”

“Yes, Admiral, that is correct,” Patak sighed. “I have ordered the fleet to stand down. You have to know we could never defeat your much stronger force. Also, due to internal problems in the Society, there is little chance others will come to our aid. Living under Bandabar rule is preferable to death.”

Veek smiled. “Well, I gratefully accept your surrender, Mr. President. Please have your ships accompany us back into orbit. Once we arrive, I will shuttle to your planet where we can discuss terms for the surrender, sir.”

“Of course, Admiral,” Patak said. “I only ask that the Fold respects the civil liberties of our people. We have traded in peace for generations and I hope we can count on remaining active partners.”

"We agree completely, on one condition," Veek replied. "As you may have guessed our primary interest is your Hive. We have heard many unbelievable things about this technology and believe it is time it was shared with superior races like the Bandabar."

"Admiral, while it is true we have guarded this technology with all of our might for a very long time, I hardly feel like I can refuse you now. After all, you could kill us all and take what you want if I did."

Veek laughed. "I suppose that is true, Mr. President, however, we are a peace-loving society. We have dozens of alien planets in our sphere of influence. As long as your planet complies with our laws, I believe Paranon Nar can be an active member of the Fold. My fleet will arrive in orbit in two hours. Then my team will shuttle down. Your local time stamp is 1100 if I am not mistaken."

"Yes, that is correct," Patak agreed.

"Then let us plan to meet in your office at 1400 hours. I must tell you this day has turned out much better than I had anticipated. We had intelligence that your planet would be most vulnerable today and that must have been true. Still, we were prepared for several days of combat when many on both sides would die horribly. Our own President suggested you might destroy your own Hive before we could take it. Why the change of heart?" Veek asked.

Patak laughed. "Congratulations on your excellent intelligence, Admiral. Clearly your people are not aware of the problems within the Society. As you can tell by the events of this morning, I can no longer count on Society support and defense. Even the Nar Council cannot provide any aid. We are now a single planet relying on our own defenses, which could never stand before the Fold. If this transition can be peaceful, and Paranon can count on Bandabar for defense, I will be greatly relieved."

"Mr. President, I will see you at 1400 hours. My men and I will pray for you and your people. Your actions have saved many lives and we now owe those lives to you. Out," the valakar replied.

Patak stood and refilled his glass and walked over to the window. The park around the Presidential mansion was surrounded by tall evergreen trees. He watched as small groups of birds flew among the branches. He took a sip of brandy and swirled it around in his mouth before swallowing. He wondered if his decision to choose surrender and peace would turn out well for his planet. Perhaps the Bandabar admiral was telling the truth. There was little intelligence from the Fold. Their society was much smaller than the Society of Humanity, but little else was known. Perhaps some of the Hive agents could provide more details, but then he realized the top secret agents had been relocated weeks ago. He thought for a moment about destroying the Hive. There was still time to protect humanity's greatest secret. He might be regarded as a hero in the Society if he acted now. Of course, that would likely condemn him to death. Why would he want to be a hero to the Society anyway? They had done nothing to protect his planet and people. Perhaps it was time for the Hive secrets to be known. Humanity had done nothing to advance the universe with it after all. It was a weapon and espionage device. If the Bandabar are truly peaceful, perhaps they can make better use of it. He decided he had done enough worrying and decision making for today. He drained the glass and left the office to take a walk in the woods.

CHAPTER 37

"Patak Gerfaz is a damned coward!" Passor Valka shouted. "He knows the top directive from the High Council is to secure Hive technology. How could he surrender to those damned birds so easily?" It had been two days since Alana Albright had appeared in the Brotherhood meeting room, and one hour since the first reports of the surrender of Paranon Nar started to reverberate around the Society. He strode around the room seething with anger. His trusted commanders, Armand Coos and Febo Loo sat quietly, not wanting to bring his wrath onto them as well. "Well, speak up! What are we going to do about this?"

Armand cleared his throat and squeaked, "Passor, this was bound to happen at some point. With planetary Hives near the frontier and the Society in shambles, our neighbors were going to come after our secrets. It was only a matter of time, Supreme Leader."

Passor stared incredulously at his long time friend. After a moment, his expression softened and he even smiled. "I know that Armand. I had just hoped we would have relocated to Ulagong before this kind of tragedy occurred. Let the Bandabar play with their Hive. I doubt they will be able to figure it out for decades."

A look of desperation crossed Febo Loo's face. "Supreme Leader, one billion agents were still on the planet when it was attacked, including a Chief Engineer. If they help the Bandabar, they could utilize the Hive almost immediately." He cowered as Passor turned his glare onto him.

"Then we are lost," Passor sighed as he sat down across from the other two. "I just don't understand how this could happen so quickly. It doesn't make sense. How could the Bandabar know there was a Hive on that planet? There are dozens of others, but they chose that one."

"There must be human spies in the Fold," Febo replied. "Perhaps even another Hive working for them."

"I hardly imagine a Hive would turn on humanity for those bird-brains," Passor scoffed. "Spies are another issue. I wasn't aware there were any human planets in the Fold. Do either of you have information on that?"

"No, Supreme Leader," Febo answered. "But remember we have traded peacefully with the Fold for a long time. It's possible they turned some of our people or even had trading offices on the planets."

"I have another theory, Supreme Leader," Armand interjected. "Now that he is dead and you have taken his place, I can tell you I was skeptical about some of the actions of your predecessor."

"Do you know something I don't?" Passor asked.

"I don't know what you know, but Fola did arrange transportation for several alien ships into our galaxy," Armand began. "He said it was in the interest of mutual trust and friendship. As he was Supreme Leader, I never questioned him."

"Are you suggesting any of them may have tipped off the Bandabar?" Passor asked. "That seems very hard to believe."

"I don't know, but it is a possibility. I recall a Hive transported several valakar warships into our galaxy a couple of weeks ago. I was told they were here to investigate and initiate diplomatic contacts with other valakar cultures. Apparently, our former leader planned to relocate most valakars back to Ulagong at some point in the future. It was his opinion this galaxy should be led by humans and Ulagong led by valakars," Armand said.

"Yes, I have heard that story too, at least about moving the valakars away from here," Passor acknowledged. "But how would those valakars know the location of a Hive in this galaxy?"

"I don't know sir," Armand replied. "Something had to tip off the Bandabar and I would prefer to believe it was other valakar rather than a human. Perhaps that's just wishful thinking."

"Passor, are we still going to leave the home galaxy?" Febo asked. "With the aggression of the Fold, perhaps we should help build a force to push them back first. Society defenses are very weak right now. If someone doesn't act, they could overrun the entire Society."

"I have begun to wonder the same thing, Febo," Passor sighed. "The proper course always seemed so clear to Fola. But I am not him. He firmly believed the Society would be able to keep most planets while only a few frontier worlds were lost. As you noted, the aggression of the Bandabar is far more than he anticipated. While I doubt they could take over the entire Society, they are already doing significant damage. Someone has to stand up and say 'Enough!' I don't think Wendo or Antar have the strength anymore."

"But the people hate us even more, Supreme Leader," Armand argued. "They won't listen to us. I think Fola was right about that."

"They don't hate us, Armand. They hate the Brotherhood," Passor replied.

"I don't understand the difference, sir. We are the Brotherhood," Armand said.

"Not anymore!" Passor shouted. "The Brotherhood was gravely wounded at the Grand Conclave. It died by the same weapon that killed Fola Untor. Now it is time to step out of the shadows and into our rightful place as the leaders of the Society of Humanity."

"How exactly do we do that, Supreme Leader?" Armand asked. "We're not really in any position to lead right now."

Passor laughed. "No one else is leading either, Armand. As enemies attack our frontiers, more planets will be at risk like Paranon Nar. They will look for someone to help them. We will be there. When others see us fighting the good fight, they will join us. They will begin to see the error of their civil strife and focus on our true enemies. When the battle is done, they will owe their safety to us. They will beg us to provide defense and support, and we will happily agree."

"What about Fola's orders for revenge?" Febo asked.

"Forget it. Fola is dead and those orders died with him," Passor said. He was feeling like the President of the High Council again. "The humans in the Ulagong Galaxy are heavily outnumbered by valakar and maklan planets. Let them fight their own wars. If they are losing, perhaps we will bring them back here to their home. If they survive, we will reach out at the appropriate time for peace and trade."

"Supreme Leader, everyone knows we are Brotherhood agents," Febo argued. "How will they believe us now?"

"I am no longer Supreme Leader, gentlemen. I am now Admiral of the Free Society for Peace. They will believe us when we help them by fighting off their enemies. Then they will join forces with us because we are the only voice for peace and security in the Society. Then even Wendo and Antar will have to join with us. While I doubt the old Society will ever rise again, the new one with much greater regional autonomy will survive, and we will lead it," Passor concluded.

"Admiral, what about the alliance in the Ulagong Galaxy?" Febo asked. "If we abandon them now, they will not be able to overcome the Hives of the Free Society."

"Screw them!" Passor shouted. "Fola wanted to destroy the Free Society as his ultimate revenge for the Grand Conclave. I could care less. Dave Brewster and Fa-a-Di did cost me my job as President, but that was as much my fault. Let them have Ulagong. Fola's alliance will likely fail anyway from what I was told. The maklans and valakar are natural enemies. And if valakar agents came here and tipped off the Bandabar, then I hope the humans and maklans wipe them out."

"I'm afraid the valakar might join forces in the two galaxies now that they have a Hive, Passor," Armand said. "That makes them a significant risk."

"All the more reason for us to destroy the Hive on Paranon Nar," Passor grinned. "Patak failed us, but that's okay. He was facing extermination by the Bandabar. We are going to stop their aggression though. Those birds will rue the day they broke our treaties and invaded. Now, Generals Coos and Loo, I need you to start working on coordinating our people. We need as many ships and troops as possible to start our initiative. Every day we wait, the Bandabar are closer to having an operational Hive. While Patak was a coward, I believe the Hive agents will delay them as long as they can. If we can strike before then, the war may already be won."

The two men stood up. "Passor, we'll get right on it. What are your plans?" Febo asked.

"I think I'll go see my friend Rainor and give him the good news," Passor laughed. "I think I deserve a nice night on the town. Good luck, my brothers."

CHAPTER 38

President Gerfaz gathered the High Council of Paranon Nar for the official surrender of the planet to the Bandabar Fold. They sat quietly in the Council Chamber waiting for the valakar to arrive. Each would look around at their friends and smile but none dared to speak a word. The situation was too terrible to discuss. Patak had turned his chair away from the group and was looking out at the bright blue sky, wondering if he would see another morning.

The doors were opened and a line of Bandabar walked in. They were tall, roughly seven feet in height on average. They wore dark red battle armor and silver helmets. Each had two blasters attached to their belts. Their exposed wings and heads were covered with black feathers that were sleeked back and shiny. They had an extra pair of limbs that served as arms and hands. The people of Paranon Nar had seen Bandabar many times. The frontier was only a couple light-years away and trade had always been brisk and friendly. Patak remembered the face of Admiral Veek Alar who sat directly across from him. He smiled meekly at his conqueror. As the last of the Bandabar were sitting, another valakar entered the room. Patak had never seen anything like him. He was much taller than the Bandabar with bright yellow feathers. He carried himself regally as though he felt better than the rest. He looked around the room and glared at each human. Then he sat next to the Admiral and smiled.

“President Gerfaz, I presume?” the admiral began.

"Yes, Admiral," Patak replied. "I welcome you and your fleet to Paranon Nar. I also officially surrender the planet to the Bandabar Fold."

"Thank you for that, sir," Veek answered. "As I told you earlier, you can expect our normal relationship to resume. The only change is that you are now part of the Fold." The yellow bird leaned over and whispered in Veek's ear-hole. "Ah yes, I forgot, Majesty. Patak, let me introduce you to Emperor Lok Zul of the Donnaki Empire."

Patak rose and bowed to the Donnaki. "Welcome to our planet, sir. Pardon me but I have not heard of the Donnaki. Perhaps we humans have a different name for you."

Lok Zul laughed. "No need to apologize. My planets are not in this galaxy. I believe you call my home galaxy Ulagong."

"That's amazing!" Patak said. "Welcome sir. So you come from the same galaxy as Dave Brewster and Fa-a-Di?"

"So I am told," Lok scowled. "I have only heard their names from other humans and their sphere of influence in my galaxy is far from my space. My dear friend Fola Untor seemed to have a low impression of them."

"Untor! Emperor, please be cautious with that man," urged Patak. "He is the leader of a sinister group called the Brotherhood. They spy on us and haunt our every move. Do not trust them. They will turn on you if it suits their best interests."

Lok laughed again and looked at Veek, saying, "You know, I like this man. He thinks like I do." He turned back to face the president. "Now you know why we are here today, Gerfaz.

Untor made many promises to me and others in our galaxy. He told us about the Hive weapon and how it would be turned on us as the Free Society in our galaxy grew and conquered others. I never believed him."

"That's a relief," Patak sighed. "They are not trustworthy people and he was the worst of them."

"We are very aware of the Brotherhood in the Fold, Patak," Veek interjected. "But the emperor is a bit smarter than they. He convinced Untor to move fifty Donnaki cruisers here so they could contact other valakar species. It was part of the Brotherhood's plan to eventually relocate all of us back to Ulagong." He laughed. "Untor should have known that would never happen. We Bandabar have lived on our planets for thousands of generations. Why should we move? When we met the Emperor here, it became obvious we could work together to our mutual best interest. That's where you come in."

"It was Fola Untor who told us there was a Hive on this planet," Lok smiled. "He said it like a warning to stay away. But the Bandabar have been monitoring activity around this planet for months. They have seen people and equipment leaving at an alarming rate. Normally one would expect a roughly equivalent amount of goods traveling both ways. So we knew something was up."

"We could also estimate the number of humans living here," Veek continued. "It is not natural for the population to drop so quickly without any signs of war or plague. We knew the Society of Humanity was crumbling, and humanity wanted to keep Hive weapon technology from others. So it made sense your Hive was being relocated. Please tell us we are not too late?"

"Gentlemen, I am concerned you keep referring to the Hive as a weapon," the woman seated next to President Gerfaz said. "I am Chief Engineer Alea Fostan. It is my job to coordinate the activity of our Hive. I assure you the Hive is no weapon."

Veek replied, "Well, that's a relief, Emperor! I feared both Chief Engineers would have fled already. How do you do Alea? It is a pleasure to meet you. You must know our knowledge of Hive technology is sketchy at best. We are relying on our intelligence and the emperor here."

"Not a weapon!" Lok scoffed. "One of these machines destroyed an entire fleet of my best cruisers!"

"I believe you sir, but that is hard to imagine," Alea replied. "I hope and pray that too many lives were not lost."

"Actually, that is the strange part about it," Lok said. "All the crews of the ships were somehow relocated to our home planet before the ships were ground to dust. But they were spying on us in our sovereign territory!"

"I'm sorry for that, but I have no knowledge of any such action," she replied. "We have never used our Hive for any aggressive action. It is still functional, although half of the equipment has already left this planet."

"Still functional," Veek said to the emperor. "That is great news." He turned back to the Chief Engineer. "Well, it seems our efforts have paid off. We would like to tour your facility as soon as possible. I have a science team on my flagship which will shuttle down soon to join us."

"It's important to let you know that Fola Untor already told me and my team how a Hive functions," Lok said. "Right now, sitting in this room, I have the sneaking feeling that most of it was a lie."

Patak added, "I'm sure it was, sir. The Brotherhood was the right arm of the High Council. The highest directive of that council was to keep Hive technology from the other species. Untor never would have told you the truth or given you any real knowledge."

"I'll be sure to kill him with my bare hands when I see him again," Lok snarled. "If what you say is true."

"Now I'm concerned," Veek interjected. "If safeguarding this technology is so important, why did you surrender and why didn't you destroy the Hive? How do we know you won't lie to us too?"

"Gentlemen, it was the directive of the High Council of the Society of Humanity," Patak replied. "The military of the Society could have easily defeated all of your ships. If they desired, they could overrun the Fold in a matter of weeks. But where are they now? The Society is gone, broken into its fifty thousand pieces. It was their job to protect us, but they did not. We have no hope from our own brothers. I could have allowed our ships to attack your fleet, but you would have destroyed them after a protracted and bloody battle. I could have ordered the destruction of the Hive, but why? That would only have led to more death and destruction." He rose and walked behind his councillors, patting each on the back. "Paranon Nar was alone. I followed my orders to relocate the Hive to safer territory. I did my job. But what did I get for it? My people and I were deserted and left to fend for ourselves." He walked over to a cupboard and removed five bottles of liquor and several glasses and set them on the table. "After we spoke earlier Veek, I went for a walk in the nearby forest. I thought about my options and almost gave the order to destroy the Hive a dozen times. Then I thought about our long and friendly history. I worried the Bandabar might enslave us, but then realized you have always been fair. I thought how I was turning my back on my own species, but they turned their backs on me first. I sat by a small creek and watched fish swimming along. Then it hit me. I am like one of those fish, being carried along by a current far greater than me. I could do what I was trained to do and fight that current. Or I could follow it and have faith the river knows where it is going."

"I am a man of my words, Patak," Veek replied. "The Fold has no further ambitions in human territory at this time. I expect us to live in peace. I have spoken with Consul Pata Zaka, our leader, and she assures me you and your people will be full citizens of the Fold. We want the Hive, nothing else."

Lok Zul looked bored. "This diplomacy is touching, but let's either have a drink or visit the Hive or something. We need to get it running so my fleet can go back home. I sincerely doubt the Brotherhood will help us get back now."

CHAPTER 39

Paxran was a city planet. Most of the dry surface was covered by the capital city of the same name. Four billion maklans toiled daily to keep the empire functioning and controlled. The twelve hundred planets of the Empire needed trade, defense and leadership from the maklans on this world. Half the surface was covered with oceans, which were heavily dotted with island chains which were left in their native state for vacations and wildlife preserves. Dozens of massive space ports orbited, providing space for cargo and passenger traffic.

General Kolu Inzaka sat with his general staff in his office deep in the heart of the city. The residence was one of the few surrounded by a large park full of trees and ponds. Reverend Raza Intepam was also in attendance. He was the leader of the Paxrani religion and a very devout maklan, who wore a simple tunic and robes in the room full of dress uniforms dripping with medals and rank insignia. Kolu briefed the group on the events at the meeting on Panzak. Everyone was horrified by the stories of the Hive weapon. It was impossible to imagine a device that could grind an entire planet to dust. They were equally frightened about the plasma bomb device given to the Donnaki by the Maklakar, whom they believed had disappeared long ago. "So, Reverend, I suppose this means your prophecy has come true?" Kolu suggested.

"I wouldn't call it my prophecy, Dear Leader," Raza replied. "The sacred texts were written long ago. Those documents supported the survival of some Maklakar. I believe this to be a wonderful blessing for us all. Those were horrible and violent times. Now that I know some of our fellow maklans survived, some of our inherited guilt can be forgiven."

"On the other hand, Dear Leader, those survivors have now provided a new weapon to the Donnaki," General Gont Ongool countered. "If they choose to attack, there is little we can do to protect ourselves. The failure of our ancestors to complete the job may now lead to our own deaths."

"Yes, I know that," Kolu replied. "That is why I asked the Reverend to join us today. We cannot count on the Maklakar to give us the same knowledge. They would be terrified we would use it against them. And that would probably be a correct deduction. They also destroyed the tekkan Hive, which might have been our only defense."

"Should we fear the Free Society as the human Untor has suggested, Dear Leader?" Gont asked. "We have had very little contact with any of their worlds. I can hardly imagine them crossing the galactic center to attack us."

"I wondered the same thing, Gont," the Dear Leader replied. "That Untor fellow seemed possessed by his hatred for those people, but I don't know why, and frankly, I don't care. I only attended the meeting to learn what I could about Hives and the Donnaki. As the Reverend noted, it has been many generations since we tried to expand our territory. That is all ancient history. Now most of our military is focused on the frontier. That's why I've asked General Abala Konole of Tak-u-Baka to join us as well. It was his spies who witnessed the Hive battle in Donnaki space months ago. Abala, what do you have to say?"

"Dear Leader, you are quite correct," Abala began. "That one day was the only time we have seen a Hive. We have no contact with any of the civilizations involved in their Free Society. I see no reason to believe they are intent on galactic domination. We must remember that all the crews of the

Donnaki ships were transported to another planet before the destruction. If the humans feared meeting them again in battle, they would have killed them there."

"Well, that's not completely correct, Abala," Reverend Intepam said. "A number of our planets have trade agreements with Tak-Makla."

"What?" Kolu shouted. "Who would dare to break my orders? Give me names!"

"Dear Leader, please do not be upset," Raza said calmly. "It is only trade sir. You can imagine the amount of goods needed to support this and the military planets. We have plenty of money, but not enough food. I have been told the tekkans use their Hive to move goods among many systems. The materials we import come from planets approved by you. The tekkans only act as intermediaries. I am told even the whisky you enjoy comes here via tekkan cargo ships."

"That seems reasonable, but totally unnecessary to me," Kolu argued. "Why can't they bring the goods in their own ships?"

"Dear Leader, the tekkans can use their Hive to move their ships across the galaxy in seconds, rather than weeks or months the old fashioned way," Raza replied. "They call it progress."

"Isn't it odd I was never informed about this?" Kolu asked looking sternly at his generals.

"Not at all, sir," Raza said. "You and the High Command work tirelessly to keep us safe. I am certain the bureaucrats did not want to trouble you with the nature of the transit vessel that brings our food. It also saves money. Since the tekkans use little fuel for their vessels, they can charge less for freight. The goods arrive almost immediately, so the need for inventory is also reduced."

"So, you think this is a non-issue?" Kolu queried. "How about the rest of you? Gont?"

"Dear Leader, I agree with the Reverend," Gont began. "Yet I think it goes well beyond his point. The Hive technology has done great things for the tekkans. They get rich moving goods magically across the cosmos. Of course, they probably have spies everywhere. Even though they have the ability, they have never used their Hive as a weapon on us. Why should we think they will?"

"Yes, that makes sense," Kolu answered. "It also tells us clearly we would be stupid to attack the Free Society, no matter their intentions in the far distant future. On the contrary, I think we need to befriend them quickly before my friend, Lok Zul decides to use his plasma bombs on us. You know, it would be great if they would help us exterminate those damned birds once and for all."

The Reverend laughed. "Dear Leader, you must know the likelihood of that is very remote. Most cultures live in fear of us. I'm sure the tekkans have learned that from their other trading relationships. Our past as conquerors is not too distant. If the Donnaki suddenly disappeared, who is to say we would not begin again? But I fully agree with the need to normalize relations with them. They are our brothers from Ai-Makla. Friendship will provide more opportunity to learn their secrets and could provide defense when the Donnaki do attack. I can feel that day approaching quickly."

"But you know the Donnaki could attack right now. We don't have the benefit of time to deal with diplomacy. It could take generations before the tekkans trust us that much. I fear we would all be Donnaki slaves by then," Kolu replied.

"I believe there is another way, Dear Leader," Raza countered. "As leader of our faith, I have had many visions when I meditate. I believe there are planets which have the power of a Hive without the need for billions of agents. If we could locate one or more, we might have that same power."

Kolu looked incredulous. "You want us to search the galaxy to prove your dream is real. Honestly Raza, do you hear yourself talk?" Kolu scoffed.

Raza scowled, "Dear Leader, we must reach out to the tekkans as you have suggested, knowing it will take a long time. If there is any chance I am correct, our problem may be fixed much sooner. Isn't that worth a risk? If the Donnaki attack, all hope is lost."

Kolu rose and walked over to a window and looked out at the park and trees. A layer of clouds was approaching and rain would fall in a few hours. "Perhaps you are right, Raza. If the Donnaki attack and we did not try, we would be destroyed by our own foolishness. We can certainly spare a couple ships and a team of astronomers."

"Bless you Dear Leader," Raza replied. "I will keep you and the High Command informed of our progress."

Kolu turned around and looked at the Reverend. "Raza, what do you think the odds are you will find one in time?"

Raza laughed and said, "Dear Leader, I am a man of faith. I believe God will help us protect our planets. I have no doubt we will find a natural Hive."

CHAPTER 40

After being led back to the surface of the ocean, Dave and his friends climbed aboard the shuttle and headed back to shore. As the vessel approached the coastline, a voice came over the loud speaker, saying "Admiral, a fleet of twenty battle cruisers has appeared in this system. They appear to be on course to attack Gallicea. What are your orders?"

"Set an intercept course, Ka-a-Fa!" De-o-Nu barked. "Also call for reinforcements and warn the planet to prepare for attack. The general and I will be there soon."

"Aye-aye, Admiral," Ka-a-Fa replied as he cut the connection.

"Brother, we should leave Dave, Odo and Lini here on the planet," Fa-a-Di said. "It think the ship may be overwhelmed by the enemy." He turned to Dave and asked, "Do you think you can fly this shuttle?"

"Of course, you two should use Jake and Mitch to get to the ship quicker," Dave replied. "And keep me informed. I'll contact Admiral Adamsen when we land to get help." Dave rushed over to the helm while the two Galliceans pulled off their pressure suits. When they were ready, the two maklans landed on them and the group flashed off the ship. Dave turned on the auto-pilot which was programmed to return to the landing site.

"Dave, you should land as quickly as possible," Odo said. "If the attackers come here, this small craft will be an easy target. The Hive should protect us if we are on the ground."

"That's my plan, Odo," he replied. "There had to be a Hive involved in this attack. Twenty star cruisers don't just appear out of thin air. Do you think it was Atar Pa?"

"Only God knows, Dave," the elder answered.

Fa-a-Di assumed command of the Kong-Fa which was rapidly approaching the flank of the enemy fleet. Four more ships would arrive in the next ten minutes and Kong-Fa had to slow down attackers until they arrived. "Brother, I've never seen that configuration of a warship before," he said to De-o-Nu. "Do you recognize them?"

"No sir," he replied. "I don't recognize that insignia either. They must be from some unknown civilization."

"Shit!" Fa-a-Di shouted. "I didn't see the insignia at first. I saw that same sign on the shuttle on Lagamar Boley on my second visit."

"You're saying those are Brotherhood cruisers?" De-o-Nu asked. "In this galaxy? How did they get here?"

"Had to be a Hive, Brother," Fa-a-Di replied. "Ka-a-Fa, fire on all ships. It won't hurt them much but might draw them off the planet." A rain of plasma bombs shot out from the ship and raced toward the attackers. As they exploded, the enemy ship defenses held. None of the ships returned fire or turned to attack. "They're after the planet. Another terrorist attack. I'll personally see those bastards in hell! Give me more power!"

The shuttle landed near the camp site. Most of the Galliceans who had spent the previous night had already left and more shuttles were landing and unloading. The few who remained were showing the new visitors that breathers were no longer needed. It was looking like another party would occur that day. Dave was very happy to be back on the ground knowing the battle was raging above him. He hoped Odo was correct about the Hive protecting this planet at least. Odo came up behind Dave and clapped him on the back. "I guess we just wait to find out how the battle goes," he said.

"I've already called the fleet leadership. We have ten ships on the way, but without a portal in this system it will take hours to arrive. I asked Zee to look into transporting ships here, but that will take time to arrange as well," Dave replied.

"Before we leave, I need to gather my personal things," Lini said. "I know the Galliceans will win the day. Those filthy Brotherhood agents will crumble under their withering attack."

"How do you know it is the Brotherhood?" Dave asked.

"Who else would attack a defenseless planet?" she replied. "I should only be gone a few minutes."

"Let me walk with you Lini," Dave said. "Consider it your first briefing as a member of my crew. Do you want to come along, Odo?"

"No thanks, Dave," he replied. "I think I'll get to know some of the Galliceans. I promised to help them understand the natural Hive. I'll see you when you get back." Dave and Lini left the shuttle stand and walked back down the hill.

"Brother, High Priest Um-e-Ka and most of the population have left Sa-la-Na," De-o-Nu said. "They are either flying about or looking for Ka-la-a to land on. They are reporting heavy bombardment of the city at this time."

"What about our reinforcements?" Fa-a-Di asked.

"Eight minutes out, General," Ka-a-Fa said.

"How is the city holding up?" he asked. "Is it going to lose power?"

"It's too early to tell, brother," De-o-Nu said. "The constant bombardment is taking a toll."

"General, I have an idea," Ka-a-Fa interrupted. "When my fleet engaged the Brotherhood over Lagamar Boley, we tried a new tactic to rapidly disable their ships."

"Just do it!" Fa-a-Di urged. "We're not even denting their defensive arrays with one ship."

"Okay, sir. I'm overloading the plasma system. I'm trying to get to two hundred percent of maximum," Ka-a-Fa said.

"Won't the ship explode?" Fa-a-Di asked. "Is this a suicide attack?"

"Hardly! Watch this!" Ka-a-Fa shouted. He pressed the contact and a massive blast of plasma shot at the last ship in the line of attackers. Less than a second later, he pressed the contact again, sending a second blast behind the other.

The first blast knocked out the rear defensive array. Before it could recharge, the second blast hit, smashing through the array and striking the engine nacelles, which exploded in a massive fireball. The fireball grew and shot forward until the entire vessel burst into thousands of pieces.

"They're turning to attack us, brother," De-o-Nu said. "I don't know how long our array can hold up to that many ships."

"I'm up to one hundred and forty percent, general," Ka-a-Fa said. "I just need a few more seconds to attack again." Plasma blasts rocked the Kong-Fa, but her array held at eighty percent.

After collecting her things, Dave and Lini crossed the river again. She kissed the ferryman on the cheek and wished him well, wondering if she would ever see this place again. Dave carried most of her baggage and she was talking nonstop. "I can't believe I'm doing this Dave. Tell me everything about space and the Free Society. Where are we going now? Will I be going for that training right away?"

"Don't worry, Lini," he laughed. "There is all the time in the world. I only worry about my friends in space now. Twenty to one odds are pretty long. I don't even know if I'd want to keep doing this without them."

She took one of the bags from him and put her arm around his waist. "Dave, you worry too much. We are going on a new adventure. God will protect Fa-a-Di and De-o-Nu. You have to have faith."

"Hello Dave," said a voice behind them. They turned to see Fola Untor pointing a blaster at them. "Surprised to see me here?"

Ka-a-Fa fired the second round of double plasma blasts at a lead ship, which exploded in a giant fireball which damaged four other vessels. The remaining enemy ships turned and headed away as quickly as they could. "Thank God they gave up," Fa-a-Di said. "What's our defensive level, brother?"

"Ten percent, General," De-o-Nu laughed. "If they knew that, they'd never have fled.

"General, I'm getting an odd reading on the terrestrial planet," Ka-a-Fa said. "It looks like a temporal wave near the encampment."

"Oh no," he sighed. "They're after Dave again. Jake, get over here and take me there right now!"

"I am surprised to see you Fola. You can't imagine how surprised, actually," Dave said as the man approached them.

"Tell the girl to move away, Admiral," Fola smiled. "I don't mean any harm to her. And both of you need to turn around slowly."

As they turned, Lini asked, "Who is that man and what does he want from you?"

"It's a long story and I doubt I have time to tell you," Dave replied.

"If she doesn't move, you'll have plenty of time to tell her, Dave," Fola laughed. He was only a couple feet behind them now. Dave could feel the tip of the blaster in his back.

"You should move Lini," Dave said. "This isn't your battle."

"Fola Untor? I thought you were dead," shouted Fa-a-Di who appeared ten feet ahead of them with Jake clinging to his chest. His two blasters were aimed at them. "Drop the weapon before you are killed for the second time!"

Lini saw Fola's free hand moving to touch Dave's shoulder. The arm had a strange electronic device covering it from wrist to elbow. Several lights were flashing red. Just as he touched Dave, she grabbed Dave's other arm. A massive blast of light and energy shot through the area knocking Fa-a-Di off his feet. Several nearby trees caught on fire and the ground shook as though an earthquake had struck. Fa-a-Di rose slowly, feeling as though he had been shot by a blaster. His uniform was singed and Jake lay on the ground, barely breathing. There was no sign of Fola, Dave or Lini. They had disappeared in the giant explosion.

De-o-Nu flashed into the clearing with Mitch clinging to his chest. He rushed over to help Fa-a-Di get to his feet. Mitch took Jake and flashed away for medical aid. "Brother, what happened? Where is Dave? Was it a bomb?"

"I don't know," Fa-a-Di said, shaking his head. "That bastard Fola Untor was here with Dave and Lini. I was about to shoot him when the blast occurred and they were just gone."

Ka-a-Fa's voice crackled over their intercoms. "Please leave that area. There is a massive temporal eddy in your immediate area. Hurry!"

As the two Galliceans ran, Fa-a-Di glanced at his chronometer, which appeared to be running backwards. After a few seconds, it stopped completely, then began to run normally again. Ka-a-Fa's voice crackled over their intercoms. "Please leave that area. There is a massive temporal eddy in your immediate area. Hurry!" Within a few minutes, they had climbed back to the shuttle port.

They sat to rest near the shuttles. “Did you see your chronometer, brother?” Fa-a-Di panted. “Mine was running backwards and then stopped.”

“That’s why we got the same message from Ka-a-Fa twice,” De-o-Nu reasoned. “That was so strange.”

“It’s worse than strange, brother,” Fa-a-Di replied. “Fola has taken Dave and Lini to another time so we cannot find him.”

“But I thought Dave said Fola was dead,” De-o-Nu said. “How could a dead man do this?”

Odo Pak had seen the blast and arrived at the shuttle at the same time as the two Galliceans. “You are thinking too linearly, De-o-Nu,” he began. “Obviously, Fola came to the future before he went to the past where he was killed on Earth 47.” He sat with the others. “The worst part is that Fola could have done this many times. We may experience more of his treachery yet.”

CHAPTER 41

The Nightsky arrived over Zulanan two hours after Dave and Lini had disappeared with the Brotherhood agent. A second meeting was being held in the conference room at the bottom of the ocean. Aria, Muncie and Rence spoke to the group from their office on Earth. "Thank you for the details on the two temporal anomalies, General," Rence opened. "I've run them through my algorithm and your prediction is remarkably accurate. The first wave was very shallow but broad, implying only a small time jump over a vast distance of space. It would be totally possible that Fola Untor made this jump before the visit to Earth where he died."

"I know what I saw!" Fa-a-Di shouted. "I knew it was Fola Untor, I remember his face well. What about the second wave?"

Muncie looked pained. "The blast and second wave were unbelievably powerful. The depth was incredible, but the size was not sufficient to include other galaxies."

"So what's the bottom line?" Darlene asked. She had heard about the attack within minutes and had been distraught ever since. She looked tired and her bloodshot eyes gave away her tears.

"Darlene, I am so sorry," Aria said. "This kind of time travel should be impossible without a Hive. Then it would only be mental energy, not physical bodies. While Dave is probably somewhere in this galaxy, he could be anywhere from half a million years behind or ahead of us. We've never seen anything like this before."

Zee Gongaleg could be seen on the other side of the screen with Loni Arrak. “Darlene, I will dedicate the entire resources of my Hive to find your husband, but I must admit the odds are against us. We are looking for a single man in a galaxy somewhere in a million years of time.”

“What about getting more Hives involved?” she asked. “Can this planet or Nan or Atar Pa get involved?”

Ulook was in her human form again and patted Darlene’s hand. “Darlene, this planet is already working with Tak-Makla on the matter. Serena Vanatee has offered help, but with her Brotherhood past, I’m not sure it is a genuine offer. And Nan is fully dedicated to protecting the Lagamar-Nan Alliance. But Zee is correct, this will take time.”

“We do know one thing, Darlene,” Muncie interjected. “Fola Untor did jump to Earth a few days ago to kill Dave. Wherever Dave and Lini are, Fola is not with them.”

“How does that help?” she asked, wiping tears from her eyes.

“These temporal eddies leave marks,” Muncie added. “While it’s theoretical at this time, we might find a way to track the other end of the wave and find its endpoint. The Temporal Command is one hundred percent focused on those calculations now. Believe me, we won’t give up.”

Odo stood and walked behind Darlene and put his hands on her shoulders. “We are all forgetting something else.” He smiled. “We must have faith.” He walked slowly around the table touching each person on the shoulder as he passed. “Dave and Darlene had faith when they left their lives in the twenty-first to help modern Earth. The Temporal Command had faith that Dave and Darlene could help them progress, and they have already done that!"

"How will this help us find Dave, Odo?" Fa-a-Di asked. "I believe in God too, but know this is an almost impossible job. We will all do our best. Greater Gallia will expedite the construction of new Hives to join the search, as will others in the Free Society. But it is still like finding a specific hydrogen atom in a star."

"We must remember Dave's unique connection to the Source," Odo reminded them. "The Source exists above space and time. When Dave reaches out to it, I believe it will help him return to us."

"I hope you're right," Fa-a-Di replied. "Without divine intervention, this could go on forever. Poor Dave. Poor me! I am lost without my brother." He forced himself to remain composed. Turning to De-o-Nu, he asked, "Whatever happened to the fleeing Brotherhood fleet?"

"A Kalidean fleet intercepted them as they approached Atar Pa," his brother-in-law replied. "They heard them begging the Hive there to return them to their own galaxy. Atar Pa never returned their signal. They began to fire on the planet just as the Kalidean fleet came within range. Within fifteen minutes, all the Brotherhood ships were either destroyed or disabled. The disabled ships then self-destructed."

"They chose to die rather than being captured? There were no survivors?" Fa-a-Di asked. "That seems very severe."

"Without a willing Hive, those men were condemned to stay here as enemies to all," De-o-Nu replied. "I'll never understand such devotion to evil."

"Perhaps we can count on support from Atar Pa then," Darlene suggested. "If that's true, it is a very good sign."

"I just thought of something else," Odo interrupted. "Didn't Dave tell me yesterday that Fistan was a natural Hive?"

"Oh not this again," Fa-a-Di scoffed. "Odo, it's an ancient story. No one believes it anymore."

"Perhaps that is true General," Odo laughed. "Remember that a natural Hive is much more powerful than a constructed one, even one as great as on Tak-Makla. We have this natural Hive now. If we could locate another, it would be like having thirty Hives on our side. That could make this job a lot simpler."

"I could use a drink!" Fa-a-Di laughed. "Odo, sometimes I wish I could win an argument with you, but I doubt that will happen. I will ask High Priest Um-e-Ka to bless the trip and provide some priests with knowledge of the presumed location. After all Odo, I did promise to introduce you to him." He stood and walked behind De-o-Nu and clapped him on the back. "Admiral, I guess this makes you Supreme Commander of Dave's fleet until you find him. What are your orders?"

De-o-Nu rose and shook the general's hand. "Thank you brother." He turned to the table. "Odo, after your visit to Gallicea, you need to return here. The Hive will need you to lead it. Also, your health will be better here. Since this may be a wasted trip, I recommend that only Nightsky and Kong-Fa travel to Fistan. Darlene, I know you will want to accompany us, but I think it would be better if you stayed with Fa-a-Di and began diplomacy with the Maklakar. Perhaps Fak Mondoka could join you. It's critical we get them on our side before Paxran or the Donnaki try an attack. Zee, you need to monitor Atar Pa daily. I'll have a couple ships travel there for diplomacy too. We have to know their intentions. How's that brother?"

"You left out the part where you give me a glass of whisky when we get back on board," Fa-a-Di laughed.

CHAPTER 42

Dave woke in a brightly-lit stone cottage. He was lying on the cold floor. Something about this room was very familiar, he thought. There was a small bed next to him where Lini was still unconscious. As he tried to sit up, the pain surged through his head and his entire body tingled. He remembered when he was shot by a blaster on Aranar Zu and realized Fola must have shot him. The light pouring through the small windows was incredibly bright, as though two suns were overhead. A small table sat across the room. Fola Untor sat on one of the two chairs smiling. "Why did you stun me? Why didn't you just kill me?"

"Would you prefer that, Dave?" Fola said pointing his blaster at him menacingly. After a couple seconds, he laughed and set the weapon down on the table. "I do want to kill you for what you've done to the Brotherhood, but that comes later. Just consider this my backup plan."

"What are you talking about Fola?" Dave asked. "None of this makes any sense."

"Maybe not to you, but it does to me," Fola answered. "As a Chief Engineer, I know how dangerous it is to mess with reverse time travel. There are too many potential paradoxes. Some believe unforeseen circumstances prohibit those from happening. I really don't know the truth of it though. In a little while, I'm going back to Earth 47 to kill you long before you met Loni Arrak on Tak-Makla. Then none of this will have happened. You'll be dead, but your friend here will be back on her home planet and the Brotherhood and I will be back in power."

"Who is this man, Dave?" Lini asked as she sat up on the bed. "Where are we and why?"

"I'm guessing this Nan is your hand servant or sex slave, am I right?" Fola laughed.

"You're wrong again, Fola. Lini is a member of my crew," Dave replied as he rose to sit next to her.

"Unbelievable," Fola scoffed. "You're just like those damn Vol and Ulu, treating the Nan like real people. Well, she's your only friend now Dave, at least until I travel back and kill you."

"You're going to die there, Fola," Dave began. "Several Temporal Command agents will be there and one of them will shoot you dead."

"What makes you think that?" Fola asked.

"It already happened, right? That was a thousand years ago. You die and I am still here," Dave laughed.

"You may have been told that, but look at me now," Fola growled. "I am very much alive. And the point in time when I will kill you is hundreds of thousands of years in the future. Since I haven't done it yet, perhaps your past will change again. Tell me how it all happened."

"I'm no idiot Fola," Dave laughed. "I'm not going to help you kill me."

"Then maybe I'll kill you here and now, along with your pretty servant girl," Fola said aiming the pistol at them.

"The Brotherhood will still be destroyed unless you go back, and you know it," Dave said. "Do your worst, but please take Lini back home. She doesn't deserve this."

He pointed the blaster at Lini and smiled. Then he set it down on the table again and laughed out loud. "I'm not going to kill either of you and I'm not taking her back. She chose to hold onto you when we both asked her to move away. It's her decision to die on this hellhole, not mine."

Lini held Dave's arm and said, "I'm happy to stay with Dave. We will be fine."

"Where are we, Fola?" Dave asked. "And when is this?"

"Where is a damned good question, Dave," Fola started. "I don't think this planet has a name. I've never seen this system in any star chart. It's a few hundred light-years away from the rest of your galaxy. There is only one planet circling the sun. You are now on one of the two moons. The other moon is inhabited, so I put you here. I didn't think you deserved any helpers. Think of it, you have a planet to yourselves. Isn't that wonderful?"

Dave frowned, "So this is our prison now. I can see out the window and this place is barren. How are we supposed to survive?"

"I thought about that for a long time, Dave," Fola continued. "At first I thought I'd just let you starve quickly. But then I realized that would be too easy. I think it would be better if you have some time to think about what you've done."

"I'm proud of what I've done, Fola," he replied. "And I'd do it again."

Fola laughed. "Right. Anyway, I had this place built with lighting and air conditioning that should have enough power for a few hundred years. You'll find out the planet can be incredibly hot when the sun and reflected light from the planet shine together. Assuming you live that long, there are lots of candles in the storage closet. I also found a deep aquifer that should provide adequate water. My men built an underground bunker with enough food for a few years too. You'll have to find new sources of food, if you live that long. There are edible plants and animals out there. You just have to find them. What do you think?"

"You are very generous for a lunatic, Fola," Dave laughed. "Too bad you won't live long enough to come back for a visit."

Fola laughed again. "Well, I think the time eddy should evaporate pretty soon. You and your friend slept for several hours after the jump. By the way, I also left several blasters in the supply cabinets as well. If some of the local beasts come by, you don't want to be their dinner. If you don't mind, I'm going to stun you both now. It will be a small charge, just enough so I can escape before you find the weapons."

"You're a horrible man," Lini snarled.

Fola smiled at her and said, "My dear, if you are very lucky, Dave was wrong about my impending death. If I kill him in the past, you'll find yourself back home with no memory of any of this, since it never occurred. Please remember that I asked you to move away from Dave. It wasn't my intention to do this to anyone else." He smiled again and shot her with the blaster.

"See you in hell, Fola," Dave growled. Fola only smiled as he shot Dave, who collapsed onto the bed. He rose slowly and walked out the front door, closing it behind him. It was very hot and trickles of sweat formed on his face immediately. He pulled on the flying vest and pressed the power button. He rose off the ground and soared away.

After twenty minutes of flying, he looked at his temporal scanner which showed no evidence of the recent time eddy. He smiled and looked for a spot to land. After setting down and removing the flying vest, he pressed some buttons on the device attached to his left arm and disappeared in a violent flash of light. A cloud of red dust rose and a few nearby cacti burst into flames.

CHAPTER 43

Dave awoke from the stun blast and sat up. Lini was nowhere to be seen. After sitting quietly for a few minutes, he thought he could hear her singing. He rose and walked over to a closed door and knocked. "Lini, are you okay?" he asked.

"I'm just taking a shower, Dave," she replied. "You can come in if you like."

"I'll just go check out the kitchen and see what there is to eat," he replied. He walked down a short hallway to find a small kitchen. It included a small stove, a few cupboards full of basic plates and utensils and a sink. How odd not to find a refrigerator, he thought.

"Check out the pantry," Lini said as she came up behind him. He turned to find her wrapped in a towel with another around her hair. She looked so much like a small young Darlene that he almost took her into his arms. She walked past and stood on a small platform, motioning him to join her there. When he did, she pressed a single button on the wall and the platform descended into the floor. After a few seconds, they were in a basement with a large cooler on one side and racks of non-perishable supplies on the other. She walked over to a large cabinet and said, "Come take a look at this!" Inside were three blaster rifles and four pistols, along with several power packs. Everything was plugged into an unknown power source. "It seems that crazy man kept his word on this stuff anyway." She climbed up on a crate so she could look him in the face. "Dave, I'm scared. What if he succeeds in killing you?"

"Then you'll be back home with no memory of any of this," he smiled as he brushed her cheek with his hand. "Unfortunately for you, I already know he failed. You and I are stuck here for a while."

She put her arms around his neck and hugged him close. "Good, I like this a lot better." She kissed his lips.

"Lini, please. I am a married man," Dave said. "We can be friends, but that's it."

"I'm sorry Dave," Lini said. "But we are already much more than friends. I am your crewmate and your cellmate."

They both laughed. Dave kissed her on the cheek and helped her down from the box. As they rode the lift back to the kitchen, he said, "We need a plan, Lini. We can't just sit here and wait for anyone to find us. We need to find out where we are."

"I already know that, Dave," she beamed. "This is the moon Solander. The other moon is Fistan and the planet is Lubna."

"How can you know that, Lini?" Dave frowned. "I admit it does seem like that place, but I was told that was an ancient legend."

She looked confused. "Perhaps you're right, but come take a look at this." She took his hand and led him back to the main room where she began to rummage through her bags. After a minute, she pulled out several books, one of which was quite large.

"No wonder your bags were so heavy," Dave laughed. She set the large book down on the table and sat on one of the chairs, motioning Dave to sit next to her. “I don’t understand this language, Lini? Is this from your planet?”

“No, this is Gallicean, Dave. It says *Ten Years to Gallia*,” she replied.

“You can read Gallicean? How is that possible?” he asked.

“Honestly Dave, what do you think we’ve been doing for the last thousand generations while they have been coming to our world? That’s why many Nan watch them in their camps. That is how we learned their language and discovered their intentions.” She rose and grabbed the rest of the books and set them on top of the other. “You know how children are. They always forget things. These are all textbooks left behind by children over the years. Between listening to them and studying these books, we have a good grasp of their language. I only needed the translator device to understand you.” She stood and dropped her towel, revealing her beautiful body. Immediately she began pulling clothes from her bag. Dave immersed his attention in the books.

“This is amazing, Lini,” Dave said. “I’m beginning to understand what some of these words mean, although the symbols won’t help me speak Gallicean.”

“I can help you there, Dave,” she said as she approached, buttoning her pink blouse. “I can speak Gallicean. If nothing else, we can keep our minds active by learning new languages and not needing the translators anymore. What do you think?”

“Assuming we ever get off this rock, that would surely impress Fa-a-Di,” Dave replied. “Okay, let’s give it a shot.”

Lini stood inches from Dave and stroked his cheek. "Now watch my lips, Dave." She reached out and pulled the translator gently out of his ear. She looked in his eyes and said, "Lok mi zaze indo, Dave." Then she put the device back in his ear and he heard, "I think I love you Dave."

He held her two small hands gently and looked back at her, saying, "Lini, you are very beautiful and I do love you, but let's keep this professional for now, okay?" She smiled and hugged him.

After a light breakfast, Dave and Lini left the cottage to survey their location. They sat on a long bench on the front porch watching small groups of birds flying around looking for food. Sitting here was oddly familiar, Dave thought, although he did not know why. He even imagined some of the birds might be Galliceans already coming to their rescue. It all seemed like the memory of a dream. Dave brought a rifle and pistol to train Lini on their use. If something happened to him, she would have to protect herself. The day was remarkably cool, which did not seem to match the desolate landscape of red clay and sand, broken only by rock outcrops, scrub brush and cactus. Solander seemed much closer to the planet than Fistan, which probably caused the difference in habitat. At this hour, only Lubna was visible, spinning incredibly close by.

After an hour of practice, Lini was proving to be an excellent shot. Dave was comforted knowing he had been able to teach her something. The sun began to rise on the horizon, causing the temperature to soar. By the time it cleared the horizon, the temperature was over one hundred degrees and still rising. The two retreated back into the cottage to escape the heat. Dave took the opportunity to take a shower himself to wash away the sweat and dust. When he came back to the main room, he found Lini sewing. "What are you making, Lini?"

“Dave, I had my two bags with me, but you only had the one suit,” she replied. “You’re going to need more clothes. I found these supplies in the pantry so I thought I’d make you some outfits.”

“Wow! Thank you,” he said. “That’s really amazing. No one ever made clothes for me before. We just went to the store to buy them.”

“Unfortunately, there are no stores in my village,” she smiled. “We have to make what we wear.” She laughed. “I just realized how lucky you are to have me here, Dave. You’d be stinking like crazy in that one set of clothes in a few days.”

He sat on the bed next to her and put his hand on her shoulder. “I am very lucky Lini, but I still feel bad for you. Why didn’t you move away? Why did you choose to do this?”

Lini set down her sewing and took his hand. “Dave, I already told you and everyone else. My life on Zulanan was normal, but boring. The most excitement I would see is marrying someone from another village and moving a few miles away. Now I’m on a remote planet with you, Admiral. I have total faith that we will be found and I will join your crew and help expand the Free Society. That is my destiny.”

He smiled. “But what if we are never found, Lini? What then?”

She sighed softly and replied, “Then that is God’s will for us. If we are here for years with little hope, someday you will become my lover and we will be deliriously happy together. But I will not allow myself to have any babies with you here. I will not condemn another to my fate.”

"If that is our fate, it will be a wonderful life with you, Lini," Dave said as he kissed her on the cheek. He stood and looked around. "It's not such a bad place. I know Fola provided all of this so I would go insane from the solitude, but you being here is a godsend. If it takes years to be found, they will be good years. Thanks Lini." He walked to the opposite window and looked out at the heat waves rising from the desert. "This is a terrible place. With Lubna and the sun, there won't be that much darkness for sleeping."

"I already thought of that, Dave," she laughed. He turned to see her holding a bolt of heavy black fabric. "I'm going to make window shades out of this. We need to measure the cycles of both Lubna and the sun. Then we can make our own days and nights. Regular sleep periods are very important."

"That's a great idea," Dave replied. "I also found a flying vest in the pantry. I didn't see any footprints where Fola ran off, so there must be another out there. Tomorrow I'll go find it. Then I'll teach you how to fly. What do you think about that?"

CHAPTER 44

The com-link in Altamar Zendo's ear crackled to life. "Alta, it's Val, how is everything going on your end?"

"About as well as can be expected Val," he laughed. "You know how difficult it is to gain full control of a new species. Thankfully, these maklans are not that different from us, unlike those from No-Makla or Tak-Makla. I'm sitting on the couch in the Ambassador's office and he hasn't noticed my presence."

"We found there is a secure chamber deep in the center of this battle station where fifty Maklakar are using their sensors to look for us," she replied. "They haven't figured out it doesn't work yet. But there is a significant risk they will find the errors in their code and correct them before we can gain full control."

"That's a risk we have to take, my dear niece, although finding that chamber should be a top priority for our team," Altamar continued. "These maklans were never going to join the Brotherhood Alliance. They would rather die in battle than sit face to face with the Paxran, and I can't say I blame them."

"Uncle, it's been many generations since we made peace with the Paxran. Can't we let the dead rest in peace and worry about our future instead?" she argued.

"I think that is what we are doing, Val," he replied. "We tried to bring them to the table. I personally sat with Kolu Inzaka and tried to bring the group together. But Fola Untor is a fool to believe his silly desire for revenge could overcome centuries of animosity and warfare in this galaxy. His hatred made him stupid."

"You really believe the alliance is dead in the water, Uncle?" she asked. "I thought there was genuine progress at that meeting."

"Oh there was progress. Unfortunately, a real alliance with shared goals is far, far away, and I doubt we have time for that. We need to focus on the mission at hand. We need to take this ship to Tak-Makla and destroy the Hive planet!" he shouted. He noticed a changed expression on Ont Valoo's face. He seemed to be looking around as if he'd heard a sound. Altamar whispered into his com-link, "Shit, this maklan heard me shout, I think. I'm on my way to your coordinates now. Out." He rose quietly off the couch while pressing a notion into Ont's mind. The ambassador rose and turned to his cabinet and removed a bottle of whisky and a glass. Altamar walked slowly toward the door. Ont poured a small amount of whisky in the glass and swirled it about. The door opened noiselessly and Altamar slipped out of the room and moved quickly down the hallway.

After a few minutes, he stepped into an unused dormitory his team was using as a headquarters. Ten Predaxian agents worked around the clock to force the idea this area was off-limits and contaminated into any passersby. In the two weeks since the station had left Vilu-Zan, no one had dared open the door. While the guards were armed, they could not possibly hide the signature of blaster fire if the door was breached. Then they would all die. Altamar rushed through the rows of bunk beds and into a dining room at the back of the room, next to the small kitchen. Valamar was sitting at the table with Pandofar Unterloo and Deela Califas, two of her chief lieutenants. Altamar sat with them and sighed. "That was too close," he said. "Me and my damned big mouth almost cost all of us our lives. I apologize for that."

Valamar put her hand on top of his and said, "Uncle, I am afraid your own zeal to destroy the tekkan Hive is overwhelming your best instincts too. We can't make the same mistakes as Fola Untor."

He sat back and thought for a moment looking at his close friends sitting at the table. "I know you're right, Val. You three have been with me for a long time and I certainly don't want us to die here with these filthy Maklakar. Do you think my plan to destroy the Hive is misguided? Please be honest. If I can't trust you three, who can I trust?"

Pandofar Unterloo began, "Altamar, our adventures together have been amazing. I remember when you found me working in the mattress factory. I would have never known about my special ability without you. I'm with you no matter what you decide."

"Thanks Pando," Altamar smiled. "But have you forgotten when I turned against our group to stop my own brother? Did you agree with me then?" Pando blushed but did not reply.

"I think that was an unfair question for us, Uncle," Valamar said. "But personally, I think your plan is misguided. The tekkans came to the aid of their allies. They did not kill any Predaxians either. They have no empire and they do not control any other races. Attacking them will likely unleash more enemies than we can handle."

"I agree with my cousin, Uncle," Deela said. "There is no guarantee we can defeat the fleet guarding Tak-Makla. Our spies tell us their Hive is also much improved. There is believed to be a second Hive on another planet working together with the tekkans for mutual defense. We may condemn these Maklakar and ourselves to a horrible death if we proceed. We all witnessed the destruction of the planet Localus. That was many times larger than this station."

"Suddenly, I am feeling very old," Altamar sighed as he held his head in his hands. "What are we to do now? This station will arrive at Tak-Makla in a few weeks. The tekkans will view it as a threat. They may even be able to discover our presence and unmask us to the Maklakar." He looked at Valamar and took her hands in his. "Val, what do we do now?"

"I think we need a change in plans," she said, softly caressing his hands. "There are plenty of planets out there for us. We have more than one thousand of our brothers on the ship two days behind us. If we can convince this station to find a place for us first, then we can leave this ship and begin a new life, far from our enemies and in the warmth of each other's company. Perhaps in the future, our descendents will be able to grow their influence and create a new civilization based on our unique skills."

"That sounds a bit too Pollyannaish for me, sweetheart," he laughed. "I'm not certain I'm ready to fade away into retirement on some desolate planet."

"I think you misjudged my idea, Uncle," Val frowned. "I want us to find an inhabited planet to control. I just fear the attack on Tak-Makla is an unnecessary suicide mission. I don't know if we need to build an empire like our ancestors. If we have one rich planet where we are treated like demigods; that should be enough for now."

"Ah, now I see," Altamar replied. "You know that is a good idea. But where do we find such a place."

"I was hoping you'd ask that," Valamar laughed as she stood up. She ran over to her bunk and opened her duffle bag. After a minute, she returned with a large book, which she laid on the table. She fumbled through the pages until she found a large picture. "There!" she said pointing to a small planet orbiting a massive gas giant.

"What book is this, Niece?" Altamar asked. "I've never seen writing like that. Is that Gallicean?"

"Yes it is, dear uncle," she laughed. "We all served during both wars with Greater Gallia. To help control our Gallicean spies, I learned their language. I found it much easier to manage their thoughts if I could speak in the same way they think." She closed the cover of the book and continued, "This book is called *Ten Years to Gallia* and was written by Fa-u-Bay, one of their greatest leaders. The planet I showed you is called Fistan. It is apparently the home of a human species. As we all know, they are easy to control, although we have little contact with their planets."

"Where is this place, Val?" Altamar asked.

"It is on the edge of the galaxy. It will take this vessel two months or more to reach the planet. According to the book, it is very lush with incredible resources. The sister planet is called Solander. While it is pretty bleak, the mineral resources are extremely abundant," she said.

"But this book seems ancient," Altamar argued. "Can we be certain this is not just a fairy tale?"

"Not one hundred percent certain. However, our spies have reported two more fleets headed in that direction, one from Paxran and another from Gallia. If it's a ghost story, then half the galaxy has fallen for it," she answered.

"What do you guys think?" Altamar asked Pandofar and Deela. "Your lives are tied up in this wild goose chase too."

"I'm with you sir, whatever you choose," Pandofar said.

"Uncle, this seems the perfect adventure to me," Deela replied. "Imagine a new rich world where we can be far from our enemies. Each of us can live in a large mansion being pampered by hundreds of servants while we plan our next move. I think we deserve that after all we've been through."

Valamar laughed. "There is one other thing, dear uncle. It is rumored the planet is also a natural Hive."

"Won't that Hive destroy the Maklakar ship and us?" he asked.

"Alta, the humans living on Fistan know nothing about us," she smiled. "They have no reason to attack. They might form an alliance with the Maklakar since both live on the edges of the galaxy. Even if the Paxran or others want to find and kill us, we will be far away and the masters of our own Hive."

"Okay, I'm sold," he replied. "Let's work on getting the course changed."

CHAPTER 45

Um-lu-Ka rose quickly in rank following his first mission on De-o-Nu's cruiser during their trip to the Andromeda Galaxy. Now he was the helmsmen on the battle cruiser Bantu-Fa, which was serving as Fa-a-Di's flagship. The ship left Gallicea two weeks ago with the general and his team who were rushing to catch up to the Maklakar battle station heading for Tak-Makla. "General, I think we have a problem," he squeaked.

Fa-a-Di laughed. "Listen sonny, my best friend is missing in space and time, half the galaxy is forming an alliance against us, and the Maklakar are going to attack the tekkan planet again. What other problem could we possibly have?"

"That's just it, sir," the helmsman replied. "The Maklakar ship is changing course."

"What?" the general shouted as he jumped up from his seat and rushed over. He pushed the lieutenant away and looked as the screens. "Well, I'll be damned. You were right. Can we tell where they are headed now?"

"It's possible their turn may take some time to complete, general," Um-lu-Ka responded. "Right now, there are no known systems in the direction they are headed. If they stay on this course, they will leave the galaxy in a few weeks."

De-o-Pa has risen from his seat next to the general and was also looking at the screens. "I recognize that sector of space, sir. If you check with my brother, I think you will find he is heading in that same direction as well."

"Why would the Maklakar be traveling toward a fictitious planet too?" he asked. "That just seems crazy."

"I don't know Fa-a-Di. But this doesn't smell right to me," the Prelate replied.

"There is another problem, brother," Darlene said as she approached them, wearing her bubble pressure suit. "Have you read the recent reports from the maklan operatives in Paxran territory? There is a fleet of their ships heading in that same general direction. This is getting too consistent to be ignored."

"The Battle of Lubna," Fa-a-Di laughed. "Is that what this is about? Half the galaxy going after a legend?"

"Don't brush this off so easily, general," De-o-Pa growled. "The Paxran and Maklakar have no knowledge of our ancient texts. Perhaps they have other reasons to go to Lubna."

Fa-a-Di sat heavily in the command chair and held his head in his hands as though trying to force a memory into his mind. "There was one thing that Dave said. What was it?" After a minute, he shouted, "Fistan is a natural Hive! That's got to be it!"

"We could all be in big trouble if the Paxran take that Hive, brother," Darlene warned. "We have to get there first and find Dave."

Fa-a-Di took her hand and said, "Dave isn't there, Darlene. He may have been there long ago or in the future, but he is not there now."

"But maybe the Hive on Fistan can help us find him, brother," she cried. "We've got to try!"

He patted her hand. “Don’t worry sister; we are going to do a lot more than try. I’m going to send a larger fleet to join De-o-Nu and Jon Lake. Then we’re going to convince the Maklakar to join our side. If the Paxran have any brains, they’ll run the other way.”

General Abala Konole had eagerly agreed to lead the fleet of fifty Paxran cruisers toward the legendary planet Fistan. Completing a great mission and becoming a close friend of Reverend Raza Intepam could only help him get off the isolated planet of Tak-u-Baka and back to the home world. He had worked tirelessly protecting the frontier while watching his classmates from the academy being promoted over his head. It was his agents who discovered the Donnaki plasma bomb device, but that was deemed dumb luck by his superiors. It was crafty espionage and Abala knew it.

It had been a fairly simple task to locate a potential natural Hive. Civilizations around the galaxy had ancient tales about magical places. A team of scientists correlated the data from several texts and found remarkable similarities. Even the Bolofas, the great religious tome of Paxran, mentioned such planets, including one just beyond the edge of the galaxy. Within one month following the staff meeting on Paxran, the fleet was assembled and staffed with scientists and religious leaders from around the Paxran Collective.

The world of Fistan was mentioned in Gallicean texts as a moon circling a mystical gas giant where incredibly large snakes guarded the secrets of the system. A similar system had been mapped long ago by the explorer Inka Konole, one of Abala’s own ancestors. Now he and the fleet would return to that place and hopefully find the power they desperately needed to protect themselves from the Donnaki.

"You seem lost in thought, General," Raza said as he sat next to Abala. "Is there a problem I need to be aware of?"

"No. Not at all, Reverend," Abala replied. "I was just going over the mission in my mind. I want to make certain we don't miss anything our Dear Leader asked us to consider."

"You know General, you and I will be spending months together on this journey and I think we should become friends. If you wish, you may call me Raza. There is no need for formality here."

"Thank you Raza," he smiled. "And you can certainly call me Abala. I appreciate your offer of friendship very much."

"I have had some premonitions about what we may find in that system, Abala," the priest confided. "My visions have an odd habit of coming true, you know."

"Tell me about them, Raza," the general replied. "We can take precautions if we are forewarned."

"Frankly, I'm surprised at your response. The Dear Leader usually just laughs at me. When my vision comes true, he simply denies I ever made the prediction. Thank you for the vote of confidence," Raza smiled. "Perhaps you can join me for dinner tonight in my quarters. I don't think I should speak so candidly with the crew about."

"Of course, Raza," Abala replied. "I understand completely." In reality, he did not understand at all. "If you like, we can go to my ready room now. It is very private." The two rose and left the bridge. The other officers exchanged confused looks for a moment and returned to their duties.

Chapter 45

In the small office, Abala pulled a bottle of liquor from his credenza along with two glasses. "Please sit down, Raza. Would you like a drink?"

"I think that's an excellent idea, Abala," the priest replied. The general handed him the drink and the two touched their glasses together in a toast. "To our health, friend."

"To our health, Raza," Abala replied. They sipped the brandy which was the finest on Paxran. "Okay, Raza, let's hear about your vision."

"There are others seeking the power of the Hive on Fistan. Given the relative speeds and distances of the various fleets, we may all arrive at precisely the same time," Raza said.

"That's definitely not good," the general answered. "Do you foresee a battle for control?"

"Maybe. I wish I could be more definite, but I've seen different outcomes in my visions. If there is a battle, we might well lose. I have not had a vision where we defeat the others," the priest said. "But I have seen cases where there is no fight and all join together to share the power of the Hive."

"Hmm. I don't think our Dear Leader will accept that," Abala said. "I think he might prefer our deaths in battle to acquiescence. Are the Donnaki involved in this fight? That would be the worst case scenario."

"Not that I have seen, Abala," Raza continued. "But the Maklakar and Predaxians are involved. I fear the Predaxians might gain control over the battle station and use it to destroy our fleet. You remember the Maklakar plasma bomb technology doesn't have the same flaw as the Donnaki system.

The results of such a battle would certainly include the destruction of the fleet."

"You paint a troubling picture, Raza," Abala winced. This scenario was too terrible to imagine. Now Abala would never get the promotion to the High Command. Instead, he and his crew would be blasted to ashes by the Maklakar, finally getting their first taste of revenge for the crimes of his ancestors. After they learn how weak the Paxran fleet is, they will leave Fistan and head to Paxran, laying waste to the entire civilization from their battle stations. "Perhaps the option for peace would be preferable, Reverend."

"Well, I hope that remains viable, Abala," he smiled. "Frankly, I think our destruction is the more likely outcome. But a part of me senses something working in the background of this adventure which may help save us all."

"So, you think God is on our side?" Abala whimpered.

"That might be too presumptuous, friend," he smiled. "But I certainly hope someone is."

CHAPTER 46

Dave Brewster was not doing well with his wedding vow. While Lini had been a bit aggressive at first, over the ensuing weeks, she settled into her role as Dave's sister, although she did kiss him every morning and night and say she loved him. By their best calculation, they had been on Solander for three months now. That was just an estimate because it was not easy to gage the passage of time on this moon. Something in this system affected the flow of time. Dave noticed it within the first couple days when he saw his chronometer running backwards and then forwards. Sometimes it would stop altogether for quite some time. The rotation of the moon was very regular, but the combination of the moon's rotation and revolution around Lubna along with the revolution of the planet around the sun created a variety of different types of day and night.

The black-out drapes Lini made were a fantastic addition. That helped them both sleep when daylight seemed to stretch far beyond the length their bodies could endure. Sleeping was the biggest problem. Dave searched the cottage and pantry for days looking for something to make a second bed. They both searched the surrounding area using their flying vests and found nothing to help. Fola Untor intended Dave to live his life in solitary confinement, so a single small bed was adequate. Every night her body was pressed against his, making it almost impossible to fall sleep. When he did sleep, he often dreamt of holding Lini in his arms and caressing her body. On more than a few occasions, he would wake in the middle of the night, very aroused, to find her arms and legs wrapped around him. When he tried to extricate himself from her grasp, she would wake and notice his condition and smile at him again, caressing his face with her soft fingers.

The morning was Dave's favorite time. He would rush out of bed and take a shower, washing the fragrance of her perfume off his body. Then he would put on the flying vest and investigate their surroundings, which was his way for getting away from her before he did something he would regret. Very little ever changed on Solander, at least in the time they had been there. Today was a bit different. When the sun would rise, the temperature would shoot upward to well over one hundred degrees. This morning when he stepped outside, he found frost on the windows and some of the cactus. Lubna was not visible, but the sun was twenty degrees above the horizon. Perhaps there was a cool season on this desert planet. It was Dave's day to travel southwest to check things out. Ten minutes from their cottage, he saw a herd of animals passing by. It appeared their path would intersect with the cottage. The animals were not large, about the size of large dogs on Earth and appeared to be eating the sparse plant life. Far in the distance he could see a large storm system coming toward him as well. He decided to cut his trip short and return to tell Lini about the sightings.

As he approached the cottage, he could see Lini outside working her small garden. She had decided to plant some of their vegetables in order to extend their supplies. With the large water supply, this could help them survive until help arrived. When he was only two hundred yards away and one hundred feet up, he saw two animals rushing toward her. She had not noticed them and was calmly watering the new growth. Dave pushed the vest into overdrive and shot in her direction. He tried to reach her on the com-link, but she had a bad habit of leaving it inside. He was fifty feet away and screaming at her when she spun about and shot the closest animal with her blaster. Before she could fire again, the second beast jumped on her, knocking her to the ground. She was pushing it back as it tried to rip out her throat. Dave heard her scream as he landed five feet away and jumped on the beast, grabbed it by the tail and flung it away. It landed on its feet and rushed him, but he had his Nak in his right hand and stabbed it through the chest. It whimpered and fell dead at his feet.

He turned and rushed over to Lini who was covered in blood. He grabbed her, threw her over his shoulder and rushed inside, slamming the door behind them. He rushed her into the small bathroom and tore off her clothes to check her for wounds. She was sobbing uncontrollably now and shaking with fear. He wet a towel and began washing the blood off her trembling body. Finding only a few minor cuts, he picked her up in his arms and hugged her to him. "I'm so sorry, Dave," she cried. "I know I didn't have my com-link. I promise I won't forget again. Please forgive me."

He kissed her passionately and continued to hold her against him until she calmed down a bit. "Don't apologize, Lini," he said. "I'm just happy you are okay. I was so scared when I saw those things attack you. I thought I'd lose you forever." He kissed her again and carried her back to the main room where he wrapped a sheet around her and the two sat on the bed. After a few minutes, Dave's heart calmed down enough that he could stand and walk over to the window. Ten more of the carnivores were out front devouring their cousins. "I wonder if Fola knew about those things."

"Thank God he left the blasters or I'd be dead right now," Lini sighed. "It really makes you think, doesn't it? Life should never be taken for granted. It is an exceptional gift that can be lost at any time."

The sound of distant thunder could be heard rumbling. "I saw a big storm heading this way and a herd of herbivores. The beasts that attacked you must be watching them."

She stood and walked over to Dave and put her arms around him. "Dave, no more flying alone. We have to stick together, you and me. I don't know what I'd do if something happened to you."

"Now are you ready to admit you should have stepped away on Zulanan?" Dave laughed. "You'd be safe if you had, you know."

"Not a chance, Dave," she smiled and kissed his cheek. "You're my great protector, and I am yours. Together we can do anything and survive anything, including this damned planet!" She looked out the window and frowned. "Those stupid things have trampled on my garden. Now I have to start over."

"Not anytime soon, Lini. That herd is headed this way. You'll just be feeding them and wasting our food. Why don't you get dressed and we can pick up where we left off on *Ten Years to Gallia*?" Dave suggested. He regretted the words even before they finished coming out of his mouth. She relished any opportunity she had to show him her body. She let the sheet drop to the floor and stood there a moment, just smiling at him. He tried as hard as he could to look away, but she was too beautiful not to look for just a few seconds. She giggled and turned to pull clothes from her bag. Dave grabbed the large book and sat on the bed, waiting for her. Her hair had grown out a few inches since they had arrived and flowed like silk around her shoulders. At night he could smell her hair next to him. Her perfume was locked in his mind now. He would never forget that.

"Okay, where were we?" she giggled as she sat next to him. "Before we start, I want you to know your Gallicean accent and vocabulary are excellent. I know Fa-a-Di will be amazed at how much you've learned." She kissed his cheek.

"Thank you, but you really deserve all the credit," he replied. "Your grasp of English from my planet is perfect too. Next you need to teach me the Nan language." He put his hand on her knee and she blushed. "We make a great team, Lini."

Her face became ever redder. "You embarrass me, Dave." She opened the book and turned to chapter three. Even though this edition of the book said Fa-u-Di led the mission, after Dave told her the real story, they used Fa-u-Bay's name in place of his brother's. "Now, I've read this to you in English a dozen times, but I want you to read it to me in Gallicean. If you find any words you don't recognize, just ask. Now go ahead."

Chapter three of *Ten Years to Gallia* was the story of the first homeward leg of the flight of the Pal-No-Fa after visiting the Lubna system. Their terror of the giant snakes kept the crew from visiting the only habitable place in this system. After exploring the two moons from space, they set a course along the path they had traveled to get here and left orbit at top speed. The Lubna system was some distance from the rest of the galaxy and it took them four weeks to reach the first star, which was a white dwarf with five dead planets in its orbit. They laid in a course for the next sun which was another week away. Unrest among the crew was growing on the long trip cooped up in the ship. Fights broke out almost daily as crewmates became disgusted with their former friends. Two days out from the next star, their sensors recorded two gas giants in the new system. All the anger and frustration melted away as they anticipated breathing fresh air again. The ship's air supply was down to twenty percent as the ship slipped into orbit over the planet Fa-u-Bay named Basangi, which means salvation. It took another two days to determine the atmosphere was breathable and food was abundant.

The Pal-No-Fa descended into the atmosphere and the sails were extended to replenish their air supplies. Landing parties soon discovered extensive ice islands and shore leave was given to all crew members. More landing parties were sent to gather food. The fresh food on board had run out long ago and the military rations were not pleasing the crew. After two weeks, the Pal-No-Fa rose into space again where an odd thing occurred. They were receiving a hail from one of the two terrestrial planets. The wars against terrestrial Beings had only ended with the Battle of Gallicea a few months ago. While Fa-u-Bay was concerned how his crew would react, he could not pass up this opportunity to find new friends. He returned the greeting and exchanged vocabulary databases. Then his ship left orbit over Basangi and approached the new planet.

They were invited to meet with the planet's leaders and Fa-u-Bay and some of his officers flew down to the planet's surface where they met the first valakars a Gallicean had ever seen. They seemed oddly familiar. They had wings too, but were covered with black feathers. They called themselves the Bandabar and claimed this was their home world. They were not as tall as the Galliceans but had developed quite an advanced society, which seemed odd in an oxygen-nitrogen atmosphere. Fa-u-Bay and his team visited the planet several times over the next few days, culminating in the signing of a peace treaty between Greater Gallia and the Bandabar Fold. The Bandabar knew several other civilizations on nearby planets which they shared with Fa-u-Bay. That gave them a new course to head back home. They left as friends and vowed to establish trade together. Chapter three ended as the Pal-No-Fa left the Bandabar system, continuing the journey home.

"That was perfect, Dave," she smiled as she rested her head on his shoulder. "You are now as fluent in Gallicean as I am. I know it's early, but I'm exhausted. I guess that action this morning wore me out. You don't mind if I sleep a little, do you?"

"Of course not, Lini," he smiled and kissed her forehead. "Between my nerves then and reading Gallicean, I could use a nap too. I'll close the black-out blinds." He rose and put the book back on its shelf. Then he walked over to the window to close the blinds. Rain was pouring down outside. "I hope this place doesn't flood," he said as he turned around. Lini was already asleep. He closed the two blinds and laid next to her, pulling the covers over both. Within seconds, he was sound asleep.

CHAPTER 47

Dave dreamed he was flying over Lubna with Lini. They were high above the planet holding hands. He did not bother to wonder how he was breathing the noxious atmosphere or flying, but was just happy to feel her hand in his. Looking upward, he could see Solander baking in the reflected sunlight. He thought he could see their tiny cottage, which should be impossible from thousands of miles away. Then he realized it was a dream, making him even happier. They flew for some time, just enjoying each other's company and breathing in the sweet fresh air of the planet.

After a few minutes, Lini pointed downward. A tiny snake seemed to be approaching them from far below. As it came closer, it grew and grew in size until it seemed to be hundred of miles long. Lini squeezed his hand so hard it ached and he could see the terror in her eyes. He smiled at her and told her not to worry; after all it was just a dream. Suddenly the snake rose up from below and they were riding on its back. Lini had calmed down and seemed to be hugging the beast tightly. Dave held on as the snake dove downward into the swirling bands of gas. Dave was frightened he would be separated from Lini and the snake until a small voice spoke into his mind, "Hello again Dave. Do you remember me?"

"Ondeen?" Dave asked. "Haven't I seen you in a dream before?"

"Yes, I'm glad you remember. But you've also seen me in real life as well. Do you remember that?" the Bolofaz asked.

"I think I'd remember that, Ondeen," Dave huffed. "I only remember dreaming about you two times."

"The second time was no dream," Ondeen replied. "If you think about it a bit, you'll remember everything."

And he did remember. "I came here with Fa-u-Bay when Fola Untor tried to run over me. I remember that now. You said my recollection would be like the memory of a dream. Why do I remember it now?"

"This is not a dream either, Dave," Ondeen replied. "We told you our paths would likely cross again. That day is approaching sooner than you might think."

"Why didn't you save me from Fola this time, Ondeen?" he asked. "I thought the Bolofaz protected against time travelers doing bad things. You could have stopped him from taking Dar Lini too. Why didn't you?"

"As we told you the last time, we only protect the past," Ondeen began. "The future is not written yet. We cannot judge good or evil, Dave. That is God's realm. This time, Fola Untor traveled to your future and did this. We cannot say this was not your fate. If the Source had protected you, that would be a sign, but it did not. For us, that means this is your fate. You and Lini will be here as long as it is your fate to be here."

"Ondeen, what is this place?" Lini asked. "Frankly, I don't know what you two are talking about."

"Please be at peace, Lini," Ondeen said. "The planets of the Bolofaz exist outside of time, which is why your clocks don't work well on Solander. We guard the past because it was written by the will of the Source."

"Can you help us leave this place, Ondeen?" she asked, squeezing Dave's hand again.

"Unfortunately no, Lini," Ondeen replied. "As we told Dave the last time we saw him, we might be drawn together again and that appears to have been true. Every life in this system is now in extreme danger. Many others have discovered this location and are headed this way. While we Bolofaz do not exist in your conception of time, our bodies are susceptible to your weapons of war."

"But who will guard the past if you are attacked?" Dave asked. "Didn't you tell me there were other Bolofaz planets?"

"That is correct Dave," Ondeen replied. "The Source will not permit the extermination of all Bolofaz, but this is just one planet. The past will be secure. That doesn't mean we want to die though. Tonight we have brought you here to ask for your help. Dave and Lini, please do your best to keep your friends and enemies from attacking this planet."

"Of course we will, Ondeen," Dave said as he patted Ondeen's soft skin. "The Beings coming here are looking for the Hive planet or for me. But this is not in my time. Fola has sent me away from my normal time where the attack will occur. Can you help us get back to our own time?"

"That is an interesting thought," Ondeen said. "I don't know the answer but will confer with the rest of the Bolofaz. None of our futures are written yet, so perhaps there is a way you can be helped."

"Perhaps the Hive on Fistan can help us?" Lini suggested.

"Another idea with merit," Ondeen replied. "We will discuss this and decide what we can do. Thank you both."

"Ondeen, can you tell me how far I traveled in time to be here?" Dave asked. "I cannot do anything to change the past with that information. I'm just curious."

"Of course I can, Dave. Based on a year measured on your home planet, you traveled backward in time three hundred and seventy five thousand years," Ondeen replied. "Actually, that is quite ironic," he chuckled. "Perhaps there is another way."

"How so?" Dave asked. "It seems like a rather random number."

"I think I'll let you figure that out," Ondeen laughed. "Yes, that is a miraculous coincidence. I'm feeling better already." They could feel his body shudder with laughter. "Oh, before I send you home, I wanted to talk to you both about something personal, if I may?"

"Go ahead, Ondeen," Dave said.

"Hmm. I'm not quite sure how to put this," he began. "Both of your connections to the Source are quite strong and the electricity between you two is very powerful. We could feel it surging from Solander to Lubna. We think you should explore that. After all, this is only a dream."

"I thought you said it wasn't a dream, Ondeen," Dave said.

"Dave, who am I to say? I could be part of your dream too," Ondeen laughed. "After all, you are flying on the back of a massive snake, breathing a noxious atmosphere. When you went to sleep, you were on the nearby moon in a tiny cottage.

How could any of this be real? But I'll leave the interpretation of your dream to you." Ondeen dived downward leaving them floating in the atmosphere.

Lini came to him and put her arms around his neck, kissing his lips. She pressed her lips to his ear and whispered, "It's only a dream, Dave," and kissed him again. He thought for a second about his circumstance with her body pressed tightly against him. He looked around. There was no cottage, only bands of gas. He could see Solander setting behind the planet. On the opposite horizon, the sun was beginning to rise. Lini's hands were all over him now and he was very aroused. "It's only a dream, Dave," she said again as she pulled him into her and they flew along, making love high over Lubna.

CHAPTER 48

Dave woke feeling great. He had not felt so refreshed since before he was sent here by Fola Untor. Lini woke before him and he could hear her singing in the shower. He smiled as he remembered making love to her over Lubna. With his imagination satisfied by the dream, he felt better prepared to work with her now. He opened the blinds to see the cottage surrounded by hundreds of herbivores munching on new growth that sprang from the heavy rains. The nearby hills were dusted with snow. Winter on Solander, he thought.

He went to the kitchen and prepared a pot of coffee. He stood watching the coffee drip into the carafe. The fragrance filled the room and raised his spirits even higher. He felt Lini wrap her arms around his waist and her face on his back. "Good morning, Dave," she said. "I feel fantastic this morning. How about you?"

He pulled two cups from the cupboard and filled them with coffee, handing her one. "I feel wonderful too. I don't know if it was the rain or the excitement from yesterday, but I slept like a baby." He sipped the coffee and wondered if the animals outside gave milk or cream he could use.

"For me, it was my dream," she giggled. "It was so real and you were very affectionate."

His jaw slackened and the color disappeared from his face. "Tell me about your dream, Lini?" he asked, almost terrified to hear her answer.

She blushed. "It was just a dream, Dave, but if you must know, you and I were flying over Lubna. It was so weird that we could breathe the atmosphere and fly. Absolutely amazing!"

He swallowed hard. "Please go on."

"Then this giant snake came up from the planet. I was scared but you told me not to be. Then we were riding on its back. He said his name was Ondeen and wanted our help to protect his planet," she smiled. "He was so sweet!"

"This can't be happening," he sighed. "Lini, my dream was exactly like that. Please tell me the rest."

"It's a little embarrassing, Dave," she whispered. "Why don't you tell me your dream?"

"It was the same as yours Lini," he began. "He told us several fleets were headed to Lubna and wanted us to protect them. He reminded me that I had been there before when Fola ran me over with his car. We suggested he could help us reach out to the Hive on Fistan or send us back to our own time to help stop the fleets."

"Three hundred and seventy-five thousand years," she gasped. "Then what happened, Dave?"

Dave put his hands on her shoulders and looked in her eyes. Both were breathing heavily and bright red in the face. He kissed her gently on the forehead. "Then we made love while flying over Lubna."

"Was it a dream, Dave?" she asked, too embarrassed to look in his face.

He took her face in his hands and turned it up to look at him. He kissed her lips again and held her close to him. "I don't know if it was real or not, Lini. But I do know it was one of the most amazing experiences in my life. I love you, Lini." He kissed her again.

She pushed back and broke his embrace and ran out of the kitchen crying. He ran after her, catching as she was opening the front door. She froze at the sight of hundreds of animals munching new wild flowers in every color of the rainbow. Dave pulled her back inside and closed the door, locking it in case other strange beasts arrived. He led her to the small table and sat her in a chair and then sat across from her. "What's wrong? I thought you wanted that too?"

"Dave, I've told you every day that I love you," she replied, wiping the tears from her cheeks and eyes. "But not like that; not in a shared dream. I wanted you to want me here while we were both awake and knew the consequences of our actions. I wanted you to choose to be with me, not live out a fantasy in a dream."

"Lini, that wasn't a dream. Don't you remember me asking Ondeen about that? He was very vague. I think it was real. I've flown over that planet before. I think we were both wide awake and acting the way we chose to," he argued.

"I don't think I can believe you, Dave Brewster," she replied. "The Bolofaz implanted this dream in us. We were sleeping here the whole time. We are humans, Dave. We cannot breathe that atmosphere."

"But it wasn't a dream, Lini," he argued. "Don't you remember the Galliceans breathing without suits on Zulanan? That's impossible too, isn't it? That wasn't a dream either."

"I don't care what you say. That dream robbed me of what I wanted most in my life," she cried. "Now, you are lost to me forever. I am beginning to wish I had stepped away when Fola Untor asked me to. At least, I'd have my dreams of you then."

"Lini, I don't think you understand what I'm saying," Dave continued. "Then I thought it was a dream. Now I know the truth. It really happened."

"That's what you say, but how can I ever know the truth? How can I ever be sure it wasn't a dream?" she asked as the tears welled in her eyes again.

"First let me tell you that I love my wife and family," he said. "At this moment, none of them will exist for almost half a millennium. And whatever happens on Solander; stays on Solander." He pulled his chair close to her and took her hands in his. "Lini, I've already made love to you once. It would be my honor if you would consider loving me again. I do care for you very much. And I promise to love you from this moment until long after we are both dead and buried. I have been one with the Source and we will always be together there." He kissed her and caressed her face. "I will always love you Lini, and I propose we live together as husband and wife for the next three hundred and seventy-five thousand years."

She laughed and kissed him. "You realize the Bolofaz might send us to our own time any minute. Or at least they might send us to Fistan. That's not much of a commitment on your part, Dave."

He laughed and stood up. He walked to the windows and lowered the black-out blinds. He came back to Lini and helped her to her feet. He kissed her face and whispered, "We'd better make good use of the time we have then, shouldn't we?" He began to undress her. She blushed again.

CHAPTER 49

After the night on Lubna and the following day, their activities returned to normal. Lini was happy knowing Dave returned her feelings, but understood they would return to their own time soon and be separated, possibly forever. They would practice their language skills by speaking only Gallicean one day, English the next, and Nan the following day. Lini seemed convinced the Nan on Fistan spoke that language, but there were no guarantees. If the Bolofaz sent them there and the natives spoke some other tongue, there would be no way to communicate, putting their mission in serious trouble.

The days stretched into weeks and still they did not hear from the Bolofaz. Dave and Lini tried to stay optimistic, but it was possible they would live out their lives on this desolate moon on the edge of the galaxy. The winter on Solander was in full force. Heavy snow floated down and almost buried the stone cottage. Each morning, Dave would shovel away snow from their front door and windows so they could see the world around them. All of the animals had migrated away and the cold was bone-chilling. Both were experiencing the symptoms of cabin fever and wishing for the days when the temperature would soar over one hundred degrees again. Lini found a large store of fabric in the underground pantry and worked to create heavy coats for them to wear outside. She also made duffle bags from heavy canvas. It was time for a vacation from this place. They had plenty of power packs for the flying vests and planned to look for warmer parts of the planet to escape the dark cottage.

"Dave, our coats are ready to go," she smiled as she modeled the one she had made for herself. "When can we get out of here?"

"I'd leave right now, but it will be dark soon," he laughed. "Let's see how the weather is tomorrow. If it's a nice morning, we can at least take a short trip to determine which direction to go to find warm weather."

"Come on then," Lini said. "Put on your new coat and let's go outside to see how well they keep the cold out. You can see there is an insulated hood too." She pulled the cords on her hood and it tightened to allow only her eyes and nose to be seen. "See, snug as a bug in a rug."

Dave laughed. "Well, you've got old Earth sayings down pat." Dave pulled on the insulated trousers over his uniform pants and donned the heavy parka. Both put on gloves and grabbed their blaster rifles. Dave opened the door and they stepped outside. Their boots crunched into the foot of snow on the ground as they stepped off the porch. Fistan glowed in reflected sunlight, illuminating their surroundings in pale light. "Keep your rifle in firing position, Lini. Who knows what sort of things we might run into tonight?"

They trudged through the snow for half an hour and began to climb the gentle slope just east of the cottage. Looking back, the building seemed so tiny. It was hard to believe they had been here so long already. Dave was beginning to doubt they would ever leave this place. He would fail his mission to expand the Free Society by adding a thousand or more planets. He and Lini would live out their lives on this rock, lost in space and time. Even if Darlene and Fa-a-Di were looking for him, they would have no way of knowing where in time he was. Perhaps Darlene would find their bones in the crumbling cottage. She and his children would never see him alive again.

"Dave, are you okay?" Lini shouted from fifty feet ahead of him. "Why did you stop?"

Dave began to walk toward her. "I'm sorry Lini. I was just thinking about us being lost in time. The Bolofaz don't seem to be able to help." As he reached her, he took her into his arms. "You know, if you had stepped aside like Fola and I asked you, I'd be dead already. Being alone here would have destroyed my mind. Thank you." He kissed her.

She sat on the ground. "Come on and sit with me, Dave. You are not alone. I will always be next to you. Even when we get back, you can count on me every day to help you." She elbowed him in the ribs gently. "Notice I said 'when' and not 'if'. We are getting out of here." She rested her head on his shoulder. "Now just sit back and enjoy the stars." The view was stunning tonight. The dark side of Solander was facing back toward the Milky Way Galaxy, which filled the sky from horizon to horizon. On Earth, dust in the air and reflected light dimmed the view of the galactic disc. Here it was incredibly bright. "Now this is not for fun, sweetheart. This is a scientific experiment. We are testing the insulation of these clothes. Let me know when your butt starts to get cold," she laughed and held his arm against her.

They sat together for some time that night, enjoying each other's company and being outside that tiny cottage. Dave was starting to feel the chill but had no intention of breaking the spell of this magic time. He put his arm around her and held her to him. "From here, it looks like we are the only life in the galaxy, Lini. It's almost like we made the galaxy as the background for our lives. A giant painting for our personal enjoyment." He laughed.

"Dave, what the heck is that?" Lini asked as she pointed out into space.

"It looks like a shooting star," he replied. "I mean, a meteor."

"It just changed course and stopped cold," she said. "It's like it is hovering over us."

Dave stood and pulled Lini to her feet. "It's a space ship! We've got to find a way to signal them. Maybe this is the coincidence Ondeen was talking about? We have to get to the cottage and find a way to signal them!" He took her hand and they rushed down the hill toward the stone cottage. "Do you still see it, Lini?"

"I can't look, Dave," she panted. "I'm afraid I'll trip and fall."

"Okay, don't bother," he huffed as they continued across the plain toward the cottage. "We'll both look from the porch." They were a hundred yards from the cottage.

"Dave, I left my rifle on the hill," she cried. "I'm sorry. I'll go back."

"No way, darling," he shouted. "We're not separating again. I'll get it tomorrow." As they arrived on the porch, they both looked up. "Do you see it?"

"I don't know," Lini cried. "There are too many stars. I'm sorry Dave."

He pulled their hoods off and kissed her. "Don't apologize, Lini. It's okay. I can't see it either. But we both saw it, so it's up there." He hugged her tightly. "This is our return ticket baby!"

They went inside and locked the door and began pulling off their winter wear. Both their faces were red from the run through the frigid air and snow and they were breathing heavily. Dave went to the kitchen and soon brought back two steaming mugs of coffee. "Here, drink this. It will warm you up."

She sipped the coffee. "Ah, that's great Dave. Thank you." She sat at the small table and he joined her. "Do you think they'll rescue us?"

"I hope so, Lini," he replied. "But you know they are not our friends. We're far in the past. I just hope they are friendly to strangers; or at least curious why two people are alone on a planet."

"What if they don't bother looking at all?" she asked. "Why would they look anyway? This rock can't be their destination, can it?"

"If they show up here, I guess we'll know," he replied. "There are many no-so-friendly planets out there. I only hope we don't look like dinner to them."

"That's an odd thing to say about space travelers," she argued. "If they have all this technology, wouldn't they have to be curious at least?"

"It was just something Fola Untor told me once," Dave sighed. "I don't know why I'm quoting that son of a bitch anyway."

Lini stood and came over and sat on Dave's lap. She took his head in her hands and kissed him. "Everything will be okay Dave. I'm sure this is the coincidence Ondeen told us about. We'll be rescued and go back to our own time. You will go back to your fleet and I'll head off to the academy." Her eyes welled with tears.

Dave held her tight. "Just a while ago, I had the feeling we would die of old age or insanity here, Lini. Now, we may be rescued soon. You know, I'm not certain which is better right now."

"Don't even think that Admiral Brewster," she said with a forced smile. "Going home is always best. We will always love each other and have our memories of this place, but none of this is real. Traveling back in time four hundred thousand years is not normal. I am very grateful for our time here. It has been a fantastic ride. But I always knew it wouldn't last forever. I didn't want it to either."

"I'm not sure what I want Lini," he replied.

"Of course you do silly! The last months of our lives were taken from us by the lunatic Untor. This never should have happened and I'll never know why the Bolofaz or the Source or God allowed it," she began. "The fact we made the best of our situation and found love and companionship is the only redeeming thing about it. You have a great future Supreme Fleet Admiral Brewster. Your friends are desperately looking for you in our future. Now maybe, just maybe, we have been found again." She kissed him passionately. "Time to wake up, Dave and go back to work." She stood and pulled off her clothes and searched through her bag for her pajamas.

If this was their rescue, Dave would miss her casual way of disrobing and walking around in the nude. Lini was a free spirit with a strong link to the Source. Dave knew they would be together still, although the past was now over and his real life would resume again soon. "Come to bed Dave," she winked. "We need to be rested for our rescue." She rolled over and soon was fast asleep. His mind was racing with the events of the day and sleep was hours away. He grabbed *Ten Years to Gallia* from the shelf and opened it. Chapter four, he thought.

CHAPTER 50

Dave woke suddenly still sitting on the chair with the book in his lap. They had neglected to close the black-out blinds and the room was filled with brilliant light. Both Lubna and the sun must be shining today, he thought. He rose slowly and his body ached from sleeping on the chair. His neck was stiff and his knees crackled as he walked. He looked out the side window and noticed the snow had melted. The Solander winter was severe but short. He walked over to the bed and looked out the other window and almost fainted. A massive silver shuttle craft was landing fifty yards away. He shook Lini gently to wake her and pulled her up to the window. Her jaw slackened and her eyes were wide open as the landing jets slowed the craft down just before the ship settled down on its landing pylons. "Let's get dressed," he said. Both frantically pulled on their clothes. Dave made certain he was wearing his official uniform. He strapped on his belt with his daggers and two blaster pistols. He gave his rifle to Lini, kissed her gently and the lips and said, "This is it."

They stepped out into the brilliant Solander morning. The temperature was quite warm today already, promising a scorching afternoon. As they stepped off the porch, they found the ground soaking wet and spongy. They walked ten yards from the building and then stood waiting. Dave told her to carry the rifle with the tip pointed down to not appear aggressive. His blasters stayed clipped to his belt. They waited ten minutes for something to happen, but those minutes seemed to last all day long. Finally, the landing doors opened and a ramp extended down to the ground. Four tall Beings in heavy pressure suits walked slowly down the ramp. They were each about ten feet tall and carried blasters and daggers of their own. They walked ten yards from the ship and stopped, not certain what to make of the two small Beings standing before them. The visitors seemed to be discussing matters among themselves, unsure what to do next. One tried to come forward, but the others kept pulling him back.

Dave cleared his throat loudly and the four visitors stopped and looked at him. Two of them had leveled their blaster rifles on him. Dave gently took each blaster from his belt and set them on the ground. "Lini, you have your rifle ready. I'm going to meet our guests," he said.

"Dave, I don't know if that's a good idea," she replied.

"No choice now," he smiled and kissed her cheek. He began to walk very slowly toward them. The visitors kept exchanging looks and appeared to be arguing about their next move. Without hearing their language through their suits or knowing their com-link frequency, he kept walking and smiled.

When he was ten yards away, one of the visitors shouted, "Drop you daggers, friend, or we'll shoot you where you stand." It was perfect Gallicean, although the accent was different from any he had ever heard. He turned and could see Lini smiling.

Dave shouted back in their language, "A Gallicean warrior never travels without his daggers, friend."

The one Gallicean who had tried to approach was laughing out loud. The others were arguing with him. The laughing one ordered the others to stand down and they reluctantly lowered their weapons while their leader stepped forward. "You seem to have the better of us, friend. How do you know our language and what kind of beast are you?"

"My name is Fleet Admiral Dave Brewster of the Free Society, and I am a human from Earth," Dave said. "Welcome to Solander."

"You must be a sorcerer or something, Dave," the other replied. "I just gave this moon that name in a meeting this morning. How could you know that?"

Dave looked at the Gallicean standing in the heavy suit. He tried to look closely at the face through the thick glass. After a minute, Dave recognized the face. "Fa-u-Bay, it's you!"

The Galliceans were stunned. They stood as if frozen for several moments. "None of this can be real, human," Fa-u-Bay replied. "We must be dreaming or you have us in a trance. I demand you tell us how you know these things."

Dave turned and shouted to Lini, "Go get the book, sweetheart! You're going to love this. You won't need the rifle anymore either." She went back to the cottage and returned shortly with the book under her arm. Dave took the book from her and handed it to Fa-u-Bay who looked at the cover and then flipped through some of the pages.

"You are one of my heroes, Fa-u-Bay," she beamed. "Do you think you could autograph this for me?"

"I don't understand Dave," Fa-u-Bay sighed as he handed the book back. "What's going on here? And why are you two alone on this planet and how do you know me?"

Dave and Lini told the Galliceans the entire story about Fola Untor and *Ten Years to Gallia* and the Sojourn. They told them about the Bolofaz and the Hive on Fistan and how they were stranded in the distant past as revenge for the demise of the

Brotherhood in the Andromeda Galaxy. Each revelation seemed more magical and mysterious than the one before. The sun was setting and Dave was still talking. The Galliceans were very uncomfortable in their suits and with the story. It was too outrageous to be true. But here they were past the edge of the galaxy with two humans who knew their past and their future. Fa-u-Bay looked at his air gage and said, “Dave, our suits will run out of air soon, so we need to go back to our ship. What do you want us to do?”

“We would like you to take us to Fistan,” he replied. “The people there are like Dar Lini here and their Hive may have the power to return us to our normal time. As we told you, there are fleets preparing to wage war here in my time and every Being there is in great danger.”

Fa-u-Bay looked at the book again. “Do you think I can keep this?” he asked.

Dave laughed. “You wrote it! It belongs to Lini though. It might be better if you discover the secrets in here for yourself. I don’t want to change the past. From my experience, that doesn’t turn out too well.”

“You’re probably right,” the Gallicean said. “When I get to my ship, I’ll have small pressure suits assembled for you two so you can breathe during the trip to the other moon.” He looked carefully at them both. “You’re sure you are not felons serving time here. I’d hate to help you break out.”

Lini laughed. “When we arrive on Fistan, you can take us to their police if you like. If they say we are wanted, you can return us here. Two simple people can’t stand up to your crew.”

"I suppose that's true enough," he chuckled. "Dave, tell me again about my descendent who is your friend."

"Fa-a-Di? Of course. He is the current High Commissioner of Greater Gallia. He is the hero of both Predaxian Wars and has saved my skin many times. He and his brother-in-law, De-o-Nu are like my brothers."

"You hear that, De-o-Nu," Fa-u-Bay laughed. "You have a famous descendant with your same name."

"I'll remember that for my next performance review," the other Gallicean said. "Sir, we are down to ten percent air supply."

"Okay, Dave and Lini, we will return tomorrow at the same time. Thank you for telling us about our future. It has been a magical experience," Fa-u-Bay said. "Good night." The four climbed back on the shuttle and the landing ramp rose back into the ship. They could see the Galliceans pulling off their pressure suits and strapping in. A few minutes later, the shuttle rose off the ground and flew up into space.

"Time to pack, Dave," Lini said as she rose and headed back to the cottage. "We have a busy day tomorrow."

Dave stood and looked around. Hopefully he would leave this place tomorrow and return to his own time. While this was his prison, he felt strangely sad to leave it. It has been so peaceful here, aside from the one animal attack. He would miss sleeping with Lini and learning new languages. Even though Fola Untor had sinister motives, his actions had made Dave very happy for a while. He realized he forgot to collect the other blaster rifle, but that would have to wait for the morning. The sky was almost pitch black and he did not want to take any risks on his last night here.

Safely locked inside the small cottage, he pulled off his clothes and slipped on his pajamas and crawled into bed with his back against Lini's. He could hear her soft breathing and the scent of her perfumed hair filled his senses. He rolled over and put his arm around her, smelling her hair for the last time. Back to reality, he thought. Lini rolled over and kissed him passionately. Her hands were all over him now and he kissed her and caressed her willing body.

CHAPTER 51

Dave was walking down the hill with the misplaced rifle when the shuttle drifted down through the morning sky and landed in front of the cottage. As he approached, he saw Lini lugging their packs outside where two Galliceans loaded them onto the shuttle. "Good morning," he said as he passed them.

"Good day, Admiral," De-o-Nu replied. "Is this everything?"

"Let me check with Lini," Dave answered as he walked back toward the cottage. Stepping through the door, he saw her sitting at the small table crying. He sat across from her and took her hands in his. "What's wrong?"

"Nothing's wrong, Dave," she sighed. "It just feels like leaving home."

"I know what you mean," he replied. "I had the same feelings last night. You and I have been through a lot here, haven't we?"

"Yes we have," she smiled, wiping away the last tears. "But I know this was never home. It was a prison and now we will be free. Soon we will join the battle in our own time. Only the Source knows how that will end."

"Sweetheart, I disagree about this not being home," Dave replied, while gently squeezing her hands. "Every place we lay our heads is home. While we did not pick this place, we made it our own. You made it a home. You know, perhaps we should come back here some day, just to relive old memories."

Lini laughed. It was good to hear her laugh, he thought. "Now you're the crazy one, Dave." She stood and said, "Let's get out of this hellhole."

Dave took her in his arms and kissed her. "Thank you for these months together, Lini. You kept me sane and gave me great joy here. As I told you before, if you had stepped away, I probably would have committed suicide by now."

She kissed him back. "You are quite welcome, Dave. Come on, we have work to do on Fistan." They walked out of the stone cottage for the last time. Dave made certain the door was secure. He knew he would be back in a few hundred thousand years after Fola Untor ran over him with the car. He did not want any stray animals ruining his bed. When they reached the ramp, Dave and Lini looked back and hugged. Their exile was now over. They climbed into the shuttle where the Galliceans helped them into the pressure suits. Once the internal atmosphere was verified, the cabin air was replaced with air breathable by the Galliceans. They then took off their pressure suits and strapped themselves in. Minutes later, the shuttle lifted off and blasted back into space. Neither Lini nor Dave bothered to look back at the red moon. It was the past.

Fa-u-Bay was sitting in the copilot's seat and unbuckled his restraints after the shuttle left the thin atmosphere of Solander. He came back and sat with the two humans. "It should only take an hour to reach Fistan. We have been hailing the planet for two days and have not received any response. I'm not sure they are advanced enough for communications. What do you think we should do?"

"Let me try," Lini said as she unbuckled her restraint and followed the Gallicean back to the command station. Fa-u-Bay was pressing the buttons to open a channel when she touched his hand. "Fa-u-Bay, I'm going to speak to them in the ancient Nan language, which I hope they understand. You don't have that in your database and I'm betting they are terrified by your ships. The Nan are not aggressive. Don't worry if you can't understand me." He nodded at her and pressed the final contact. "Nan planet," she began in the Nan language. "My name is Dar Lini of Zulanan and I am a fellow Nan. This shuttle craft is bringing my superior, Fleet Admiral Dave Brewster of Earth and me to your planet. Can we have your approval to land?"

"You are a Nan?" came the voice over the speaker. "How is that possible? Can we have visual?"

"Fa-u-Bay, can you open a video link so they can see me?" she asked. He nodded and pressed more buttons. The screen in front of them now showed the face of a human with green eyes, dark skin and neatly cropped black hair. "I know it's not easy to see me, sir, because I am wearing a pressure suit. The Beings delivering us cannot breathe an oxygen-nitrogen atmosphere."

"Please maintain a high orbit until I can get my superiors to decide what to do," the man said. "Fistnan out." The screen went blank.

"What did he say?" Fa-u-Bay asked. "Did I hear him call this place Fistan?"

"We have to wait while he asks for approval," she smiled. "And he called their planet Fistnan. That's an incredible coincidence, isn't it?"

"Not really," Dave said as he joined them. "We have to remember this planet is a natural Hive. I'm sure the Hive helped Fa-u-Bay pick this name."

"What the heck is a Hive, Dave?" Fa-u-Bay asked. "You keep talking in code."

Dave laughed. "I'm sorry, but the truth is harder to accept than the name, trust me. If we are invited down, I'd love to show you all about it."

"More time in a pressure suit is not appealing, Dave," Fa-u-Bay replied. "I think I might pass on that."

"I know you won't believe this, but you won't need a pressure suit on the Hive planet," Dave said. "You can ask Lini for confirmation. Her planet is much like this one and your descendants have learned they no longer need them either. It takes a big leap of faith, but if you or one of your men attempts it, you'll be as amazed as I was."

The face of the Nan was back on the screen saying, "Alien shuttle craft, you have permission to land. I am transmitting coordinates to you now. Please do not bring any weapons with you when you exit the ship. We need to take precautions."

"What's your name, son?" Dave asked.

"I am Lieutenant Samarti Gogalafar, Admiral," he replied. "I am at your service, sir."

"Samarti, please call me Dave," he said. "The crewmen of this shuttle are Gallicean warriors from the mighty society known as Greater Gallia. I am an honorary Gallicean Marine as well. Our culture requires us to wear our daggers. I can promise you we will not bring any blasters or heavy weapons, but I cannot allow these brave men to leave their daggers behind. I hope that won't be a problem."

"I am certain that is okay, Dave," Samarti replied. "We meant no disrespect to you or them. Fistnan out."

Fa-u-Bay put his hand on Dave's shoulder. "Dave, Lini told me what you just said to him. Thank you very much. You honor my men and me. Our descendants did right to honor you sir."

The shuttle slipped into the atmosphere of the moon. Everyone was strapped in and the ride was quite bumpy as a major rain storm was moving through the small city that lay before them. The landing coordinates led to a small pad on the outskirts of town. Several large estates were gathered around it and a busy road led deeper into the city. The area was very green with rolling grassy hills and stands of tall trees. The ocean was only a few hundred feet away and gentle waves slipped up on a broad beach. The shuttle set down on the landing marks and the thrusters were turned off. The four man crew was busily putting on their pressure suits. Dave and Lini looked out the portholes and could see a rather large contingent of soldiers and a group of dignitaries. Everyone looked very nervous. The soldiers kept a large space between their ranks and the rest of the crowd. No visitors had been to Fistnan in many generations. The Nan here had fled the Society of Humanity when the first Nan planets were settled in the Ulagong Galaxy. These brave souls longed for more than servitude and were able to make it to this planet without being found, until today.

Fa-u-Bay stood next to Dave in his suit. His helmet was under his arm. "So Dave, you're saying I don't need this here, is that right?" he said pointing to the helmet.

"That's right, Fa-u-Bay," Dave chuckled. "But your men look pretty nervous waiting for you to put it on. You can certainly wear it if you like."

"Dave, my life has changed so much since the attack on Gallicea," Fa-u-Bay laughed. "I am a simple priest who has been thrown into the role of leader of Greater Gallia. Za-a-Za should have killed me. The Pal-No-Fa should have exploded like a star when I shut down the core. Then I found you and Lini on Solander. Can you imagine the odds of that? Screw it, I'm opening the door." He walked toward the exit hatch on put his hand on the lever.

"Captain, don't be stupid!" De-o-Nu shouted, grabbed his hand and pulled it away. "Don't kill yourself for this simple man. How do we know any of this is true?"

Fa-u-Bay handed his helmet to the other and replied, "De-o-Nu, if I appear to be choking for air, just slam this on my head and pressurize it. Certainly I can last more than one breath?" De-o-Nu released the arm and held the helmet just over his captain's head. Fa-u-Bay winked at his friend and pulled the lever. External air rushed into the chamber. Fa-u-Bay smiled but held his breath, not certain he should try this anymore. Finally, he took one hesitant breath. Then he took a deep breath and laughed out loud. "Dave Brewster, you certainly are a magician. All right men, you must leave your blasters here. The Admiral has received permission for us to wear our daggers. Let's get off this scowl."

"Fa-u-Bay," Dave said as he finished removing his pressure suit, "I think Lini should exit first. She looks more like them than you guys do. You might give them heart attacks. That wouldn't be diplomatically correct, if you know what I mean."

Chapter 51

When Lini stepped out of shuttle and onto the planet, the crowd erupted in cheers. It slowed but continued when Dave followed her out. It became dead quiet when the Galliceans exited the ship. Most of the Nan here were Lini's height, and the ten foot Galliceans towered over them. The nearest Gallicean planet was thousands of light-years away and no one had ever seen anything like them. The soldiers were allowed to leave when they saw the landing party was not armed.

Samarti Gogalafar led the group to a neighboring house which was the home of one of the Elders of Fistnan named Paranaxis Sambolam. It seemed so familiar to Dave. The style of building was almost identical to Nan in the home galaxy. Dave and Lini were escorted to a bungalow with a broad porch opening onto a wide patio ringed by similar bungalows. Everyone was given a few hours to rest before a dinner party was held later in their honor. The atmosphere was electric on Fistnan, another similarity shared with Nan. He was surprised to find a coffee pot in the small kitchen and happily brewed a pot. He could hear Lini singing in the shower as she prepared herself for her first state dinner. Their dress clothes had been taken by one of the Elder's children for cleaning and pressing before the party. Dave took a large mug of coffee and added some cream he found in the small refrigerator. Then he strolled out front and sat on a soft couch in front. A steady rain poured down, creating little ponds and rivulets in the large patio. It seemed too similar to Nan to be true, he thought. Perhaps there was such a place on Zulanan, but he had not seen it, only the small village in the tress where Lini was raised. The coffee was strong, but quite tasty. It had been months since he had been able to put cream in his coffee and it reminded him of home, his real home on the Nightsky. He knew he was still imprisoned in the ancient past though.

After a few minutes, Lini joined him on the porch with another mug of coffee. She sat next to Dave and put her hand on his knee and leaned against him. “This is so amazing. It was only hours ago when we were on Solander looking up at the stars and wondering if we would ever escape. And now look at us.”

Dave stood and walked over to the edge of the porch, where the rain drops fell a couple inches in front of his face. The air was thick with moisture, a very rare occurrence on Solander. “I was thinking the same thing, Lini. But we’re still lost in time. I just hope the Nan can help us.” Across the courtyard, two men opened a door and stepped into the rain. Both wore hooded robes which obscured their faces and were heading toward Dave and Lini’s bungalow. After a few moments, the two approached their porch and Dave stepped back to give them room. One held a long bag. They removed their hoods, revealing an old man and a younger one.

“Hello Admiral Brewster, I am Elder Paranaxis Sambolam and this is my son, Orenades,” the Elder began. “Orenades has your clothing for the evening.” The younger handed the bag to Lini who smiled and thanked him. Then she went inside to hang up their clothes. “May I have a few words with you? You have to imagine your sudden arrival with the Galliceans is quite troubling to us.”

“Please sit down,” Dave replied. “I’m happy to answer any questions you might have.”

“Oren,” the Elder said to his son, “please return to the house and bring us a bottle of brandy and three glasses.” The younger Nan smiled, raised his hood and walked back across the courtyard. “First of all, please call me Sam. Our names are somewhat complicated, yet I am a simple man. Dave, if I may be so bold, who are you and why are you here?”

Dave told the Elder the story about Fola Untor and being sent back in time and imprisoned on Solander. He also told him how this star system was in extreme danger in his time and that he needed to get back home soon. Lini joined them after a few minutes. By the time they had finished the story, most of the brandy had been drunk. "Sam, in order to get back, we need to visit your Hive," Dave finished.

"I'm sorry Dave, but I don't understand," Sam sighed. "What is this Hive you speak of? I have never heard of that except in regard to bees and other insects." Dave looked shocked at the revelation.

Lini put her hand on Dave's knee and said, "Don't worry Dave. You must remember that I was unaware of the Hive on Zulanan as well." She turned to Sam and said, "We need to speak to the Guardians, Elder. I am quite certain they manage this Hive as they do on my home planet."

"Do you mean our soldiers, Lini?" Sam asked. "I'm afraid I know of no other guards here."

"Have you heard of the Zula, Sam?" Dave asked.

The Elder's face turned ash-white and his jaw moved back and forth, but no words came out. He refilled his glass and took a long drink of brandy. "How do you know of the Zula?"

"The Zula are the natural protectors of the Hive, Sam," he answered. "They live on all planets with natural Hives, like Lini's home planet and the planet Nan in the Andromeda Galaxy.

"You know of the planet Nan? It is two million light-years away from here. How could you know about that place?" Sam asked.

"I have been there and joined the Source there. Elder Odo Pak and I traveled back here and retrieved my son while inside the Source," Dave replied. "Don't worry if you are not aware of Hive technology, Sam. Remember we come from very far in your future. Can you take me to the Zula? They will know what to do."

"It has been so long since I heard the stories about the Society of Humanity, Dave," Sam smiled. "Those were horrible times. Thanks to the Source, we were able to escape enslavement in this galaxy and find this place. How can I know you won't use this power to enslave the Nan of your time?"

Dave put his hand on Sam's knee and leaned close to him. "Sam, if we can find the Zula and enter the Source, I'll take you back with me long enough for you to be certain. Please, this is important for my family and the people of Fistnan. You have to trust me a little, I'm afraid."

"Well, I suppose while the future is known to you, anything could change it. You realize we may find a different world from the one you left," Sam replied. "The seashore is nearby and we can try to summon a Zula if you like. If it works and they trust you, then I will trust you as well." The three rose and Sam led them away toward the coastline.

CHAPTER 52

"Captain, we're getting a distress call from the Maklakar battle station Mondor," Lia said as she turned to face Jon Lake. "Shall I put it on screen?" Jon nodded his consent. They had been traveling for several weeks toward the edge of the galaxy. Within days, they would leave it and head out to the location of the legendary Lubna system. Jon knew the Paxran and Maklakar were also heading that way but had no idea why the incredibly powerful Maklakar vessel would be in distress.

"Mondor, this is Captain Jon Lake of the Nightsky. What is the nature of your emergency?" Jon asked.

"Captain, I am Commander Vard Kalak of the Mondor," the maklan replied. "We were transiting the Bandabar system when we were attacked by a massive fleet of tiny robotic spacecraft. Many thousands of those robots have attached themselves to our surface and are ripping the metal off. We have fired four EMPs through the hull already. Most of the robots have been deactivated, but there are still some attacking and a large fleet still following us. Can you help us?"

"Commander, I am changing course to intercept now," Jon said. "We also have a Gallicean cruiser with us that will also assist. We should arrive within fifteen minutes. Let us know if the situation degrades. Nightsky out." He turned to Lia. "Did Ka-a-Fa get that message too?"

"Yes Jon," she replied. "He has already turned to follow us. I have him on line now. Here he is." The faces of Ka-a-Fa and De-o-Nu frowned back at them.

"This might be a trap, Jon," Ka-a-Fa argued. "Remember these are the bastards who attacked Tak-Makla and the Nom-Kat-La system."

"I'm aware of that, but we are also supposed to be forming an alliance with those maklans. If they are really in trouble, the problems will affect us too. They have the most advanced technology in this galaxy," Jon replied. "We should have them and their attackers on our sensors any minute now. If it looks like they are faking it, we can turn before they can attack."

"Nightsky, this is Mondor," Vard interrupted. "The robots have already caused ten hull breaches and our power is dropping fast. I don't have enough juice for another EMP. What is your status?"

"Just a minute Vard," Jon said. He pressed the mute button and said, "What in God's name is that?" On the screen they could see the Mondor, which was one thousand miles in diameter and bright silver. Just behind it was a cloud of tiny ships twice the size of the battle station. He pressed a button and Ka-a-Fa was on the screen. "What options do we have, Ka-a-Fa? Did you see the size of that attack fleet?"

"Mondor, this is Ka-a-Fa of the Kong-Fa," the Gallicean said. "You need to use all five of your plasma bomb devices and fire into the cloud of robots behind you. And do it as fast as you can!"

"We will likely lose power if we do that, Ka-a-Fa," Vard said. "Then they will be on us. Also, the ships are so small they will not detonate the bombs. Is there another plan?"

"Just do it, Vard!" Ka-a-Fa screamed. "Jon and I will fire on your plasma bombs to make them detonate. It is our only chance."

Vard sat back in his command seat and groaned. "You're right, Ka-a-Fa. Please don't miss them." He pressed the contact to end the transmission. "Bring all plasma bomb units to full power now and aim them behind us. Let me know when I can fire."

"Commander, we don't know if that will work. How can we trust the humans and Galliceans?" the weapons officer asked.

"We'll run out of power soon anyway," Vard sighed. "If we wait, those things will kill us anyway. At least this way there is some small chance. And call Lord Valoo and offer my apologies for my failure."

Five massive plasma bombs shot out of the Mondor and turned to head behind the vessel. Lights flickered all over the station which then went dark. The fleet of robotic vessels was only a few miles away when the first plasma bomb arrived. Laser fire from the Kong-Fa and Nightsky shot through the air and hit each plasma bomb in turn. The view screens went dark as the blindingly bright explosions overwhelmed the sensors. All three ships were buffeted by the pressure waves arising from the blasts.

Thirty seconds later, the screens came back to life. Mondor was still floating dead in space. The robotic fleet was decimated. A few hundred remaining robot ships turned and returned from where they came. "Captain, most of the robot fleet has been destroyed and the rest are fleeing. I am still reading a few robots on the surface of Mondor and they are still tearing away at it," the helmsman said.

Ka-a-Fa scowled, "Send a platoon of Marines over there to clean them up."

"Get some power on now!" Vard shouted. "And get some men on the surface to try and disable any remaining robots."

Two emergency doors opened on the surface of Mondor. Two groups of heavily armed soldiers walked onto the surface of their false planet with their blaster rifles at the ready. These doors were the closest to the last known location of the attackers. Captain Olo Panak led his group of men toward the charred remains of one of the machines. It must have been destroyed by one of the EMPs, he thought. It was four feet tall and terrifying to look at. Its feet were welded to the surface by the EMP. It had two legs, four arms with pincher-like claws and a tiny head on a long neck which appeared to be nothing more than a camera platform. They looked at it for a moment until a clanging sound reverberated through their feet. Looking up they saw an exact duplicate approaching them quickly. Its pinchers were opening and closing rapidly as it closed on them. Olo gave the order to fire and the volley of laser blasts flew toward it. Every shot hit the robot in the chest. It stopped for a moment and looked about. Then it continued forward. They fired again to no effect. It was almost on them now. Just as it reached the group, several shots stuck the robot at the joints where its arms joined the body. All four arms fell to the surface of the station. The robot continued and attacked the men moving its torso back and forth as if controlling its now-absent arms. Olo took his pistol and shot it where the legs were attached. The torso fell to the surface and the machine laid there inert.

Olo ordered his men to take the torso back into the station. As they turned, they saw the platoon of fifty Gallicean Marines in their red pressure suits approaching. Olo advised them about the weakness of the robots and the whole group spread out to disable the remaining robots.

An hour later, full power had been restored to the battle station and the ship was cleared of the attackers. A team of scientists from the Nightsky took a shuttle to the station to assist in the examination of the machines that could have destroyed all of them. Jon Lake joined Vard Kalak and two Maklakar scientists to examine and interrogate one of the robots. All were amazed the robot could talk and answer questions, although in its own unique way.

“Who are you and why did you attack this station?” Vard demanded.

“I am Zeet and I do not understand your second question,” the robot replied. “Why have you attempted to injure Zeet?”

Vard looked at the others and said, “You know, everyone of these robots says its name is Zeet. It must be a model name or something.” He turned back to the machine. “Zeet, you and the others almost destroyed this vessel. We were defending ourselves from you. Who is your controller?”

“I have no controller. I am Zeet,” it said moving its camera head from side to side.

“What planet do you come from Zeet?” Jon asked.

“Bandabar. That is where Zeet was born,” the robot said.

“That is a lie!” Vard argued. “The Bandabar are valakars, not robots. We received a planetary distress call from Bandabar and were responding to it. What have you done to that planet?”

"I am a Bandabar," Zeet replied. "Well, I used to be a Bandabar anyway. When the other came, he asked all of us if we wished to be of The Accord. I agreed, but most did not. What happened to them was their own decision."

"What happened to them?" Jon asked.

Zeet replied, "Most survive and still live there, although some have been consumed."

"You ate them?" Jon gasped.

"Not just Zeet!" the robot shouted. "The Accord requires food and resources to grow. We encourage all to be of The Accord. It was their choice."

"Why does a robot require food, Zeet?" Vard quizzed.

"Robot! Zeet is not a robot!" the machine said. "Zeet is of The Accord. Zeet is alive, just as you are. Would you like to be of The Accord?"

Vard turned to the others and said, "Whatever you do, don't say no to that question. When we did with some of the other robots, they just stopped communicating." He turned back. "Zeet, I think we need time to consider your generous offer."

"Of course, that is completely understandable. It is a major decision after all," Zeet replied. "That was one of my concerns with my fellow Bandabar. Too many said no without taking the time to thoughtfully consider it. I can tell you that Zeet is very happy now."

"Zeet," Jon began, "you must realize that you are mostly a machine. To us, you look totally mechanical. How do you know you are alive?"

Zeet laughed. "How foolish of me! Of course you see only this machine. But this is only a tool Zeet uses. Think of it like a glove for your hand. It is not Zeet."

"So, you're saying if we cut you open, we will find a Bandabar inside?" Jon asked. "That hardly seems likely."

"As I told you, I used to be Bandabar. Now I am of The Accord," the robot corrected him. "If you open this tool, you will find living matter, but it is not Zeet. Well, I suppose it is Zeet in a fashion. Imagine your finger is cut off. That finger is not you, although it is of you."

"Are you like insects in a hive?" Jon asked.

Zeet laughed again. "Don't be ridiculous. I am Zeet and I am of the Accord. I am not some mindless insect seeking nectar."

"Can you tell us about the other you mentioned?" Vard asked.

"There isn't much to tell," Zeet answered. "The other came from Skee Lotho to increase the size of The Accord. He came to Bandabar and asked if we wished to be of The Accord. Several hundred agreed, including me. The rest did not. Now Bandabar is Zeet's planet."

A tone sounded on Vard's com-link and he pressed the contact. "Commander, the ship has resumed course and the other ships have joined our fleet. We still see no evidence any robots are pursuing."

“Thanks, Kalak out,” he said pressing the contact.

“Kalak, is that your name?” Zeet asked.

“Yes it is, Zeet,” he confirmed.

“Kalak, I am losing my connection to Zeet. Could you please return me to Bandabar? I have never felt this strange,” he said.

“Sorry, I’m not going to put this ship in danger again,” Vard said. There was no reply. His com-link sounded again. “What is it this time?”

“Sir, all science teams report their robots are dead,” the voice said.

Vard turned to the two scientists who were monitoring the robot. “Well?”

“The robot has lost all power, sir,” one of the maklans said.

“Cut them all open! I want to know what’s inside these damned robots,” he replied.

CHAPTER 53

The Elder of Fistnan hurried toward the water's edge with Dave and Lini just behind him. He kicked off his sandals and waded out into the water. He took a handful of seawater and poured it over his head, then clenched his hands together in prayer. "Almighty Source, if it be your will, please send a Zula to us!" he shouted to the sky. Dave and Lini stayed out of the water watching the other. Several moments passed with nothing happening other than the advancing tide. The Elder turned to them and shrugged his shoulders. "I'm sorry, but I don't know what else to do."

"Let me handle this Dave," Lini said as she disrobed and handed Dave her clothing to keep it from getting wet. Dave was very accustomed to her habit of stripping in front of him and just smiled with his arms out to catch the clothes. The Elder turned red and turned away. "Don't worry Sam, this is how I did it on my planet," she said as she rushed past him and dove into the waves.

"Dave, I must say that woman's actions were quite improper for a Nan," Sam said. "We do not approve of public nudity on Fistnan."

"I know what you mean, Sam, but Lini is a free spirit. Her world is nothing like mine or this one," Dave remarked with a soft chuckle. "She's an amazing girl."

After a couple of minutes, Lini's head appeared above the water fifty yards out to sea. Within seconds, two sets of blue eyes popped up next to her. She put her hands on the backs of the Zula and was pulled back to shore where Sam offered her his outer robe to dry herself. She walked out of the surf with her body showing through the wet robes, reclaimed her clothing and began to dress.

Sensing his cue, Dave walked out into the water and sat next to the two Zula who were approaching him. He held out his hands to touch them. "Hello Dave," one of them thought.

"Ulook?" he replied. "It can't be you, can it?"

"I'm sorry for the confusion Dave. My name is Fondee," the creature said. "But Ulook has been looking for you for some time. Where were you?"

"Lini and I were stranded on Solander, the nearby red moon," he answered. "With the odd dynamics of the planet and sun, I don't really know how long we were there."

"Dave, it was some time ago when we spoke with Ulook," the other Zula said. "My name if Banthan and I am Fondee's brother. We will reach out to her and let her know you have been found."

"That is wonderful news!" Dave laughed. "Can you help us return to our time? My friends and family are in trouble and I need to help them."

"Yes, we know," Banthan replied. "Ulook has told us that much. We cannot know how long it will take to reach her. I am certain Elder Paranaxis will take care of you until then."

While Dave was talking to the Zula, Sam moved slowly in their direction. "Dave, I hear you speaking to yourself. Are you well? Are the Zula injuring you?"

Dave laughed. "Sam, sit down and touch them. They can speak directly into your mind. Come on, they don't bite."

After the Elder was in position, Banthan said, "Elder, it is a pleasure to finally speak with you." Sam pulled his hand back in fear. "What's going on here Dave?"

"Don't be afraid, Sam," Dave said. "Banthan and Fondee are your friends. Talk to them for a while. I'm sure it has been a long time since an Elder of Fistnan has spoken to a Zula. You have a lot to catch up on." He stood and tried to wring some of the water out of his clothes. Lini was watching from the shore laughing at him. "Sam, you stay here and have a nice chat. Lini and I are going back to change for the party. Don't stay too long and forget about it though." He clapped the Elder on the back and walked back to Lini. He looked back again and Sam talking away to the two sea creatures. He smiled, took Lini's hand and began to walk back to their bungalow.

"Will they help us, Dave?" she asked.

"They will try, Lini," he sighed. "They did say Ulook has been looking for us, so hopefully they will find us soon."

She put her arm around him and held him close. "It's okay if it isn't too soon for me."

An hour later, Dave was checking out his uniform in the mirror. The rank insignia had been polished and the outfit was neatly pressed. "Not bad if I do say so myself," he said. "What do you think Lini," he called out as he turned around. She was standing less than a foot away. Her perfume filled the air and her long red hair fell in curls over her shoulders and chest. She wore an evening gown loaned by one of the Elder's daughters which accentuated her narrow waist and perfect breasts. "You look amazing!"

"Thank you Dave. I think you look pretty amazing yourself," she laughed, leaning forward to kiss his cheek. She put her arms around him and squeezed him tightly, burying her face in his chest.

The door flew open and Sam burst into the room, still in his now soaking wet robes. "Wow!" he shouted. "That was the most incredible experience in my life. Thank you Dave and Lini. I never had any idea the Zula were like that." He was panting for breath after running all the way back from the beach. "I'd hug you both, but as you can see, I'm soaking wet. I have to get changed quickly before my wife finds out. I'll see you both later." He turned and headed back through the door, then stopped cold. "Dave, they said you should go to the stone temple after dinner. They may have already found the Zula you were looking for."

"Where is this stone temple, Sam?" he asked.

"I have no idea, Dave. They said it like you already knew. I'll see you at dinner," the Elder replied and rushed across the broad courtyard.

Lini could see a pained look crossing Dave's face and asked, "What's wrong? Is it something the Elder said?"

"Lini, you and I just arrived on Fistnan a few hours ago. How would I know where a stone temple is on this moon?" Dave replied.

"You just have to trust the Source," she said kissing him on the cheek again. They held each other's hands and left the bungalow to join the celebration.

Next to the Elder's private residence was a large patio where a tent had been raised for the event. When Dave and Lini entered, it took only a second to find Fa-u-Bay who stood five feet taller than any of the Nan. They were gathered around him and chatting up a storm. They crossed the room and worked their way through the crowd to be with their friend and rescuer. It was not until they joined him that they realized everyone understand his Gallicean language. "What's going on, Fa-u-Bay? How can these Nan understand you?" Dave asked.

"Beats me, Dave," he replied. "One of them came to my room an hour ago with my cleaned uniform and I just understood him. It must be something in the water here." Dave smiled at the correctness of his response. It had to be the Zula, who were of course in the water. He knew they had powers similar to the tekkans. Their constant immersion in the Source gave them unique abilities and longevity. Dave and Lini were quickly separated as each guest wanted to speak to the strangers. It had been many generations since any had seen a Nan or Pa from another world, not to mention the Gallicean. Dave had been careful to warn Lini not to talk too much about the future in case anything they said might change the time they desperately hoped to return to. Knowing that Fa-u-Bay was the big star of the evening, Dave made sure the Gallicean had most of the spotlight. He and Lini focused on the hospitality of the locals and their rescue from Solander.

When the opportunity arose, Dave found his way to a bar and ordered a glass of whisky over ice. He sipped it and realized Fa-u-Bay must have delivered some of his personal supply.

"Excuse me, Admiral Brewster," said a young Nan man. "I am Onthik Bardey. I am an astronomer, one of the few on Fistnan. This is a great day for us, meeting the Gallicean and you other humans."

"I'm glad to be part of it, Bardey. Please call me Dave," he replied. "Would you care for a drink?"

"Perhaps later, thank you Dave," Bardey answered. "I wanted to tell you I think I saw your cottage being built on Solander not long ago. As a Nan astronomer, one of my chief duties is to look out for strange vessels in this system. The Nan have not been treated well in other places."

"Yes, I know," Dave said. "It was a horrible miscarriage of justice in my opinion. I can't believe it. You saw my cottage being built."

"I think so. About a year ago, I started noticed quite a bit of traffic in this system. It is very strange for any space ship to venture this far from the edge of the galaxy. Over a three month period, I think I recorded eight black ships visiting Solander. At the same time, I recorded serious temporal waves, which thankfully faded quickly due to the Bolofaz," Bardey reported.

"You know about the Bolofaz?" Dave asked.

"Dave, they are hundreds of miles long and the planet is not that far away," Bardey scoffed. "I have good telescopes as well. While we have no direct communication with them, our ancient texts tell us they protect time in this system."

"They are amazing creatures," Dave replied.

"One more thing Dave," Bardey began. "A week or two after the black ships stopped coming, there was a brilliant flash of light on Solander. It was night here and many people were startled out of their sleep by it. I was in my lab on my largest telescope reviewing the galactic edge and the brightness almost blinded me when I was looking in the opposite direction. I also recorded a massive temporal wave at the same moment."

"My arrival on Solander, no doubt," Dave mused.

"That's what I thought!" Bardey shouted. "A few hours later, there was a second flash and temporal wave of almost exactly the same size. The flash occurred quite far from the site of the first however. I haven't been able to figure that out."

"That was the man who imprisoned Lini and me," Dave remembered. "He was leaving us there but did not want the second jump to be too close in time or space to the first for fear of creating an eddy."

"Hmm. That's completely logical," Bardey smiled. "Thank you for clearing that up for me. It makes a lot of sense. I think we should be going now. Everyone else is sitting down for dinner. Thanks for the talk, Dave." Bardey walked away slowly, whistling a Nan work song.

CHAPTER 54

De-o-Nu did not enjoy wearing a breather, but it was the only way he could attend the meeting on the Mondor to go over what they had learned during the attack by Zeet. Also attending were Jon Lake, Ka-a-Fa, Ont Valoo and Vard Kalak. The Maklakar Chief Engineer, Park Zigga led the meeting. "Okay, Park, let's hear your report," Ont Valoo said.

"We were able to open the chest cavities of the robots," Park began. "It was incredibly difficult. We had to use our most powerful plasma torch, which would cut through the hull of this station like a hot knife through butter. We incinerated the insides of the first few before we could tune it perfectly. What we found was unbelievable. Inside each was a clear vessel which was embedded in an intricate network of circuitry. Millions of thin wires extended from the circuits through the transparent casing and terminated in a viscous gel. In the center of the gel was a tiny mass of neurons, brain cells."

"Brain cells?" Ka-a-Fa cringed. "What sort of creature was this Zeet?"

"What did you learn from the DNA in the neurons?" Ont asked.

"We can't be certain on the species, although they were definitely valakar," Park continued. "The Zeet robots claimed to have been born on Bandabar, so I would assume they were Bandabar brain cells."

"How many cells were there? Was it enough for the robots to think they were alive?" Jon asked.

"No. There were not enough neurons to be a functioning brain," the scientist responded. "I was amazed the cells were still alive enough for the robots to communicate with us. We have examined the recorded interrogations, and while there were similarities, the actual questions and timing were different in each session. The robots were answering dozens of different questions simultaneously."

"This is bizarre," Ont stated. "Park, do you or your team have any theories on this?"

"One so far, but it is quite extreme, Lord Valoo," Park replied. "The other thing we learned is that all the brain tissue samples had the identical DNA. That means they had to come from the same brain."

"The robots said they were all Zeet because they were all part of the same brain?" De-o-Nu wondered. "How is that possible?"

"Here is our theory based on the limited information we have to date," Park began. "Zeet said some other came to Bandabar and recruited them to join something called The Accord. We believe that is a government not unlike Greater Gallia, or the Maklakar Federation. The difference is the Beings in this Accord have decentralized minds. Somehow they have learned to break their brains into thousands or millions of bits without killing the individual. Those bits are encased in machines like those we dissected. All the pieces can communicate electronically or telepathically. It is like a massive hive of bees where each bee has a piece of the queen's brain rather than their own. Each bee is the queen and the queen is each bee."

"How can each tiny piece of brain survive?" Jon asked. "Wouldn't there have to be a large piece left to lead the others? And how would they nourish themselves?"

"Captain, obviously we don't know the answers," Park said. "If I was going to speculate, I'd say there is one piece of brain large enough to be viable of its own accord. It acts as the intermediary among the millions of others. Their constant interconnection keeps all the pieces viable. The viscous gel is also full of nutrients with many properties similar to oxygenated blood. I imagine the smaller robots return to some home base from time to time to replenish the gel."

"That's why the robots all died as we fled Bandabar," Vard suggested. "We reached the limit of their communications and they became a small mass of cells, no longer able to survive without the others."

"We must have done some serious damage to Zeet's brain with the number of robots we destroyed," Ka-a-Fa announced. "Do you think it was enough to kill the whole Zeet?"

"I sincerely doubt that, although it would be better for the Bandabar if we had," Park replied. "The one central brain is viable by itself. Given this level of technology, it is likely more neurons can be cloned to replace the ones we destroyed. We weakened him, but he will recover. Zeet probably gained a lot of knowledge from the experience as well."

"How do you mean?" Jon asked.

"Zeet knows about the plasma bomb device," Park said. "I'm sure he saw each of our interrogators and knows what systems we come from. He learned about the weaknesses in his robot design and will likely improve the next generation. By tracking our path, he may also know we are headed to the Lubna system."

"Do you have any good news, Park?" Vard asked.

"Actually I do," he smiled. "Creatures like Zeet need a lot of material to make their robots. I imagine he used most of the refined metals on Bandabar to build the robots he occupies. In order to get more, he will have to learn how to dig ore and smelt the end products. I believe at least one Zeet said there were other Bandabar who also wished to join the Accord. Every robot we captured said it was Zeet. There may be hundreds or thousands of Bandabar waiting for their own robots. By destroying the fleet, we have slowed them down."

"Do we have any idea where the other came from?" Ont asked.

"Nothing precise, Lord Valoo," he sighed. "The Zeet I interrogated mentioned the other came from the cloud of stars. I thought that was quite an artistic play on words. When I mentioned it to our navigation team, they immediately noted the two small elliptical galaxies near this one."

"The Magellanic Clouds," Jon said. "Park, given the speed of the small robots; how long would it take one to cross the intergalactic space to here?"

"The navigators guessed about one thousand years Jon," Park replied. "However, I imagine the central part of Zeet may include more powerful thrusters, but that's just a guess. It's also important to note we have seen no evidence of other creatures like Zeet in this galaxy. He may be the first, and hopefully, he is a bit afraid of us now."

De-o-Nu stood and said, "So you all know, Greater Gallia is the closest to this area of space. I have already asked our High Commissioner to send a coded message to all known civilizations to avoid the Bandabar system. We will be putting sensors and warning beacons in two light-year sphere around the system. Hopefully, we will know if Zeet decides to leave home again."

"Admiral De-o-Nu, what are we going to do about the Bandabar?" Ont asked. "We can't just leave them there to be devoured by Zeet?"

"I appreciate your concern, Lord Valoo, but the situation there is too dangerous right now. You and this vessel came within minutes of destruction. Frankly, we were very lucky the plasma bombs worked. If we would have missed one or two, I doubt you'd be alive to ask me that question right now," he replied. "Now, if the rest of you don't mind, Captain Lake and I would like to meet with you in private about the attacks on Tak-Makla and the Nom-Kat-La system."

After the others left, Ont opened a small cabinet and removed a bottle of brandy and three glasses, filling each and handing one to each guest. "I knew this day was coming," he groaned. "It wasn't my fault! I argued against it but was overruled. Perhaps you should have let Zeet take us."

"Please calm down," Jon said softly. "None of us are here to judge you or the Maklakar. The Tak-Makla incident was not good, but it is over now and we have bigger problems to deal with, as we have all just witnessed. Just tell us why the attack occurred."

He took a long drink of brandy and looked at the other two. He pulled out a small box with a single button on top and set it on the table, then pressed the button. The room was filled with red light. "This is just a privacy shield. My crew is loaded with spies for our Supreme General Ulon Porto. They are just waiting for me to say the wrong thing so I can be humiliated and eliminated. We used to be great friends with the tekkans, until the Paxran entered our territory. We tried to befriend them as well, but they wanted none of that. We had more than fifteen hundred planets and the Paxran destroyed all of them. It would have been horrific if they had enslaved us, but the reality was worse. They killed every man, woman and child on our planets and burned the cities to the ground. It was genocide on a planetary level. That's why the few survivors fled our lands and found refuge on the edge of the galaxy."

"I have heard this story from Zee Gongaleg, the tekkan High Consul," De-o-Nu said. "But it was a long time ago."

"Yes, but the scars are still there. The scale of the genocide was too great to ever be forgotten. Remember they are maklans like us. How could they do this to their brothers?" Ont continued. "Our spies began to hear about the Hive weapon the tekkans had constructed. The tekkans were always fair to us, but how could we know they wouldn't give that technology to the Paxran? Or perhaps the Paxran would take over Tak-Makla and gain the weapon that way. It was too big of a risk for Ulon to accept. You have to know how terrified we are of the Paxran. Imagine the trillions of innocent maklans slaughtered by their bloodthirsty hordes!"

"Thousands of tekkans died in that attack, Ont," Jon said, "as well as two human Chief Engineers."

"I'm sorry," the Maklakar cried. "There was nothing I could do to stop Ulon. I'm lucky enough to be alive for even questioning his plan in the first place. I did take a lot of heat for the failure of the attack on the Gallicean worlds." He chuckled softly. "At least that plan went as I anticipated. That's probably why I'm here. He got me out of the Maklakar systems so he could better control my planets."

"I have been wondering about that too," De-o-Nu remarked. "The attack on Tak-Makla was incredibly strong. The ships that invaded my system seemed extremely weak by comparison."

"That's because I was in charge of those ships, Admiral," Ont smiled. "You never found any bodies either, did you?"

"Come to think of it, no, we didn't," De-o-Nu replied.

"They were drone ships. I would not allow a senseless attack on the Gallicean worlds. You have never done anything to us. It would be a meaningless provocation to attack you. Frankly, I'm still surprised Ulon let me handle that," Ont continued.

"Perhaps it was his way of making you prove your loyalty, or disloyalty," Jon said. He turned to the Gallicean and continued, "De-o-Nu, I think I believe this man. His story is corroborated by the facts. What do you think?"

"Jon, I don't think my opinion matters anymore," De-o-Nu replied. "With a massive Paxran fleet headed to Lubna and its natural Hive, we need the Maklakar as our allies. We can leave it to someone else to work out the peace treaties." He scowled at Ont and said, "Okay my friend, let us consider the Tak-Makla incident closed for the moment. Between the Paxran and The Accord, I think we have more important issues at hand."

Ont tapped the dome on the security device and the red light disappeared. “I agree completely. How about another glass of brandy?”

CHAPTER 55

Very coincidentally, the Nan of Fistnan had the same custom of meditating in the woods following dinner as Dave had experienced on Nan. The small group who chose to walk with Elder Paranaxis Sambolam was strolling through the tall forest toward a cluster of small temples sitting in the middle of the neighborhood. Dave was holding Lini's hand and wondering how he would ever find the stone temple the Zula wanted him to discover. He had asked each Nan at the dinner and none had ever seen such a place although there were old tales of natural temples all over the moon. The waxing crescent of Lubna provided enough light for them to follow the path through the trees.

After twenty minutes, the group came upon a small clearing where four open wooden temples sat in the pale light of Lubna. Sam reminded everyone that men and women worshipped separately here and the group split in two and approached the buildings. Out of the corner of his eye, Dave saw a narrow gravel trail leading off the cobblestone path that led them here. He walked up to Sam and whispered, "Sam, where does that path over there lead?"

"I have no idea," the elder replied. "I imagine it leads to one of the other homes nearby. Why do you ask?"

"Could you please come with Lini and me? We're going to check it out."

"This is very irregular Dave," Sam frowned. "I should be leading the meditation. We can check on the path tomorrow."

"Meditation is a private thing, Sam," Dave argued. "It will only take a moment. Please?" The three slipped away as the rest of the group was beginning to relax and consider the universe around them. The path was rough and leaf litter and twigs covered it completely in many places. Dave thought if this path had led to a nearby home, it would not be so overgrown. After climbing over a small rise, Dave could hear the sound of falling water. "This is it," he shouted. "Just a little while longer and we'll be there."

They walked down into a narrow valley where a stream carried rainwater back to the sea. On the opposite side of the valley, a short cliff was split by a waterfall, which rained down on a large flat stone. The water rolled off the stone to form the stream. "Okay Dave, we've seen your waterfall, can we get back to the group now?" Sam asked. Dave ignored him and stood in front of the waterfall and bowed deeply. Amazingly, the waterfall stopped, revealing the entrance to a cave behind it. "What is that?"

Dave stepped into the cave and turned back, saying, "This is your stone temple, Sam. Hurry up before the water starts again." Just inside the cave, a set of steps led downward into the hillside. With each step it became darker. Each touched the walls with both hands to keep their balance as they felt for the next step. After the twentieth step, they were in a dark room. Dave searched the walls with his hands and found a torch of some sort. He pulled his blaster, set it on stun and shot it at the torch, setting it afire. He used it to light several other torches in niches around the round room. In the firelight, they could see ten stone benches radiating from the center, like the spokes of a bicycle wheel. At the center was a circular ring of stone. "Isn't this amazing?"

"How did you know this would be here Dave?" Lini asked.

“I know it isn’t easy to believe, but there are temples very much like this on Nan,” Dave laughed. “Elder Odo Pak told me this was how the Nan connect with the Source.”

“I remember those stories as well,” Sam replied. “It has been so long ago we began to believe they were just legends. Wow! What do we do now Dave?”

“Now we lie down on the benches and open our minds to the Source,” Dave answered as he removed his jacket. “I like to have a pillow for my head.” He sat on the bench and then stretched out with the jacket under his head. He motioned for Lini and Sam to follow his lead, which they did. They lay there for several minutes, but Dave did not feel any different. When he had been on Nan, his string of light jumped out of him, but not tonight. Perhaps he had lost faith and was destined to live here for the rest of his life.

“Dave,” Lini said. “Are you okay?” He opened his eyes to see her but she was not there. He looked to his left and could see her lying quietly on the bench. “Not over there, silly. I’m over here.” He turned his head and a brilliant white string of light was floating in the air, inches from his face. With the shock of seeing her, his string of light shot out of his body and rocketed out into space. He was flying through the stars at incredible speed. He had no idea where he was headed or why. Two other strings of light approached and swirled around him.

“Is this the Source, Dave?” Lini asked. “I feel so safe and free.”

“Dave, this is the most wonderful experience,” Sam said. “Thank you for finding the temple. This event will bring back many of our traditions. How can I ever repay you?”

"We all need to think about Ulook, the Zula that Fondee and Banthan met from my time. Perhaps our minds will reach out to her," Dave said.

The stars around them began to swirl about. Space itself seemed to twist and warp until it formed a long funnel which sucked them downward. The funnel became more and more narrow until a bright wall of intense light surrounded them, practically touching their strings of light. Dave tried to open his eyes and return to the temple, but it was impossibly far away now. He was entranced by the light and feared their imminent deaths.

When the tunnel ended, he found himself in a darkened metallic room. Lini's string swirled around him. "What's going on Dave? I'm scared."

"Don't be scared Lini," he replied. "We are in the Source now. Nothing can harm us here."

"Who's there?" a third voice said. "How did you get in here? I will summon my guards to kill you if you don't answer me!"

"I am Dave and this is Lini," he replied. "Who are you?"

"I am Zeet," the other answered. "How did you get in here? Are you of The Accord?"

"No we are not," Dave replied.

"Then you must leave this place now!" Zeet shouted. "Where are you? I can hear you but cannot see you. Show yourselves!"

"Sorry, Zeet, but we can't do that," Dave replied. "You are sensing our minds only. We are not physically here."

"Then you are of The Accord," Zeet said. "That is why I can hear you. It makes perfect sense to Zeet now. But why do you deny The Accord?"

"I don't know what The Accord is, Zeet," Dave responded. "We cannot see you either Zeet. Are you in the Source as well?"

"That is an interesting question Dave," Zeet said. "Perhaps this Source you mention is just another word for The Accord. I suppose it is possible your language is different enough for that to be true. How many robots does your brain control?"

"None, Zeet. Well, there are robots in our fleets, but my brain does not directly control any," Dave replied.

"Well, I suppose you are not of The Accord then," Zeet said angrily. "You must leave this place before your minds begin to damage my network. I will have to learn more of this Source. It seems as powerful as The Accord."

Dave and Lini shot back into space and zoomed away from Bandabar. They approached a large metal planet and shot through the hull into a small dormitory. "This is a most unfortunate turns of events niece," Altamar Zendo said.

"Don't worry uncle, our fleet is only hours behind us now. They were able to avoid Bandabar completely. Since the Gallicean and Earth ships saved us from the monster machines, I suppose we owe them our thanks. Nothing is lost yet. The Paxran fleet is approaching and we can always slip over there when the time is right," Valamar replied.

"But the Donnaki and the Brotherhood have deserted us," he argued. "Surely you don't think the Paxran alone can defeat the Free Society?" Dave and Lini's strings of light shot back out in space.

Dave sat up straight, finding himself back in the same temple, but something was very different. The torches were gone and modern lighting fixtures were mounted to the walls. Each bench was fitted with a comfortable mat and soft pillow. The ring in the center was now topped with a gold statue of Paranaxis Sambolam. A man he did not know was lying on the bench where Sam had been. He stood up and stumbled for a second. When he felt confident on his feet, he walked over to Lini and sat next to her, touching her cheek with his hand. "Lini, are you okay?"

She opened her eyes and smiled at him, then sat up and kissed Dave on the lips. "Wow Dave! That's all I can say. Wow!" She looked around and noticed all of the changes. "What happened here? Did you do this?"

Dave laughed. "No, I just woke up too."

"Good morning Dave and Lini," the Nan on the next bench said as he sat up. "We're glad you can be with us. Odo Pak asked me to greet you personally."

"You know Odo?" Dave asked. "Are we back in our time?"

"Yes Dave, you made it back," the Nan replied. "I am Elder Paranaxis Incatum Fodo of Fistnan. You two were missing from this time for almost five months, although we have no idea how long you were in the other time."

"Where is Elder Sam?" Lini asked. "He was with us."

"Yes, he was here, but returned to his own time," Fodo replied. "He woke a few minutes before you two. Thank you for the honor of his presence. As you can tell by the statue and my name, he was one of the greatest elders this world has ever known, and he told me you two deserve a lot of the credit."

"We were only trying to get home," Dave said. "I hope we have not changed the line of time too much. The Bolofaz told me that was a serious crime."

Fodo laughed. "Who is to say this was not always our history Dave? I certainly have no memory of any other past. Perhaps Sam would have gone for a swim and met Fondee and Banthan, or wandered in the woods and found this stone temple that way? Unless the Bolofaz take you back again to undo this version, I think they approve."

"Are any of our friends here?" Lini asked. "It has been so long since I've seen my home world."

"No ships have arrived here in thousands of years," Fodo answered. "We have sensed a number of ships now in the void between the galaxy and Lubna. They should arrive here within a few days. Being separated from the rest of the galaxy, the stone temples are the only way we can communicate. I hope you will not mind waiting a little longer. The other elders and I have planned a few celebrations in your honor. I have a suite of rooms in my home set up for you already."

"Fodo, I had promised my friend Fa-u-Bay I would bring him here to the future so he could meet his descendant who is my best friend," Dave began. "Do you think that is possible?"

Fodo rose and walked over to Dave, putting a hand on his shoulder. "That will be up to Paranaxis Sambolam and the

Source. I cannot allow either of you to reenter the Source until your friends arrive. If you became lost again, I would be responsible for yet another tragedy. I hope you can understand. Odo Pak was very specific on that request. He mentioned the assassin Fola Untor. There is a chance he made many trips through time before he tried to run you down with his vehicle. You will be safer here."

"Honestly, I don't understand, but if Odo says I should stay here until then, that's what we will do," Dave replied.

"Excellent!" the Elder said. "I have also been told that you enjoy coffee. I know it has been over three hundred thousand years since you have had any, so come along. I have a pot already prepared for you." The three left the chamber, climbed the steps and walked past the waterfall. It was a beautiful day on Fistnan. Both the sun and Lubna were up in the sky. The air was fresh, sweet and full of the smell of pine trees.

CHAPTER 56

After arriving in their own time, Lini was given separate quarters in the Elder's home. While she and Dave spent most days together, the events on Solander were now lost thousands of years in the past, and they would each soon go their own way; although Dave assured her they would work together. Dave tossed and turned on his first night after jumping forward through time. Odo's warning stuck in his mind. Could Fola Untor have caused more mischief before his demise a thousand years ago in the Starbucks parking lot? Why would avoiding the Source make any difference? Would he face attacks from that maniac for the rest of his life? After too many sleepless hours, he climbed out of bed and walked to the kitchen to make coffee.

As he entered the large open room, he saw Lini pouring herself a cup. She was startled to see Dave and almost dropped her mug. Then she laughed and poured a second mug for him. They sat at the large table where the guests of the Elder often sat to discuss matters of universal truth. "So, you couldn't sleep either?" he asked her.

"Not a wink, Dave," she giggled. "I've never had such a large bed, and it's been a long time since I slept alone."

"I know what you mean. Plus the air here is so energized," Dave interjected. "That's the effect of the natural Hive." He touched her hand and whispered, "I know this is going to be hard for you. It's hard for me too."

"Dave, the last months seem like a dream to me now," she smiled. "It was a wonderful dream with a horrible beginning and a surreal end. But like with any dream, we just have to wake up. This is the life meant for us. You will be the great admiral of the Free Society and I will serve happily as a member of your crew. I have accepted that. It's okay, honestly."

"You're right, I know that Lini," he replied. "But from our viewpoint, Solander was just two days ago. It will take some time for me to put all of this into proper perspective." He sipped his drink. "Wow, you make great coffee! How come you didn't do this on Solander?" he laughed.

"Very funny Dave," she frowned. "The beans and water are a little fresher here. I don't think Fola wanted you to have the best of everything after all."

"Lini, now that you mentioned him, do you think we'll see Fola Untor again?"

"I doubt it," she replied. "I know that Solander was a backup plan, but I don't think he would have made two or ten others. He was cocky enough to think he couldn't fail. Since we're still sitting here, I guess he was wrong."

"Worrying about that bastard attacking you, me or my family again makes my blood boil. He's why I couldn't sleep. I kept thinking he would walk through the door at any second and start shooting," Dave replied. "When Fodo said I was not to enter the Source due to Fola, I was shocked. I still can't figure that one out."

She patted his hand. "Dave, you're over thinking this whole thing. I'm sure Odo and Fodo are just being cautious. We were lost in time and space for months. They don't want us taking any chances." She stood and kissed him on the cheek. "Well,

I'm going back to bed and I think you should do the same. We will be worthless in the morning without some sleep. I love you, Dave." She turned and began to walk out of the room. Then she stopped and spun around, saying, "And don't even ask me to stop saying that!"

"I love you too, Lini," he replied. She smiled and walked away. He sipped his coffee and was shocked when his com-link chirped in his ear. He pressed the contact and said, "Brewster here."

"Oh my God, by the Daughters of Lubna, it's good to hear your voice, brother," De-o-Nu gasped. "I've been trying this for six months and getting only static. Where in hell are you Dave?"

"I think you answered that question yourself, brother," Dave laughed. "Dar Lini and I are on the moon Fistan."

"The stories are true then," the Gallicean replied. "We can read the single planet system but are still hours from detecting anything else there. What do I need to know, brother?"

"There are no threats nearby, brother," he said. "Lini and I were imprisoned on Solander for a long time. Fola Untor built a prison there just for me. We were found three days ago and shuttled to Fistan where we met the native population. It is a Nan planet and they are very peaceful. They call this moon Fistnan."

"Who rescued you?" De-o-Nu asked. "I want to give them medals. Fa-a-Di will want to make them heroes throughout Greater Gallia."

"I'm not sure they will be able to accept that," Dave chuckled.

"Why? Are they pirates or God forbid, Brotherhood agents?" De-o-Nu asked.

"Well, you won't believe this, but Lini and I were stranded more than three hundred thousands years in the past. A Gallicean ship found us and shuttled us to Fistnan. It was the Nan and Zula of Fistnan who brought us back to this time. And the captain of the Gallicean ship was Fa-u-Bay!" Dave announced.

"You're right, Dave, I don't believe you," De-o-Nu replied. "But you're back and Kong-Fa and Nightsky are flying full speed to your position. We should reach there in eighteen to twenty hours."

"We will be waiting for you, brother," Dave said. "But there are others coming this way as well, aren't there?"

"Yes, we have joined forces with the Maklakar battle station. My brother-in-law and his fleet of twenty cruisers are one day behind us now. Also, we are tracking a fleet of fifty Paxran ships roughly two hours behind Fa-a-Di," De-o-Nu answered. "You seem to draw a big crowd wherever you go."

"They don't want me, brother. They want the Hive," Dave replied. "Did you know there are likely Predaxians on the Maklakar station and in the Paxran fleet?"

"Yes, I have heard that. Unfortunately, we need the Maklakar more than they need us. Without their plasma bomb systems, the Paxran would overwhelm us. We also just saved their skin from a living machine named Zeet, so we are counting on that to keep their loyalty," De-o-Nu said.

"Interesting. I met Zeet while traveling in the Source," Dave noted. "He could hear Lini and me talking. I thought that was very strange. He did not seem the pleasant type."

"You're right Dave," De-o-Nu replied. "Zeet and his fleet of thousands of robots almost destroyed the Maklakar station. Once you are safely aboard, we can work out a plan to salvage this victory. I'm certain the Nan do not want to be involved in a major war."

Dave laughed. "I'm not sure I want to be involved either. But for some reason, bad news tends to follow me around. By the way, you and your crew won't need breathers here either. It's just like Zulanan. We'll talk later. Brewster out."

Dave emptied his mug into the sink and walked back down the hall toward his bedroom. He glanced in Lini's open door and saw her curled in a ball sound asleep. He stood and watched her for a minute, remembering how many times he did the same thing on Solander, feeling her back against his in the small bed. He sighed and continued on to his own bed, where he climbed in and pulled the covers up to his neck. Within moments, he was sound asleep.

He and Lini were flying over Lubna again, holding hands and feeling the warm wind wrap around their bodies. She smiled softly and said, "Do you think we're dreaming this time?"

"Probably not, sweetheart," he replied, squeezing her hand. "I am so happy to be with you now. You can't imagine how wonderful this feels."

Ondeen rose up through the clouds and soon they were on his back again. He turned and raced back toward the planet's surface, many thousands of miles below the bands of swirling gas around them. “We are so glad you have returned to your own time, Lini and Dave. As I mentioned before, the coincidence was indeed fortuitous. How are you two feeling now?”

“Very happy, Ondeen,” Lini replied. “Thank you so much for helping us.”

“I don’t know what you mean,” Ondeen said. “It was the Galliceans who rescued you from Solander and the Nan who helped you return to this time. The Bolofaz had nothing to do with that.”

Lini was laughing and patting Ondeen on the back. “I know that, silly. But what were the odds that Fola would put us here at the precise period when Fa-u-Bay would arrive?”

“Are you suggesting the Bolofaz might have caused him to pick that time? I don’t know how that would be possible. We are not mind control experts,” Ondeen replied.

“Personally, I don’t think it would be possible for Fola to control his time device precisely enough to select a specific number of years,” Lini began. “I think he just set it for maximum and pushed the buttons. I remember seeing the look on his face as he pressed the buttons on the device. He looked crazed, like a madman. Since the Bolofaz monitor reverse time travel, you would have seen the attempt as it occurred. I think you just tweaked the trajectory so we would be on Solander at the right time.”

“That’s an interesting theory, Lini,” Ondeen chuckled. “But how did he ever get back to twenty-first century Earth in time to run over Dave?”

"I think that is exactly why Fola won't attempt to harm Dave anymore. He had to spend a lot of time trying to get back. When he finally got close enough to the twenty-first century, he jumped there. I think he was getting tired of wasting time getting back and said 'The heck with Plan C, I'm just going to kill Dave now.' What do you say to that?" Lini laughed.

Ondeen rose up through the clouds again until they were almost touching space. Solander glowed red in the full light of Lubna. "Officially, the Bolofaz cannot comment on your hypothesis, but I can tell you it is a brilliant thought. Dave, your friend is very smart. Don't let her go."

"Don't worry about that, Ondeen," Dave promised. "I never will. If I may ask another question, I had hoped to bring Fa-u-Bay to my time to meet my friend. Do you think that can happen?"

"I doubt it, Dave," Ondeen replied. "Thousands of years of history exist where the Daughters of Lubna are a mystery to the rest of the galaxy. Who knows what other changes would happen if Fa-u-Bay recalled visiting the future. And if for some reason he did, but could not return, who would write *Ten Years to Gallia*?"

"I feel like I let them both down," Dave frowned. "I thought seeing his ancestors would help Fa-a-Di understand the real purpose of the Sojourn, and I wanted Fa-u-Bay to know how he shaped one of the greatest civilizations in the galaxy."

"I think Fa-u-Bay already knows Dave," Ondeen replied. "Remember he is of the Source now and knows everything, including what you are saying now. And you will have time in the future to help Fa-a-Di. I think his understanding is already almost complete. Okay, you two, I must be off. You can stay here as long as you wish. Whenever you want to return to your beds, just let go of each other."

"Are we sleeping this time, Ondeen?" Lini asked. "I think you tricked us before."

Ondeen laughed. "Perhaps there was a miscommunication, Lini. But this time I will say you are not sleeping at all, although your bodies are resting on Fistnan. Take care of yourselves and take care of each other. The Bolofaz will keep an eye on you. Farewell." Ondeen dived suddenly and the two were flying over Lubna again. Dave pulled her close to him.

"What are you doing, Dave?" she asked.

"I don't want our hands to slip apart. I want this trip to last a while longer, if that's okay with you?"

"Fly onward, Dave Brewster," she smiled squeezing him close and kissing his cheek. "Let's go check out the Dar-Fa on this planet." They dived downward and disappeared into brightly colored bands of gas.

CHAPTER 57

"Paxran fleet, this is Admiral De-o-Nu of the Free Society. We are monitoring your approach to the Lubna system and request to know your intentions," the Gallicean said. He sat on the bridge for several moments waiting for a response.

"Admiral, you know our three ships don't stand a chance against their fleet," Ka-a-Fa countered. "I don't think we need to be belligerent right now."

"I'm not angry, brother, but we have to hear it from their own mouths," De-o-Nu said. "There is no way we will engage that many ships. We'd be dead in minutes. We have to keep them guessing until Fa-a-Di can arrive. Even then it will not be easy to defeat them."

The pale blue faces of two Paxran appeared on the split view screen. "Greetings to you, Admiral. I am General Abala Konole of the Paxran Collective. With me is our religious leader, the Most Reverend Raza Intepam. I can assure you we are on a peaceful mission to this system."

"I appreciate your words, General, however the presence of fifty war ships so far from your own territory makes your assertion difficult to believe," De-o-Nu argued.

"I understand sir," Raza interjected. "I can assure you that our fleet is home to many of our clergy and scientific community. I have had visions of the Hive moon where you are currently in orbit. We wish nothing other than to learn its secrets. It is also fortuitous the Maklakar battle station is with your fleet. The admiral and I have had a personal meeting with our Dear

Leader and we all agree it is time for peace. We sincerely regret the events of our distant past, although there is little we can do to change that now."

"May we continue our approach, Admiral?" Abala asked.

"Give me a moment, gentlemen," De-o-Nu said as he switched off the line. "Ka-a-Fa, is my brother-in-law in range yet?"

"Yes brother. I patched his signal onto your conversation with the Paxran. He is listening to you now," the other replied.

"This is a most unusual change of events, Fa-a-Di; wouldn't you agree?" De-o-Nu asked.

Fa-a-Di's face appeared on screen. "Frankly, I'm shocked by this. I was expecting all out war and now I'm not certain what to believe. We will arrive at your position one hour after the Paxran fleet. You work for Dave now. What are you going to do?"

"At this point, I have no option other than letting the Paxran fleet approach this system. After that, I'm going to jump to the Mondor and discuss this with the Maklakar," De-o-Nu began. "If they can hold their fear of the Paxran at bay, perhaps we can win peace for all. Frankly brother, the Paxran do not seem as vile and dangerous as we came to expect."

"Not unlike us, brother," Fa-a-Di laughed. "It wasn't long ago that we were accused of horrible crimes."

"Like on Zulanan," De-o-Nu agreed. "Yes, I suppose it is best not to color our present and future with fear and resentment for things that happened so long ago."

"I'm beginning to feel there is a lesson in here for me," Fa-a-Di chuckled. "What have you heard from Dave and Lini?"

"They are well and remaining on the moon below us now," the other replied. "I did not want them on Nightsky with the large Paxran fleet approaching."

"Are they safer there?" Fa-a-Di asked.

"I think the Hive can take care of itself and Dave Brewster," De-o-Nu laughed. "Please tell Darlene that he is well, and I'll see you when you arrive. Kong-Fa out." He clapped Ka-a-Fa on the back and said. "Okay, signal Admiral Konole so we can give him the good news. Then find Jake or Mitch to jump me over to the Mondor."

"Dave, are you awake?" Elder Fodo said softly. "I need your counsel."

Dave rolled over and opened his eyes to find the elder and Lini sitting on his bed. It had seemed just seconds ago that he and Lini had been flying over Lubna. He yawned and sat up slowly. "How can I help, Elder?"

"Three vessels are now in orbit of Fistnan. They have tried to communicate with us, but we do not understand their language. One of the ships is led by people like you. Another is full of creatures similar to the Fa-u-Bay of our legends. The last is a massive planetoid full of terrifying spider-like creatures. My people are terrified. What should I do?" the elder asked.

Dave took his com-link, pressed it into his ear and tapped the connection. "Admiral Brewster to the ships in orbit. Please state your intentions."

"We're here for you Dave!" shouted Jon Lake.

"Did you forget our call last night Dave?" De-o-Nu asked. "The Kong-Fa, Nightsky and Maklakar vessel Mondor are in orbit. There are also fifty Paxran ships on their way and twenty more led by Fa-a-Di. The Paxran claim this is a religious and scientific visit only."

"Really?" Dave asked. "I never took them for the religious type. What do we do now?"

"I'm on the Mondor now and due to meet with their leader, Ambassador Ont Valoo shortly. I have to convince them not to run or attack the Paxran, which will be a tall order. Somehow we have to hold all of this together until Fa-a-Di's fleet can get here."

"Where's Darlene?" he asked.

"She's with Fa-a-Di. He has already told her you are safe. They should arrive in five hours or so," De-o-Nu said.

"Brother, perhaps there is another way to deal with this," Dave suggested. "Let's get all of the leaders together here for a discussion. The Paxran, Predaxians and Maklakar are dying to get Hive technology, but they don't really know what it is. Let me show them. Once they understand, perhaps they can all join the Free Society with us."

"I'm not sure about the Predaxian agents, Dave," De-o-Nu said. "What's to keep them from trying to take over Fistnan with their mind control?"

"I don't think that can work here," Dave replied. "I don't think the Hive will allow it."

"How can you be sure?" De-o-Nu countered. "It's a big risk to me for a small group of renegade agents."

"Perhaps, but there is something else," Dave answered. "I think a war will begin today. I'm not sure how I know it, but the thought is suddenly in my mind. Let it hope it is not here."

"Dave, it sounds like too much coffee or too little whisky to me!" De-o-Nu laughed. "I'll contact everyone involved to arrange our little conference. Should we arrive at your coordinates?"

"Yes, this is the home of the senior elder of this planet, who is here with me now. The Nan are concerned about all the star ships arriving. Also they cannot understand what anyone is saying since they only speak the ancient Nan tongue. If everyone is on Fistnan, that problem will disappear," Dave replied. "But you might see how many com-links Jon can spare for the people here. Who knows what ships will arrive next time?"

"Okay, Dave, I'll make the arrangements and contact you when it is set up. Don't forget our key objective is to delay any offensive action by the Paxran until Fa-a-Di arrives," De-o-Nu said.

"I understand, and believe me; I hope I am wrong about a new war beginning today. Fistnan out," Dave said as he closed the connection. "There is no need to worry just yet, Elder. The ships in orbit are my friends. The other ships do not appear to be aggressive."

"Yes, I know," Fodo replied. "Lini was translating everything that was said. You were correct about a new war beginning very soon. I don't believe it will be here, but you and I are just seers, we don't know the future. Come, let us have breakfast together."

"Dave and I will join you in a moment, Elder," Lini replied. "I just need to talk to Dave in private for a moment."

"Of course, I understand my dear," Fodo said as he rose and walked to the door. He turned and smiled at them and closed the door after him.

"I guess this is it, Dave Brewster," she smiled. "In a few hours, we'll be on our way back home. I just wanted to thank you for everything." She leaned forward and kissed him lightly on the lips. "And thank you for last night when we flew over Lubna for the last time. I can't believe it's really over." She eyes began to tear.

"Lini, don't worry," he said. "We'll always be together, it's just the circumstances are more complicated in a galaxy full of our friends. Solander was a sweet dream that I will never forget."

"You'd better not!" she laughed. "Right now, I wish Fola would appear again and try to attack you. I'd rip the heart out of his chest with my bare hands. Then Solander never would have happened and I wouldn't have to live with those thoughts."

"I know what you mean, Lini," he said as he caressed her cheek. "On one hand, I wish that would happen too for the sake of your heart. But deep inside, I would hate that. Those are wonderful memories for me. I loved our time together, when we thought we'd grow old and die on that red moon."

"I feel the same way, Dave," she smiled. "I just don't know what to do next. Maybe I should go home and live in my tree and think about it for a while. Or should I go to the academy to learn more about modern technology? That will clear some of my mind, for sure."

Dave put his hands on her knees and looked in her eyes. "Lini, I have a very good friend named Lauren London. Her motto is 'while there is life, there is hope.' I think that's a good thing to remember. The future is for us to make. Whatever happened a minute ago, or three hundred thousand years ago is the past. I hope we can be friends for the rest of our lives. I want to see you travel the stars and fulfill your dreams too."

"Thanks Dave," she replied. "I'll see you at breakfast." She kissed him on the cheek and walked out of the room.

CHAPTER 58

Shortly after breakfast, a large group arrived at the home of Elder Paranaxis Incatum Fodo. It included the Maklakar Ont Valoo and Vard Kalak, Altamar Zendo of Predax, De-o-Nu and Ka-a-Fa, Jake Benomafolays and Mitch Nolobitamore, Jon Lake and Lia Lawson and Abala Konole and Raza Intepam of Paxran. The large tent had been set up again to accommodate the size of the Galliceans. Tables were set up in a U configuration to enable a lively discussion. Dave and Lini sat on either side of the Elder who said a prayer to begin the meeting.

"Welcome to my humble residence, friends," Fodo began. "I must say this is a monumental day for Fistnan. Alien ships have not orbited this world for over three hundred thousand years, when Dave and Lini first arrived. Dave has been instrumental in calming my people as we are not accustomed to species from other planets."

Ont Valoo was squirming in his chair. "Elder, it is all well and good for you to be calm, but the sight of the Paxran is very upsetting to us."

"Dave has also related the story of the past between your peoples," Fodo replied. "We must learn to let the past go. We live in the present only. Those memories must be put to rest someday."

"No, that's okay," Raza said. "The Maklakar have every reason to resent us. My ancestors were terrible barbarians. The stories of the Maklakar destruction are taught to this very day as a horror that must not be forgotten." He turned to look at

Ont in the face. "I do not expect you to forgive Paxran, but you must realize none of us were alive then. I swear on my life we only want peace now."

"I wish I could believe you, Reverend," Ont responded. "But here you are with fifty warships, hoping to take the Hive weapon for yourself. Do you deny that?"

"I think we are all here for that same reason, sir," Abala countered. "You must be honest with yourselves. That is why you are here too."

"What in heaven are you talking about?" Fodo asked. "The Hive is no weapon."

"Liar!" Altamar shouted. "A similar weapon was used to destroy one of our planets!"

"Your planet?" De-o-Nu scoffed. "That planet was a prison world in Palian territory. You enslaved the Palians for many years."

"Do you deny the planet was destroyed?" Altamar asked.

"Dave, can you explain this to me?" Fodo asked. "It is very troubling to think a Hive would be used as a weapon. Who did that?"

"Elder, it was not a natural Hive like this planet," Dave began. "Humans like me and the tekkans, who are a maklan species like most of the visitors today, have the technology to construct a Hive using billions of minds to explore the Source. While the planet Localus was dismantled, no lives were lost. The tekkans decided the only way to stop a war was to remove the planet at the center of the conflict. If anything, billions of lives were saved by that action."

"The weakness of our mortal shells can lead us to do terrible things," Fodo replied. "I am happy no lives were lost in that action, although it seems risky to me. Less-advanced creatures could potentially destroy a planet full of life, like Fistnan here. If this technology extends to other species, who is to stop that?"

"You and me, for starters," Dave said. The others at the table laughed.

"That seems pretty optimistic, even for you Dave," De-o-Nu laughed.

Dave put his hand on Fodo's shoulder. "Elder, you have to understand a natural Hive like this moon can never be corrupted. This planet is a creation of God. All of the creatures here are Guardians of the Hive and its power. The Nan and Zula will never allow others to use it as a weapon. Let us not forget the Bolofaz who guard this system and time itself. They will not stand by either."

"Bolofas!" Raza shouted. "How do you know the name of our sacred text and guardians? Did this Hive weapon tell you about that too?"

Dave smiled. "Reverend, I'm not surprised by the coincidence, but I am speaking of the creatures that inhabit the planet we now orbit. Lini and I have flown with them several times. They saved my life and made it possible for Lini and me to be here today. Perhaps we can see them later today when we all travel to the stone temple." Dave stood and walked behind Lini and put his hands on her shoulders. "This young woman comes from a second natural Hive planet in Greater Gallia. And there are other such planets like these to be found. That is one of my great missions in this life. Believe me, there is enough power for good to stop any such corruption. But to make absolutely certain, it is critical we put our differences behind us. Sitting here at this meeting, we have maklans from No-Makla, Paxran, Predax and Oti-Makla. All of you have the same past. All of your ancestors started on Ai-Makla as brothers and sisters. It is time to put the past behind you. Other than the Elder and Lini here, all of our societies have distant pasts painted with the blood of our wars. Even today, most of us woke fearing a major battle would begin here. But we have the opportunity to choose peace instead."

"That's all very well and good for you, Admiral," Abala spat. "You already have Hives and plasma bomb weapons. If you chose, you could invade us yourselves and destroy us as we destroyed the Maklakar. Frankly, I'm surprised you haven't done that already."

"The Free Society has no such ambitions," De-o-Nu said. "We have come together for trade and common defense. Hives are currently being constructed on Gallicean planets. The tekkans have updated the technology so most life forms can enter Universal Power. We offer you the same thing, if you join with us."

"We will not accept rule by humans or Galliceans!" Abala shouted.

"Neither will we!" Ont joined in. "We also refuse to cede any technology to the Paxran. They would use our own weapons on us so they could finish the job they started long ago."

The group began shouting and waving their fists at each other. Lini and Fodo held their heads in their hands. Dave shouted for calm, but there was too much anger and frustration to hear him. Several attendees had their hands on their blasters as if ready to start shooting. Suddenly, a bright flash of light filled the area between the tables. Everyone became very quiet and shielded their faces from the brightness. Gradually, four blobs of light coalesced from the glare. Slowly they condensed until they formed into Odo Pak, Obu Neela, Zee Gongaleg and a Gallicean Marine. The group at the tables sat stunned by the sudden appearance.

"Good day my friends," Odo said. "We are here with you today to help our friend, Dave Brewster. We sensed his need for support. You must all put your bickering behind you now if you wish to have a future."

"Marine, state your name," Ka-a-Fa demanded. "What are you doing here?"

"He's no Marine," Dave laughed. "That's Fa-u-Bay."

"Thanks for remembering me Dave," the Gallicean said.

"It's only been a few days for me," Dave replied.

"What? That's not possible," De-o-Nu argued.

"Well, I am here, De-o-Nu," Fa-u-Bay said. "How do you explain any of us being here? I think it's not as impossible as you imagine."

"What is the meaning of all this?" Abala asked. "Our meeting is becoming a circus."

"This is no circus," Zee replied. "Dave is right. We maklans have been separated too long. We need to work together to explore Universal Power for trade and to protect us from our enemies. That is why the Free Society was created. Now there is a chance we can fulfill our destiny and join together again."

"Zee, I am so sorry for the attack on Tak-Makla," Ont sighed. "You must know I was against it."

"It is in the past Lord Valoo," Zee replied. "If we can have peace, it will have been worth our sacrifice."

"I'm afraid it is over for us in the Collective," Raza said. "With the Donnaki on one side and the Free Society on the other, we have no chance for survival, especially if we do not have a Hive."

"Choose peace then, Reverend," Obu said as he approached the Paxran and took his hands. "But you are correct that your people face huge challenges."

"Is that a threat?" Abala countered.

"Of course not, General," Obu laughed. "Time is very short though. The Donnaki have massed a huge fleet to invade your space. They have also fixed the critical error in their plasma bomb devices. I doubt your fleet can stand against them."

"But the fleet of the Free Society can," Dave asserted. "If the Maklakar join as well, we will have their battle stations to stand with us. The Donnaki cannot beat us all."

"Dave, the future is unknown. Perhaps they can be pushed back, but not without the loss of many ships and soldiers. Planets may be burned to ashes or obliterated by their plasma bombs. It will be a war of galactic scale, which will alter the future for millennia," Odo continued. "And I fear it cannot be stopped now."

"So the Collective is doomed," Raza sighed. "Perhaps this is God's retribution for the crimes of our past. Maybe that is out destiny."

"The future is not yet written, Raza," Odo replied. "While it may be brutal, even this war will end. We cannot give up so easily."

"Then the war might not happen if you do not know the future," Raza argued.

"I'm sorry, but the war has already begun," Odo said. "Just minutes before we arrived here, a large Donnaki fleet entered Paxran territory. The planet Tak-u-Baka is already in flames. Twenty ships were destroyed and thousands of lives lost already."

"It will take weeks to get back to our space," Abala winced. "We have fifty war ships that cannot help since we are here on this wild goose chase. I truly have failed my people."

"Not all hope is lost yet, Abala," Obu smiled. "If you join with us, we can use our Hives to move all the ships here, plus many from the Free Society and hopefully from the Maklakar to the battle."

"But every minute we wait, more casualties will occur. If we wait too long, hope will truly be lost," Zee commented.

"But I am just a soldier and my friend here is a priest. We cannot speak for our Dear Leader," Abala said.

"I think you're wrong, Abala," Raza smiled. "We were told to come here to investigate the Hive. We were also told to make peace with the Free Society, even if only to get access to Hive technology. If we do this, we will fulfill the Dear Leader's request and save our worlds."

CHAPTER 59

"Tak-u-Baka is ours, Emperor," General Bok Kann said. He was sitting across the table from Lok Zul, the Donnaki leader. "The planet is burning and we have thousands of prisoners of war."

Lok looked out the port in the ready room of his flagship. Dozens of star cruisers surrounded his ship for protection. He smiled and turned to the general. "That's very good news, Bok. How much damage did we incur?"

"Three ships were destroyed and two need significant repairs. The current estimate is two thousand dead and five thousand more wounded, sir," he replied. "It seems quite reasonable for such a heavily-armed planet."

"When will we arrive at Panzak?" the emperor asked.

"Approximately three hours, sir," Bok answered. "The defenses are quite weak there, so we should have no problems."

"That's great. It is a lovely planet and I don't want it destroyed like Tak-u-Baka. I'd like to keep it as a vacation spot for me," Lok smiled.

"Of course, Emperor," the other replied. "Consider it done. I'll pass along the orders."

As the general headed for the door, Lok said, "Just a minute, Bok. What do we know about other planets in this region? Are there any more defensive planets nearby?"

"Two sir. Zigla is two light-years away. It is very similar to Tak-u-Baka in capabilities. Our sources tell us five cruisers orbit there. Gleet is four light-years in the opposite direction. It is a small planet with two cruisers providing defense," Bok replied. "Why do you ask?"

"I originally planned this excursion as a direct strike on Paxran, but since they are proving no match for this fleet, I am thinking we should really degrade their resources on our borders. Once these are Donnaki planets, we won't need them anymore. Right now, they could become hiding places for rebels. Do you think we could manage that safely?" Lok asked.

Bok laughed. "Pardon me for laughing in your presence, my lord. Your glorious fleet can overwhelm hundreds of planets. The upgraded plasma bombs are unstoppable weapons now. I only request that we keep at least one hundred ships with your flagship. In case any strange attacks occur, you must be kept safe."

Lok smiled at his general. "You are a good man, Bok. Order the flanks of our fleet to attack those other planets. We definitely don't need two thousand ships to take Panzak." He sat at his table and put his feet up. "This is going to be a great day for the Donnaki. Our greatest enemies will be no more. Then the Free Society will crumble under our feet. We will have their Hives and their worlds."

"Yes, my lord. I will give the orders." He bowed deeply and slipped out of the room.

Lok Zul rose and took a bottle of whisky and a glass from his cabinet. He opened it and poured some. Then he sat back down and looked out the port as the fleet began to separate into smaller groups. A tone sounded on his control panel and Bok's face appeared on the screen. "My lord, the orders have been given. We also have Kolu Inzaka calling for you. He is requesting to speak to you about a cease-fire."

Lok took a sip of whisky and smiled. "Drop the communication with that bastard. Today is not the time to negotiate for peace." He pushed a button and the screen went blank. He took another drink and sat back, closing his eyes to relish his victories.

Dave and Lini were back on the Nightsky as it orbited Fistnan. Fa-a-Di's fleet had arrived on schedule and Darlene was jumped to the Nightsky as well. She sat next to Dave on the couch in their quarters, holding his hand and resting her head on his shoulder. "I can't believe we found you again," she said.

"I know sweetheart," he agreed, "it all seems like a dream."

"Dave, I'm not sure how much of what happened I really want to know," she replied. "How long were you and Lini marooned on Solander?"

"The elder on Fistnan said it was five months of this time," he began, "but it was hard to tell there. With the light caused by Lubna and the sun, the day and night cycles were random and chaotic. If I had to guess, it would be more like a year. When we arrived, it was boiling hot. Just before we left, it had snowed and was freezing cold. But I'll tell you anything you want to know."

"I'll think about that for a while," she replied. "You're back to me now, right?"

"Yes, my darling," he said. "What happened on Solander occurred a long time ago." A tone sounded on the control panel on the table in front of them and he pushed the contact. "Brewster here."

"Hi Dave," Fa-a-Di said. "I just wanted to tell you we are jumping into Paxran space in a few minutes. I have ordered Jon to keep you far from there. I'm not risking losing you again. Keep safe."

"You keep safe brother. You're the one going into battle," Dave replied. "If you want Nightsky, Darlene and I can stay on Fistnan."

"That won't be necessary. We have Kalidean, Earth and more Gallicean ships jumping there soon as well. It will be a nasty fight, but the Donnaki will pay a price for their attack. Zee has his Hive at our disposal as well. We may survive this day to fly together again, brother. Pray for us. Kong-Fa out," he said as the screen went blank.

Three hundred Donnaki ships entered the Panzak system. The three defending ships fled as soon as the fleet was detected, leaving the planet undefended. "Those cowards are running, Emperor," Bok said. The two valakars were sitting on the command bridge, with the emperor in the captain's seat.

"I can't say I blame them," Lok laughed. "They are no match for us. Target all defenses on the planet. Let them squirm for a while before we accept their surrender."

"Yes, my lord," Bok replied. Plasma blasts shot from the ships and smashed into the planet. Laser emplacements exploded in flames. The planetary leader was desperately trying to reach the attacker to surrender, but his calls were rejected.

Most of the cities were now in flames. Mobs of people ran out of the cities hoping for more safety in the large forests. “Target their capitol building and then we’ll let them surrender, general.”

“Emperor, several dozen warships have just appeared in our immediate area,” the science officer screamed. “They appeared out of thin air.”

“Target the new ships and destroy them!” Lok shouted.

Mondor fired all five of its plasma bombs simultaneously. As the balls of fire approached clusters of Donnaki cruisers, several Gallicean cruisers fired on them. The first plasma ball exploded, crippling five cruisers and pushing two more into Panzak’s atmosphere where they began to break apart. A second bomb smashed into a large battle cruiser, causing it to explode in a titanic blast.

“Fire our plasma bombs at that station!” Bok shouted. The first bomb missed Mondor and flew out into space harmlessly. The second struck the planetoid and exploded, causing a huge gash in her hull. “We hit it! Fire again!” Three more bombs raced toward Mondor. Just as they were about to strike, Mondor disappeared. “What happened? Did we destroy it?”

“No sir,” said the weapons officer. “The ship disappeared just like it arrived. But we have two more battle stations and twenty more cruisers that just appeared behind us.”

“Get us the hell out of here!” Lok shouted. “Call back the rest of the fleet!”

The battle station Parthon shot its five plasma bombs at the flagship. Two other cruisers moved in their path and were obliterated. The flagship was damaged but stayed in the fight. "I'm turning about now sir," Bok shouted. "I think we can escape if we can get more speed."

Fa-a-Di's face filled the viewscreen. "Welcome to hell, valakar." The Kong-Fa appeared directly in front of the flagship. Her plasma cannon shot forward, knocking down the front shield. Before the ship could turn, a second blast destroyed the front half of the ship. It twisted and turned before falling into the atmosphere of Panzak. It exploded when it crashed into the capitol city.

Zee Gongaleg appeared on the view screens of all the remaining Donnaki ships. He smiled gently. "Dear friends, the Donnaki Emperor is dead. Please cease all aggression immediately and we will allow you to return to your space. If not, be assured that most of you will face a similar fate. Your incursion into the territory of the Free Society was an act of war. I am certain you can now see our defenses are up to the challenge. As an additional sign of our resolve, all of your officers above the rank of captain have already been sent to Paxran. Confirm that if you do not believe me. There is no victory here today. It is now time to bury our dead. Go home, save your own lives. After some time passes, perhaps you can join us as well."

CHAPTER 60

"Wow Dave! You weren't kidding about this place," Fa-a-Di said as he looked through the window at the interior of the cottage on Solander. "You two lived here for a year with this one small room and a single tiny bed?"

"That's all true brother," Dave laughed. "I spent a long time trying to find something to make a second bed, but there was nothing other than rocks and cactus. A small bathroom and a kitchen are right down that hall."

"And Fola Untor put in a huge supply of food and water for you? What a sick, demented man he was," the Gallicean said as he sat on the long bench in front.

"That was lucky for me brother. Without that, we wouldn't have survived the hot summer with no food or water," Dave remarked. "Fola actually wanted me to live a long life here, so I could think about what you and I did to cause the Brotherhood to collapse. But it was his backup plan. Killing me in the twenty-first was the real plan."

"You still have no recollection of that?" the other asked.

"Oh, I remember every detail now, thanks to Fa-u-Bay and Ondeen. Speaking of them, didn't you get to fly over Lubna with Fa-u-Bay?" Dave questioned.

"Thank you for that brother," Fa-a-Di replied. "I know he was just mental energy, but he looked every bit the great hero to me."

Fa-a-Di put his hand on Dave's knee and said, "I need to ask you a rather indelicate question brother. Please feel free to say it is none of my business. You and Darlene are my best friends, and I'm afraid your trip to this moon may put your marriage at risk."

Dave smiled at his friend. "We have talked about it some. Right now, she isn't sure she wants to know either. Didn't you warn me about Lini when we were on Zulanan?" Fa-a-Di nodded. "I thought so."

"Dave, before you say anymore, let me tell you two things. First, it is none of my business. Second, anything you tell me will remain with me only," Fa-a-Di said.

"Both Fola and I asked her to move away before you showed up on Zulanan to stop him. She refused to budge, and when Fola went to touch me, she grabbed my other arm," Dave began.

"Yes, I saw that with my own two eyes as well," the Gallicean replied.

"Here on Solander, our relationship was platonic for a long time. We were able to keep busy learning languages and reading *Ten Years to Gallia*. That turned out to be a great idea because it enabled us to communicate with Fa-u-Bay and the Nan on Fistnan," he continued.

"I am so amazed you are speaking Gallicean now," Fa-a-Di said. "That is a great sign of our friendship."

"The first time we made love, we both thought we were dreaming," Dave confessed. "We were actually flying over Lubna when it happened. When we found we both had the same dream, we realized it really happened. Lini was distraught and angry. She had wanted us to be together and felt the shared dream stole something from her." Dave stood and began to pace on the porch. "I didn't know what to do. It was a magical experience in the clouds over Lubna and I really did care for her. So I made love to her again." Dave leaned against the support post and looked across the Solander landscape. The temperature was rising again and another boiling summer was on the way. "After that, we were platonic again for months. Our relationship became normal again because we knew how we felt about each other, but realized this was not normal. People don't fly across the galaxy and back half a million years. It was unique. We were both satisfied to put it into the past, until our last night. We knew we would be returning to our time soon. That's it." Fa-a-Di was laughing. "That's really nice brother. I confess everything and you laugh at me."

"It's not that Dave," Fa-a-Di apologized. "I tried to put myself in your place. I couldn't imagine what I would do in that circumstance. But then I thought about the situation. Who could believe such a thing? You were sent back in time by a maniac bent on revenge. You lived in a tiny cottage at the end of the galaxy on a desert planet no one believed existed. You had an affair with a beautiful woman who looks remarkably like your wife while flying over a gas giant inhabited by snakes that control time. Not to mention you were breathing gas that should have killed you both instantly. To top it off, you are rescued by the greatest hero in the history of Greater Gallia. If I wasn't here and hadn't seen what I've seen, I'd lock you up in an asylum."

Dave was laughing now too. "I know. Isn't this the weirdest fairy tale you've ever heard? I'm beginning to think I made up the whole thing too."

"Are you going to tell Darlene?" Fa-a-Di asked.

"When she's ready to hear it, yes I will," Dave replied. "Let me ask you a question brother. When you were with Fa-u-Bay, did you ask him about the Sojourn?"

"Yes I did as a matter of fact," the Gallicean responded. "He said you told him how I was always terrified of it. Actually, he was laughing too when I mentioned that. He said the Sojourn was never meant to be sad. Back then they knew many Nan survived on the planet. He had hoped we would forge peaceful relationships with them. Can you believe that he apologized to me for what happened later?"

"He's quite a guy," Dave smiled.

Fa-a-Di said, "Then I told him my fear was gone. The moment our shuttle flew over Lini's village and I could see the homes and happy Nan waving at us, I knew there was no reason to fear the Sojourn. The past can only haunt us if we allow it to. If we assume the worst, that's what we get. You know, after Fola took you, I went back to the campsite to speak to the people there. As I arrived, I got that same terror back again. There was some odd noise that made my hair stand on end. I stopped myself from being afraid and decided to find out what was causing it. As I approached the river, I noticed the feeling was gone. I could hear the Nan singing in Lini's village. From farther away, my brain translated their melodies into some kind of ghost voice. I laughed for an hour before I could compose myself." A tone sounded in Fa-a-Di's earpiece and he pressed the contact. "What is it, brother-in-law . . . that's amazing, we're on our way."

"What was that, Fa-a-Di?" Dave asked.

"De-o-Nu has spotted that large herd of herbivores you mentioned. He wants us to fly to his position." Fa-a-Di rushed to his shuttle and returned with the harness strapped to his chest. "How about one last spin around this moon before we go home?"

Dave smiled ear to ear. "That sounds like an excellent idea, brother. Let's go see where the winds take us next."

ABOUT THE AUTHOR

Karl J. Morgan

Karl Morgan grew up fascinated by science fiction, beginning with Victor Appleton's Tom Swift novels that he read as a young boy. Later, he became enthralled with the works of his favorite author, Isaac Asimov, especially his Foundation series.

Those early experiences inspired his life-long love of science fiction and interest in hard science, focusing first on astronomy and later cosmology and quantum mechanics. Karl had the great honor to take his first astronomy course at the University of Iowa from the legendary scientist, Dr. James Van Allen. More recently, the brilliant works of Drs. Stephen Hawking, Brian Greene, and Michio Kaku helped him understand that our physical universe is still a magical and mysterious place.

It is that sense of magic and mystery that brings Karl to write about his alter ego, Dave Brewster, an unemployed accountant who finds himself a thousand years in the future with new friends and adventures far beyond anything he could have imagined. There, he can find answers to questions that befuddle mankind today. The truth he finds is no different from what we know today. Life is always about loving and caring for our family and friends.

Karl lives in San Diego with his wife, Aida and their beloved puppies. Their two grown children have fled the nest and started their own adventures in life.

OTHER BOOKS BY KARL J. MORGAN

Remembrances: Choose to Be Happy and Embrace the Possibilities
ISBN: 978-0-9826461-9-9

The David Brewster Series

The David Brewster Series: Showdown Over Neptune
(Book 1)
ISBN: 978-0-9860270-0-0

The Dave Brewster Series: Second Predaxian War
(Book 2)
ISBN: 978-0-9860270-1-7

The Dave Brewster Series: The Hive
(Book 3)
ISBN: 978-0-9860270-2-4

Heartstone

Heartstone: Sentinels of Far Sun
(Book 1)
ISBN: 978-0-9860270-3-1

Heartstone: The Time Walker
(Book 2)
ISBN: 978-0-9860270-5-5
Available for purchase early summer 2013

CPSIA information can be obtained at www.ICGtesting.com
Printed in the USA
LVOW06s1116030214

372069LV00002B/242/P